ABOUT THE AUTHOR

Brought up in Lincolnshire, Judith Thomson studied Art in Leicester before moving to Sussex, where she still lives. She is passionate about the seventeenth century and has gained much of her inspiration from visits to Paris and Versailles. In her spare time she enjoys painting, scuba diving and boating.

Follow her on:-
Judiththomson.com
Judiththomsonsite.wordpress.com
Judiththomsonblog.wordpress.com
and on Twitter @JudithThomson14
Facebook: Judith Thomson Books

FLOWERS OF LANGUEDOC

Judith Thomson

Matador
9 Priory Business Park,
Wistow Road, Kibworth Beauchamp,
Leicestershire. LE8 0RX
Tel: (+44) 116 279 2299
Fax: (+44) 116 279 2277
Email: books@troubador.co.uk
Web: www.troubador.co.uk/matador

ISBN 978 1800460 911

British Library Cataloguing in Publication Data.
A catalogue record for this book is available from the British Library.

Printed and bound by CPI Group (UK) Ltd, Croydon, CR0 4YY
Typeset in 11pt Bembo by Troubador Publishing Ltd, Leicester, UK

Matador is an imprint of Troubador Publishing Ltd

1642

PROLOGUE

Cardinal Richelieu forced a smiled as the King approached him in the company of a beautiful young woman. Richelieu had seen her before, of course, for Madeleine Pasquier, with her tumble of blonde curls and her vivacious manner, had made quite an impression since she had come to Court, and the Cardinal noticed everyone, particularly those who King Louis liked.

The only fault he could find with Madeleine was the fact that she was a Protestant, and from Languedoc, the most rebellious region in France.

All Protestants were protected by an edict established by the King's father, which had granted them the right to worship as they chose, but the Pope had many times urged Richelieu to have it repealed.

However, the Cardinal's interest was in France, not in Rome.

There were European wars to fund, and the Protestants, for all their religious shortcomings, were hard-working and successful businessmen. They were the backbone of the country's economy – and they paid their taxes. Many had converted voluntarily, of course, following the example set by some of the Protestant aristocrats, who realised that it was the only way they could keep their positions at Court, since the Court's religion was the King's. That was the very reason the Cardinal encouraged them to send their sons and daughters to Court, but Madeleine, despite enjoying the favour of the King, showed no signs of complying.

If she could only be married into a good Catholic family, he thought as he looked at her. What a coup it would be if just one of the proud, defiant Pasquiers converted. He still had hopes.

Those hopes were dashed as soon as King Louis spoke.

"Alas, it would seem we are soon to be deprived of one of the jewels of our Court, your Eminence."

"Indeed?"

Madeleine curtsied to him, raising her bright blue eyes boldly to his, almost as though she was reading his thoughts.

"She has asked my permission to wed our English envoy, Lord Sidney Devalle."

Richelieu had no particular regard for the English and scant sympathy for their King, who had sent Lord Devalle with a report upon the troubled situation which was beginning there. The Cardinal had not forgotten that it was the interference of the English which had encouraged the Protestant town of La Rochelle to defy King Louis fifteen years before. Now King Charles was having problems of his own. Fortunately, his Queen was Louis' sister and a staunch Catholic, so the Cardinal knew he could rely upon her to exert the best possible influence over her husband.

"A fine young man, and from a noble family, I understand," he said smoothly. "How soon will you be leaving us, mademoiselle?"

"Lord Devalle is to travel home next month, your Eminence. I hope to accompany him, if my father will agree to it."

"But I have to agree to it first," King Louis reminded her, taking her hand and raising it to his lips, "and I am not sure I can bear to let you go!"

Madeleine laughed, but Richelieu suspected that persuading the King to let her leave France and marry a Devalle was going to be the least of her problems.

And he was right!

❧

"It is out of the question." Pasquier glared at his daughter.

"But why?"

"For many reasons. To begin with, his father is a madman. I have heard he is kept chained to his bed."

"I am not marrying his father."

"And what of your children? Would you bring the Devalle sickness into our family? It has been with them for many generations. This could taint our line."

"Sidney and his brothers do not have it," Madeleine reminded him.

"And there's another thing, he is the third son. What will he inherit after they have taken the best from the estate?"

"It is a wealthy family," Madeleine said, "wealthier than ours. Some would reckon him to be a good catch."

"Well I do not." Pasquier went over to the window. "Look out there, daughter. What is before you?" He indicated the sunny slopes, stretching before them almost as far as the eye could see, neatly planted with ripening vines. "Our vineyard. Yours and your brother's inheritance. You have no need of anything the Devalles can offer you. We are an honourable family who can rival any in France for breeding."

"And we are Protestant," she flashed back. "You don't know what it is like at Court now. The Catholics look down their noses at us. The only way to advance there is to become one of them."

"The Pasquiers will never be apostates."

"I know that, father, and I have kept the promise I made to you when I went to Paris, but it is hard. The King is good to me, he is kind and pays me compliments but I know that, if I am to remain at Court, he will have me marry a Catholic."

"Then come home," her father said simply. "I sent you to Court in the hopes of your making a good match but, if that is not to be without selling your soul to the devil, I will find you a husband here. There are plenty in Languedoc who will be proud to join their families with ours, and none will 'look down their noses' at you here."

"But I don't want to be here," Madeleine said stubbornly. "I have already found the husband that I want and I wish to follow him to England."

"Why would you want to go to England now, of all times?" Her father asked. "The place is in turmoil. Even down here the news reaches us that half the country is fighting a war against their King."

Madeleine shrugged. "It will not last long, so Sidney says. There are plenty loyal to King Charles. Sidney and his brothers intend to fight with the Royalists, and you should admire him for that."

"I do not admire him for proposing to put my daughter in danger," her father said, "or is it the thought of that which appeals to you? You think this will be a fine adventure, I suspect, joining the fight for a noble cause."

Madeleine kept silent, but she had to admit, if only to herself, that was a part of it. She had found life in Languedoc too dull and life at Court too shallow and frivolous at times. It was as though a doorway to the rest of the world had suddenly opened for her, with the prospect of a husband, a new country and the possibility of a little excitement.

"Well?" her father demanded. "Have you nothing to say, for a change?"

"Only that he is a Protestant and from as good a family as mine, or any at Court, and that you should at least do me the favour meeting him and judging him for yourself."

"I have no wish to meet him, nor do I ever intend to meet him." her father said coldly, "and I tell you now, Madeleine, that if you go ahead with this match against my will then, not only will you marry him without a dowry but, from that day I shall never agree see you again, nor will you be permitted to have contact with your brother or any other member of this family. Furthermore, I will refuse to acknowledge any issue from the marriage to be my grandchildren."

Madeleine looked at him, stunned. She had expected resistance from her father, knowing him as she did, but not such harshness. The lack of a dowry did not trouble her, insulting though it was, for the Devalles were rich and she knew that Sidney would be prepared to take her as his wife without her portion, but to have to break completely with her own family was a blow. It was of no use to appeal to her mother, she knew, for her mother always did as her father said. They all did. They always had. She fought back the tears that were rising in her eyes, determined to show no weakness in front of him but gradually the shock at hearing his words was replaced by anger at this unjust treatment from a parent who was prepared to cut her out of his life forever if she disobeyed him.

"So be it," she said quietly.

The tears came when she got back into her own bedchamber, the room that had been hers since she was a little girl and which she would now be leaving forever, and they came in the form of great shaking sobs. Nanon, her maid, put her arms around her and held her close until they had subsided.

Nanon was only fifteen years-old, three years younger than Madeleine, but she had proved herself to be not only reliable and discreet but a true and loyal friend, who adored her young mistress.

"It seems I must choose, Nanon," Madeleine said sorrowfully, when she was able to speak again. "It is to be my family or Lord Devalle."

"Do you love him?" Nanon asked.

"He is a good man, and he will make a loving husband, I am sure of it."

Nanon put her head upon one side and studied her without replying.

Madeleine was not able to pretend, not to Nanon, at least.

"The truth? I think I *could* love him," she said slowly. "What I think I will love most is to see a little more of life. Won't it be exciting, Nanon, to go to another land, to meet new people, to be away from Languedoc and the vineyard, and the Court too, where the Cardinal looks at me as though I was a piece of horse manure stuck beneath his boot!" She imitated the supercilious way Richelieu had of peering down his long nose.

Nanon giggled at that. "You are dreadful!" she reproved her.

"I know, but I don't like him, Nanon, and I don't trust him. The King is sweet and has been good to me, and yet I am uneasy there. I know it is but a matter of time before I am persuaded into some match that he thinks is suitable. If I don't do this, I shall have to remain in Languedoc and marry the son of one of my father's friends or, worse, spend the rest of my life in the Louvre, at the mercy of a Catholic husband and his family. I would still be estranged from my own family then, for you know my father would not accept that proposition any more than he has the one I made him. At least this way I get to choose my own fate."

"Just so long as you have properly reasoned this out," Nanon said demurely.

Madeleine glanced over at her and caught her maid's knowing smile.

"And yes, it would be a fine adventure too," she admitted, laughing. "Shall you come with me?"

"Wherever you go, I go," Nanon said staunchly.

"Then, my dear Nanon, we go to England!"

Sidney was wrong. The Civil War in England raged for another eight years and claimed the lives of both of his brothers, so that he and Madeleine eventually became master and mistress of High Heatherton, the family's large estate in Sussex. She bore him two sons although, sadly, she did not live long enough to see either of them grow into manhood. The oldest, Henry, showed early signs of being cursed with the family sickness.

The second son was Philip Devalle.

1689

ONE

Philip was a soldier, and he was going back to war.

He looked across the fields towards High Heatherton. Philip had grown to love that house, even though his childhood there had been so miserable, terrorised as he had been by his older brother, Henry. Henry was locked away in Bedlam now, where he could do no more harm, and the estate belonged to Philip.

Parts of it had been destroyed by fire by the time it finally became his, but he had restored it all, as well as setting up a profitable business selling the timber from High Heatherton's vast acres of woodlands to the boat builders at nearby Shoreham. He was proud of his efforts, and well he might be for he had made those who lived and laboured on his estate into a happy community. He had given High Heatherton back its spirit.

His own small family was happy there too. He looked down fondly from his horse at his seven-year-old daughter, Maudie, sitting confidently upon the plump little pony he had recently bought her. He wanted nothing more at this moment than to remain here with her and his wife, Theresa.

"What do you see?" he asked Maudie.

"I see our house and our fields and our sheep up on the Downs."

She was right. From their vantage point they could see all of those things.

"And I see John Bone," she added, laughing. "He is waving to us!"

Philip saw him too. Indeed, the giant of a man was hard

to miss, even from a distance. John had been his boyhood companion during the dark days when he had been allowed no friends outside of the estate for fear that folk would learn the truth of his brother's sickness. John was his farm manager now, as loyal to him as he had always been and a great favourite with Maudie, who was waving back at him enthusiastically.

"All this may be yours one day," Philip told her as they trotted their horses down the hill to meet John. He was beginning to fear that perhaps Theresa would be able to bear no more children after her recent miscarriage.

John took the reins of Maudie's pony when they reached him, although he stayed well clear of Philip's horse, Ferrion. The magnificent black stallion had been trained for war and was never really docile with anyone but Philip or with Philip's manservant, Thomas, who was the only other person who ever dared to ride him.

"So you are leaving us tomorrow, Lord Philip?"

John still used the title with which he had addressed him when they were boys, and Philip was fine with that, even though he was now a duke. John, as his first friend, would always be allowed a little familiarity.

"Sadly, yes," he said.

He had hoped to spend Christmas at High Heatherton this year and invite every worker on the estate to share a feast in the great hall, a tradition that would be kept by other landowners across the length and breadth of England. It was a tradition that had not been kept by his own father for fear of Henry's unpredictable nature displaying itself, and for the few years that Philip had owned the property it had never been possible. The previous year he had been in London at Christmastime with the King, helping to keep the peace in the capital, which was still unsettled from the events which had so recently caused King James to flee the city and 'Dutch William' to take charge. He had even spent one Christmas in the Tower, awaiting trial for treason!

Next year, perhaps? Philip never considered the possibility that he may not return from a campaign, but this campaign in Ireland was going to be unlike any he had fought during his time with the French army. This time, as well as King James' Catholic Irish troops, it was French soldiers he would be fighting, and that was not a prospect that he relished, for Philip was half-French himself and felt as much at home in France as he did in England.

"I'll take care of everything whilst you are away," John assured him. He never allowed himself to consider that Philip would not return either.

"I know you will." Philip said gratefully. It was good to feel that he could safely leave his estate in John's dependable hands.

"Give those Irish bastards hell!"

"I'll certainly try to send a few there, John!"

Back at the house he saw his trunks being carried out by Jonathon and Ned, his Negro coachmen, to be loaded onto the coach ready for the next morning's journey. Theresa came through after them, carrying a thick woollen cloak, and she greeted him with a smile.

"I thought you might need this tomorrow. It will be cold in the morning when you leave," she said. "Thomas has packed your trunks, since, according to Bet, I am too fragile to do anything at the moment!"

Bet was the housekeeper at High Heatherton but she had once been Theresa's maid and was insisting on taking care of her mistress at the moment, even though she had only recently given birth to a baby girl herself.

Philip knew well enough that, despite his wife's delicate build, she was strong and had always been far tougher than she looked, but he was taking no chances with her health after what had happened. Theresa meant the world to him and he had been desperately worried about her when she had lost the baby she had only just begun to carry.

He tucked a wayward strand of her red hair behind her ear. "Just do as you are told and let Bet take care of you whilst I am away."

"Thomas still wants to go with you," she reminded him as they walked out to the stables together, where Philip removed Ferrion's saddle and wiped the mud from the horse's legs himself.

"Well he's not going," Philip said decidedly "and neither are you, my faithful friend." He stroked Ferrion's forelock affectionately. He had decided that his companion from so many battles in the past was growing too old now to cross the sea and help him fight this latest war. "Thomas will look after you whilst I am away," he told his beloved warhorse.

Thomas was waiting for him when he went in, as Philip had been expecting that he would be.

"Won't you change your mind, my Lord," he pleaded, as soon as he saw him.

Philip shook his head. "Sorry, no,"

Although Thomas was only in his early twenties, the servant had been with him for a long while, for Philip had taken him in when Thomas was a boy, an urchin of the streets, being chased by the law for cutting a purse. He had repaid Philip's kindness many times over, proving himself to be a loyal member of his household, and the truth was that Philip had grown fond of him, far too fond to risk taking him into what promised to be a bloody skirmish.

"I'm not afraid to come," Thomas protested.

"I know that, but I would be afraid for you, every minute," Philip said. He had trained Thomas to ride with the army he had raised to help King William when he first landed in England, the previous year, but that had been a very different proposition than the one he was facing now. "You've never been to war and I fear that Ireland will be no place for any man not tried and tested in battle. Morgan, though, is a different matter," he said, as his Welsh steward came in, with his own possessions packed and ready for the journey.

He had met Morgan whilst they were both serving in the French army and Philip had never gone into battle without him by his side. Nor would Morgan have allowed it.

It was still dark when they left the following day, a foggy November morning. Theresa and Maudie were there to see them off, and Morgan's wife, Bet, holding their baby in her arms. Thomas was there too, and he put a comforting arm around Maudie, who could not stop two tears running down her little face. The two women did not cry, for they had seen their menfolk off to fight before, although they had both hoped that those uncertain years were behind them, but neither could find the words to say, now that the time had come.

It was Thomas who broke the tension of the poignant moment. "You'd better come back soon," he told them. "I can't look after everyone all by myself!"

Philip smiled at him gratefully. He knew full well that if the worst happened Thomas, despite his youth, would do his level best. He picked up his daughter and kissed each of her damp, rosy cheeks, then held Theresa to him feeling the beating of her heart against his chest. "Goodbye, Tess," he said quietly. "Do as Bet tells you. And take good care of yourself."

"You're telling *me* that?" Theresa said, with a shaky little laugh. "You're the one off to fight."

He kissed her forehead, her eyelids and, finally, her lips, then determinedly pulled away from her. "Don't worry, sweetheart. It's only the Irish!"

Morgan's goodbye to Bet was swift and silent. Neither were people who ever openly showed their emotions, and yet, Philip knew, they were a devoted couple, even more so since their tiny baby had finally made them into family after six childless years of marriage.

Before he climbed into the waiting coach he turned back to his young manservant and put a hand on each of his shoulders. "Forgive me, Thomas?"

"This time," Thomas said with grin. "But don't ever try leaving me behind again."

"I won't," Philip promised him.

He sincerely hoped that he would never again be called upon to take up arms for his country. Philip had quite another plan for his future, a plan which would have to wait for a while, he feared.

At least until King William put paid to the hopes of his father-in-law, King James, ever regaining the throne of England.

∽

Philip watched the hills of Ireland growing ever closer as they approached the bay of Belfast.

"What the hell are we doing here, Morgan?"

"Fighting James again it seems," Morgan said morosely.

"I seem to have been doing that half of my damned life. I thought to be rid of the bastard when I helped him flee the country."

Philip, with King William's approval, had been instrumental in aiding James' escape to France the previous year, when James' continuing presence in England had become somewhat of an embarrassment to William, who had been invited to come over to take James' throne. James might still have been in France had not King Louis equipped him for war and sent him over to Ireland to fight to regain that throne.

The results had been disastrous, so far as Philip was concerned, for William had used the move as a reason to declare war with France. He had joined an alliance of other European countries who feared France's increasing powers and now the allied forces were fighting on France's borders. For Philip, to fight against his mother's countrymen was bad enough, to fight them in her country was unthinkable, and he had made that plain to King William.

So he had been posted to Ireland.

He had brought with him 500 men. They were reinforcements for the ten thousand troops that Marshal Schomberg had taken over with him in the Summer, but Philip knew that Schomberg had lost more of those men through dysentery than he had from the fighting they had done. As he watched his own soldiers disembarking from the troop ships in the Bay of Dundalk, near to Schomberg's camp, Philip could not help but wonder how many of them he was leading to their deaths, from disease or from the battles still to come.

Philip and Morgan were met by a pleasant young English captain, called Armitage, who was to escort them to the camp. He was leading two horses.

"I have purchased these for you," he said. "I hope you will find them satisfactory for the time being. There were few decent ones to be had here."

"Does the cavalry not have some horses to spare?" Philip asked in surprise.

"I fear not, Colonel. The Irish officers have hired most of them out to the local farmers," Armitage explained. "A lot of the carts we had have disappeared as well but I have managed to find a few to transport your equipment."

Philip exchanged looks with Morgan, who raised a bushy eyebrow.

"I know this is probably not what you expected but I have done the best I could, Colonel," Armitage said hesitantly.

"I am sure you have, Captain, and we are grateful for it, believe me," Philip assured him. "And, if it makes you feel a little better, my expectations were not particularly high!"

He learned a bit more about the state of affairs at the camp as they rode along, and it did not sound good. The men were apparently still dropping like flies from disease and many of those who had been shipped to the hospital at Belfast had died before they had even reached it.

The camp itself appeared to be situated in the middle of a marsh, which Philip thought might be partly responsible for the spread of the sickness. He lost no time in reporting to his commanding officer, Marshal Schomberg.

The Marshal had also served in the French army, although Philip had never previously served under him. The battle-hardened veteran was in his late seventies now, but he still cut a powerful figure.

Schomberg put him at his ease right away.

"I am delighted to see you, Colonel Devalle. Your reputation as a soldier is well known to me, which is why I particularly asked for you to join me in this godforsaken place."

Philip was flattered that Schomberg thought so highly of him as to have specifically requested to have him on the campaign. Whether he was grateful for it, though, was another matter!

"How bad are things here?" he asked him.

"You may judge when I tell you that, in a lifetime of military service, I have never known troops as untrained or undisciplined as these Irish." A career soldier, Schomberg had fought for many different countries during his adventurous life. "As for the officers, I told the King that he would be better served if these Irish Colonels were as able in war as they are in pillaging the country. I needed a commanding officer who has been properly trained in the French army. Perhaps, now, we can instil some discipline into this ragtag bunch they have given me."

Philip grimaced. It appeared he was going to have his work cut out if he was to going to knock these troops into any kind of shape. "Will the men fight?"

"I believe they would if they were properly led and equipped. They didn't even have shoes when I first arrived here and the pikes with which they had been issued were so rotten that they broke in your hand. To makes matters worse, the soldiers I brought with me from England are succumbing daily to this flux.

It seems to me that the English are so delicately bred they die as soon as you take them out of their own country."

Philip smiled at this tactlessness, whilst Morgan, standing behind him, muttered something barely audible in his own Celtic tongue.

"He's Welsh," Philip explained, "so he is probably agreeing with you!"

"I intended you to accompany me when I first came here but I was informed that you had gone to France," Schomberg said. "I was even told that you were dead!"

"There was an attempt upon my life," Philip said, "and it was put about that my attackers had succeeded but, as you plainly see, they did not."

"What the devil were you doing in France anyway? We are at war with them."

"It was declared whilst I was there. I went at the invitation of King Louis."

"And what did he want with you?"

"He graciously offered me the vineyard which had belonged to my late mother's family, the Pasquiers, before they were dispossessed. They were Huguenots."

Philip knew that Schomberg, who was a German Protestant married to a French Huguenot, had left France after the Revocation of the edict which had protected the rights and properties of French Protestants, even though Louis had been prepared to make an exception in his case.

Schomberg nodded. "He's no fool, King Louis," he said. "He offered you their estate, did he? In exchange for what? Not fighting him in his own country, I'll warrant. He could tolerate you fighting the army he sent over here with King James but he could not permit a Hero of France to lead the allied forces encroaching upon his boundaries."

And that was exactly the truth of it.

"I accepted his offer," Philip told him, unsure of how the

Marshal would react to that, after the man had abandoned everything he had in France for his religious principles.

He need not have worried. Schomberg only laughed. "You are no fool either," he decided. "One thing we can be thankful for is that King Louis has now sent the Comte de Lauzun to lead King James' forces."

Philip had thought that an odd decision on Louis' part. "Whatever can have induced him to appoint Lauzun?" Philip had known the little Comte well when Lauzun had spent some time in the English Court. "Louvois can't stand him." Louvois was the French Minister for War.

"He did once serve under Turenne, though, like yourself," Schomberg pointed out.

"That was in his youth. He was in prison for years after that," Philip reminded him, for Lauzun's impudence in attempting to marry the King's cousin, Mademoiselle de Montpensier, who was the richest heiress in France, had led to his falling foul of Louis.

"I think you would find that it was probably Madame de Maintenon who persuaded the King to put him in charge," Schomberg said.

Philip had good reason to dislike Maintenon, for he had discovered that she had been the one behind the plot to take his life, although he'd had more sense than to openly accuse her. As she had married Louis, albeit in a secret ceremony, she wielded a good deal of power behind the scenes.

"Even so, Lauzun is not fit to be a general," Philip reckoned. "He must have forgotten what little he ever knew about soldiering after all these years."

"You are probably right, thank goodness, but King James' wife is friendly with Maintenon and probably asked her to intervene for him. You know he helped the Queen escape from England with her son?"

"Yes, I do know. I was there," Philip said.

Schomberg looked at him in surprise. "You were?"

"It's not common knowledge, but I came upon them quite by chance, on the riverbank," Philip said, recalling the dark, wet night when he had met Lauzun with Queen Mary Beatrice and the little Prince. "I helped her into the boat that rowed her across the Thames to where her coach was waiting to take her to safety."

"Why did you do that?" Schomberg said.

Philip didn't even know the answer to that himself. It had just seemed to be the right thing to do and he had never regretted it. "As I told her Majesty at the time, I trust I shall never sink so low as to menace women and children."

Schomberg nodded his approval. "Quite right. You are an honourable man, but there are many who would think you were wrong, when you had such valuable hostages at your mercy."

"But King Louis is not one of them," Philip pointed out, "and anything which advances me in his esteem is to my greater benefit."

"So it would appear," Schomberg said dryly.

TWO

A brick hurtled down, seemingly out of the sky.

Giles' reactions were still as fast as those of the soldier he had once been. He threw himself onto the ground and rolled to the side. The missile thudded harmlessly into the turf beside him, but it had missed his head by mere inches.

Ahmed, Giles' Negro servant, reacted just as swiftly as he sprang forward and started off toward the building, covering the ground with a speed that left the onlookers wide-eyed. Without pausing he began to scale the scaffolding that surrounded Kensington Palace. Terrified workman scrambled to get out of his way, but Ahmed paid no attention to any of them. He had sighted his quarry and the man would not escape him.

He climbed up to the third storey and saw him pressed against the wall. The chase was over.

By the time Ahmed got the man back down to the ground, at the point of his knife, Giles was on his feet, unhurt, though somewhat shaken by the experience.

The palace guards rushed forward and took charge of the prisoner, although, from Ahmed's expression, he would have infinitely preferred to deal with the man himself!

Giles heard a woman cry out and the next instant his wife, Marianne, came hurtling toward him, heedless of the wet lawns and newly planted flowerbeds.

She threw her arms around him and clasped him to her tightly. "I thought he had hit you."

Giles managed a shaky laugh. "As you see, he didn't. It was close though."

"I know. I saw it all, Giles, I was at an upstairs window looking out at the gardens."

"The gardens you have just trampled through and have got all over your shoes and skirt?" Giles said despairingly. "Are you ever going to start behaving like a countess?"

Marianne glanced down at her muddy satin shoes and her damp skirt, stained now with splatters of earth, then looked up at him and laughed when saw that he was smiling. "Why did that man try to kill you?"

"I have no idea." Giles was not without his enemies, he knew. A rebel who had once fought with the Duke of Monmouth against King James' forces, he had also been one of the foremost members of the expedition which had enabled William to take James' throne the previous year. It was on account of that he had been made the Earl of Wimborne. There might be plenty amongst James' supporters who had cause to want him dead, since Giles had opposed him twice, but, even so, the method chosen for the attack seemed a little crude.

"You had a narrow escape," she said

"As did my assailant! I half-expected Ahmed to cut his throat on the spot."

"What stopped him do you think?" Marianne was well aware of Ahmed's fierce protectiveness towards her and her husband.

"I have been trying to teach him that the wild ways we once followed in Morocco will just not do for the English Court of a king like William!"

Giles had been a slave trader in Morocco, after barely escaping with his life following his part in the Duke of Monmouth's doomed rebellion. That was where he had first encountered Ahmed and met Marianne, a Frenchwoman who had been captured by the Moroccan pirates in a raid on Marseilles and sold into slavery in Meknes. Giles had got them both out and had offered Ahmed his freedom but the former slave had preferred, like Marianne, to remain with the man who had helped them to escape a cruel master.

"It would have been a strange twist of fate indeed if I had survived a bloody rebellion and the rigours of the Sahara Desert only to perish upon the lawns of Kensington Palace!" Giles reckoned.

"Well I think you should just have let Ahmed cut his throat," Marianne said decidedly.

"I'm not quite sure how that would fit with William's idea of turning the unruly English into a civilised nation!"

Ahmed came to join them and Marianne linked arms with them both as they walked up towards the palace together. Their shared experiences would bind the three of them tightly forever.

"I didn't know you were in the house," Giles said.

"The Queen is fussing about getting the rooms ready. She wants to spend Christmas here."

Queen Mary had been so insistent upon moving into her new residence without delay that William, overburdened with other matters at the moment, had delegated to Giles the task of putting pressure on Christopher Wren to get the alterations finished quickly. The problem was that William also wanted Wren to complete the work on renovating Hampton Court. Aware, though he was, of Wren's problems, Giles had no choice but to obey if he was to satisfy the impatient Royal couple.

"The scaffolding won't be down by then," he warned, for it was already the first week of December.

"I don't think she cares."

Giles didn't care either. He was past caring about the whole thing.

"Must we stay in London for Christmas?" Marianne asked him. "I thought perhaps we go could down to High Heatherton and be with Theresa."

Theresa was Giles' sister.

Giles sighed wistfully at the prospect of escaping from the pressures of the Court and taking his wife and their little son, Will, to spend Christmas in Sussex, but he feared he would be expected to be at the King's side over the festive period.

"I wish we could."

"But it will be such a sad Christmas for her, with Philip away, and she has not long got over losing her baby. Surely William will understand."

"I very much doubt he will."

William was not a very understanding person. He was cold and distant, even to those he claimed to think highly of, like Giles.

"Well Philip thinks he is expecting too much of you," Marianne said, as they parted, Giles to inspect the progress of the building work and Marianne to re-join the Queen, "and I agree with him."

She found Queen Mary supervising the unpacking of her china collection. Her taste for the blue and white pottery she loved had started quite a craze in London, as had the little pug dogs which were running around the place now, getting in everyone's way. Marianne thought them rather sweet and always made a fuss of them but the Queen beckoned her over as soon as she saw her and took her to one side, away from the hearing of the servants.

"How is Lord Wimborne?"

"A little shaken but unharmed, your Majesty."

"I thank God for it. I don't believe I could have endured to have his death upon my conscience as well."

Marianne looked at her, puzzled. "I'm not sure I understand, your Majesty."

"The guards have questioned his attacker and it transpires that he did it because he believed Lord Wimborne to be responsible for the death of his brother."

"His brother, your Majesty?"

"Yes, he was one of the workmen who died when the roof collapsed here."

It made more sense to Marianne now. Under so much pressure from both the King and the Queen, Christopher Wren had resorted to some faster methods of construction. Unfortunately, these had resulted in a roof collapsing at Kensington Palace and a wall at Hampton Court. Three workmen had died as a result and there had been a public outcry. As the Surveyor of the King's Works, Wren had been made to attend a court of enquiry but Giles' name had been linked to the disaster too. Marianne felt a stab of anger that the Queen's folly had led to him being put in danger.

Queen Mary's next words made her angrier than ever.

"I have decided that, under the circumstances, he will suffer no punishment for what he did."

Marianne was certain she must have misheard. "No punishment?" she repeated. "What if he had hit his target and my husband's brains had been dashed out on your lawn, your Majesty?"

"Then the fellow would have been hanged but, as it is, I feel we should show leniency."

Marianne had always felt sorry for Queen Mary, who had been forced to leave Holland, which she loved so much, and return to England which she no longer thought of as her home. Her feelings for the Queen changed somewhat as she realised that Mary's decision had been made purely to ease her own guilt, for she would have known well enough that it was hers and William's actions which caused the death of the man's brother, even though Wren and Giles had got the blame for it.

"You understand, I am sure." The Queen returned to the sorting of her china. The matter was obviously satisfactorily resolved so far as she was concerned.

Marianne did understand. Only too well.

∽

"I am considering returning to Holland," William told Giles without preamble, when he saw him later that day.

"Indeed?"

Giles was not finding William an easy man to serve. Apart from his ungracious manner, he was prone to bouts of pettishness when things did not go his way. Which was often.

"I don't believe any could blame me. Not after Parliament has dealt me such an insult."

Parliament had, that month, put onto the Statute Book a Declaration of Rights, which William considered to be a curb upon his royal powers, for it took away, amongst other things, his ability to execute any law without their consent. He was still displeased with Parliament for refusing to grant him a revenue for life, without which he considered he was not a proper king at all, but this last move, Giles knew, had been the final straw.

"I cannot work with these English politicians," William said petulantly. "Nothing but intrigues from morning till night. They would rather fight among themselves than do any business and they oppose me at every turn. There is nothing I can do to please people, it seems, even when I take your advice and show myself off to them."

William did not make many public appearances. He blamed his asthma, which had worsened since he had been forced to live by the river at the palace of Whitehall, but Giles knew that the real reason was simply because he had no desire to meet his subjects. In October he and Philip had accompanied him to Newmarket, hoping that if he was seen attending the races, as King Charles had used to do, it might help his popularity a bit. William had managed to lose a fair amount of money there, but he had none of Charles' wit or charm and it seemed the trip had been in vain. Even the lavish combined birthday and anniversary celebration, that had been held at the beginning of November, did not seem to have endeared him to his courtiers, mainly, Giles suspected, because it had been obvious that William was not actually enjoying it!

"I have problems enough in Holland at the moment," William continued, "so I believe it might be better if I went back to rule my own country and left the Queen here to rule hers. The people like her far better than they like me, so I am sure she could manage extremely well."

Giles very much doubted that she could. It was true that Mary was more popular, indeed it would have been hard for her to be less popular than her husband, but she had made it perfectly plain that she had no interest in politics or any desire to become involved in governing the country. Ever since she had been back in England she had been totally absorbed in domestic matters and would happily tell people that she knew nothing of state affairs.

However, he knew that William was not really concerned with what he thought, so he did not bother to offer his opinion.

He suspected he could guess at the real reason William had wanted to see him, and he was right.

"One further thing, I wish you to use whatever influence you have with the Whigs to dissuade them from opposing my Indemnity Bill when it is reintroduced next month," the King said.

William had already tried and failed with that Bill, which would have offered amnesty for all previous political crimes, and was not at all in the interests of the Whigs, since it most benefitted the Tories.

"That may not be such an easy task, your Majesty."

"Nevertheless, I would have you try, for I can do nothing with these wretched Whigs, William said. "They are a constant source of trouble to me, with their endless arguing and complaining."

The Whigs had good cause to complain, in Giles' view. It was mainly through the effort of the Whig party that William had been invited to come over to take the throne in the first place and they could have expected some reward for that but instead, although he was governing with a coalition of the two political parties, William still gave most of the high offices to the Tories, many of whom had supported King James.

"Perhaps they would complain less if they felt you appreciated them more, your Majesty," he suggested mildly.

"If I gave them more power, you mean? Frankly, I don't trust them."

"And you trust the Tories?" Giles said sceptically.

"I don't trust them either. I have heard that some are secretly in touch with my father-in-law."

Giles had heard that too. "Then why rely on them?" he said.

"Because they have shown themselves in the past to be the ones more loyal to the Crown."

That might well have been true in the past, but the problem now was that many saw William as a usurper to the throne.

Giles and Marianne had travelled over to Holland the year before, where he had helped to train and prepare William's invasion force. He had been at his side when they sailed to England and done more than most to ensure the success of the expedition when they arrived. Yet here he was now being forced to listen to the King whining that he was not being given enough respect and asking him to work against the interests of the very people who had helped to put William where he was.

"That will be all. I leave the matter in your hands," William said.

But it was not quite all, so far as Giles was concerned.

"I understand that my assailant this morning is to suffer no punishment for his crime, your Majesty."

"That was a regrettable incident," William said.

"It was a plain attempt at murder, your Majesty. That was what it was," Giles said firmly.

"But there were certain unfortunate circumstances that needed to be taken into account," William said.

"Such as the fact that I was carrying out your Majesty's orders when I instructed Wren to hasten the work upon the building?"

"You were unharmed," William said stiffly.

"By luck, or by the grace of God, whichever you prefer to call it," Giles said sarcastically, for he guessed that the Queen, a deeply religious woman, felt that her leniency would somehow compensate in the eyes of the Almighty for her causing the deaths of the three workmen.

Giles already realised the futility of trying to reason with William. In truth he cared little if the man lived or died, for he had been in far more dangerous situations than he had that day, but Giles had been a manipulator all his life and he knew exactly how to turn this to his own advantage.

"Lady Wimborne is still in a state of shock over the incident for, unfortunately, she witnessed it from a window in the Palace," he told William. "I believe it might be beneficial if I were to take her to spend Christmas with my sister, who has been unwell since she suffered a miscarriage."

William looked displeased, as he had expected, but Giles stood his ground, knowing that there had rarely been a better time for him to ask for a favour, since William was obviously feeling a little awkward about the matter. "It will be a difficult enough Christmas for her as it is, with Philip in Ireland," he stressed.

William sighed irritably. "Oh, very well, but you are to be back before twelfth night. I can't manage without you for longer than that. Have you had word from your brother-in-law?" he asked, as Giles turned to leave.

"We have. It seems that affairs are in a bad state there, your Majesty."

"Schomberg's reports tell the same story. I may have to raise more troops next year."

Giles had guessed that William's talk of returning to Holland was no more than a peevish threat, for he could easily send his lifelong friend, Hans Bentinck, who he had made the Earl of Portland, back to Holland to deal with the troublesome Regents of Amsterdam. Christopher Wren had already confided to Giles that William had asked him to design a portable wooden building, suitable to be taken upon campaigns, so Giles knew that what was really in the King's mind was to go over to Ireland himself to lead his new troops.

And that would no doubt mean that he would have to go too!

Philip was pleased to receive Giles' letter, by way of one of their frequent supply boats, telling him that he and Marianne would be spending Christmas at High Heatherton. He knew how much Theresa would love to have their company, although the news made him long to be home even more. He had spent most of his life at Court or on the battlefield but this campaign was reinforcing what he already knew – at heart he was no longer either a courtier or a soldier.

But he was good at what he did. He had managed to instil some discipline into the men during the short time he and Morgan had spent in Ireland, although it had been an uphill struggle. Those English troops who were still fit to fight were, in the main, raw and needed considerable training if they were ever going to survive a pitched battle. As for the Irish, he had no co-operation from their officers, who plainly resented him, whilst the regiments that were formed of French Huguenots refused to accept any authority but that of their own commander, Caillemot. In addition, it had rained ceaselessly since they arrived and the already swampy ground had turned into a quagmire. More men were going down with the sickness every day and there was little that could be done for them in the camp.

He had managed to improve their morale a little by improving the standard of the men's food, which had been virtually inedible when he arrived. It had not taken him long to discover that the

Chief Commissary was as corrupt as everyone else and had been stealing the bulk of the money allotted to him for the men's provisions.

However. putting decent food in their bellies was only a part of the solution, as Philip realised.

In the wet, miserable months the rest of the army had already been in Ireland they had barely engaged with the enemy, even though, apparently, James' forces had sometimes been in their plain view and the Jacobites had sent out skirmishing parties. Philip could understand the General's caution, in view of the poor health of the men, but he reckoned it had robbed them of their fighting spirit. Schomberg had once hoped to be spending Christmas in Dublin but, as December wore on, it had become very evident that it was not to be. James' forces had fallen back to Ardee now, which was only a few miles away, but Schomberg still refused to be drawn out to fight them.

Philip suspected that King James' forces were probably not in a much better state than their own. There was only one way to find out for certain though, and that was to infiltrate the camp, which appeared to have become their Winter quarters.

"What do you think?" he asked Hugh Armitage, who he had appointed his aide. "Shall we pay them a visit?"

Other than Schomberg's son, Meinhard, who showed promise of being as good a commander one day as his father, Hugh was the only officer there who he rated highly and Philip liked him. He rather reminded him of himself when he had been a young captain.

Hugh's face lit with enthusiasm at the prospect of an adventure. "Will the General allow it?"

"Probably not. I thought to tell him afterwards!"

"That might be best," Armitage agreed, laughing.

"We go in secret then, just you, me and Morgan." Philip knew that, no matter how much he might disapprove of the idea, Morgan would have followed him through hellfire if he asked it of him, let alone an enemy camp in Ardee! "We can pose as Frenchmen."

There were some French uniforms in the camp, taken off the Jacobite soldiers who had died in one of his few encounters with the enemy and Philip, as a senior officer, had unquestioned access to anything he wanted.

"You do speak French, don't you?" he asked Hugh, as they tried them on.

"Hardly any," Hugh admitted.

"Then you had better leave the talking to me or Morgan. Preferably me," he added, with a sidelong glance in the Welshman's direction. Philip spoke the language like a native, for he had learned it from an early age and had spent so many years in France, both in the army and at Versailles, but Morgan, though he understood it perfectly, and was fluent in the language, as was everyone in Philip's household, somehow managed to speak French with a determinedly Welsh accent!

The three of them left as soon as it began to grow dark, which was about half past four on that damp December afternoon. Philip smiled at Morgan, staunch beside him, as ever. "Another tale with which to amuse our grandchildren one day, my old friend!"

They approached the camp boldly, without reining their horses. Philip was relieved to see from their uniforms that the four sentries at the gate were Irish, for he did not want to draw too much attention to them from the French. He was even more relieved to see that the sentries, far from being alert, sat hunched up together in a meagre shelter and barely glanced up at them.

"Patrol returning," he said curtly as he swept through with Morgan and Hugh on either side of him.

One of the guards beckoned him on with a dismissive gesture and spat some unintelligible words after them.

Hugh grinned. "I may not speak too much French, Colonel, but I don't need to understand their language to guess that his remark was something along lines of 'bloody Frenchmen'."

"Yes, I rather got that impression too!" Philip guessed there would be little love lost between James' local recruits and the well-trained and efficient French battalions.

This became evident once they were inside the perimeter, for they could see that the French were in an entirely separate part of the camp.

There was not much sign of movement as they walked their horses between the Irish huts, in which they could see men drinking and playing cards. The occasional sound of female laughter demonstrated that other activities were being carried out in some of the huts, but nothing of a military nature!

"If Schomberg had attacked tonight we would have taken the lot of them," Hugh reckoned.

Philip felt inclined to agree with him. There seemed to be little discipline amongst the troops, so far as he could tell, and certainly no sign of any commanders. What was perfectly plain, however, was the obvious animosity between the French and the Irish. Several curses were muttered after them and other Frenchmen who were passing by. They all responded in kind and Philip, who could curse as fluently in French as he could in English, decided to do the same, since it was obviously expected of him!

"Would any of the French officers recognise you?" Hugh asked, as they approached the French army's quarters.

"Possibly. Lauzun would for certain." Philip could imagine how thrilled the French General would be to capture such a prominent member of Schomberg's forces as himself.

From his expression, Morgan obviously could imagine it too. "You had better make sure it doesn't happen," he said grimly.

Philip laughed. "Now where would we be if I never took any risks?"

"At home in England?" Morgan suggested, which, Philip knew, was probably true, for if he had not taken the risk of helping William to seize James' throne then he would never have been awarded the dubious honour of being appointed to lead troops against the Jacobite army.

Philip was not too concerned. He suspected that the Comte de Lauzun, like King James, would be nowhere near this muddy camp but comfortably ensconced in some local manor house, and even if any of the officers who had served with him during his time in the French army had been assigned to this godforsaken outpost, he doubted very much that they would recognise him dressed, like he was, as a common soldier.

It was fully dark by now. As Philip had hoped, by the sputtering lights of the lanterns fixed in front of the tents, no-one was likely to pick them out as strangers amongst the numbers of Frenchmen there. They dismounted and he left Morgan and Hugh with the horses whilst he went over to a group who were sitting around a camp table at the entrance to one of the tents, sharing a bottle of wine.

"Can you spare a measure for a thirsty man?" he asked, in French, taking a vacant seat at the furthest point from the light.

One of the soldiers pushed the bottle toward him and he took a swig from it, as they had done, suppressing a grimace, for it was sour to his palate.

The talk was of Boisseleau, one of their major-generals in the south, who had established a training camp in Cork to drill the Irishmen and teach them to take care of their weapons.

"A waste of time," decided one. "He'll never make soldiers out of this Irish scum."

"Ungrateful bastards, and cowards the lot of them," put in another. "It only takes a single cannon shot to get the whole battalion on their bellies!"

They all laughed at that and Philip laughed with them, taking another drink from the bottle, which had been passed to him again.

"What do you expect from an army who makes officers out of anyone who can raise a hundred followers?" the soldier sitting next to him sneered. "No wonder they don't take orders when the men giving them know no more how to fight than themselves. And where are those officers now?"

That was a question Philip had very much wanted to ask.

"Drinking, and whoring in Dublin, that's where," the soldier continued, taking the bottle Philip offered him. "Celebrating what they see as a victory because Schomberg's army have not been able to march any further south. And who is it that have stopped them? Not the damned Irish, that's for sure!"

Philip was smiling as he went back later to re-join Morgan and Hugh. "If it's any consolation, the morale here is as bad as amongst our own troops," he told them, and they hate the Irish as much as our men do. They seem to regard a posting in Ireland almost as a disgrace, and they have little loyalty to James. Most of the money King Louis supplied him with he has kept to himself and their conditions have been even worse than ours. The only reason they moved down from Dundalk was that the huts there were uninhabitable and they are suffering from the sickness that is affecting our own men. I could even feel sorry for the poor bastards!"

"But they *are* the enemy, Colonel," Hugh reminded him as he held the reins for Philip to mount.

"I know. An enemy I have led, an enemy I have fought beside, Hugh, the same as Schomberg has, and who, like him, I now must kill or be killed by. Fate plays some strange games with us, does it not?"

"What will you tell Schomberg?" Morgan asked him as they rode back towards the sentries at the gate.

Philip considered this. "Nothing," he decided. "We could attack Ardee tomorrow and we might take it with ease, but it is only the French troops who will defend it bravely. They will be slaughtered for a cause they do not believe in and a country they detest, whilst the Irish soldiers run around in chaos and their officers are safe in Dublin."

Morgan nodded his agreement. He had once fought for France, as a piquer under Philip's command, and Philip knew that he, too, respected the courage and ability of the French troops.

Philip turned to Hugh, who was riding silently between them. "I will meet them on the battlefield, Hugh, and I will play my part, have no fear of that, but I hope it will be in a battle worthy of the name. If we attack their camp whilst they are in disarray then we may kill sufficient men to win the day, but for me that would be no well-earned victory and it would not end this damned war. You must make your own choice, however, and I give you full leave to report what we have discovered to General Schomberg, in case he wishes to take advantage of the situation."

"I'll not tell him, Colonel. I agree with you," Hugh said. "There would be little honour in overrunning the Jacobite camp. I did not join the army to sneak up upon unprepared and ill-led troops. Let them stand and fight us and we will then prove ourselves to be the better soldiers and win the war honourably."

"Well said, young Hugh!" Philip was pleased with him and pleased, too, at his own decision. They passed through the sentries at the gate once more, two of which appeared to be asleep in the shelter this time, or perhaps drunk. Philip snarled a French obscenity at them as they rode away, smiling as he heard a gruff reply hurled after them.

Giles was predicting that William would soon be joining them. If he did, and if he was the soldier he had once been, Philip knew things would soon change. He also knew that these Irishmen and their officers, who were now enjoying the delights of Dublin and refusing to obey James' orders to return to their regiments, had absolutely no idea of what was to come.

No idea at all!

THREE

∽

"Christopher Wren showed me the house he has designed for William to take upon campaign," Giles told Marianne. "It is ingenious, made all of wood, in sections that can be quickly put up and taken down and it can be carried on a couple of wagons."

"Fancy that! But where will you be sleeping my love?" she asked him, laying her head upon his shoulder. They were sitting in a quiet spot in the gardens of Kensington Palace on a fine May morning, with Will on a blanket at their feet and Ahmed, ever watchful, standing over him.

"In a tent, I suppose," Giles said ruefully. "It won't be the first time and at least it is Spring in Ireland now."

Giles knew from his brother-in-law's occasional letters home what awful weather the troops in Ireland had been forced to endure throughout a wet, cold Winter there.

"I still wish you weren't going."

Giles sighed. "And so do I, but the matter must be settled and William feels he is the only one who can do it."

"And what do you think?"

"I think he's right, but whether he is fit enough is quite another matter."

"The Queen is afraid for him. She is making herself quite ill over it." Marianne, like the rest of the Queen's ladies, was having to endure Mary's melancholy moods and bouts of sickness brought on by her worry. "Not only does she fear that he will die, but she is convinced that the worry is going to kill her too. She had a sore throat the other day and put all her affairs in order,

30

just in case! Still, I suppose it can't be easy to face the prospect of your husband fighting your father," she allowed.

"William worries about her as well, or at least about leaving the kingdom in her hands. Not that she'll have any real power, of course. He has more sense than to give her that and even the council have been instructed that any matters which can wait should be delayed until his return."

The King had arranged for a council composed of five Tories and five Whigs to govern in his absence with Mary nominally at its head, although Lord Shrewsbury, the Whig that William had most wanted to be a part of it, had just resigned. Giles was sorry to see him go, for the Earl had been in Holland with William even before Giles himself arrived there and was a person who could be relied upon, but Shrewsbury was worn out by the constant conflict between the Tories and the Whigs.

Giles knew exactly how he felt.

He had resisted all attempts to lure him into politics. His natural sympathies were with the Whigs but he had no desire to become involved in their never-ending struggle for power and see his own health deteriorate through it, as Shrewsbury's had done. He had no desire to be a soldier again either, if it came to that, but he had not had much choice in the matter.

Giles had achieved all of his ambitions; the son of a country squire, he had been determined to rise above his birth and he had succeeded. He had a title, he had power and he had managed to accrue a little money. What he did not have was freedom. At that moment he felt he would have given a great deal to be in a position to do what Shrewsbury had just done – turn his back on the whole mess and retire to his country estate.

"We're going to buy a house when I get back," he said determinedly, "and we are damn well going to live in it, like a proper family."

They had talked about that often but there never seemed to be the time or opportunity to actually do it, with them both so caught up in their Court duties. He knew that Marianne was growing unhappy and that her attitude toward the Queen had changed since the incident of the brick last December.

"Yes, we will," Marianne agreed. She smiled as she saw a familiar figure approaching them. "Here's Luc!"

"Good. I asked him to join us here," Giles said.

"Lady Wimborne, you are without doubt the loveliest sight to be seen in these gardens," Luc told her gallantly, "if you can call them gardens," he added with disdain.

"They are Queen Mary's pride and joy," Marianne reminded him, watching indulgently as he squatted down to play with Will.

"That's as maybe, but you cannot tell me that these Dutch flowerbeds could ever rival the splendour of Versailles."

Luc Santerre was French. He was also, so he claimed, Philip's illegitimate son, although Philip always refused to acknowledge that!

Giles had met him under strange circumstances the year before, in Paris, and he had taken a liking to the young Frenchman and brought him back to England to join his household. Luc was useful to him, for he was popular with the younger set at Court and was often able to illicit information Giles himself would have been unable to obtain, but there were some who resented the presence of a French Catholic now that matters had reached such a pitch in Ireland and Giles was unsure of how safe Luc would be in London once he himself had left with William. That was one of the things he wanted to speak about whilst he had the chance.

"Now that we are all here, there are some matters which must be discussed," he said, indicating that Luc and Ahmed were to sit beside them on the stone bench. "The King speaks of leaving for Ireland at the beginning of next month, so there is not much time."

Luc looked at him expectantly, but Giles shook his head. "No, Luc, I am sorry but I have decided I shall not take you with me, nor you, Ahmed," he said, "and I will accept no arguments about this from either of you. You are both precious to me," he added in a softer tone, seeing their disappointed faces, "almost as precious as Marianne and little Will, and I will not put your lives at risk."

Ahmed, obedient as he had always been to Giles' wishes, said nothing but he was unable to conceal his sadness at the prospect of being separated from his beloved master.

Luc was less compliant, as Giles had expected.

"But I have always wished to be a soldier, my Lord, you know that and it is in my blood. I should be there with you and my father."

He always spoke of Philip as his father, even though none of the others ever openly referred to him as such, no matter what their private thoughts on the matter might be, but Giles did not trouble to correct him on this occasion.

"No Luc, you should not be there. I intend to help you to be a soldier one day, if that is what you truly want, I will even buy you a commission when it is time for you to go to war, but this is not the time and it is most definitely not the war. Unfortunately, I don't feel I can leave you here in London either, not without my protection at the moment."

Luc's face fell even further at those words. "You are going to send me back to France, aren't you?"

"Why, no," Giles said in surprise. "I would never do that. You are a part of my family for as long as you wish to remain with us. I am going to send you to Sussex."

"Sussex?" Luc repeated, as Marianne and Ahmed looked questioningly at Giles. "Do you mean to my father's house?" He had never been invited there.

"I have decided that it will be far better for you all to be at High Heatherton with my sister whilst I am gone," Giles said. "Ahmed and Luc, I would like you to protect and care for Marianne and my son when I am away and," he added quietly, "if

I should not return, which is a possibility that must be faced, then I am asking you to share that responsibility for as long as you live. I will not insult either of you by asking for your oaths upon this, for I know the affection you feel for them both, but you should know that my entrusting them into your care is a token of the high esteem I have for the two of you."

There was silence as he finished speaking, a silence broken only by the gurgling of young Will, who had crawled to the edge of his blanket and, taking advantage of the temporary inattention of his minders, was about to set off across the lawn. Giles scooped him up and sat him upon his knee. He was not much given to sentiment, but he loved his wife and child, and the words had needed to be said, although he knew that neither Ahmed nor Luc would ever have permitted any harm to come to them.

"You have my oath upon it, whether or not you require it," Luc assured him, whilst Ahmed merely bowed his head as a sign of his assent.

Marianne, looking tearful, took his hand in hers. "I will be happy to go to High Heatherton, my love. I have no desire to remain here without you."

"That is settled then. We will travel to Sussex tomorrow." Giles, business-like once more, got to his feet and passed his son to Marianne. "All I have to do now is to inform the King that, instead of leaving with him, I shall be catching up with him along the way."

He made it sound easy, but Giles could well imagine how pleased William was going to be with him when he was informed of that plan!

Giles joined William at Chester.

He scarcely recognised him. The monarch he had left in London had been ailing, undemonstrative and with a perpetual look of annoyance on his pale face. In his place was a smiling, enthusiastic man who greeted Giles warmly.

"Pleased you could join us, my friend! I trust you managed to get your wife and son settled in Sussex."

"I did, thank you." Giles made him a small bow, for he knew how much William disliked any extravagant demonstrations of deference, which he always considered false. "Your Majesty is looking well."

"And I am feeling well," William assured him. "Better than I have for months."

"It seems that being a soldier again agrees with you." Giles said.

"Indeed it does, in fact I would say that being back on campaign is a perfect pleasure to me, Giles, for I am sure I understand that far better than I understand how to govern England!"

They attended a service in the Cathedral and, as they filed out afterwards, Giles managed to speak with Robert Southwell, who had travelled up with William as Secretary of State.

"What's happened to him, Robert?" he asked him.

"You may well ask! He seemed to change as soon as we left London and he's been positively genial all the way. He's even been talking to us!"

"Perhaps it's the relief of leaving all the courtiers and politicians behind?" Giles suggested.

"You may be right, but there's something else that's helped. Everywhere we've been the crowds have come out to cheer him. It's been like a royal progress, with women fighting to kiss his hand whenever he got out of his coach."

"Really? That's what it was like when he first came to England." Giles had been at William's side when he had landed at Brixham and had made the journey to the capital with him. "It seems he has rediscovered his popularity."

And that, he realised, could well be the answer.

After dinner he went with William's party to Hoylake, to inspect the fleet that was to take them over to Ireland. There were forty ships ready to transport the huge army that was going with them, composed not only of English but also Scots, Danish, French Huguenots and Brandenburgers, as well as William's own famed Blue Guards, who were supposed to be the finest cavalry in Europe.

"What do you think?" William asked him as they looked over the infantry and cavalry troops. "Do you not reckon that with such soldiers as these we shall send King James running back to France with his tail between his legs?"

"I'm confident of it, your Majesty." Giles had not yet become accustomed to William's new affability, but he liked it.

"So am I. Combined with those men Schomberg commands, I feel we are assured of victory. You will be pleased to see your brother-in-law again too, I expect."

"I will, your Majesty."

"And so, will I. He is an able commander, as I am aware, having first met him as an enemy!" William said with a smile. "It will not be long now. I am impatient to be away."

Impatient or not, the winds were unfavourable and they had to wait for another couple of days before Cloudesley Shovell, who was leading the ships, deemed it safe to depart. Giles accompanied William on his yacht, the 'Mary', when they set sail, early in the morning, but they had not gone far when they ran into thick fog.

The order came to cast anchor. Giles glanced over at William, half-expecting to see the all too familiar frown of irritation on the King's face but, although he was obviously frustrated by yet more delay, William seemed to take it in his stride.

When they got going again the waves were high, reminding Giles of the crossing they had made from Holland, when they had braved the November storms nearly two years ago. On that occasion William had been violently seasick throughout the journey, but even that had changed and when they finally entered Belfast Lough and dropped anchor in Carrickfergus, he looked fit and well.

Giles climbed down into the rowing boat after him and they were rowed ashore to the old Norman keep. There was a crowd there waiting to greet him and a spokesman came forward, dressed in the solemn black attire of a Quaker.

He seemed an odd choice to Giles. He knew little of the strange sect but he did recall that they refused to use titles, or even doff their hats as a sign of respect. The man did neither, although he did go so far as to remove his hat and lay it upon a nearby stone before addressing his King.

"William," he said, "thou art welcome to thy kingdom."

The others who had accompanied William ashore looked horrified but Giles smiled. He guessed that William, detesting, as he did, any excessive shows of homage, would rather like that. He was right. William did not seem in the least put out and greeted the man courteously.

Marshal Schomberg was waiting for him by the side of the Lough and Giles watched as they left for Belfast together, their coach surrounded by the cheering crowds.

It had been a long while since Giles had seen any action and, much as he was missing Marianne and little Will, he found himself sharing the King's pleasure at the prospect. If nothing else, it made a change from appeasing disgruntled politicians and supervising building works!

Philip received orders from Schomberg to bring the troops to Loughbrickland, to join with William's forces.

It was a mighty army that assembled there.

"Do you know, Morgan, for the first time I think we might actually win this ridiculous war and be able to go home," he said to the Welshman, squinting against the bright June sunshine as he tried to catch a glimpse of his brother-in-law amongst all the confusion. "Can you see Giles anywhere?"

"I dare say you will find him wherever you find the King," Morgan said.

William was surrounded by his officers but, as Philip rode nearer, he spotted Giles' distinctive auburn hair.

"There he is!"

Giles saw Philip too, and left William's side to ride over to him.

It was a happy reunion. They were close, for Philip had also been Giles' patron and had introduced him at Court. As he looked at him now, he remembered the ambitious sixteen-year-old, self-possessed, even at that age, who had so determinedly attached himself to him. Giles had always known exactly what he wanted and had seen Philip, in those days, as a way of achieving it, but he had been a protégé that would have made any patron proud. Philip was proud of him still for, although he had a scar upon his cheek which had long ago spoiled his good looks, Giles cut a magnificent figure in his uniform.

"We've been worried about you," he told Philip.

"There's been no need," Philip assured him. "We have seen little real action. How's Tess?"

"Fit as she ever was and talking of bearing you another child one day! I took Marianne and Will down to stay with her whilst I am away."

"Excellent!" Philip liked the thought of them all being together.

"Bet and your daughter are well too," Giles told Morgan, who had stayed back a little whilst they talked. He and Giles had never got on all that well, but they respected each other, nonetheless, and were bound together by their common love for Philip. "Bet keeps the household together, as ever."

"And Thomas? I hope he has forgiven me for leaving him behind!" Philip missed his cheery young servant.

"Thomas looks after everyone and everything," Giles said with a smile. "Between him and John Bone your estate is running very smoothly, and profitably, without you."

"That's good, because, when I get out of this blasted place, I shall be leaving Heatherton once more, for I intend to go to Languedoc."

"I'm not sure what William will say to that!"

"He can't surely doubt my loyalty after this." Philip indicated the preparations for war going on all around them.

"There's something else I should tell you," Giles said, a little hesitantly. "I left Luc at Heatherton too."

"Of course you did!"

Philip was not entirely surprised, for he knew how protective Giles was of Luc.

"To be honest, I was worried for his safety without me there. French Catholics are none too popular in England at the moment."

"I can imagine. I am surprised he didn't want to come with you."

"Oh, he did, but I would not hear of it. He and Thomas can commiserate together about missing all the action. Ahmed was even less happy about it but I left him behind too. My Ahmed is no soldier. He has sworn to protect me for the rest of my life but, in a battle, I fear that would just get him killed."

Giles had not had Philip's many years of experience on the battlefield but this was not his first time in action. He had fought with the Duke of Monmouth at Bothwell Brig, against the Covenanters, and later had been at Monmouth's side in the disastrous battle of Sedgemoor, after which he had narrowly escaped with his life.

"The miserable bastard actually looks cheerful for a change," Philip remarked, seeing William talking quite animatedly to those around him.

"He's been a different person on campaign," Giles said,

and told him how William had been behaving throughout the journey.

"Why the hell can't he be like that at home?" Philip wondered. "It might not be so hard to get the people to like him!"

"Maybe we are just trying to make him into the kind of king he is not," Giles said. "The one we want him to be."

"You mean a copy of King Charles without the deceit?" Philip said dryly. "I think the truth is that he was not cut out to be the ruler of a country, at least not one like England. He is a soldier really, and a good one. I know that, having fought against him in the past. I think we will finally see him at his best. If he doesn't get himself shot of course," he added, for he remembered William as being a bold commander, always at the forefront of the action and often reckless in his disregard for his own safety.

William noticed him then and called him forward to introduce him to Colonel Bellingham, an Irishman who was to act as William's aide-de-camp during the campaign.

"You will find Colonel Devalle as able a soldier and commander as you could wish," William told Bellingham. "I was nearly the death of him once, when our troops met on opposite sides whilst he was serving in the French army," he added with a smile, "but, fortunately, he survived to serve me."

Philip was pleased at the compliment and pleased, too, that Morgan was out of earshot, for he would not have trusted the Welshman not to mutter something impolite in his own tongue. It had been Morgan who had saved Philip's life that day, when he had dragged him free during a cavalry charge after Philip's horse had been killed and he had been trapped beneath it.

"We are delighted see your Majesty," Philip said, "and with such an impressive force. Are we to march soon?"

"I assure you I have not come here to let the grass grow under my feet," William said. "We shall soon see whether our enemy wants to fight."

Even as the troops filed past him for inspection, shots could be heard in the distance from the direction of Carlingford, and Philip feared that James' troops were destroying yet another town in their wake as they marched south.

The following day they left Ulster and began the ascent of the Moyreagh Gap, which took them through steep mountains. It was swelteringly hot but there was no shelter along the way for the sweating troops as they marched and struggled with the heavy wagons of equipment along the stony, narrow tracks. It took them three days to reach the town of Newry, but there was little respite for them there, as the Jacobites had raised it to the ground the previous year. There were occasional glimpses of the enemy, but only small raiding parties, sent to harass them rather than to be a real threat, and they plodded on.

Philip was summoned to William's side as they grew nearer to Dundalk, the site of their previous camp. Scouts had reported that King James had returned there.

"I have a mind to inspect his position," William told him. "I would have you accompany me, since you know the terrain well, and I would value your opinion, if we should need to attack."

They set off at a fast gallop, accompanied only by Hugh Armitage and a few of Philip's own cavalrymen, for William had not wished to make his presence obvious, or to be hampered by a great troop. Philip enjoyed the ride immensely. They were in sight of sea from there, and of the fleet that was following them, waiting to take them home after the battle, and it was invigorating to feel the cool sea breeze after the scorching heat they had endured on the slow trudge from Belfast.

When they arrived at Dundalk, they found that the Jacobites, also, had abandoned it.

Philip sent Hugh, with two of the men, to check the surrounding area. Whilst they were gone, he thought he would take advantage of the rare opportunity of being alone with William to recommend the young captain for promotion.

"He has been invaluable to me since I arrived here," Philip told him. "The level of training and the discipline amongst the troops was worse than you could possibly imagine."

"So Schomberg has informed me. He has blamed that and sickness, as well as the severe Winter, for his lack of action, but I must say I expected more of him. I began to wonder whether I had been right to rely on the man." William said with a momentary return of his old petulance.

Philip had become a little impatient for action too, but he was not about to be disloyal to his commander. "All of it is true, your Majesty. I respect him and I respect his decisions."

"You defend him, which does you credit," William allowed, "but caution will not settle this dispute. We must attack and attack immediately, if we can but find our enemy. Here comes your captain it seems," he said as the three horsemen came into view. "Hopefully he has something to report. You have ever been a good judge of men, Philip, so I promise to observe him closely during this campaign and ensure that he receives his due reward."

"Thank you, your Majesty."

Hugh did indeed have something to report. They had encountered a deserter from James' army, who had told them that James had headed towards Ardee, about fifteen miles further south.

"What did you do with the man?" William asked him.

"I let him go, Sire. He said his family lived nearby and he feared for them if the Jacobites came through."

"You did right," William said approvingly, with a small nod in Philip's direction. He had given orders to his army that there was to be no plundering or acts of violence against the population, but James' forces seemed to be obeying no such restrictions.

When they reached Ardee that became obvious once more. It had been devastated. The houses were stripped of everything of value and they had not left the few people who remained, mostly the old or the sick, with anything to eat. Philip ordered some food to be distributed amongst them but there was little to spare, for they had only brought five days' provisions with them, expecting that it would be possible to buy supplies along the way, and even the flour for making the soldiers' bread was already running low.

They did not remain long at Ardee. The scouts William had sent ahead came back with the welcome news that James had at last made his stand.

On the south bank of the River Boyne.

FOUR

༄

As the mist slowly rose from the river early the following morning the Jacobites' tents, near the little walled town of Drogheda, were clearly visible, their standards hanging motionless in the still air.

Giles stood with William on a hilltop, watching as James' soldiers erected breastworks along the river bank. "I am glad to see you, gentlemen," William remarked, almost to himself. "If you escape me now then the fault will be mine. Let's take a closer look at them, shall we?" he suggested, mounting his horse.

Philip was inspecting a ford in the river at Oldbridge when Giles and William, with the rest of his staff, rode down to the river. It would have been the obvious place for their army to cross were it not for the enemy troops, who were already watching them from the other side.

"Should he be here?" Philip said to Giles, seeing William riding in full view of the enemy. "Lauzun's over there, I spotted him."

"Are you sure?"

"Oh yes, I'd recognise the cocky little bastard anywhere."

"I think we should pull back now, your Majesty," Giles suggested, returning to William's side. "General Lauzun is watching us."

"Then I think we should let him see how little we are worried by his preparations," William said. "We will stay here and eat some breakfast."

"What the devil is he doing now?" Philip asked Giles in frustration as he saw a camp table being erected and food being carried out to the King.

"He is tempting fate, that's what" Giles reckoned, looking nervously at the opposite bank, which was thickly lined with willow trees. "We have no idea what is behind those trees."

Philip agreed with him, but there was nothing they could do about it. They both declined William's invitation to join him and kept a close watch on the enemy camp as William and his staff had their breakfast, in full view of James' army.

It was not until William got back on his horse that Philip saw, coming out from between the willow trees, the sight he had been dreading.

Two cannons.

"Get him away from here!" he shouted.

But it was too late. The first gun fired. Prince George of Hesse, who was at William's side, fell to the ground as his horse was killed beneath him.

At the second shot William slumped down over his horse's neck, blood staining his coat. He had been shot in the shoulder.

"God in Heaven! Move the silly sod out of range," Philip ordered his men, for those nearest to the King seemed to be milling around him in a state of shock.

A huge cheer went up from the Jacobite camp and Philip guessed that they thought William had been mortally wounded. He knew how nearly that had been the case.

A field dressing was being hastily applied to William's shoulder, which was bruised and bleeding.

"That came close enough," William said, showing him the hole in his coat.

"Indeed it did, your Majesty," Philip said heavily. He actually felt quite annoyed that William would so wantonly put himself and his officers in danger for the sake of what, in Philip's view, was a silly piece of bravado.

William's next words angered him even more.

"I don't suppose your precious King Louis ever gets that close to enemy fire."

The words were said lightly but their point was not lost upon Philip. William was well aware of the high regard that Philip had always felt for the French king and he never missed a chance to make a snide remark against the enemy he hated so much. In fact, Philip had more than once gone into battle with Louis and he had found him as fearless as any commander he had ever followed when facing the enemy, but the difference, so far as he was concerned, was that Louis was first and foremost a ruler, with far too great a sense of responsibility to his country to expose himself to any unnecessary risks.

cℓℓ

The camp was a hive of activity when Philip rode through in the evening on his way to the council of war that William was to hold with his senior officers.

Every soldier's equipment was being cleaned and checked and Philip knew that even the raw and untrained troops he had been given at the start of this campaign were as ready for battle now as they would ever be.

He stopped by one of the campfires and watched the men melting the lead which they had managed to strip from anywhere they could whilst on the march. They were making bullets, which would be put into paper cartridges with gunpowder. It was a familiar sight to him and one which brought back many memories. The prospect of the coming fight did not trouble him. Philip had always faced battle with anticipation rather than nervousness, but mixed with that was an overwhelming sense of relief that matters had finally come to a head and that this war, which he vowed would be his last, would soon be over.

The sergeant in charge of the men barked an order and stood to attention as he passed by, but he indicated that they should continue their work. Tomorrow, he knew, the soldiers would be biting the top off those paper cartridges and loading their weapons ready to fire at the enemy. As he looked into their sweating faces, he could not but wonder how many of these men would be going home.

Schomberg and his son, Meinhard, were already present at the meeting and Philip went over join them. The old General looked unhappy. William, on the contrary, was positively ebullient. When word had reached the men that morning that he had been shot, many had thought he had been killed, so he had ridden around the camp, amid loud cheers, to prove to them that he was still alive.

This demonstration of his popularity had obviously worked wonders for his self-esteem for, despite his wounded shoulder, William was on top form, smiling and confident as he took his place at the table. From Schomberg's expression, Philip guessed that he was as unimpressed with the King's irresponsible lack of caution as Philip was himself.

"He no doubt thinks he is invincible now," Philip said quietly to Giles, who, although only a Major, was present as a member of William's staff.

"That's all we need!"

"Colonel Devalle inspected the river crossing at Oldbridge earlier today," William said. "May we have your opinion, Colonel?"

"It certainly could be crossed there at low tide, "Philip said, "but it is not the best choice, in my view."

"And why is that?" William demanded.

"Because we would be crossing right into the heart of James' army. The soldiers in the water would be at the mercy of their cavalry the whole way, and even those waiting to cross would be in danger, for the Jacobite cannons are quite capable of reaching us from across the river. As we discovered this morning," Philip added pointedly.

William had the grace to nod his acknowledgement to that. "Then what would you suggest, Colonel?"

"There is another ford at Rosnaree, a few miles west of Oldbridge, which might be a better place to cross. It would also give us the opportunity to attack James' flank and, if we could capture the pass of Duleek, we might stop him escaping to Dublin."

William considered this as he studied the map spread out before him. "Is the ground not marshy there?" he asked.

"It is," Philip conceded, "but it would still be a better place, I feel."

"Surely a man honoured by King Louis as a Hero of France does not fear coming head to head with the enemy," Caillemot, the commander of the French Huguenot regiment, said sneeringly.

There was a sudden silence around the table.

Caillemot had shown resentment toward him from the start but Philip had no intention of getting drawn into a pointless exchange of words with him. He knew he had nothing to prove concerning his military record or his loyalty to William's Protestant cause and he certainly had no apologies to make for the acclaim he had received during his service to the Catholic King of France.

"Any man who does not fear the French cavalry is a damned fool, your Majesty," Philip said, ignoring Caillemot completely, "but what I most fear is that your army will not be unified in its actions tomorrow."

It was a valid point, for the Huguenot regiments were still unwilling to follow anyone but Caillemot.

"I understand your concern, Colonel. Our army has been recruited from many countries but I shall endeavour to ensure that we will act as one, regardless of our nationalities or our personal feelings toward one another," William promised. He turned back to the map. "What about the bridge here, at Slane?"

Slane was four miles away and a little to the west of Rosnaree.

"Some could cross there," Philip allowed, "although the land upon the other side looks boggy."

"I was not thinking of sending the main force," William said.

"If we send a detachment over the bridge it will draw some of the cavalry away, then we may have a better chance of crossing at Oldbridge."

"We will still lose men," Schomberg put in. "It is madness to cross in full view of their camp."

But William's mind was made up. Despite the old general's objections, it was decided that a small force, headed by Schomberg's son, would leave in the early hours of the morning and cause a diversion to draw the Jacobite flank. The infantry would cross at Oldbridge.

Schomberg stomped off to bed in disgust.

At nine o'clock the following morning the army assembled for the crossing. Philip, Giles and Hugh had been up for most of the night, though none of them felt tired as they checked the men for the final time. Philp had ensured that each soldier was wearing a sprig of green in his hat, to be easily distinguishable from James' men, who wore a white feather, for he knew that, amid the smoke and chaos of battles, it was sometimes hard to tell friend from foe. The men seemed in good spirits. Word had come back that Meinhard's troops had successfully forced their way across the bridge at Slane, and the Irish soldiers who had been guarding it had fled, which put Schomberg in a better mood. They had been unable to take the Pass of Duleek, however, since a detachment of French soldiers had been sent to meet them, but William was pleased nonetheless, since that meant a reduced number were left to stop them crossing the river. But there was still the dreaded French cavalry.

William had been up since one o'clock in the morning, but he looked ready for battle as he was helped onto his horse, wearing his Star and Garter, although it was plain that his shoulder still troubled him.

Giles' troop was to ride with him whilst Philip was to fight under Schomberg, which pleased him, and he clasped hands with Giles as they parted.

"May the day go well for us both," he said.

Giles smiled. "At least one of us will have to make it home, to take care of the families!"

Giles and Morgan, who was at Philip's side, nodded to each other and then he was gone.

It was the first time Philip had ever been in a battle with Giles. He was slight of build, like his sister, and even in his uniform and fully armed he suddenly looked very vulnerable to Philip. The adventurous life his brother-in-law had led had proved that he was well able to take care of himself but Philip still had an uneasy feeling as he watched him ride away.

Morgan watched him go too. "He knows what he is doing," he reminded Philip quietly, and yet Philip sensed the same thoughts were in the Welshman's mind.

But he had never been one to indulge in premonitions and he knew it was the very worst thing he could do now.

"If course he does," he said briskly. "One should probably never go into battle with family – or old friends," he added, with a sidelong glance at his Welsh companion. Philip rarely gave a thought to the danger he would be exposed to at such moments, but two of the people who were dearest to him in the world would be exposed to it too on this day, and that was not an easy thought.

Hugh was to lead some of the infantry, which were to cross in four lines at the ford. Philip found him at the head of his men and looking well prepared for the fight ahead. "Well, young Hugh, it seems we are to have a real engagement at last."

"I'm ready for it," Hugh told him eagerly.

Philip laughed. "You are more than ready, Captain, and, if you acquit yourself well, which I am sure you will, I think I have persuaded the King that you might end the day a Major."

Hugh face lit with delight at the news and Philip thought what a fine-looking officer he made, straight-backed and handsome, with his dark curls and an infectious grin.

"Thank you, sir. My father will be so proud." Philip already knew that Hugh came from a military family. His grandfather had died at Naseby, fighting in the Royalist army, and his father, like Philip himself, had fought against William in the Dutch Wars. "My mother will be proud too. She never wanted me to be a soldier you know." Philip hadn't known that. "She feared to lose me, I suppose."

Philip could not remember his own mother, who had died when he was little more than a baby, and he wondered whether, had she lived, she would have been worrying about him now. He had lived his whole life without her there to witness his successes and his misfortunes, but he hoped she would have been proud of him. He brushed the thought aside. He had work to do and as he went to join Schomberg he knew that, like Hugh, he was ready to do it.

William's Blue Guards crossed first, under heavy fire from the trees and from some neighbouring empty houses.

They made it across and were engaged immediately with Irish troops. The Danes and the Huguenots went next, but were driven back by the French cavalry. Philip recognised the cavalry commander, Richard Hamilton, who he had known from his days at Court but who had recently defected to the Jacobite side. He saw no sign of King James.

As Philip waited impatiently for his own orders to go, he saw the Huguenots suddenly milling in confusion and realised that Caillemot was down.

Schomberg saw it too. His eyes met Philip's for a fleeting moment and then he drew his sword.

. "Forward men, these are your persecutors," he shouted, galloping into the water to take Caillemot's place to lead the Huguenots against the French Catholics they hated.

Philip waited no longer. He drew his own sword and, with Morgan at his side, he led his troops into the water and joined the mêlée upon the opposite bank. They had both trained for war alongside these French soldiers they now were fighting and Philip knew how skilled they were and how brave they were, but none of that mattered. He had to drive them back or kill them and he did his job, as he hacked and thrust at those in his path, and Morgan, armed with a pistol and his knife, did his.

They both saw Schomberg fall. The general was surrounded by swordsmen, attacking him viciously. Philip disengaged to go to his aid, but then a shot was fired which took the old soldier in the neck.

Philip's first reaction was of disbelief, that this famous warrior, the survivor of so many battles, had died fighting here, in such an action as this. The fury that overwhelmed him spurred him on to fight with even greater ruthlessness as he cut through the human wall that was opposing them.

The banks were steep and muddy where William was crossing, surrounded by his fiercely loyal fighting men of Enniskillen. Giles, a little further along the river, successfully reached the southern bank and was immediately engaged by the French, but when he managed to glance back it seemed that William appeared to be struggling. His horse was stuck and Giles feared William's exertions might bring on one of his asthma attacks but he saw one of the huge Enniskilleners lifting the King bodily from the saddle whilst another freed his horse. Giles turned his attention back to his own problems. He did not share Philip's feelings for the French, he had no loyalty whatever to King Louis so he fought the soldiers, which the French king had sent over to Ireland, with relish. But Giles did not care for either Ireland or the Protestant cause. Giles wanted one thing only, to defeat James and to return home to his wife and child.

Once the cavalry had forced their way over the Boyne the infantry began to cross. They were well in range of the Jacobite guns along the shoreline now and were suffering a heavy bombardment.

Philip saw that William had made it to the southern bank and was in the thick of the fighting, using his sword in his left arm. But the infantry now appeared to be in trouble. Even as they struggled out of the water, they were being fired upon by grenadiers, hidden in the trenches on either side of them. Shouting orders to his men, Philip took an attachment over and gave them support.

The sun was high in the sky by the time all of the infantry were on the southern bank. They now outnumbered the enemy. The rout of the Jacobites had begun.

They ran leaving their guns and equipment behind.

William was leading the chase himself and Philip was relieved to see Giles with him. He decided to find Hugh before he followed. He had managed to glimpse him leading his men across, but he had lost sight of him after that. He and Morgan rode back to the shoreline, and it was then that he saw him.

He was lying on the trampled ground near what remained of the trenches. He had been shot by the grenadiers.

Philip threw his horse's reins to Morgan and went to him, lifting his head from the mud, which had matted in his dark hair. One glance told him that Hugh was already dead. They were too late to save him.

Philip gently laid him back down, fighting the wave of emotion which rose within him. Still reeling from the shock of Schomberg's unexpected death, this was an even worse blow. He had taken to Hugh and seen such promise in him. Now it was gone, wasted, like so many of the young lives, on both sides, that were being lost that day.

"Damn William, damn James and damn this godforsaken country," he said passionately.

Morgan echoed his sentiments.

They joined the chase. The Jacobites ran for the high ground and tried to make a stand around the walls of the church at Donore.

Philip was pleased to catch up with Giles again there. He looked as hot and dishevelled as himself and there was some blood upon his coat, but it was not his blood.

William divided his troops and moved in upon James' forces, but with the smoke of the muskets and the closeness of the opposing armies it became difficult to tell who was who, even with the green sprigs that the men had been ordered to wear in their hats. Philip caught a brief glimpse of James, watching the battle from the top of the hill.

Men on both sides were nearly dropping from exhaustion by the middle of the afternoon, for the hot sun was blazing down upon them and the battle had been raging for nearly eight hours. Philip's endurance had been tested in longer battles and in worse conditions than this one and he fought on. He was no longer fighting for William, he was fighting for Hugh and for Schomberg, and it was that thought which gave him the strength to continue.

Finally, surrounded on three sides by their enemies, the Jacobites retreated and made a run for Duleek.

The order came to pursue, but the disciplined French cavalry maintained their formation and kept them at bay with a courageous rear-guard action that Philip could not help but admire. They held until the last infantryman had made it through the Pass before taking flight themselves.

Then the rout began in earnest.

FIVE

William was leading the pursuit himself, despite his wound and a grazed leg, where a bullet had shot away part of his boot. Philip had been left in charge of the battlefield around Donore, where he was to restore order amongst the scattered soldiers and see to it that the wounded from both armies were moved and properly tended.

Giles would have very much preferred to stay behind and help him, but it was not to be.

William had insisted that he accompany him and ensure that any of the Jacobites who laid down their arms were given quarter. Even so, many of the stragglers were shot as they tried to run or to hide amongst the hedgerows and in ditches, and there was not too much that Giles could do about that.

They had been pursuing them for a few miles when a group of Jacobite soldiers broke cover and ran into a neighbouring field that led to some woodland.

"Leave them!" Giles commanded, as several of his own men veered off to follow them.

Most turned, albeit reluctantly, and returned to him, but there were three who did not.

Giles was in no mood to tolerate defiance amongst his men. He had hardly slept the night before and he had fought a fierce battle in the burning sun. He was hot and he was tired, and he vowed that these three would be punished when he got them back to camp.

"Carry on," he ordered the others, "I will catch you up."

He turned off the track and entered the field himself but, at first, he could see no-one. Then he heard shots, not from the woodland but close by and he swung round, drawing one of his own pistols. Too late Giles saw, in the growing dusk, that the fleeing Jacobites had not made for the woods at all but had arranged an ambush for the soldiers who had followed them.

And Giles had ridden straight into it.

It was nearly eleven o'clock at night by the time William returned. Philip had managed to get some semblance of order into the camp and had set up a field hospital. He had also placed guards around the perimeter of the battlefield to prevent the kind of rabble who followed every army from stripping the dead of their belongings.

He was ready for his bed but he dutifully rode up to make his report to William. He found him surrounded by his friends and by those who had joined him on the chase. Philip was weary and it took him a minute before he realised that Giles was not among them.

He rode through the crowd. "Your Majesty?"

William looked at him. Even by the flickering lights of the lanterns, Philip could read the expression on the King's face, and his heart sank.

"Where is he? Where's Giles."

"I'm sorry, Philip, truly I am."

Philip stared at him, unwilling to accept the words that he feared were coming next.

"What has happened to him?"

"It appears he went after three of his men who were chasing some Jacobite deserters. None of them were seen again but I was told that several shots were heard and so, sadly, we must presume him dead."

"Presume him dead?" Philip said incredulously. "Was no-one dispatched to search for him?"

"I did not realise what had happened until we reassembled at Naul, in readiness to return. "It was dark by then and there was no way we could have found him."

"And you never tried? You just abandoned him?"

"I had no choice," William said stiffly.

Philip looked with disgust at the unfeeling monarch who could so cold-heartedly dismiss the fate of one who had done so much for him as Giles had done.

"Of course you had a choice."

"Have a care, my Lord," William warned him, looking displeased at being addressed in such a manner.

But Philip was beyond concern for the King's feelings or for any fiddling points of etiquette. He cared only that his brother-in-law might be lying injured in the dark in some deserted field and at the mercy of the scavengers who were only too happy to finish off wounded men in order to rob them.

"Where did this happen?" he demanded.

William looked at him uncertainly, but a soldier pushed forward.

"It was near a bridge, Colonel, about two hours' ride from here. Major Fairfield told us to carry on and he would follow."

"Thank you." Philip turned back to the King. "I will look for him."

"No." William's voice rose angrily. "No, you will not. You, my Lord, will remain at your post. I will be sending out search parties for any survivors at first light."

"That may be too late," Philip said grimly.

He grabbed two lanterns from the men surrounding them and passed one back to Morgan, who had ridden up behind him.

He knew that to defy William in front the other officers and the men would probably herald the end of his military career, and forever lose him the King's favour at Court, but all that mattered to him was finding Giles. And he *would* find him. If he was alive then he would save him and if he was truly dead, then he would bring his body back before it was defiled. He owed that to Theresa and to Marianne, and he owed it Giles.

"I am your commanding officer and we are still fighting a war." William said quietly. "I forbid you to leave this camp."

Philip looked at him disdainfully before he wheeled his horse around. "Your blasted war was not worth the lives of General Schomberg or Captain Armitage, and it sure as hell is not worth the life of Giles Fairfield."

William's reply, if he made one, was lost to him as he and Morgan galloped off into the night.

It was difficult to judge how far William's troop would have got in the time the soldier had estimated. For one thing the men had been in hot pursuit of the enemy and, for another, it would have been daylight. There was a moon that night, for which Philip was grateful, but the lanterns cast little light upon the rocky track. The two hours passed and then a third, without any sight of a bridge but shortly after that Morgan called to him to halt.

"Listen," the Welshman said. "I hear water."

Philip could hear it now too. It sounded like a stream rushing over stones. They walked their horses a few paces further and then Philip saw what he was looking for – the outline of a small bridge.

They crossed over the stream, which divided a grass field in two. By the light of the moon they could just pick out what looked like woodland in the distance on the far side of the field, and there was a gap in the hedgerow by the side of the bridge. It would have been the perfect place for the fleeing Jacobites to turn off the road.

"This has to be it," Philip said, steeling himself for what he feared he might find.

"I think so too."

It was quiet, deathly quiet. If this was truly where the attack took place there was no sign or sound of life.

They dismounted and, leading their horses, they walked into the field.

There was nothing to see at first glance and the only noise Philip could hear still was the gurgling of the stream, which was running alongside of them.

Then, as his eyes became more accustomed to the gloom, he saw a dark shape on the ground.

Morgan saw it as well. It was a body.

They held their lanterns high as they approached and Philip forced himself to look at the face of the man lying on the ground.

It wasn't Giles.

"There's another!" Morgan moved a little way off and Philip saw him peering over a second body. The Welshman shook his head. "This one is one of theirs."

"So Giles and his men put up a fight of it."

"It would seem so."

Philip set off in the opposite direction and found two more, both Jacobites. and both shot cleanly through the head. Despite the circumstances he smiled to himself. Giles had always been an excellent shot and he could imagine him coolly firing at his attackers for as long as he was able.

They found the other two of Giles' men over by some bushes, both dead. There was still no sign of Giles.

"If he died, he died here, Morgan," Philip said.

"Then we will find him and we will know," Morgan said firmly.

Leaving Philip to search amongst the undergrowth, Morgan headed back towards the stream where the ground dipped down a little.

A moment later Philip heard the words he had both wanted to hear and yet dreaded.

"He's over here!"

As he followed the flickering light from Morgan's lantern Philip said a silent prayer, a thing he had not done in a very long while.

His stomach churned as he looked down at Giles. Even by the lantern light he could see the blood in his hair. A trickle of it had run down his face and dried upon the old scar down his left cheek. He had plainly been hit over the head, and hard, but he also had what looked like a gunshot wound in his thigh. A great deal of blood had come from that and the grass beneath was slick with it.

Philip knelt down and bent his ear to Giles' mouth, scarcely daring to hope that he would hear a breath.

He did.

It was so faint a breath that he thought his hopes must be tricking his senses. Then he heard another.

"He's still alive," he said huskily.

Morgan listened too. "He is," he agreed.

They looked at each other and Philip knew the same question was in both their minds.

But for how long?

Philip spoke first. "We can't get him back like this. We'll likely kill him if we try to move him on a horse. You need to find us some transport."

Morgan looked at him dubiously and Philip knew that he was unwilling to desert him, vulnerable and alone, in this remote place.

"I can't risk leaving him, Morgan. It will begin to get light in an hour or so and we know what will happen then. It is a mercy that these bodies have not been found already."

Morgan said no more but mounted his horse and set off across the field.

Philip took off his coat and also the gold sash he was wearing around his waist, as part of his uniform. He bound the sash tightly around Giles' leg wound, which seemed to be still oozing blood, and laid the coat over him. Although the night was warm, Giles felt cold to the touch, which he feared was not a good sign.

Then he waited. He kept alert, for he knew that when daybreak came so would the scavengers with their sharp knives ready to slit the throats of any unfortunates who still breathed and with sacks ready to steal their weapons and valuables. Even, sometimes, their boots and the very clothes upon their backs.

This would not be Giles' fate. Not whilst he was there to protect him.

He had a water canister in his saddlebags and he topped it up from the stream and poured a little onto Giles' face and into his hair, where the blood had congealed. There was the flicker of a reaction when the cold water touched his skin, and Philip bent down closer to him. "Talk to me, Giles," he said, willing his brother-in-law's eyes to open. "You've been hurt, but we are going to get you to safety. Morgan has gone to find a cart to take you back to camp."

It did seem, as Philip spoke to him, that Giles was becoming aware that he was there. With sudden inspiration, he fetched something else out of his saddlebags, something which he thought might be of more help than the water – a small flask of brandy.

He touched the bottle to Giles' lips and poured a tiny amount into his mouth. The reaction was almost instanteous. Giles coughed so hard that Philip feared for a moment he would choke, then the grey eyes flew open and stared at him in shock.

The result was even better than Philip had hoped for and a wave of relief flooded over him. Giles was not out of danger yet, he knew, but it was a start.

"Stay awake, Giles, Philip told him, as his eyelids began to close again. "Look at me."

Giles did open his eyes again, and this time there was a hint of recognition in them. "Philip?" He managed a weak smile. "You found me."

"Well of course I found you. What do you think, that I was going to let you die out here? Theresa would never let me hear the end of it! Don't move about too much," he ordered him as Giles tried to sit up. "You have lost a lot of blood."

Giles looked down at the makeshift bandage around his thigh. "Your Colonel's sash?"

Philip shrugged. He doubted he would need it anymore. At the very least he thought William would demand his resignation. "Does your leg hurt much?"

"Yes, it damn well does," Giles said, laying his head down again, "and my head is thumping like a drum."

Philip held the brandy bottle back up to his lips.

"I can't stand the stuff," Giles reminded him, pulling a face as more of the fiery liquid was tipped into his mouth.

"Stop complaining! It brought you round, didn't it?" Philip took a swig of it himself. He had relied heavily on the spirit during a period when he had been in great pain from an old injury and he thought it might help to dull Giles' pain too.

Just as he had feared, as the early light streaked the sky there were signs of movement by the bridge he and Morgan had crossed. Philip counted five shapes silhouetted against the pale colours of the dawn. There had been no weapons by the soldiers' bodies and he guessed that the surviving Jacobites had taken them, along with Giles' pistols, but he knew these ghouls would already be armed and he took out his own pistol, positioning himself so that he could aim over the top of the steep bank.

Philip regarded scavengers with revulsion. During his years in the army he had heard of injured soldiers being beaten to death with their own muskets by such creatures, so he had no compunction about killing them, even the women, but a shot would draw them to him and put Giles in even greater danger.

"Lie still," he told him.

He could hear their voices as they set about their loathsome work and he gritted his teeth. Each of the men he and Morgan had found were already dead, which was some consolation to him as he saw their possessions being shoved into the sacks.

They had not seen him yet, since he and Giles were down by the water's edge, but he knew it could only be a matter of time before they spotted his horse, which he had tied to a tree by the stream.

The stallion was trained for war, and had served him well during the campaign, but he was more skittish than his old warhorse, Ferrion. Philip winced as he heard the animal whinny softly.

One of the men spun round at the sound. He called to the others and they began to walk in Philip's direction. He could stay concealed no longer.

He got the closest of them in his sights and fired. The man dropped down and the rest moved more cautiously, but they were still coming for him and one fired a return shot.

He heard a scream and the shooter fell, a knife embedded in his back.

The other three turned and, leaving their companions, ran for the safety of the woodland.

"Nicely timed," Philip said, climbing up the bank as Morgan was retrieving the knife he had thrown. "I see you haven't lost your touch! How did you know they were here?"

"I didn't, but I thought it a fair bet," Morgan said as he went back to where he had left the horse and cart, which he had commandeered, in the name of King William, from the first farmstead he had come across. He'd also had the forethought to demand a blanket from the farmer, who had been too terrified at being awoken in the middle of night by a fearsome-looking Welshman to argue!

The journey back was slow. Morgan drove as carefully as he could and Philip followed, leading Morgan's horse. Giles had fallen asleep, for which Philip was thankful, for the jolting would have hurt him, despite Morgan's best efforts to avoid the worst of the ruts and boulders in the road.

Philip's eyes rarely left the pale figure who lay motionless in the rough vehicle. So many thoughts went through his mind as they travelled. He and Giles had not always agreed. Whilst it had been Philip who had first introduced him to the Duke of Monmouth, Philip had not joined the Duke's rebellion. That had caused a rift between him and Giles, who was convinced that, with Philip leading the cavalry instead of Lord Grey, the battle at Sedgemoor might have had a different outcome.

Giles had been an outlaw during the remainder of James' reign, which was the reason Philip had first involved him in William's plans, although, as he looked at his brother-in-law now, he wondered whether he should have done so.

The camp was stirring by the time they got back, although there was not a great deal of activity. Men were sitting outside of their tents, idly chatting in the early morning sunshine, or staring ahead with dazed expressions. Philip knew they would all need a day of rest to recover from the previous day's hard fighting.

Every man looked up as the cart went through and Philip guessed that the whole camp had heard of his altercation with William the previous night. A ragged cheer came from a group of his own men, a cheer that was quickly taken up by all they passed.

They went directly to the field hospital. Word must have already reached the surgeon, for he came out to meet them, looking nearly as tired as Philip felt.

Two orderlies lifted Giles from the cart, under the surgeon's watchful eye, and carried him into the tent.

Philip went to follow but the surgeon stopped him.

"Your actions have saved his life, Colonel. The rest is up to me."

Philip knew that he was right and reluctantly turned away.

"When did you last sleep?" The surgeon demanded.

Philip honestly did not know. He had lost track of time and days. He had seen Schomberg and Hugh die since he had last slept, he knew that, and he had fought and killed men on the battlefield. Now he had accomplished what he had set out to do and brought Giles safely back, the energy he had found to do it drained away from him and he realised he was feeling much like some of the men he had seen sitting outside their tents.

"I'm not sure," he admitted.

"As I thought. Rest now," the surgeon told him. "There is nothing you can do here."

Philip nodded.

"And Colonel," the surgeon added as he and Morgan walked away, "You are good men, both of you."

Philip smiled at that as they made their way back to his own tent.

"He doesn't know us very well, does he, Morgan?"

Giles was sleeping when Philip went back to the hospital tent to see him that afternoon. He had slept for several hours himself and felt restored.

The surgeon appeared to have done a good job of removing the bullet from Giles' leg, which was now strapped in bandages. There was another bandage around his head, and Philip was surprised to find that the surgeon was more concerned with that injury than the bullet wound.

"He can't see properly and he cannot bear the light," he explained to Philip, "He is confused too. It is possible that his memory has been affected."

Philip, who had assumed that a crack on the head would be the least of Giles' problems, looked at the surgeon in dismay. "He will recover from it, won't he?"

"He will live," the surgeon stressed, "thanks to you, but he may not recover all of his faculties. He received a savage blow to his head, you know. It is a miracle his skull was not smashed."

"But you have treated such injuries before, have you not?" Philip asked him anxiously.

"There is no treatment, Colonel. Time may heal him, but he should be sent home, for there is nothing more that I can do for him here. You should probably wake him now. A man should not be left to sleep too long after his brain has been shaken."

Philip went over to Giles and woke him gently. The afternoon sun was bright, even through the canvas of the tent, and Giles flinched as he opened his eyes.

He looked pleased, though, when he saw who was sitting on his bed, although it did seem to Philip that he was looking over his shoulder rather than directly at him.

"You saved me, Philip. You and Morgan came to search for me, even though William had forbidden it."

"Now who told you that?" Philip had not intended Giles to discover the fact that William had not tried to find him.

"The orderlies, but it is apparently all round the camp. I hear they even cheered you when you brought me back. That won't endear you much to William!"

Philip smiled. "Possibly not. How are you feeling?"

"I'm not in too much pain, but I feel a little sick and my head aches," Giles admitted.

"I'm not surprised! Can you recall much about what happened to you?"

Giles shook his head, then winced. "Remind me not to do that! I only remember feeling the shot go into my leg. I must have fallen from my horse. I suppose they stole that."

"And your pistols, I'm afraid."

"Bastards! I thought I could hear water when you first woke me."

"You could. They clouted you across the head, with the handle of a musket, judging by the force, and you must have rolled down the bank of the stream. You were lucky, they probably couldn't be bothered to go down and check whether you were still alive."

"I wouldn't be if it were not for you, I realise that," Giles said, reaching out to clasp his hand. Philip took his instead, since Giles seemed to be having trouble focusing on him.

"Can you see me?" he asked, thinking back to what the surgeon had told him.

"I can see two of you, actually," Giles admitted, "but I'll not complain, for you are the most welcome sight I could wish to see here."

Philip left him to get some rest and went back to his tent, where Morgan had a message to give him.

"Apparently King William wishes to see you right away."

Philip had been expecting that. He told Morgan everything the surgeon had said as the Welshman helped him on with his coat. It was yet another hot day and he had been walking around in his shirt sleeves, but that would not do to present himself to William, especially on this occasion, although he no longer had his gold sash to complete his uniform. "He used to be the best shot I have ever known, and now he can't even see straight," he said sadly. "They are going to send him home."

"It's the best place for him," Morgan reckoned. "Bet will take care of him, and her potions will do him a damn site more good than anything that can be found in this camp."

Morgan's wife, Bet, looked after the health of all the family and everyone upon the estate. She was proud of her medicinal herb bed, from which it seemed she could prepare a potion to cure any complaint. Although her concoctions were not always very palatable, they were invariably effective!

William still wore a bandage on his shoulder and he looked strained. He greeted Philip stiffly. "How is Giles? I hear the surgeon wants to send him back to England."

"Yes, your Majesty. His leg wound should heal, I understand, but it may be some time before he fully recovers from the injury to his head."

"That is a pity. He is a valuable member of my staff," William said. "He was fortunate that you managed to save him," he added, a little awkwardly. "All the same, as one of my senior officers, your open defiance of my orders did not set a good example to the men, but Giles is your brother-in-law and I was perhaps not as reasonable as I might have been."

Philip realised, with surprise, that William, if not actually making an apology, was at least attempting to justify his actions, which he had not expected.

He thought he had better be gracious.

"On a day such as that had been, your Majesty, I think it small wonder that we were both a little overwrought."

William gave a half-smile. "Indeed. You and I have spent too many years at war, both as enemies and friends, not to understand what battle fatigue can do. I had been seventeen hours in the saddle and you had fought gallantly and led Schomberg's forces after he went down. I have just now commiserated with Meinhard upon the loss of his father. I know his death, and that of your captain, was a great blow to you. On account of that I am prepared to put the matter behind us on this occasion."

Philip made no reply to that, for he sensed that William had not said all he wanted to say. And he was right.

"I have always known that I would never completely own you, Philip Devalle," William continued. "Whilst you have shown me more loyalty than you did either of my predecessors, I am well aware that your true allegiance is with King Louis, which is one of the reasons this war is so abhorrent to you. Nevertheless, by fighting against your old comrades in the French army you have adequately proved your support of the Protestant cause in Ireland, but you have played your part now, so far as I am concerned."

He paused and Philip wondered what was to come.

William must have seen his apprehension, for he held up his hand. "I am not about to discharge you from my army," he hastened to assure him. "I would be a fool indeed to do that, when I am certain to have the need to call upon you again at some time in the future, but you have served me here for eight months now and I know from the reports sent to me from General Schomberg that you were greatly responsible for preparing the raw troops for battle. I have received word today that King James has already deserted his army and left for France, so it is my intention to march to Dublin as soon the troops can be organised. You, however, I am quite certain, would much prefer to return to England with your brother-in-law."

Philip could hardly believe his luck. Nothing could fit more perfectly with his plans!

SIX

⌀

When Philip and Morgan had set off for Ireland, on a cold, dark November morning, Winter had been fast approaching, but now High Heatherton was at its Summer best. The trees in the orchard were heavy with ripening fruit, the pastures where the cattle and sheep grazed were lush, and the formal garden, which had become Theresa's own special project, was bursting with colour.

Philip laughed at her enthusiasm as Theresa proudly showed him the neat flowerbeds, bright with marigolds, pinks and periwinkles, as well as the rosebushes, which were her pride and joy. She had created a little rose arbour, too, at the end of one of the paths and from beneath the profusion of red roses they could see the kitchen gardens and Bet tending her thriving herb patch, with Marianne by her side.

"Motherhood suits Bet, I think," Philip said, for their sharp-tongued housekeeper seemed to him to have positively mellowed since the birth of her baby daughter.

"Having Morgan home suits her too," Theresa said. "Bet, Marianne and I have been a comfort to each other these past months with our husbands all away fighting."

"If it is any consolation to you, Tess, I promise that was the last time for me."

"How can you promise that, my darling? You are a soldier and if William commands you then surely you will have to go."

"I'll find some way," Philip vowed. "I've had my fill of war."

He had written to Hugh's parents since he had been home, giving a glowing report of their son's behaviour and his bravery, hoping it might be some small comfort to them in their loss, but his and Schomberg's deaths, especially for such a cause, had sickened him and Giles' narrow escape had further determined him that he was never going to fight again if he could help it. News of the war had reached him from London, of course. William had been well received in Dublin but, on the continent, Waldeck had suffered a sound defeat at Fleurus, in the Spanish Netherlands, at the hands of Philip's old commander, the Duc de Luxembourg, and, whilst he had been away, the French navy had won a victory off Beachy Head, less than 30 miles along the Sussex coast from High Heatherton.

Philip no longer cared about any of it.

Bet and Marianne came up, carrying some branches in their baskets that they had cut from Bet's rosemary bush. "For Giles," Marianne explained, showing them the tiny mauve flowers amongst the spiky, fragrant leaves. "He must take these with some bread and salt first thing in the morning, before he eats anything else."

"And what will that do?" Philip asked her.

"Bet says it will help to clear his sight and it will strengthen his brain."

Giles' leg wound was healing nicely with the aid of Bet's salve, which she always prepared every Spring from primroses. However, he had not completely recovered from the blow to his head, for his sight had not yet returned to normal. He was still finding it difficult to concentrate as well and, Philip knew, he was getting increasingly frustrated by his own inadequacies.

Bet had taken over his care, as Morgan had predicted she would. With her determination to get him well and her sound knowledge of the old cures, Philip thought he could be in no better hands. Also, he knew, Bet had always had a soft spot for Giles, even when he had been a precocious young man, and would never have let another tend to him.

It was not the first time she had been called upon to treat

Giles. She had healed, as best she could, the dreadful scar that had ruined his once handsome looks and she had cleaned and bound a sword cut on his arm when he had been a fugitive, fleeing from King James' soldiers after the Rebellion.

"We need a few of those red roses too," Bet said, brandishing her clippers. "He is complaining of a headache today so we are going to boil some in wine for him. I am teaching Marianne a few things she may need to know when they leave us. We can't risk putting him in the hands of a member of the so-called medical profession, who kill more of their patients than they heal." Bet had no time at all for doctors, with their purging and bloodletting.

Philip agreed with her about that, for he reckoned that it was a doctor's treatment which had caused the death of a dear friend of his many years before.

"Are you in such a hurry to return to the city then?" Philip asked Marianne.

She shook her head. "I don't ever want to go back there but Giles feels he is a burden to you."

"That's nonsense!" Philip said. "You know you are both welcome to remain here as long as ever you want and, besides, there can't be too much for him to do in London with William still away."

"Can't you persuade him to stay?" Theresa asked Philip. "You have more influence on him than anyone else."

"Which isn't saying a great deal," Philip said, for Giles had always known his own mind. "Leave him to me. I have a proposition to put to him, if he is well enough to hear it now."

"Thank you," Marianne said gratefully. She put her arms around him and gave him a little hug. "And thank you for bringing him back to me."

"It was a wonderful thing you did for him, my Lord," Bet said, when she had laid the roses in her basket beside the boughs of rosemary.

"Why, thank you, Mistress Bet!" Philip said, amused, for Bet had often seen fit to criticise his actions in the past.

"Morgan told me how you defied the King and disobeyed his orders."

"I could never have saved Giles without your husband to help me," Philip stressed.

"There are a lot of things you could never have done without my Morgan," Bet said loyally.

"That's true," Philip admitted.

"And now, I suppose, you'll need him to help you run your French vineyard."

"I most certainly will, Bet! In fact, I don't believe I can manage it without him."

"Nor do I," she retorted as she walked away. "Someone with your fancy upbringing might know how to behave at Court or how to fight a duel but you never learned anything really useful, such as how to grow things!"

"I fear she's right," Philip said ruefully to Theresa. "But I have to try, you do see that don't you, Tess?"

"Of course I do. In any case, I feel certain it will prove to be a lot less hazardous than some of the other enterprises you have been involved in," Theresa said. "At least this one should not land you in the Tower!"

Philip found Giles sitting outside in the sunshine, although he was beneath the shade of one of the trees, for bright light still troubled his eyes. Maudie was next to him, playing on the lawn with little Will and keeping an eye on Gwen, Bet and Morgan's baby daughter, who was sleeping on a blanket nearby. Maudie, who lately had very much taken charge of the two babies, and Giles as well, put her finger to her lips as he approached. "I have only just managed to get Gwen down to sleep," she whispered.

"I just want to take your uncle for a walk," Philip told her, "if you will allow it!"

"Certainly. He needs to exercise his leg, Bet says so."

"I pity the man who gets your daughter for a husband," Giles said, when they were out of earshot. "A more determined female I have rarely seen."

"She's wonderful, isn't she?" Philip said proudly. "And destined to go far, I feel. I will try to find a husband worthy of her when the time comes!"

"Maudie for a wife and you for a father-in-law? Poor sod!"

They both laughed and walked along in companionable silence for a while beneath a shady avenue of chestnut trees. Giles still needed to use a cane for support but he hardly limped anymore.

"How is your leg?" Philip asked him.

"It doesn't hurt now. I thought I might try to ride again."

"Good idea. Have you had any thoughts about what you are going to do when you've recovered?"

"I was thinking of buying a house in town. I have a little money put aside but if I wait for William's return, I shall never have the chance to do it."

"Is that what you really want, to work for William again?"

"No, to be frank I have had enough of him and of the politicians for a while, but what choice do I have? Some of us, remember, will never inherit a vast estate with an income sufficient to sustain our needs."

Philip let that one pass. He knew it had always irked Giles that he had not come from a wealthy, aristocratic family, but had needed to work hard and use all of his ingenuity to acquire the title and position he now held.

"But if you go back to London now then you will have to serve Queen Mary, who will no doubt insist that you to be part of her council."

Word had reached them that the Queen was struggling with her new responsibilities, and with some of the men William had appointed to advise her.

"I know." Giles passed a hand across his brow. "I dread that prospect too but I can't stay here forever, Philip, even though I know how much Marianne would like that."

"Not forever, maybe, but for a few months more. I need you here, Giles."

"For what? I am a useless invalid," Giles said irritably. "I might be able to ride soon but I cannot read properly or aim a pistol and my head aches unmercifully at times."

"Bet and Marianne are preparing a potion for that as we speak. And you had better take it," he added with a smile, "or you will have my daughter to contend with as well!"

Giles smiled too. "I am not ungrateful to you all, truly, Philip. Theresa has been magnificent and I owe you my life, but I cannot continue to live on your charity."

"So pay me back," Philip said simply. "You are not the only one staying away from London and taking advantage of William's continued absence, you know. It is my intention, as you are aware, to go over to France this month. I shall be taking Morgan and Thomas with me and, although John Bone has done a magnificent job of keeping High Heatherton going for me during these last months, I cannot expect him to do it much longer. He has the farm to manage and, besides, the timber business needs a shrewder head to handle it, as he would be the first to admit. What I am asking you, Giles, is whether you will consider running the estate for me whilst I am away."

Giles looked at him in surprise. "Me? But I know nothing of such matters."

"Giles, I really can't imagine that a man who has fought desert tribesmen in the Sahara, negotiated with slave traders and bested Moroccan pirates is going to have the least trouble in dealing with timber merchants or obtaining the highest prices for the wool from my sheep! Even I managed it for a while, when I first acquired Heatherton."

There were a great many things Philip had needed to do himself when the estate had finally become his, for there was much that had needed doing and he had been penniless then. With the aid of Morgan, Thomas and his childhood friend, John, he had succeeded. He had even worked alongside his own labourers cutting the timber, which was the lifeblood of the estate, and which had eventually provided the income which had enabled him to restore it all.

"Are you asking me become your steward?" Giles asked in amusement.

"Hardly! What I am asking for is your help. Thanks to King Louis, I am now the master of my mother's family estate which, with any luck, I shall be able to turn back into a profitable enterprise, one that might one day benefit us all. But I cannot do it alone. Morgan will have to take charge of the work that will be required at the vineyard and I shall need to spend a great deal of time in France."

"A country with whom we are at war," Giles reminded him.

Philip made a dismissive gesture. "Louis will grant me safe passage. Think about it, Giles. This could be the perfect solution for the two of us."

Giles stopped walking and leaned upon his cane to look at him. "You're serious about this, aren't you?"

"Never more so."

"You are not just feeling sorry for me?"

"Pity? For you?" Philip shook his head. "Never. You would always get by, Giles. You were a selfish little bastard when I first met you and you have always known exactly what you wanted and how to go about getting it. This is a proposition that will benefit us both and, with any luck, will distance us from William for a while. I have no wish to fight for him again and, I imagine, you have even less desire to be at his beck and call when he does finally return."

"When did you think of this?" Giles demanded. "Is it since I was injured?"

"No," Philip assured him, "but it was whilst we were in Ireland."

"You never mentioned a word of it before. The truth now."

"The truth is that it was after William forbade me to go looking for you," Philip said quietly, for he did not like reminding Giles of the fact. "I decided there and then that he didn't deserve either of us. My life and yours have been inextricably bound together ever since you first persuaded me to become your patron and I promised myself that, if I found you alive, I would devise a way that we could work together for our mutual benefit and to hell with William, his whining politicians and his Court."

Giles was silent for a moment and Philip wondered if he was going to turn his suggestion down. He hoped not, for he had meant what he said, but he knew that Giles would never take any decision without weighing it up and deciding how it would best benefit him. Unlike Philip himself, Giles was not a gambler.

"You are asking me to risk displeasing the King who gave me an earldom and elevated me from being an outlaw to holding one of the highest positions in his entourage."

"And who almost got you killed," Philip reminded him.

"You've nearly done that a couple of times!"

That was true. The scar Giles bore upon his face was the result of the part he had played in one of Philip's past schemes, and on another occasion, but for Thomas' help, he would have been arrested for treason.

"Well you will hardly be put at risk this time," Philip pointed out. "You will be as safe in Sussex as you would be in London. Safer, perhaps, since I gather that people throw bricks at you there! The greatest problem you are likely to have here is ensuring that you get the best price for your timber, which can't surely be anywhere near as risky as haggling with Arabs over the price of slaves. Besides, if you take Ahmed along with you then I doubt you'll have many arguments! You can always use your injuries as an excuse to William," Philip reminded him. "He would take you back at any time, I'm sure, if that is what you eventually decide you want. He'd be a fool not to, after all you've done for him. It might even do him good to discover what it is like to manage without you for a change. What do you say?"

"I'm tempted," Giles admitted, "and I know how happy it would make Marianne. She hates our London life and we get so little time there to spend with Will. When are you hoping to leave for France?"

"That rather depends on you."

"Oh, it would do, wouldn't it! You always have the damnedest ways of persuading people to go along with your plans."

"Do it for your sister, if not for me," Philip said craftily. "She and Bet are as capable as they come, but with the harvest beginning they have their own work to do, helping and organising the women on the estate. There are crops to be picked and stored as well as preserving to be done if Heatherton is to be entirely self-sufficient throughout next Winter. I can't leave them to cope alone at such a busy time."

Giles gave him a sidelong glance. "You'll be telling me next that you can't go if I don't agree to stay here! Very well. If this really means that much to you, then I will run your estate whilst you are away."

"Thank you." Philip was delighted. "In that case I will be travelling to Paris next week. I was thinking of taking Luc with us too, if you can spare him. I doubt he'll be much help here and it might be a good idea to have a Frenchman with us."

"But you are half-French," Giles pointed out.

"Even so, there may be some who might object to my claiming the property."

"Object to a Hero of France?" Giles said archly. "Hardly likely! Take him if you want, but why don't you just admit that, whether or not he is your son, you have come to like him?"

Luc's appearance in their lives had been a shock to everyone, not least to Philip himself. He had sired a few bastards in his wild, younger days but he had hardly expected any of them to actually confront him in France and claim that he was their father! Were it not for Giles' decision to take Luc back to England, Philip would have been happy never to have seen him again but Luc had grown on him a little lately and he had to grudgingly admit, if only to himself, that it was entirely possible that the young Frenchman could be his offspring. Especially since he seemed to have inherited his blonde hair and blue eyes.

"He might be a useful person to have around," he said, which was all he was prepared to say on the matter!

Philip's house in Paris meant a great deal to him. It was the first house he had ever owned, bought with the aid of a generous gift from King Louis, in appreciation of his service in the French army, fighting in the Dutch Wars. When the Edict which had protected the Huguenots was revoked Louis had been persuaded by Madame de Maintenon, who detested Philip, that he should be treated no differently than the French Protestants, who were being forced to sell their properties. Fortunately, the King's brother, Monsieur, was a friend of Philip's and disliked Maintenon quite as much as he did. Monsieur had bought the house and now rented it back to him for a nominal sum.

As soon as Philip got to Paris, he paid him a visit at the Palais Royale and Monsieur, was thrilled to see him again.

"I've been so worried about you and Giles, fighting in that dreadful place," he told him. Giles was a close friend of Monsieur's as well and he was horrified when Philip described his brother-in-law's injuries.

"Shouldn't you have been worrying about King James?" Philip said, for James was Louis' and Monsieur's cousin.

Monsieur shrugged. "I don't like him as much as I like you two and, besides, I don't suppose he did much fighting."

Monsieur had done some fighting in the past, indeed he had once been a Lieutenant-General at the Battle of Cassel and had personally led a charge that had won the French a significant victory against William's Dutch troops. That had been over twenty years ago and he had been acclaimed as a hero, but poor Monsieur had been a victim of his own success. The people of Paris had turned out to cheer him when he returned and Louis had begun to fear his brother's popularity. Their uncle Gaston had caused trouble throughout their father's reign by his attempts to usurp power and, determined this would not be his fate, Louis had forbidden Monsieur to ever hold a position of importance again.

He was still a popular figure at Court though, for Monsieur was attractive and witty. Deprived of any better use of his talents, he concentrated on organising balls and receptions, and he had grown more and more outrageous as time went by. He was privy to every intrigue and scandal that took place and he regularly fell in and out of love with handsome young men. He had been unashamedly in love with Philip for years and, although Philip did not return his passion, he was genuinely fond of Monsieur, who had been a good friend to him.

As well as purchasing his house for him, Philip knew that Monsieur had been instrumental in persuading Louis to grant him the Pasquier estate. He would never forget those and the many other favours Monsieur had done for him during the years they had known one another, and he would always be loyal to him.

"My brother will be expecting you to attend upon him immediately at Versailles but, after that, I insist that you spend a few days here with me," Monsieur said. "After all, it has been a whole year since I saw you."

Impatient though Philip was to travel down to Languedoc, he knew that he owed the First Gentleman of France this courtesy.

"Of course, Monsieur."

"I would like to see Luc sometime too," Monsieur said. "I always liked him."

"Yes, I know you did." Philip said heavily. Luc had once been part of Monsieur's set, placed there to spy upon him, so it had turned out, by Louvois, the King's Minister of War.

He became aware that Monsieur was studying him closely, and evidently finding it difficult to conceal his amusement.

"What is it?" Philip asked him.

"Are you going to tell me now?"

"Tell you what?"

"The truth about Luc. At first you did not like him, you made that perfectly plain, and the next thing you are taking him back to England with you."

"Giles took him, not me," Philip reminded him.

"But Giles does nothing without good reason, we all know that, so tell me, who is Luc, and why is he so important to you?"

"He might be my son," Philip admitted reluctantly.

Monsieur gave a shriek of laughter.

"How priceless! So that is the secret!"

"I doubt it will be one much longer," Philip said dryly, for Monsieur could not keep even the smallest secret.

"I'll not tell a soul." Monsieur pledged.

Philip regarded him with exasperation. "Yes, of course you will!"

Since King Louis had come under the influence of the religious and disapproving Madame de Maintenon, the Palace of Versailles had become more restrained. When Philip had first visited it, as a young man, he had thought it the most exciting place in the world but he sensed a change in the atmosphere now.

The Hall of Mirrors was still filled with gossiping courtiers and he could see yet more exquisitely dressed figures promenading in the gardens that were visible through its tall windows, but he thought they all seemed a little subdued. He was beginning to understand why Monsieur's lavish parties at the Palais Royale were so popular with courtiers who still wanted to have a little fun.

As he walked the length of the magnificent gallery on his way to Louis' closet, he glanced up at the ceiling, which was decorated with paintings depicting the past victories France had won since Louis had been in power. One of them showed the crossing of the Rhine and Philip could not resist a wry smile for he had been there, fighting the Dutch troops of William of Orange, who was now his king. That had been Philip's first campaign, and it was where he had made a name for himself and been acclaimed a hero.

Philip thought King Louis looked more careworn than when he had last seen him and he wondered whether the war that he was waging with the allied troops on his borders was beginning to take its toll. Even so, to him, Louis would always be magnificent. Philip had a greater respect for the French king that he had ever had for either King Charles or King James and, although he had helped to place William on the English throne, in Philip's eyes the Dutchman could not compare with him as a monarch. William had been right when he had said that Philip's true allegiance was with Louis, despite the inconvenient fact that France was now England's enemy.

Philip made him a low, elaborate bow, for Louis, unlike William, demanded a proper show of homage from his courtiers. He also preferred them to be decorative, and Philip had always been good at that. He was dressed for the occasion in a coat of dark blue velvet, trimmed with silver lace, beneath which showed a long, cloth of silver waistcoat, covered in blue, embroidered flowers.

Louis nodded approvingly at the sight of him.

"Elegant as ever, Philip. It is good to see you again."

"I would have returned sooner but I have been a trifle busy, your Majesty!"

"Yes. Annoying my cousin in Ireland, so I hear."

"I fear so, your Majesty, although I did not see too much of King James whilst I was there," Philip said truthfully. "I trust he managed to get back safely?"

Louis gave him a sharp look but Philip kept his expression bland.

"I was saddened by Schomberg's death," Louis said, changing the subject.

"As was I, your Majesty. He was a great man and a brilliant commander."

"That he was. I never wanted him to leave France, you know. I only hope your Dutch king appreciated his service as much as I did."

Philip thought probably not. The old general had told him that William had been impatient at their lack of progress in the months before the King had arrived in Ireland, even though they had been hampered by constant sickness and the need to train their raw troops, but he kept that to himself.

"I saw him fall," he said instead. "He died heroically, as you would expect." Philip also refrained from reminding Louis that Schomberg had died leading the French Huguenots against their Catholic countrymen.

"You seem to have emerged unscathed, as usual," Louis said, "and now I suppose you have come back to France to remind me of my promise to you."

"I may have been forced to fight your troops in Ireland, your Majesty, but I have not, and will not, fight them on French soil," Philip assured him. "I have kept my part of the bargain,"

"So you have, and I shall keep mine," Louis said, "but what do you intend to do with your mother's vineyard when you have taken possession of it?"

"I intend to grow fruit, your Majesty."

"Do you indeed?" Louis' searching blue eyes met his for a moment. "You are not going to cause me any trouble, are you, Philip?"

"When have I ever done so, your Majesty?"

"You mean apart from landing yourself in the Bastille a while ago and coming close to being assassinated in Paris only last year?"

"I can hardly be blamed for either of those misfortunes, surely," Philip protested, "since on each occasion I was the victim of other people's spite."

On the last occasion it had been Madame de Maintenon's spite which had caused the attempt upon his life, as they both well knew, although neither would ever speak the words out loud. Louis because of his insistence upon the royal family being always united in the eyes the world, and Philip because he had more sense!

"Perhaps not, and yet trouble does seem to seek you out, Philip Devalle."

"How much trouble can I possibly get into running a vineyard in Languedoc, you Majesty?"

"We will see, won't we?" Louis handed him two documents. "These are for you. One is the deed to the Pasquier estate, the keys of which are being held by the Intendant of the region. The other has my own signature upon an order that will give you and your family and servants safe passage across the whole of France, regardless of the war that at present wages between our two countries."

"Your Majesty is gracious," Philip said, as he accepted the papers. "I shall be ever in your debt."

And that, of course, was exactly what Louis had in mind, as Philip well knew!

SEVEN

∽

Whilst he was in Paris, Philip had a visit from his old friend and army comrade, Armand St. Jean. There was no-one he could have been more pleased to see. He had first met Armand when they were young captains in the French army serving with Condé and fighting against the Dutch. They had both distinguished themselves in battle under the command of the famous general and both risen to positions of high command. Philip had eventually returned to England but Armand had continued his career until a bullet had smashed his knee five years before and forced him to retire from active service.

"I little thought King William would permit you to come to France whilst our two countries are still at war, my friend," Armand said, as he accepted the glass of brandy Philip poured him. Brandy drinking was a habit they had both acquired in Holland.

"I doubt he would if he knew! So far as I am concerned, my part in this unfortunate war is now played. I have done my duty, even William acknowledged that, and an unpleasant one it was too. Do you realise that, but for the misfortune which robbed you of command, it might easily have been you who I would have faced on the other side of that damned river?"

Armand nodded. That thought had obviously occurred to him too. "Thank God it never came to that. If it is any consolation to you, James returned here a broken man."

"He should be broken," Philip said savagely. "He deserted his troops and ran back here to save himself. He left them in disorder and he left them to die. Those Frenchman fought bravely for him, Armand, and for a country whose people hated them. What is more they stood when most of the Irish fled. They deserved better and I wanted no part in their slaughter."

Philip realised that Armand would understand, better than any, how hard it had been for him to fight French soldiers.

"King Louis received him back without reproaches but I know he feels his defeat is a disgrace which reflects upon France, as James' allies. It is certainly difficult to believe that, with our troops at his disposal, the man abandoned Ireland."

Although Armand was a Catholic, Philip knew he had no liking, or respect, for King James. He did not even refer to him as the King of England, as most Frenchman did. Armand had been a soldier all his life, proud to fight for his country, and plainly could not comprehend James' behaviour.

Philip showed him the two documents Louis had given him.

"He still loves you then," Armand said with a smile.

He himself was not so well placed in Louis' affections, despite his illustrious years in the service of France. Armand, who was the Comte de Rennes, had been a widower when he left the army and, at the start of the Huguenot troubles, he had married the daughter of his Protestant neighbours before they had escaped to England. It had been a marriage of convenience, a title and protection for their daughter, Marguerite, in exchange for their land and the money he needed to restore his own neglected property, but such unions were frowned upon, especially for an aristocrat, and such a renowned soldier as himself.

Louis had never really forgiven him, even though Marguerite had become a convert, and when Armand had protested at the brutal treatment Louvois' soldiers were inflicting upon the local Protestants the King had devised an appropriate punishment. Armand had been appointed to oversee the Intendants of the various regions to ensure that no further tales of brutality could besmirch what Louis had hoped would be the peaceful conversion of his Huguenot subjects to his own faith.

For Armand this meant spending long periods away from home, and away from his young wife, who he had come to love very much, but he had little choice in the matter.

"And how do you fare?" Philip asked him.

"My duties are nearly at an end. The King has decided there are insufficient Protestants left in France to warrant my protection."

"But you don't think so," Philip guessed.

"There are still pockets of resistance, particularly in your region," Armand said, "but I don't tell him all I know."

"In Languedoc?"

"It was always the most troublesome province. I've heard tales of rebel bands hiding in the mountains and forests of the Cevennes."

"Brave men," Philip said.

"Foolish men," Armand corrected him. "They won't win, Philip. Madame de Maintenon has so much poisoned the King against them that he will not rest until every Protestant in France is converted, imprisoned or dead. Those that openly defy him now will be destroyed. There is no more that I can do for them."

"You have done enough," Philip reckoned. "So what happens to you now?"

"I pray I am permitted to retire at last to La Fresnaye." La Fresnaye was Armand's family estate. "Marguerite is with child," he added proudly.

"That is wonderful news!" Philip was pleased for his friend, even though it was a painful reminder of the baby Theresa had lost the year before.

"I thought it was time La Fresnaye had an heir," Armand said. His dark hair was greying at the temples, but he was only in his late thirties, like Philip, although the last few, trying years seemed to have aged him. "All I want now is a little peace."

"I hope you get it." Philip said sincerely. "You deserve some happiness."

"Alas, my friend, we rarely get what we deserve, I find! How simple the path of our lives seemed when we made our plans, all those years ago," he said wistfully. "All I ever wanted to be was a soldier. I was never much of a scholar and I had no desire to be a courtier or run an estate. I was determined to have a life of adventure and I accepted that I might one day die upon some battlefield but this," he indicated his wounded leg, "I never did envisage or that, on account of it, I would be forced to complete such a distasteful task. Enough of my troubles. When do you leave for Languedoc?"

"As soon as Monsieur will let me," Philip said. "It is my intention to make first for Montpellier, where I will need to introduce myself to the Intendant."

"That would be de Basville."

"You don't like him," Philip guessed, from Armand's expression.

"Frankly, no, and he doesn't like me either. Many of the Intendants object to my insistence upon their treating the Protestants fairly."

"Do you know what happened to the Pasquiers?" Philip said, forcing himself to ask the question that had sometimes troubled him.

"They got out. When I realised who they were I made sure that de Basville did not hinder them."

"Thank you, Armand," Philip said warmly. Whilst he had no affection for the Pasquiers they were, after all, his mother's family, and he had not liked the thought of them becoming victims of the anti-Protestant violence that had swept through the country.

"It was the least I could do, although it did not endear me to de Basville, of course. They had to leave everything behind, but I heard they had reached the coast safely and taken ship to the Americas. I dare say he would have preferred to have made an example of them as they were a prominent family."

"Tell me about him. I need to know who I am to be dealing with."

"He has run the province like his own little kingdom in the five years he has been in charge," Armand told him "He has given the military command to his brother-in-law and all the administrators are his own men."

"And Louis allows this?" Philip said in surprise, for the King usually liked to keep a tight control on everything that went on in the regions.

"Languedoc is a long distance from Versailles," Armand reminded him. "Many of these officials take advantage of that and King Louis allows it, so long as matters run smoothly. De Basville has an impressive record of conversions to his credit, so he is left alone."

Philip nodded, understanding. During the period after the Revocation some Intendants were more vigorous in their persecution of the Protestants than others. "He was a cruel bastard," he guessed.

"One of the worst, I fear, although he claims now, as do they all, that he was simply obeying the orders of Louvois, but he is a Jesuit, and there are none who hate the reformed religion more. By the time I arrived there most of Languedoc had been subdued so I know only what I have been told about his methods, but you must judge the man for yourself. He will be no friend to you, though, since he is a close friend of Madame de Maintenon," Armand warned him.

Philip feared he was right.

It took the better part of two weeks to travel down to Languedoc, although neither Philip nor his three companions minded the journey too much, for it took them through parts of France which none of them, including Luc, had ever seen before.

During the long hours spent together in the coach, Philip had the chance to get to know him a little better. Monsieur was right when he had said that Philip had disliked the young Frenchman at first, for Luc had shown an almost obsessive interest in him and made his resentment very plain. It was not until later that Philip had learned of Luc's claim to be his son, which had explained a lot.

It transpired that Luc's late mother had once been a pretty actress on the Paris stage and Philip had enjoyed a brief liaison with her nearly twenty years before, when he had been a young soldier on leave from the French army, but, so far as he was concerned, this was no proper proof that he was Luc's father.

Giles had discovered that Louvois, the Minister of War, upon hearing who Luc purported to be, had seen a use for him and presented him to Monsieur, whose friendship would allow him a place at Court, with a chance of meeting Philip. In exchange Louvois, who had agents everywhere, employed him as his spy inside the Palais Royale, although Philip had never divulged that to Monsieur, who he knew would have been terribly hurt. That was not the first that Giles had heard of Luc Santerre, however. At the outset of the war with France, Luc had been recruited to send any information gleaned from his privileged position at Monsieur's side to King William, which was why Giles, fearing for Luc's safety, had offered to take him to England. It had been much against Philip's own better judgement but, whether or not Luc was his son, he had certainly proved himself to be a staunch ally when Philip had sought out the men who had tried to kill him on his last visit to Paris.

That was why he had brought him along now. And that, he told himself, was the only reason.

Once they arrived in Montpellier and their trunks had been unloaded at the Inn of the Three Crowns, in the centre of the city, Philip purchased a sturdy horse for each of them at a nearby stables.

Morgan and Thomas returned to the inn whilst Philip stayed behind to pay for the animals, but he noticed that Luc had hung back.

"Tell me about these Pasquiers, my Lord," he begged him, as they walked together along the Rue Rebuffy to the inn. "All Lord Wimborne knew of them was that they would never have anything to do with you."

"That is the truth of it."

"But why?"

"The Pasquiers were a well-established family, accepted at Court. In fact, my mother was a favourite of the old king," Philip told him with a touch of pride, "and considered to be a great beauty. I think they were hoping for a better match for her than my father."

Luc bristled at that. "But the Devalles are a noble line."

Philip smiled at the passion in his voice. "Indeed they are, Luc, but it is also a line tainted, in the opinions of some, by the 'sickness' that has afflicted several generations of us," he reminded him. "They feared it might affect their grandchildren."

"That was wrong of them," Luc said hotly.

"My brother is a raving madman," Philip reminded him. "That is the only reason I was able to inherit High Heatherton."

"But you are not mad."

"Even so, they made it very clear that they wanted no connection with me."

"Not even when you became a Hero of France?" Luc cried incredulously.

"Not even then, nor I with them, frankly. Not after the way they treated my poor mother. They broke all contact with her when she went to live in England. She must have been very sad at times."

"Did she ever speak of them?"

"I have no memory of her, to my great regret. She died when I was only three years old and my father rarely spoke of her,"

Philip told him, with a sigh. "If it were not for Nanon I would know nothing at all about her."

"Nanon?"

"She was my mother's maid and her friend. She went over to England with her and stayed there, for my sake, after my mother died. Dear Nanon." Philip smiled at the memory of her. "She brought me up, she taught me to speak French and she cared for me until I left home, when I was twelve."

"Twelve is a young age to leave home, my Lord," Luc reckoned.

"Not if you have a brother like Henry." Philip shuddered at the memory. "She told me she was going to return to Languedoc and see if the Pasquiers would take her in. I hope they did, for I believe she had no family of her own."

Philip had wondered recently what might have happened to her if they had taken her in. Nanon had been a Catholic but, since no Protestant had been allowed to employ a Catholic after the Revocation, he supposed that she would have had to leave them. If she was even still alive, that is. He felt a little ashamed now that he had never bothered to try and contact her during all those years.

"I think you have learned quite enough about me for the time being," he decided. Philip had never enjoyed talking about his childhood, and he rarely did.

"There is just one question I would ask, if I may, my Lord, for it is something which troubles me," Luc said.

"And what is that?"

"The Devalle sickness. Is it possible that I might have inherited it too?"

Philip was about to remind him, yet again, that it was not certain that Luc was his son, but he saw the genuine concern on the young Frenchman's face and thought it was not the time. "It is entirely possible, but I would say, unlikely," he said instead.

"But I sometimes have fits," Luc reminded him worriedly.

"I know you do, but that is not a sign, not if my brother and grandfather were typical. If you suffered from the same affliction as Henry then the disease would have manifested itself long before now and in violent and irrational ways. I used to question my own sanity when I was younger," he confided to him. "It is only natural, after all."

"But sometimes, when I get really angry, I don't know what I am doing," Luc said quietly. "It is as if a blackness comes around me and, for a moment, I seem to lose all sense of reason."

Philip had also experienced that. "I have been known to lose control at times," he admitted, "but I have learned to tell the signs and get the better of my emotions. You will too, with practice. Occasional irrationality is not madness, Luc."

Luc looked relieved. "Thank you, my Lord. But how do I learn to tell the signs?"

"Those who care for you will see them," Philip said, recalling how both Morgan and Giles had saved him from himself in the past. "Rely on Thomas," he advised him. "He misses very little and he makes a good and loyal friend, but we all watch out for each other in this family. Of course, it may be that you are not a Devalle in any case," he could not resist adding, as they entered the inn and joined Morgan and Thomas at a table. although he softened the remark with a wink.

"I had better make myself known to the Intendant first, I suppose," Philip said, after they had eaten a meal. He was not much looking forward to that but it was a courtesy he knew he must observe, and, more importantly, de Basville was in possession of the keys to the chateau.

"Do you need me to accompany you?" Morgan asked.

"No. I think I can cope with a bureaucrat with too great an opinion of his own importance," Philip said.

"In that case, I thought I ought to try to discover a little about the wine trade, since it seems you are all looking to me to know how to run the estate," Morgan said heavily.

"Can Luc and I ride over and take a look at the house?" Thomas asked him eagerly.

"If you like. Only try not to annoy the locals too much," Philip called after them, as the two young men whooped for joy and rushed off to saddle their horses.

He watched them go with an indulgent smile then turned to find Morgan looking at him with much the same expression.

"They need a little exercise after being cooped up in that coach for so long," he offered, by way of explanation.

"Of course they do, my Lord."

That was only part of it. What Philip felt Thomas and Luc really needed, what they all needed, was a new venture to embark upon. Les Jacinthes was a project that was exciting everyone.

Including Morgan, although he knew the Welshman would never admit that!

De Basville was everything that Philip had expected, after his conversation with Armand. A supercilious-looking man of around his own age, and one who was obviously well aware of the prestige of his position, he nevertheless greeted Philip with the deference due to his rank. Despite that, it was evident to Philip that his presence in Languedoc was not exactly filling the Intendant with joy!

"I received word from the King of your coming," he said stiffly.

Even if he hadn't, Philip guessed the news would have travelled swiftly across the region, through de Basville's network of paid informants.

The Intendant took a leather bag from a strongbox in the room. "I have been requested to present you with the keys to the property and to render you every assistance."

Philip smiled, guessing at how much that must have pained the man. "Thank you."

He opened the bag that de Basville had somewhat ungraciously passed to him and took out an impressive set of keys, the keys to, Les Jacinthes, the property to which the French side of his family had never even invited him to visit.

"Did you know the Pasquiers?" he asked the Intendant.

"Not well. They left shortly after I arrived. I knew *of* them, of course. They were one of the most important families in the region. The old man was already dead before the troubles, otherwise I think it might have killed him."

Philip could not bring himself to care too much about the feelings of a grandfather who had never even wanted to meet his English grandson.

"The place has been closed up since then?"

"Yes, by order of the King, although a relative of mine, tried to buy the land," de Basville said, somewhat testily, "as well as your Catholic neighbour. You may find he is none too happy that it is has been given to another member of the family," he warned.

Philip didn't care much for the feelings of his neighbours either. "People will just have to get used to it, won't they?"

"No doubt, when they realise who you are, they will treat you with respect, my Lord."

"They had better," Philip said pleasantly, as he rose to leave.

He had paid his necessary courtesy call and received the keys to the property, so he saw no reason to prolong the interview, but the Intendant evidently felt it his duty to establish some further rapport with him, unwelcome though that duty appeared to be.

"Let us understand each other, my Lord," de Basville said. "I was never in favour of the Revocation, but I received my orders and my appointment from King Louis, who I have always been proud to serve."

"As have I," Philip said.

"Precisely. Since we are both loyal servants of the King, and have both benefitted so much from his favour, I feel we should endeavour to work together as much as possible."

Philip would dearly have loved to point out that, in his case, he had not earned Louis' favour by rigorously persecuting innocent Frenchmen, but he guessed this was de Basville's way of offering, if not exactly his friendship, at least his co-operation. He knew better than to trust anyone associated with Madame de Maintenon, of course, but he thought he had better play along. For the moment.

"As you say. I intend to visit the chateau tomorrow," he told him, in the spirit of co-operation, and also because he guessed de Basville would soon enough be made aware of it. "I have sent two members of my household ahead to see if it is habitable."

"It has not been looted, if that is what you mean, my Lord," de Basville said, looking a little put out. "This province is under my control. It is a respectable and law-abiding area. Your friend, the Comte de Rennes, was appointed to oversee the actions of Louvois' soldiers, as you know, and the people here are not savages. Even so, it may be that your men will find them less than welcoming. I trust they will not run into any trouble."

"They are both well able to take care of themselves," Philip said, unconcerned, for he had never had cause to doubt the courage or prowess of either Thomas or Luc. "They will make no unfriendly moves towards our neighbours but, should the need arise, they are both well capable of defending themselves."

The pair arrived back at the inn shortly after Philip and he beckoned them over to the table where he was sitting with Morgan, who had already returned from making his own enquiries.

"How did it look?" he asked them impatiently.

"Impressive," Thomas said. "There are no signs of damage, although I could not see inside for all the windows are shuttered and the doors are locked."

"So all was well?"

"Fine, apart from the fact that whilst I was inspecting the back of the house Luc ended up in a fight!"

"The man came at me with a sword," Luc protested. "What was I supposed to do?"

"De Basville did warn me about our neighbours," Philip admitted, "but I little thought they would be there waiting for you."

"I don't believe he was your neighbour, my Lord, for he said I was trespassing upon his land and asked me who I was," Luc said.

"His land? What did you tell him?"

"That I was the son of Philip Devalle, the hero of the Rhine."

Philip glanced over at Thomas, who raised his eyes to heaven.

"And that was when he attacked you, when you told him that?"

"Yes. I was doing well until Thomas appeared and ordered us to desist. The man ran off when he saw there were two of us."

"He certainly was doing well," Thomas admitted, "but I was not sure how running a man through with a sword would fit with your instructions not to annoy the locals!"

Philip was grateful that the dependable Thomas had been on hand to control the situation.

"Who the hell was he to accuse you of trespassing on his land?" he wondered.

"He didn't say, my Lord, but he was obviously no admirer of yours," Thomas said.

"Obviously! We will see if he reappears when we ride over there tomorrow, Morgan."

"Perhaps we should come with you," Thomas said. "He may not be alone next time."

Philip looked over at Morgan, who was a pretty fearsome-looking individual to any who did not know him, with his shaggy black hair and swarthy looks. The fact that half of his right ear was missing seemed to add to his menacing appearance and armed, as he usually was, with his trusty knife he was not a person most would challenge lightly. "Oh, I think we'll cope," he decided. "Besides, I want you to explore Montpellier tomorrow, Thomas, and use your unerring talent for seeking out the lowest elements of every city! Search the taverns and the streets and discover what is really happening beneath the surface of this 'respectable and law-abiding' place."

Thomas' past as a thieving urchin of the streets had many times stood Philip in good stead when it was necessary to discover the seamier side of a city's life. It existed in both London and Paris, and he doubted that Montpellier would prove to be much different, despite de Basville's claims.

"I'll go with him," Luc offered.

"No, you won't," Philip said. "You'll get into far too much trouble. This is something Thomas will be better doing alone. I have another job for you in any case."

"What job is that?" Luc asked eagerly.

"One that only you out of the four of us could do," Philip told him. "There is quite another aspect to Montpellier, one which might pose even more of a problem to me, so I need someone who can observe it from the inside. Tomorrow is Sunday. You are a Catholic and I need you, Luc, to go to church!"

EIGHT

The following day Philip and Morgan set out for Les Jacinthes. Whilst they rode, Morgan talked about what he had learned the day before. He had said little about it the previous evening, and Philip had not pressed him, knowing that Morgan would tell him everything in his own good time, when he'd had the chance to consider it properly himself.

"I talked to some of the workers in our neighbour's fields. It would seem to me that, at the beginning at least, it would make sense to have our harvest processed off the estate. There is an Abbey called Fontfroide, near Narbonne, who have been producing their own wines for centuries and those I spoke with seemed to think the monks there might be prepared to help with ours."

Philip liked the idea but Narbonne was days away, especially at the pace a horse and wagon could travel the country roads with its perishable load.

"Surely that's too far to take it."

"Not upon the canal," Morgan told him, with a hint of triumph in his usually expressionless features.

"You mean 'Riquet's ditch'?" Philip laughed. He had often heard the courtiers at Versailles referring to the Canal Royale by that mocking name during the many years it was being dug and constructed, but the canal was finished now, although Paul Riquet, who had designed and built it, had not lived to see it completed.

"Exactly. It would mean we only have to get the fruit as far as the port of Marseillan. From there a barge could take it to where it could be easily transported a few miles to Fontfroide."

Philip looked at him admiringly. "That's brilliant, Morgan."

Morgan accepted the praise with a shrug of his shoulders.

They rode on until they reached what Philip guessed must be the outskirts of the estate. They paused for a moment and took in the view. There were rocky, wooded mountains in the distance and they could see occasional flashes of sunlight reflecting on what looked like the sparkling water of a stream running down towards the gently sloping fields. They were still planted with vines but, even from the road, he could see what five years of neglect had done to the once neat rows of fruit. When they had gone a little further, Philip caught his first glimpse of the chateau itself, half-hidden by the line of trees in front of it.

It was not so large, nor so grand as High Heatherton, but it was attractive, built in the pale, golden-coloured local stone and with a pinkish, tiled roof. Most importantly, to Philip, it had once been the home of his mother. He did not dare to hope that there was anything left in it which he could associate with her, for he doubted it was little more than an empty shell of a building, but just to know that she had once lived there was enough to make it a special place to him.

He turned to Morgan, the companion who had been staunch beside him, whatever he had attempted, even when the Welshman had disapproved of his ventures.

"Well, Morgan, what do you think? Have I been a fool to take the risk of coming here?"

Morgan's expression softened as he glanced up at the house and then across the fields of pathetic-looking fruit. "No," he decided. "I don't believe you have."

Philip looked at him in surprise. "Don't tell me that you actually believe this to be a worthwhile enterprise!"

"Probably the most worthwhile you have ever attempted, my Lord."

That was encouragement indeed from Morgan.

"In that case, my old friend, how can it fail? Come on, let's get a closer view of the house."

All was as Thomas had said, the windows were shuttered and the doors locked but the place looked none the worse for being abandoned and there was certainly no sign that any had tried to break in.

Although the vineyard had shown obvious signs of neglect, the formal gardens behind the house were surprisingly tidy.

"It is almost as though someone has been watching over it," Philp said quietly to Morgan, "just as someone is watching us now."

"I got that feeling too." Morgan's hand was already on the hilt of the knife at his belt.

They both looked over to the woods which ran just behind the house.

"Perhaps we are about to meet Luc's attacker," Philip suggested. "Surely he will have more sense than to try to take the two of us."

"Unless, of course, he is not alone this time."

"Shall we find out?" Philip indicated the trees at the edge of the gardens. "He has to be in there."

"He may have a pistol," Morgan warned, as Philip stepped out onto the open lawn.

"If he had wanted to kill me, I dare say he could have picked me off a dozen times whilst we have been in this garden." He raised his voice. "We know you are there. Come, show yourself."

For a moment there was no sign of movement then, from out of the trees, a man stepped forward, his sword held ready. He was blonde, like Philip, and quite tall.

Philip held his arms to the side, showing that his own sword was still in its scabbard, although that did not mean he couldn't produce it swiftly if the need arose.

"Approach," he told the stranger. "We mean you no harm, unless you intend to threaten us, as you did a member of my household yesterday."

The man came closer, slowly but not with any caution. More, with a touch of arrogance, Philip thought.

He stopped a few yards away and faced them defiantly. "By what right are you here?" he demanded.

"I own the damned place."

"This is Pasquier property."

"It is now Devalle property," Philip corrected him, "and I am Philip Devalle."

"I know who you are." The man almost spat the words and brought his sword up in front of him.

Philip saw Morgan tense. The Welshman's hand had not left the weapon at his belt and, as he withdrew it slowly, the stranger took a step back.

"Who is this, your bodyguard?" he asked sneeringly, but Philip could detect a touch of nervousness in his manner now.

He knew he had to diffuse the situation if was not to get out of hand. Morgan was, outwardly, an impassive individual but if any danger threatened his master then Philip had reason to know that his reactions were swift and deadly.

He put a restraining hand upon the Welshman's arm.

"This," he said, "is Morgan, who is my steward and my closest friend. I tell you now that he will kill you without a second's hesitation if he thinks you mean me ill, so I suggest you sheathe your sword. That's better," he continued, when the man had sulkily done as he asked. "Now that I have given you our names perhaps you might return the courtesy and tell me who the hell *you* are."

"I am your cousin, Antoine Pasquier."

Philip had not expected that.

"My cousin?"

"My father was your mother's brother, Guy Pasquier."

Nanon had certainly told him that his mother had a younger brother but, for some reason, it had never occurred to Philip that he might have cousins.

Morgan took a step back, studying them both together. "I reckon he might be speaking the truth."

"Why should I lie?" Antoine demanded.

"Quite a few reasons I can think of," Philip said. "In any case, I understood from de Basville that the Pasquiers all escaped at the beginning of the troubles."

"De Basville? You have spoken with that devil? You should have killed him while you had the chance."

Philip exchanged looks with Morgan. "That's all we need, another hot-headed Frenchman! Why did you attack Luc?" he asked Antoine.

"He said he was your son."

"Yes," Philip said with a sigh. "He tells me that as well, but that was no reason to attack him."

"So is he your son or not?"

"Maybe," Philip allowed.

"A bastard?"

"Decidedly he is a bastard. Whether he is mine is a different matter but the point at issue here is why you ran at him with a sword."

"Because no mad Devalle whelp is entitled to inherit Les Jacinthes, and that includes you."

"He's a Pasquier, alright," Philip said to Morgan. He spoke the words calmly but an anger was welling up inside him, an anger at the way that his mother had been treated by this haughty family, and at the way that he had never been accepted as a part of them. He decided to put things straight.

With a lightening movement, he swung round on Antoine and kicked him full in the stomach before the Frenchman had time to draw his sword again. Philp drew it for him as he lay on the ground, pulling it out of its scabbard and hurling it across the path. He withdrew his own and threw that on the ground also, before dragging Antoine to his feet. "You want to fight, Antoine Pasquier? Then fight me, not a boy."

Antoine staggered back as Philip's first punch caught him on the jaw, but he quickly recovered and came at him, hatred burning in his eyes.

"You have no right to this place."

"I have every right," Philip said, dodging with ease the blows Antoine was attempting to rain down on him. "I have my mother's right, she who your precious family disowned." He landed another punch, and it was a good one, which almost knocked Antoine back onto the ground. "That was for her. Come on, if you want to finish this. If not then either behave yourself or crawl back to wherever you have been hiding ever since the rest of the confounded Pasquiers sailed for the colonies."

"How did you know about that?"

"I know about it because the Comte de Rennes, who was appointed to ensure that the Huguenots in every region were treated fairly, discovered their plans and persuaded de Basville to turn a blind eye."

Antoine rubbed his jaw gingerly but made no further attempt to retaliate. "For what reason would de Rennes do that?"

"He is a friend of mine. The reason they were allowed to leave without hindrance is mainly on account of the fact that the Comte knew they were my relatives."

"And I am expected to thank you for being their salvation, I suppose," Antoine said sullenly.

"You can keep your thanks. I want nothing from any of you," Philip said.

"Except our property. What kind of man are you who would seek to profit from the misfortunes of your own family?"

"My family? Do you mean the family who did not seem even aware of my existence?" Philip flashed back. "The family who did not once invite me to visit them in all the time I was living in France?"

"Oh, we were aware of you," Antoine assured him. "It is

hard to ignore the existence of a Hero of France, but we wanted nothing to do with you."

"Yet here you are."

"I needed to see what kind of a man would steal a property from its rightful owners."

"And now you know. Like it or not, Antoine, all of this belongs to me now." Philip made a sweeping gesture that encompassed the house and grounds and the slopes of the vineyard beyond. "The Pasquiers forfeited their rights to it when they defied the King."

"What of you?" Antoine demanded. "You don't appear to have suffered under the new laws."

"As it happens, I did. I lost my house in Paris," Philip said. "This estate, however, was granted to me as part of a separate bargain, one which was struck between King Louis and myself, and I intend to keep the place if I have to fight every Pasquier left in France."

"There are no others," Antoine told him. "My sisters and their families went to the Americas with my father and mother."

"Why did you not go with them?"

"Because I vowed to stay and fight for the Huguenot cause."

Philip looked at him with fresh eyes. Armand had talked about the pockets of resistance left in Languedoc but he had never considered that any of the Pasquiers might be rebels.

"You cannot fight King Louis," he said quietly.

"That's all you know," Antoine cried. "We have lost our properties and our freedoms, and many have lost their lives, but we will not give in to tyranny. I know where there are still men who are prepared to fight and I am planning to join them."

"I admire your courage," Philip said honestly, "but I believe this defiance will likely cost you your life."

"Do you intend to give me away to de Basville then?"

"Of course not. You can take yourself off and do as you please, for all I care, just so long as nothing interferes with my plans to restore this vineyard."

"What do you know about managing a vineyard?" Antoine asked sneeringly.

"Practically nothing," Philip admitted.

"Then you will fail. I have helped to run this estate since I was a child and I know how hard it can be, even when you know what you are doing."

Morgan, who had kept silent so far throughout all their exchanges, stepped forward. "Then perhaps, before you leave to join the others, you would care to share your knowledge with us."

Philip knew it was his turn to keep silent now and trust in the Welshman's intuition, as he had so many times before.

Antoine looked at him in astonishment. "Why would I do that?"

"Because this place, which was once your home, is evidently still dear to you. That is why you come here, to watch over it and see it comes to no harm," Morgan guessed. "You must always have known that it would never be yours again. Be thankful, then, that the new owner is no Catholic interloper, chosen by de Basville from amongst his cronies, but a Protestant, like yourself, and one who, whether or not you accept him to be part of your family, is probably the only Protestant in France who would be permitted to acquire it."

Philip hid a smile. Morgan did not speak much but, when he did, he always made good sense. They had been together for so long that each could read the other's thoughts and he knew the part that he must now play in the conversation.

"I think the motives you attribute to my cousin are too noble, Morgan. You may believe he is here because of love for Les Jacinthes, but I reckon he is so consumed by hatred that he wants only to thwart whoever possesses it. I suspect he would rather have the house a crumbling ruin and see the fruit rot on the vines than have anyone else thrive here, especially me."

"No, that's not true," Antoine cried passionately. "I planted some of those vines with my own hands and nurtured them until they bore fruit. They are like children to me. I would never want to see them die."

"Then help us to save them," Philip said.

Antoine looked at him uncertainly. "You mean work with you?"

"Why not?"

"I am a fugitive from the law," Antoine reminded him.

"Well I doubt that any would think of looking for you here, but I will have none of your rebel friends anywhere near Les Jacinthes," Philip warned him.

"You would still be taking a great risk, and so would the rest of your household," Antoine said. "De Basville's spies are everywhere and there are heavy penalties for harbouring Huguenots."

"In that case we shall just have to make sure that no-one discovers you." Philip said.

"And how will you do that?"

"I don't know," Philip said patiently. "I haven't thought it out yet. But as for the rest of my household, they are all well used to the taking of risks, having spent so many years with me!"

Antoine looked from one to the other, his conflicting emotions evident upon his face.

"You would be working mainly with Morgan, not myself," Philip told him, in an effort to persuade him to go along with Morgan's idea, which could solve a great many problems for him. "He is a son of the soil, whilst I, plainly, am not, which is why he is here. In fact, since I will have to return to England on occasions, you and I may not be forced to endure each other too much, which, I fancy, will please us both."

Antoine still looked doubtful. "I am afraid I am already endangering the life of a Catholic friend who has been protecting me."

"Then stay at the house."

"You mean I would be able to live here again?" Antoine said slowly.

"I don't see why not, in fact you can escort us around it now, if you wish." Philip produced the set of keys that de Basville had rather unwillingly given him.

He started off toward the house, then noticed that Antoine still stood as though rooted to the spot.

"Well?" he asked. "Are you coming or not?"

"How do I know I can trust you?"

"Oh, for God's sake!" Philip cried in frustration. "You are a harder man to befriend than you are to fight." He turned away from him. "We are wasting time here, Morgan. You were wrong. He evidently wants no part in helping this estate to live again."

"I didn't say that," Antoine protested, hastening after them. "Don't be so unreasonable."

"Unreasonable?" Philip muttered, without slowing his pace. "That comes well from a blasted Pasquier!"

∽

Thomas was waiting for them at the inn when Philip and Morgan returned. He burst out laughing when he heard their tale.

"He's your cousin? Are there any more of your relatives likely to come forth and surprise us, do you think, my Lord?"

"I sincerely hope not," Philip said with feeling. "The two that have already found me are quite troublesome enough! On that subject, where's Luc? He should have been back by now. The church is only around the corner."

Thomas laughed afresh. "Don't worry. Surely even Luc couldn't get into much trouble going to church!"

Philip was not so sure, but it was not long before the young Frenchman entered the inn and joined them at the table where they were seated, tucked away in the corner.

"How long do these services take, for goodness sake?" Philip asked him.

"I stayed behind after Mass to introduce myself to the priest," Luc said.

"I trust you didn't tell him I was your father."

"Oh no. I told him I was Louvois' nephew visiting the region from Paris," Luc said blithely. "He was very accommodating after that!"

"I'll bet he was!" Whether or not Philip was prepared to acknowledge Luc as his son, he could not fault his ingenuity. "I can see why claiming kinship with Louvois instead of me might have been advantageous. So, what did you discover from this accommodating priest?"

"I discovered that he is a worried man, my Lord. It transpires that almost half of his flock were once Huguenots, and have now converted to save their lives. It is compulsory for them to attend Mass and to take the sacrament, but he knows they only pretend to be genuine converts and he is afraid that they will bring trouble upon themselves and him."

"What kind of trouble?"

"De Basville has appointed an Archpriest called du Chayla as his Inspector of Missions," Luc said. "This man has trained his own priests, who will take over a parish if it is not succeeding in keeping its newly converted parishioners in line, and those men are cruel, my Lord. They seek out those they believe to be the ringleaders and hand them over to du Chayla, who keeps them prisoner in his house and tortures them before he kills them."

Thomas nodded. "I have heard that name today too, my Lord. There cannot be a more feared man in Languedoc."

"I hate bloody priests!" Philip had little regard for religion and none whatever for Catholic ministers who could perform such atrocities and still call themselves men of God.

"Not all priests are evil," Luc insisted. "I found Father Perrault, at Ste. Anne's, to be a likeable enough young man. He is doing his best to protect his congregation from themselves, but he fears he will soon lose his position and then they will be at the mercy of a successor chosen by the Abbé du Chayla."

"No doubt he is fearful of what you might divulge to your 'uncle' as well!" Philip said.

"I did promise I would give a good report of his behaviour," Luc told him, smiling, "but, truly, he is not a bad fellow. He confided to me that he is the third son of an aristocrat and only became a curé to please his father. I think there are a probably a great number like him who want no part in persecuting their fellow Frenchman."

"Let's hope you are right." Philip turned to Thomas. "And what did *you* discover?"

"That the region is a hotbed of insurrection."

"Is it now?" After his conversation with his cousin, Philip was not too surprised.

"There is a whole network of people supplying the rebels hiding out in the Cevennes. They are taking them food and weapons right under the very noses of the authorities."

"Weapons? Where the hell are they getting those?"

"It seems like, as with most places, you can get anything you want here if you know the right people," Thomas said, "and in Montpellier that is a family called the Tartours, who operate from a house in the Rue de Bayle, not far from Luc's church. They run everything and any thief working in the city, from the lowliest cutpurse to the most expert picklock, must pay them dues, or face the consequences."

"And this right under de Basville's nose?" Philip asked, amused.

"They protect their own, my Lord, a bit like Alsatia."

"What is Alsatia?" Luc asked.

"It's an area of London that our Thomas knows well," Philip answered for him, "where criminals of the worst kind hide out and the law never ventures in. Because he was once one of their own, they sheltered him, when he was on the run from the law after I was arrested."

"Like the Cours des Miracles in Paris?" Luc suggested.

"Very like," Thomas said, for in that district, between St. Denis and Montmartre, a thriving criminal fraternity still operated, despite the best efforts of the Paris police chief, La Reynie, to suppress it.

"And how did you find all this out?" Philip wondered.

"I let it be known I was a thief and wanted to ask permission from the family to work an area of the city," Thomas said. "I was told Emile Tartours would take half my gains until I had proved my worth but that I might do better, if I had the nerve for it, running guns and supplies to the Huguenots in the mountains. It is risky with du Chayla on the prowl, but apparently they pay well and are planning to rise up against the authorities when they are ready."

Philip cursed. "That's all we need, to get caught up in a religious war. I am pleased with both of you," he told the two young men.

"What about you and Morgan, my Lord?" Luc asked. "Did you run into any trouble at the house?"

"Nothing we could not handle," Philip assured him.

Thomas looked from one to the other, when Philip said no more. "Well aren't you going to tell him, my Lord?" he asked impatiently.

"Tell me what?"

"We encountered the man who attacked you," Philip said. "He turned out to be my cousin."

It took Luc took a second to digest that information. "But that means one of my own relatives tried to kill me!"

He looked so horrified that Thomas and Morgan could not keep straight faces.

"You are beginning to learn, Luc," Philip said, as solemnly as he could manage, "that it can sometimes be quite dangerous to be a Devalle."

NINE

༄

Philip was agreeably surprised to find that, far from being an empty shell, Les Jacinthes appeared to be much as would have been when the Pasquiers left it.

There were signs of haste, certainly. Empty boxes had been left open, boxes that might have once have contained jewellery or precious keepsakes, the contents of clothes chests had been scattered about when their owners had selected which few items they could carry and books were lying crookedly on shelves where other, more favoured ones, had been removed to accompany them on their long journey into the unknown.

But there was little that Philip could find which might have once belonged to his mother, not even in the room Antoine said had once been hers. He had half-hoped to discover a little of her childhood there, a doll, perhaps, a sampler she had embroidered, or at least a portrait of her as a young girl but it almost seemed as though the family had expunged the memory of her from their home and from their lives, and any remnants of sympathy which Philip might still have had for the once great family, who had been brought so low, disappeared with that discovery.

He decided to occupy her room, nonetheless, when they moved into the chateau. Antoine moved back into what had been his old bedchamber and Morgan chose the room nearest to Philip but Thomas and Luc, with the enthusiasm of youth, raced all over the house inspecting every room before they selected which ones they wanted.

Antoine regarded their behaviour with disapproval but the opinions of a Pasquier were not of much consequence to Philip, although he did stress to both him and Luc that there was to be no recurrence of what had happened between them at their first meeting, no matter what provocation either gave the other.

He had decided that Antoine could pose as one of the companions he had brought with him from England. For working outside the house, Philip decided to buy him a dark wig and ensure that he always wore a hat pulled well down over his eyes. Even so, he dared not take the risk of employing anyone who might recognise him and report his presence to the authorities.

This meant that they were going to have to do all the work themselves, which he had not bargained upon. Leaving Morgan to assist Antoine, he, Thomas and Luc set about some of the other tasks that needed to be done outside the chateau.

There was a well close to what had once been the kitchen garden, an ancient one, Philip guessed from its construction, made of stone and roofed over with a giant slab of granite. Philip was relieved to discover that the water in it was clean and sweet and he put Luc to work to clear it of the leaves and debris that had accumulated during it years of disuse.

He found a job for Thomas too. There was a little stone building in one of the fields that had been built to house equipment but it had deteriorated badly, its door rotted off its hinges and gaping holes where the roof tiles had fallen through. Thomas, who had lovingly restored the long-disused stables at High Heatherton when they had first moved there, set about its repairs with a will.

Morgan and Antoine were making good progress, meanwhile, along the rows of vines, pruning and tying back those which could be saved. There was little Philip could do, or wanted to do, to assist them, but he was more than happy to draw water from the little stream which ran along the foot of the mountains and transport the buckets to the vines in the horse and cart he had purchased for use on the estate. He also loaded up the cart with the debris that their work was making, which he took away to burn.

"I little thought my lofty cousin would soil his delicate hands with such rough work," Antoine sneered, watching him drive a cartload away.

"You don't know him very well," Morgan said, looking up from his own task. "Do you imagine High Heatherton was the fine estate it is today when he first got it? One wing of the house had been gutted by fire with most of the contents ruined, where the rooms had been left open to the weather. The fields and woods had been neglected for years and those tenants who had remained were near starvation, for his brother had given them no money to replace livestock or to sow new crops.

He restored it all, working alongside his own labourers to cut the timber from his woods, which he sold to raise the money to rebuild the house and make the land around it profitable again."

"I didn't realise," Antoine said, in a chastened tone.

"Then don't ever judge him," Morgan said harshly. "Your cousin is a man to respect and to admire. He is brave, he is honourable and he is the finest person I or any man could ever hope to serve."

"Yet he is loyal to King Louis, who persecutes those of our faith," Antoine countered.

Morgan shrugged his shoulders and continued with his work. "Is any man perfect?"

"I suppose I'll have to send for some household staff from High Heatherton," Philip told the others crossly after the first week of shifting for themselves.

That was another thing he had not bargained on and for which he blamed his cousin. Luc had proved himself to be a reasonable cook, for his mother had taught him, but it was obvious that they were going to need someone to take care of them and the house.

"I know a person who might be prepared to help," Antoine said, sounding a little reluctant. "Someone who would not betray me."

"I trust it is a Catholic someone," Philip said severely. "I don't propose to open my house to anyone else who is hiding from de Basville."

"She's a Catholic," Antoine assured him, "and she is the person who was hiding me before you came. I will fetch her tomorrow if you like."

"Will she be prepared to work for a Protestant do you think?"

"I'm certain she will work for *you*," Antoine said cryptically.

Philip frowned at the almost resentful tone which had entered his cousin's voice and wondered who the woman might be. A sweetheart, possibly, he guessed. That might account for it.

Antoine left very early the next morning, taking the horse and cart. When he returned, Philip saw that a slight figure wearing a large straw hat, which shaded most of her face, was sitting beside him. Philip sent Luc out to greet her first, thinking that the presence of a Frenchman might put her more at her ease, and carried on poring over the plans of the vineyard, which he had spread out upon a table in the garden.

He was aware of a woman's soft footsteps approaching him down the stone path and he glanced up, ready to greet her.

It was not Antoine's sweetheart. Her hair was grey and, although still good-looking, she was plainly in her sixties All the same, Philip's heart leapt when he saw her.

"Nanon?" he said disbelievingly.

She made to curtsey to him, but Philip gave her no chance. Instead he put his arms around her and kissed her upon both cheeks. She was laughing, and her eyes brimmed with tears of joy.

Philip felt emotional too.

"Dearest Nanon, I never thought to see you again."

"Nor I you, and what a magnificent sight you are, Lord Philip. So handsome, so elegant," Her voice wavered and she turned her head aside to hide the tears that had begun to flow down her lined cheeks. "Forgive me, I am overwhelmed."

"By me? Surely not!! You, who used to scold me all the time!"

"I never did." she was laughing now through the tears.

"You were usually cross with me for something or the other, as I recall," he teased her, "but I forgive you all of it now for you taught me your language and brought me up to be a young gentleman."

"You were always a young gentleman," she insisted, "and the best master I could ever have wished for. You treated me kindly. I loved your mother and I loved you."

"I'm grateful that you did," Philip said quietly. "Without you there my childhood would have been even more miserable than it was. You were the only one who gave a damn about me and made my life bearable."

"I think your father loved you in his way."

"No, Nanon. If he had loved me, he would have kept Henry away from me. My father knew how I was suffering at his hands and yet he allowed it to continue rather than admit to the world that his precious elder son was sick and should be put where he could do no harm. Look only at what he did to you after I left."

The last time they had met was when Nanon had come to say goodbye to him, whilst he was a pupil at St. Paul's School in London. The reason she had come home to France was because Henry, no longer having his younger brother to torment, had attacked her instead.

"I was just glad that you were out of his reach," she said, shuddering at the memory. "I feared that he would kill you one day."

Philip had often thought that too at the time, for he had received some vicious beatings at his brother's hands and would always bear the scars upon his back to remind him of them.

"Well he's where he can't hurt either of us now," he said. "I had the bastard locked up in Bedlam, where he can do no harm to anyone."

"And now you are the master of High Heatherton, which is how it should be," she said. "To think you used to hate it there."

"It has become a happy place, and I will take you back there one day, if you wish," Philip pledged. "You can see it as it should always have been, and you can meet my wife, Theresa, and my little daughter. She is named Madeleine, after my mother, though we call her Maudie. The only problem is that they will love you so much that I doubt they will ever let you leave!"

Philip spoke the words lightly, but he was quite sincere. Now that the Pasquiers had left, he guessed Nanon would have no-one to take care of her as she grew older. He felt he owed her a debt of gratitude for the gentle care she had given him during his childhood, but, more than that, now she had come back into his life he did not want to lose her again. Theresa, he knew, would welcome her with open arms and she would be safe there, certainly safer than she would be in Languedoc if de Basville ever discovered that she had been harbouring Antoine.

"I would like that," she told him, the eyes which a few moments ago had been damp with tears now sparkling with excitement at the prospect. "I have often regretted that I ever returned to France at all, if I am honest. The Pasquiers agreed to take me back, which was good of them, although your grandfather threatened to dismiss me on the spot if he ever heard me speak your mother's name. Your uncle Guy and his wife were nice to me though and I looked after their children. The two girls were good as gold but Antoine was always such a troublesome boy. So very different from you."

"And yet you have been risking your life to protect him?"

"What else could I do? When the family left, they gave me a small amount of money, all that they could spare, and I rented a little house on the outskirts of the town. I took him in because he had nowhere else to go."

"He should have gone with the others," Philip said.

"I told him so, but he wants to fight, he says."

"That's his choice, but he had no right to put you in danger."

"I couldn't turn him away. Besides, he was the only link I had left to your mother and to you, for until today I had no notion you were even in France."

"You did not know I was the new owner of Les Jacinthes?" Philip said incredulously "Antoine never told you?"

"Not a word, or I would have come to see you sooner."

"I will never understand these Pasquiers, Nanon. Do you know the first time that I met him he threatened me with a sword?"

"I'm not surprised! He was ever ruled by his passions, that boy, and, remember, he was brought up to hate you. I think he was jealous of you too; of your success and the affection he knew I still bore you."

And that, Philip realised, explained the resentment in Antoine's manner when he had offered to fetch her.

"Damn him! The sooner Morgan has no more need of him and he is out of our way the better," Philip said, with feeling. "Let him follow his noble cause, if that is what he wants. He will probably die for it, then he will be less trouble to us all."

Nanon put her head upon one side and smiled at him. "You don't wish him dead. I still recognise in you the child I raised and I know you are too noble for that. He is your cousin, after all, your own blood."

"I put but little store on blood, Nanon," Philip said. "My father, my brother and my wretched Pasquier cousin count as nothing compared with those I hold dear and choose to have close to me. Morgan and young Thomas, both of whom I brought with me from England, are dearer to me than any Devalle or Pasquier. They are part of my family, as are you, together with my precious wife and child, and I have a brother-in-law in England who is more like a brother to me than Henry ever was."

"What of the handsome French boy who came to meet me?"

"Luc? Antoine tried to kill him too, by the way. In truth, I don't know who Luc is, but his mother was an actress I knew long ago in Paris."

"You have a love child?" Nanon said, in mock horror.

"More than one, I suspect. I have not exactly been an angel, Nanon!"

"I never thought you would be, not with your looks! I bet the ladies of the Court threw themselves at your feet, didn't they?"

"Most of them did," Philip admitted, modestly

"Do you recall how I used to tell you they would eat you up alive? All you wanted in those days was to go to Court and join the army. You have done it all now and you are a great hero. I'm so proud of you," she said, taking his two hands in hers. "You are everything your mother would have wanted you to be."

"I hope so," Philip said with feeling.

"So, for her sake and mine, you will try to be friends with your cousin Antoine, won't you?"

"I'll try, Nanon," Philip promised resignedly. "You're right, I do not want him dead, but I could wish him to be a little more…" he searched for the word, "…manageable."

After he had introduced Nanon to Thomas and seen her settled in her old quarters, Philip went in search of his cousin and found him out in the vineyard, talking with Morgan. They both looked up as he approached.

He made straight for Antoine and Morgan stepped swiftly aside.

Without a word he slammed his fist into Antoine's jaw, knocking him to the ground.

"What the hell was that for?" the Frenchman shouted, struggling to his feet.

"For putting Nanon in danger. She could have been imprisoned or even killed if any had discovered you in her house. And this," Philip dealt him another blow, which knocked him back onto the hard earth again, "is for not telling me about her until today."

Antoine glared up at him. "I would have told you if you'd asked about her, but you didn't."

And that was true. Philip had not thought to ask after her, although he felt a little ashamed of it now. Not that he was going to admit that to Antoine.

Morgan was watching the two of them, his features expressionless, as usual.

Antoine started to get to his feet for the second time, looking at him warily. "Are you going to do that again because, if you are, I may as well stay where I am."

"No." Philip reached a hand down to help him up, then turned and walked away. "She says we have to try to be friends."

Theresa greeted Matthew Stebbins, King William's envoy, politely. He had sent word ahead of his coming, which was fortunate, since it had given Giles the chance to prepare for his visit.

"Is your husband at home, my Lady?" Stebbins asked her.

"I'm afraid not. Philip is visiting friends some distance away," she told him, with her most winning smile.

"No matter, it is mainly Lord Wimborne that I came to see. How is he?"

"His wound still troubles him and his eyesight is not what it was," Theresa warned him.

"Still? That is most unfortunate, my Lady."

"You will excuse us if it is a little dark in here," she said, as they entered the room. "My brother is very sensitive to light."

The curtains were partially drawn across in the room where Giles was sitting with Marianne.

Maudie came in to join them and seated herself upon a little footstool near his feet. She glanced up at him conspiratorially, then rested her chin upon her two hands and watched their visitor.

"King William is back in England, my Lord," Stebbins said to Giles. "He sends me to request your early presence back at Court, but it would appear that you are still indisposed."

"I fear so," Giles said regretfully. "My injured leg can scarce support me without a cane."

"That is sad news indeed, my Lord, and I understand from your sister that your sight has been affected also."

"I am apparently still suffering from what is called a concussion," Giles explained. "I'm afraid I would hardly be an asset to King William at present."

"Have you consulted a physician?"

"The very best to be had here," Giles assured him. That much, at least. was true for, in Giles opinion, Bet was more knowledgeable than any local physician that they could have called. "I am told I must be patient and let nature affect its own cure in its own time. How is the King?"

"He is well, my Lord, and in good spirits, despite his defeat at Limerick."

Giles had not received word of that, although he had heard that the French army had now returned home and he had thought, when he heard the news, that William would have little to fear from the Irish troops. William had obviously thought the same when he had decided to besiege the town of Limerick but it seemed that the Irish General Sarsfield and the French governor of the town, Boisselot, had refused to surrender. Stebbins described how the King's troops had been harassed night and day, in atrocious weather that had turned the ground into a swamp.

Giles was sympathetic. He recalled Philip's tales of the constant rain in Ireland during the Autumn and Winter.

"There were several cases of fever," Stebbins told him, "and King William dreaded a repetition of what happened to General Schomberg's forces. Then Sarsfield led a raid upon a vital load of ammunition coming to the King's troops from Waterford. They killed nearly all the escort, before they spiked the guns and blew up the powder. There were no more of the big guns to be had so his Majesty decided to make a last attempt to attack with what they had, but the citizens refused to give in. Even women and children were fighting and, in the end, he was forced to abandon the siege."

Giles was thankful he had managed to miss that, but he could guess how galling it must have been for William, for it was the first defeat the King had suffered since he had gone to Ireland.

"And how was he received back in London?"

"Oh, as a hero, my Lord. There were bonfires lit and effigies burned of King James and even of King Louis."

Giles smiled as he imagined Philip's reaction to that!

Stebbins took a document, bearing the King's seal, from the pocket of his coat and held it out to him. "He sent you this letter, my Lord."

Marianne took it from him. "I will read it out to my husband later, sir."

"Of course, my Lady."

"Thank you, Mr. Stebbins." Giles struggled to his feet, wincing, as the envoy made to take his leave.

"Let me help you, uncle," Maudie leapt up and handed him his cane, then took hold of his other arm.

"Please don't trouble to see me out, Lord Wimborne," Stebbins said hastily. "I would not wish to cause you any suffering on my account."

Maudie stayed at Giles side until Stebbins' carriage had gone around the circular drive and out toward the lane. Then she collapsed upon him in a fit of giggles.

Giles shook his head at her despairingly, but his lips were twitching.

"Let me help you, uncle?" he said, attempting, unsuccessfully, to look stern. "You are a little minx!"

"I know," Maudie said cheerfully. "It worked though, didn't it? The idea just came into my head."

"I thought she was magnificent," Marianne said, laughing.

"And so were you, Aunt," Maudie told her. "Saying you would read the King's letter to him was a clever touch."

"I thought so too," Theresa said as she came back to join them. "How lucky you are, Giles, to have three females here to aid you in your scheming!"

"You all did well," Giles admitted, "and as for you," he said to Maudie, handing her back his cane, "you are every inch your father's child! Even so, I fear I won't be able to put off returning to London for much longer, now that William is home." He took the King's letter from Marianne and quickly scanned it. "Lord Shrewsbury is once more back in the King's service, it seems. No doubt he couldn't stay away from the Queen any longer." Word had it that Shrewsbury had conceived quite a passion for Mary, and some even said she returned it, although Giles had always doubted that. "If William's got him then I am sure he can manage without me for a few more weeks at least!"

"I think you are quite enjoying being the lord of the manor," Theresa teased him.

Giles smiled. It was the truth, and he was more surprised by it than any of them. He realised how much Marianne was enjoying their life there too and he had made a decision that he knew would please her. "I have decided that, rather than buy a house in town, I will find us one in the country," he told them. "It won't be nearly so grand as this, of course," he said hastily, as Theresa and Maudie delightedly embraced Marianne, "and we shall need to be close to London, but I feel it would be better for Will. And any other children we may have," he added. "Now, Maudie, would you please ask Jonathon and Ned to have the horses harnessed to the coach and ready to leave immediately."

She sped off straight away. Even though he was now fit and well, she rarely left his side and was always eager to help him.

"I want to get to the shipyard, before it closes tonight," he explained to Theresa and Marianne. "The Navy lost seven ships at Beachy Head, remember, so there has never been a better time to negotiate a price for our timber but, unfortunately, I am not the only one trying to sell it to them!"

TEN

༄

Philip and Luc presented themselves at the imposing arched gate to the Abbey of Fontfroide, where Philip hoped to come to some arrangement with the Abbot for processing his crop. Antoine had disagreed with his choice, as the monks at Fontfroide had once been cruel persecutors of the Cathars, another religious sect, but Philip was far more interested in the services they could provide now than he was in events that had happened five hundred years before, so he had ignored his cousin's protests.

Leaving Morgan in charge of Les Jacinthes, they had travelled to Narbonne by coach. The journey had taken them nearly three days and had further convinced Philip of the wisdom of their decision to utilise the Canal Royale to transport their first harvest as far as Capestang, since wagons loaded with heavy barrels would take far longer.

The had hired a couple of horses for the last few miles of their journey to Fontfroide, feeling the need for some exercise and fresh air, and, after one of the lay brothers had taken the animals to the stables, they proceeded into the main courtyard of the yellow and grey sandstone Abbey.

"The Abbot is expecting you," the old monk who came to greet them told Philip. "He is in the Chapter House, about to hold Prime and give the brothers their tasks for the day. If you will wait in the Cloister, he will send someone for you."

"What's Prime?" Philip asked Luc as they made their way there.

"The first prayer of the day. Listen."

They could hear singing coming from the Chapter House

on the opposite side of the Cloister. It was melodic and, just for a moment, as Philip looked out through one of the openings at the flowerbeds of the Cloister garden, still colourful in the Autumn sunshine, he experienced a rare sense of peace. Even so, he had never been able to understand why a man would voluntarily lock himself away for the whole of his life, even in such a beautiful place as this. Philip's own life had been exciting and eventful. Not all of his experiences had been pleasant, by any means, but some of the worst of them had been the brief periods when his freedom had been taken from him, once when he was imprisoned in the Bastille and once when he had been held in the Tower of London.

"Do you really think they will agree to turn our crop into wine?" Luc asked him as they walked around the Cloister, their boot heels sounding unnaturally loud on the stones in this place of silence and sweet singing.

"For a price, yes. They have been making their own wine here for centuries, apparently."

"Still, my Lord, I am surprised that they would enter into any arrangement with a Protestant right now, and particularly one from a country with whom they are at war."

"La Rochefoucauld is what they call a commendatory abbot, which means he is a businessman," Philip reminded him. "He runs the Abbey for profit, most of which, I suspect, goes to line his own pockets. Do monks have pockets, by the way?" Philip wondered, thinking of the old monk in his long robes.

Luc gave him a pained look. "I hope you have not brought me with you just to ask me silly questions, my Lord."

Philip laughed. Luc was such an earnest young man that he enjoyed teasing him a little at times. "Not at all. I brought you here to lend me a little credibility! Do something Catholic, will you, when we meet the Abbot?"

La Rochefoucauld was everything Philip had expected. A shrewd-looking man, he had a professional smile that softened his features as he greeted them.

Luc dutifully went down upon one knee to receive a blessing and La Rochefoucauld murmured some Latin words as he made the sign of a cross on Luc's brow.

"Your son is a fine young man, my Lord," he said to Philip, evidently noticing the resemblance between them. "I apologise for keeping you waiting, but there were more mea culpas than usual today."

Philip thought that this was probably not the time, or place, to pass comment on Luc's lineage. "Mea culpas?" he said instead.

"After the work has been discussed there is a public confession for those who feel they have broken any rules of the establishment."

That piece of information made it harder than ever for Philp to understand why any man would want to devote himself to the Abbey. "As I told you in my letter, we are expecting to produce a small crop this year at Les Jacinthes and I am hoping we can come to some mutually beneficial arrangement."

"I am sure we can, my Lord. Follow me and I will show you our storeroom, where your barrels will be kept. What is your crop?" the Abbott asked, as they walked along through a passageway.

"Mourvèdre."

The Abbot nodded approvingly. "That makes a good wine, high in acid and with a fine flavour, although it is the better for a little ageing. With Mourvèdre we would need to ferment the fruit still on their stems."

Philip attempted to look knowledgeable but he realised he had failed when the Abbot burst out laughing.

"You don't know much about this, do you, my Lord?"

"Not really," Philip had to admit with a smile, "but fortunately I have those who do."

The Abbey's storeroom was impressive. It was a low, vaulted chamber which was entered by a massive archway that stretched from one side of the room to the other. The air was cool in there and Philip could see piles of barrels stacked one upon the other as well as fresh food supplies.

"We are fortunate to have our own well here and we can produce most of our food ourselves." La Rochefoucauld explained. "Of course the lay brothers provide the greater part of the labour, but the monks are expected to contribute also, when they are not at prayers."

Which, Philip guessed, would be for the greater part of their day, and part of their night also, since Luc had told him that the monks were woken from their sleep to pray as well. The Abbot, however, looked well rested and prosperous.

Even though Philip had scant regard for clerics of any rank, whether Catholic or Protestant, he felt a grudging respect for this powerful man who was running an ancient Cistercian monastery as a thriving and profitable business.

He knew that la Rochefoucauld had the measure of him too. Philip was a member of a Huguenot family, forced from their livelihood by the Catholic church, who was as willing to do a deal with their enemies as the Abbot was with him.

A deal with the devil!

"That went well," Luc said, as they mounted their horses and set off back to Narbonne.

"It did," Philip agreed, for he had managed to strike a satisfactory bargain with the Abbot. "We just need to ensure that we produce a good crop next year."

"Morgan seems to have that under control, my Lord."

"Morgan always has things under control," Philip said. "He even seems to be able to manage my wretched cousin! Everything is fine."

When they arrived back at Les Jacinthes, however, it was plain to Philip that everything was not fine.

There was something uncharacteristically reticent about Morgan's manner. The Welshman might not talk a lot but, when he did, he was always direct.

"Has all been well whilst I have been away?" Philip asked him.

"Yes, my Lord."

Philip regarded him closely. "What are you not telling me Morgan? Come on, out with it, man."

"I let some of your cousin's friends stay here on their way to the mountains," Morgan admitted quietly.

Philip looked at him in horror. "You did what?"

"It was just for one night, my Lord, and none saw them come or go. Thomas had no part in this," Morgan stressed. "He was against it but he was in Montpellier when they arrived and I had already agreed to let them in."

"And what of my cousin, who promised me this would not happen?"

"Antoine swore he had no notion they were coming, but they were such a pathetic bunch, with women and small children amongst their number, and I did not feel that I could, in all conscience, turn them away."

"Damn it, Morgan," Philip cried out in frustration, "I thought I made myself clear on this."

"They are victims of injustice," Morgan reminded him.

"So they might be, but this is not our fight and I have no intention of making it our fight."

"You have supported less honourable causes," Morgan pointed out.

"Well I am not supporting this one," Philip said firmly. "That is not why we are here, Morgan."

"I know."

"You have sympathy for them, don't you?" Philip guessed.

"They have been badly treated and they are honest, hardworking people."

"Who pray for the death of the King! Do I need to remind you, Morgan, that Louis is not, and never will be, my enemy? If the King of England cannot make me see him as one then, be assured, this motley group of rebels will not. He is my friend and benefactor. Without him we would not have been protected during King James' reign and I would not be the owner of this property now. It is unlike you to be so sentimental."

"Perhaps it is because they remind me of my own people."

The Welshman rarely spoke of his homeland, or his upbringing, but from the little Philip had been able to discover about him, he had been brought up in the Celtic mysticism of what he called 'the old faith'.

Philip could sympathise with the rebels too, but he knew he could not afford to be party to anything which might jeopardise his position. It was already precarious, in a land that was at war with his own and where only the protection of King Louis kept any of them safe. Thomas and Nanon had also been put at risk by Morgan's well-meant action and he felt he had to be brutal, much as it pained him.

"Do they mean more to you than I do?"

Morgan looked hurt. "How can you ask that?"

"I can because I need to know," Philip continued remorselessly. "We have been together for too many years not to be honest with one another now and, save for Theresa and Maudie, there is no-one who means more to me than you, but you must stand with me on this or not stand with me at all. I would never betray Antoine or his friends but neither will I be seen to be helping them. You must make your choice."

"My loyalty to you comes before everything, my Lord. I have proved it often enough."

"Yes, you have," Philip agreed, in a gentler tone, "and there is no man I would rather have at my side. I respect your views, my friend, truly I do, but I fear another kind of war will start with us in the middle of it if we are not careful. Now I will have words with my blasted cousin and then, perhaps, we can get on with what we are in Languedoc to do, which is running this estate."

He found Antoine suitably chastened and so apologetic that he felt inclined to accept what Morgan had told him about his innocence in the whole affair, but he felt uneasy about it all the same.

A note delivered to him from de Basville the next day did not make him feel any better.

He showed it to Thomas, who was usually abreast of anything going on in the town.

"What do you make of this? He is inviting me to visit with him, and God only knows why. He has not done so since I first arrived here and it is plain he can't stand the sight of me."

Thomas pulled a face. "The word is that Abbé Du Chayla is expected to be arriving in Montpellier and will be staying with de Basville. That can't be a coincidence. I'll warrant he is the one who wants to meet you."

"That's all I need! Especially after what occurred here in my absence."

"I am sorry about that," Thomas said, a little awkwardly. Philip smiled at him fondly. Another might have immediately disclaimed any part in the incident and placed all the blame on Morgan, but he knew that Thomas would never do that.

"It was not your decision, so I understand. Besides, if Morgan had made up his mind then I doubt you would ever have been able to change it, Thomas. The question now is what am I going to do about this invitation?"

"I reckon you had better go," Thomas said.

"I fear you are right. I had better take Luc with me again.," Philip reckoned. "He played his part well with the Abbot and I think it might useful to have a good French Catholic in attendance if I am meeting the Archpriest of the Cevennes!"

∽

Thomas' suspicion was right. When they were shown into the Intendant's residence, three days later, Philip found de Basville in the company of a sharp-featured man wearing a long, grey wig and dressed in the dark robes of a cleric. Even before they were introduced, Philip had guessed that this was the infamous Abbé du Chayla.

He greeted Philip with an icy politeness but little deference, the piercing, dark eyes above his long, thin nose plainly assessing him, whilst his thin lips were pursed in obvious disapproval.

Philip, who had no intention of giving the Abbé the satisfaction of thinking that his imperious manner had disconcerted him, returned his greeting with a curt nod and turned his attentions to de Basville.

If Intendant de Basville had presumed that Philip would be unnerved to find himself in the presence of his Inspector of Missions he was to be disappointed.

Philip introduced Luc to him as a member of his household and talked of the progress they were making in the vineyard, for all the world as though he considered this to be nothing more than a friendly get-together of neighbours. De Basville was plainly embarrassed at the way he was ignoring du Chayla, which gave Philip the added satisfaction of knowing that he was putting both of them out of countenance.

At last the Abbé could endure it no longer.

"Are you a Catholic?" he asked Luc in a voice loud enough to talk over the conversation of the other two.

"Yes, Father. Whilst I am staying in Languedoc, I attend Mass regularly at Ste Anne's in the Place de Pelisse," Luc told him.

"Father Perrault's church," du Chayla said deprecatingly. "I have heard reports that his converts are not performing their duties with sufficient zeal."

"I have never noticed that to be the case," Luc said. "Indeed, I rather believe most of them are growing stronger every week in their desire to follow the true faith."

Philip hoped that he would not overdo it in his desire to protect the young priest he knew Luc had come to like.

"If you say so." Du Chayla did not sound convinced. "But tell me, Santerre, how does a good Catholic like yourself ensure that your soul is not risking eternal damnation by your working in a Protestant household?"

Even de Basville looked a little shocked at such a direct insult to Philip, but Luc was unfazed.

"I go to confession!"

Luc's flippant response had lightened the situation a little and du Chayla actually managed a tight-lipped smile.

Philip was unperturbed by the barb but, as he studied the Abbé, he could not help thinking that, of all the detestable men he had ever met, and there had been a few, this so-called man of God was probably the most odious.

It had not escaped his notice either that du Chayla seemed quite taken with Luc and, whilst that might prove to be beneficial, Philip could not dispel a feeling of disquiet. Whatever was the purpose of the meeting, and he was sure it had a purpose, he was keen to have an end to it.

It seemed that de Basville was of the same mind. "The Abbé owns a property in the Cevennes region, at Le Pont de Montvert, my Lord," he said conversationally.

Philip guessed this might be the notorious house where Luc had told him prisoners were taken to be tortured.

"So I have heard."

"The area is a viper's nest of rebels," du Chayla put in. "If they can get to the forest, they can use hidden tracks that only they know in order to gain the safety of the mountains and, once there, ten of them could hold off a hundred of my soldiers."

Philip raised an eyebrow at the use of the term *my* soldiers, although he said nothing.

"It is the truth," de Basville put in. "The mountains are virtually impregnable. If they form themselves into a fighting force there, they can stop an entire army."

"And do you have reason to believe that they are doing that?" Philip asked, recalling what Thomas had told him of the trade in arms and food.

"Who is to say what they are planning?" du Chayla said "They are mutinous and they are meeting in secret to follow their foul faith. If we are to stop more joining them, we need to prevent them reaching the Cevennes. It is a daunting task but a necessary one if we are to carry out the King's wishes and hunt out these heretics," he ended piously.

If he thought that bringing King Louis' name into it would impress his point on Philip, he was wrong.

"I understood from my friend, the Comte de Rennes, that the Intendant has already been rigorously pursuing that aim for five years," Philip said meaningfully, turning to de Basville, who looked put out.

"Despite the rumours that may have reached the Comte's ears, I can assure you there is not a province in the land where Huguenots have been more fairly treated," de Basville insisted.

"And there lies the problem, I fear," du Chayla said. "Gentler methods have failed. The time has come to take harsher actions and, with God's help, I will scour the land of the wretches who refuse conversion. Furthermore, Jesuit priests that I have trained myself will be installed in any parish whose converts are not being made to take the Sacrament, or are not being properly educated in the Catholic faith."

He looked over at Luc as he said those words and Philip suspected that Luc's friend would not be remaining in his position for much longer. He was beginning to wonder what any of this had to do with him, for he was certain that if there was least suspicion regarding Antoine or the recent visitors to Les Jacinthes then du Chayla would not have hesitated to mention it before now. He was soon to find out.

"I have been appointed by Intendant de Basville to supervise the building of roads throughout the region, in order to give better access to the remoter farms and villages. Many of them could be only be reached by goat tracks before but the new roads will be wide enough to allow soldiers and cannons to pass through. No-one will escape me then, and none will be able to harbour them without my knowledge, but this is a harsh terrain and we are encountering many difficulties."

"Yes, I imagine you are."

Philip could see where this was going now.

"To the north of your property there are substantial woods where fugitives could safely hide on their way to the mountains. I desire your permission to take a road through your estate which would enable me to reach those woods by a less circuitous route," du Chayla said.

"You do see that it would be of great assistance to us," de Basville put in, when Philip did not immediately reply.

"I can certainly see that," Philip said, "but I am afraid I must decline your request."

"Decline, my Lord?" Du Chayla's thin pretence at pleasantness vanished in a trice.

"That is what I said, gentlemen. This is not my concern, and nor is it my intention to become involved in French affairs. I am here solely as the proprietor of a vineyard and it is in that capacity alone that King Louis has been gracious enough to ensure me of his protection. It is not my place, nor my desire, to become embroiled in any other matters whilst I am in France."

"I might have expected that. Your family were Huguenots." The Abbé almost spat the words.

"They were, but my family are not your problem," Philip said firmly.

"No. They were allowed to escape justice." The Abbé cast a furious look at de Basville. "An example should have been made of them and, instead of that, the vineyard is now in the hands of another Protestant in the family."

"As you say."

"I could disregard your wishes and bring my road through your property in any case."

"I wouldn't advise it," Philip said quietly, standing up and indicating to Luc that they were leaving.

De Basville rose too, evidently thinking he had better be seen to exert some authority over his Inspector of Missions. "If that is your final word upon it, my Lord Southwick, then so be it. You are in this country as a guest of King Louis and, as such, your wishes will be respected in this matter."

Du Chayla, however, could not contain his rage. "What the King gives the King can take away," he reminded Philip.

Philip turned toward him. "Are you threatening me, du Chayla?"

The Abbé's hard, dark eyes locked with his and Philip sensed pure malevolence in their expression, but the priest dropped his gaze first.

"Threaten a Hero of France? I assure you, my Lord, that my words were intended as advice, not as a warning."

But Philip knew differently. He also knew this was a dangerous man.

⁌

"Arrogant bastard!" du Chayla fumed. "He will regret crossing me, I can promise you that."

"I don't like him being in Languedoc any more than you do," de Basville said, "but before you decide to take any action against him you should consider who he is."

"He is an English Protestant and a member of a Huguenot family that you allowed to escape justice." Du Chayla almost snarled the words.

De Basville looked uncomfortable. "He is also beloved of King Louis and a favourite of the King's brother," he reminded him, as well as being a close friend of the Comte de Rennes, who has made my life so difficult over the years he has been supervising the treatment of Huguenots. It was he who put pressure upon me to let the Pasquiers go, doubtless for Devalle's sake. Even so, I could never have predicted that the King would give him the wretched place and that I would have to put up with him living here. I had plans for disposing of that estate, profitable plans."

"Maybe they could still come to fruition, if you help me," du Chayla said craftily.

"I'll not touch him. Not while he has the King's protection."

"And what if he lost it? What if something should occur to make the King doubt the wisdom of his decision. You have friends at Court do you not? Powerful friends?"

"You are referring to Madame de Maintenon no doubt."

"Indeed I am, for there can be few people better placed to influence King Louis, and there is no-one in France, I am certain, who hates the Huguenots more than the woman who persuaded him to revoke the edict which protected them."

"And no-one who hates Philip Devalle more either," de Basville allowed. "I think it likely that she was behind the plot to assassinate him last year. Nothing could be proved against her, of course, but one of her close friends was arrested and Madame de Maintenon feared the affair had discredited her in the eyes of the King."

"Then we shall have to give her something which will enable her to have her revenge, won't we?"

De Basville still looked unsure. "I have a position to uphold here," he reminded du Chayla. "and Versailles leaves me alone. I cannot afford to become involved in a plot against Devalle which might fail and hazard my own standing with the King."

Du Chayla looked at him disgustedly. "You will only need to turn a blind eye."

"Very well," de Basville said, after a short pause. "That I can do."

❧

"Was it wise to refuse him permission" Thomas wondered, when Philip had told the others about their visit.

"Probably not, but the last thing I want is to have dragoons on my property, especially dragoons under the authority of an evil sod like du Chayla."

"What are you going to do, my Lord?"

"I am going to do nothing," Philip stressed. "I don't believe he would have the temerity to force the issue but, in case he does, I intend to send a letter to Armand to warn him of the situation about to erupt here. He is about the only person in France who I can truly trust."

"Well I am going to warn Father Perrault," Luc said decidedly.

"Be careful with that," Philip said. "He is obviously already known to du Chayla, who I presume must have one of his spies amongst your friend's congregation."

"What should I do?" Antoine asked.

"You should carry on doing exactly what you are doing. Since I doubt that du Chayla is capable of subtlety, I am guessing he has no idea who you are or that you are here. There must, however, be no repeat of what occurred whilst I was away," he stressed, looking at him and Morgan, who both began their assurances, but Philip held up his hand. "That incident is now closed," he told them, and will not be referred to again, but we must all be extra cautious from now on."

ELEVEN

⚶

Philip looked with satisfaction at the sign he'd had made to replace the one which had been pulled down after the Pasquiers left. The new sign proudly bore the words 'Chateau Les Jacinthes. Domaine Pasquier-Devalle'.

Even Antoine had not been able to object to that!

He looked, too, at the rows of neatly pruned vines in the part of the vineyard that Morgan and Antoine had so far managed to restore.

"You have done well, my friend," Philip told Morgan, "and I am grateful to you."

"I could not have done it without Antoine," Morgan said honestly.

"And there's another thing, you have endured the company of my troublesome cousin all these weeks!"

"He's not the easiest of people to work with," Morgan admitted, "but we have grown more used to one other now. He is not such a bad fellow really when you get to know him a little better."

"I'll take your word for that."

Although, for Nanon's sake, the pair had tried to appear friends, it was still a wary relationship. Antoine's temper could rise at the least provocation, it seemed, and Philip was not prepared to put up with that, especially on the occasions when his cousin's anger was directed at Thomas or Luc. Philip had become protective of them, knowing the potentially perilous situation he had put them in by bringing them to an enemy country to live amongst such hostile

Catholic neighbours as de Basville and the soldiers who served du Chayla. He and Morgan had been in threatening situations for the greater part of their time together and accepted it as a natural part of life but, although he knew that both young men were dismissive of the danger and that neither of them wanted to be anywhere but by his side, he felt responsible for them.

"You will notice there are some vines that we could not save and those will need to be replaced in March, but there should still be sufficient of these old ones bearing fruit in this section to give us a decent harvest next year," Morgan explained.

"Excellent! And what needs to be done now?"

"Nothing. The work is finished for this year."

"So we can go home for Christmas?"

Philip recalled only too well the previous Christmas that he and Morgan had spent, cold, wet and miserable in Ireland and he wanted to spend this one at High Heatherton if he could.

Morgan smiled. He evidently felt the same. "Indeed we can, my Lord."

Philip went to find Nanon, who was busy, as usual. Thanks to her efforts, Les Jacinthes had been transformed. She had chopped wood, cooked their meals, kept the house clean and taken care of them all as though they were her own little family which, in a way, Philip knew, they were.

"Morgan tells me there is nothing of any significance to be done here until the planting of the new vines in Spring so I am planning to spend Christmas at High Heatherton," Philip told her. "I would like you to come with us."

"I would like that too, very much." The years seemed to fall away from her as her face lit at the prospect and Philip thought she looked just like the Nanon he remembered from his childhood, but her elation was short-lived.

"What of your cousin?" she said. "We can't leave him here on his own. He is sure to get into trouble if he so much as goes to town to buy food."

"Damn the man!" Philip had not even given thought to what would happen to Antoine if they left. What was very obvious to him, however, was what would happen to Nanon if du Chayla's soldiers came to the house in his absence and discovered Antoine there with her. "I suppose I could take him to England with us," he said, although he did not much relish the prospect of having him at High Heatherton.

"No, you can't," Nanon said firmly. "There are strict penalties for helping Huguenots to leave the country. It is far too risky."

"I am already taking a risk just by having him here," Philip pointed out, "the same as you did when you took him into your house. The man is a wretched liability to us all."

"But I am unimportant," Nanon protested. "You are a public figure and du Chayla would delight in bringing you down. You would be playing right into his hands."

Philip shrugged. "That is a chance I will have to take, for I am determined to go home and I won't leave you here with no-one to protect you."

As it happened, the problem was solved for him. Antoine listened to his suggestion in obvious surprise.

"You would be prepared to hazard so much for me?" he said, sounding quite unlike his usual, belligerent self.

Philip was tempted to tell him the truth, that he was only making the offer to save Nanon from the consequences of her soft-heartedness, but Antoine was plainly touched by his suggestion and he decided not to spoil the moment.

"If you wish to accompany us you will be made welcome at High Heatherton," he said instead.

"I thank you, cousin, truly I do, but I have already decided that the time has come for us to go our separate ways."

It was Philip's turn to be surprised now. "You are leaving us?"

"There is little more I need to teach Morgan. He will be quite capable of dealing with the planting of the new vines without my help and I thought to follow my friends to the Cevennes."

Philip looked at him in amazement. "Do you have a death wish? You know what is happening there. Du Chayla's soldiers are scouring the forest for rebels making their way to the mountains."

"Nevertheless, I must try to reach the others, for we need as many able-bodied men as we can get if we are ever to defeat our oppressors."

"You can't defeat them," Philip said flatly. "Your enemies are the most powerful people in the land and they have thousands of well-equipped soldiers at their command. You and your tawdry bunch of rebels are untrained men, armed with whatever weapons that you manage to get smuggled through to you. They have no chance of success, Antoine, why can't you see that? You will die with them."

"Then I will die in good company and for a good cause," Antoine said stubbornly.

Philip raised his eyes to heaven. "And they call the Devalle's insane! Come with us to England, Antoine. You could live safely for the rest of your life in a Protestant country, or you could take ship from there to the Americas and find your family."

Antoine was silent for so long that Philip thought he might be seriously considering the suggestion, but then he shook his head. "I can't, Philip. I could not live with myself if I turned my back upon a cause which means so much to me. You, of all people, must surely understand that."

"Me? Why would I understand?" Philip wondered.

"Because you have risked your own life to uphold the Protestant faith often enough. Were you not once imprisoned in the Tower for aiding the Duke of Monmouth in a plot to replace his Catholic uncle as the successor to the throne? Did you not raise an army to support Dutch William when he seized that throne from King James and did you not, only this year, fight in Ireland for the rights of Protestants suffering from Catholic oppression?"

Put like that Philip could see how, to someone who did not know him well, he might appear to have had more noble motives than was actually the case!

"I am no champion of Protestant causes, Antoine," he said gently. "I supported Monmouth not because he was a Protestant but because he was my friend and also because, by doing so, I served the interests of the Earl of Shaftesbury, who, in return, helped me gain my estate. As for the reason I raised an army for William, that was because, during James' reign, we were virtually prisoners on that estate."

"But you did lead troops for him in Ireland," Antoine persisted.

"Only because, had I not volunteered for Ireland, I might have been dispatched to fight with the Allies on France's borders, which would have broken the agreement I had with King Louis and most likely lost me Les Jacinthes."

Antoine was silent for another moment while he digested that and then, unexpectedly, he burst out laughing, the first time Philip ever remembered hearing him do so.

"You are a clever bastard, aren't you, Philip?"

"I have needed to be for I have fended for myself since I went to Court at thirteen and I was penniless for a good part of my life. Even as a child I was alone," he pointed out, "for, unlike you, I never knew a mother's love. I had only a brutal brother and a father too weak to protect me from him. Thank God I had Nanon to care for me."

"What happens to Nanon now?"

"She stays with us," Philip said decidedly. "There will always be a place for her with me whether I am in England or in France. It is my turn to care for her now, and I promise I will do so, for the rest of her life."

"That's good. I love her too, you know, although I have always realised that you were her favourite."

"You resented me for that," Philip guessed.

"That and other things. Truly, I think I envied you," Antoine admitted.

"You did?" Philip said in astonishment. "But surely you had everything here."

"Everything except my freedom," Antoine said ruefully. "Our grandfather was a tyrant of a man, one who needed to totally control others. The way he disowned your mother was cruel but at least she got to do what she wanted, even if the cost to her was to lose her family. I had no such choice. My life, as my father's only son, was mapped out for me before I could even walk. I was to stay here and learn to run this vineyard. My own desires were unimportant to him. Nanon told me that you always wanted to be a soldier, which is what you were able to become. I wanted to join the army too but he forbade it. It was my duty as a Pasquier, he impressed upon me, to take over this estate upon my father's death. My whole life has been spent here, Philip, and for what?" He smiled wryly. "To see my famous cousin come and take everything from me, not just the vineyard that should have one day been mine but the entire purpose of my life. That is the main reason I resented you."

Philip was stunned at his revelations and it occurred to him that this was, ironically, the first time they had properly talked to one another.

"Yes," he said quietly, "I can see why you would but, surely, it would have been so much worse to have your life's work pass into the hands of a Catholic friend of de Basville. You know that I will do my very best for this place and that I will love it for the sake of my mother. I am, after all, half-Pasquier. If you come to England with me now, I will purchase a commission for you in King William's army," he promised him. "He has troops of French Huguenots under his command and you will have plenty of opportunity to fight beside them against the forces of the Catholics that you hate so much. How old are you, thirty-five? It's not too late to have that life you always wanted, Antoine."

This time Antoine did appear to be considering the suggestion but Philip was not too surprised when he shook his head.

"I would still be turning my back upon those brave enough to make a stand here and, besides, by travelling with you I would be risking the liberty, or even the lives, of you and your household. You have taken enough chances for me these last few months and I am more grateful than you could know for the sanctuary you have given me and for the opportunity to help restore the vineyard. It is time for me to leave now, for I know I am leaving everything in safe hands. I'm talking about Morgan's hands, of course, not yours," he added, with a smile.

Philip smiled too. "Of course! When do you go?"

"I thought tonight."

"Very well," Philip said resignedly. "I'll not make any more attempts to change your mind. May good fortune shine upon your endeavours, Antoine Pasquier."

"Thank you, cousin. I am pleased we finally met."

"So am I," Philip said.

And he meant it.

Antoine left through the woods a few hours later, taking one of the horses and as much as he could carry in his saddlebags. Philip wondered if they would ever meet again, but he doubted it.

The following day they left their remaining horses in the care of the ostler in Montpellier and, after informing de Basville of their departure, Philip, Morgan, Thomas, Luc and Nanon boarded a coach to begin the long journey home to England.

King William's birthday, on the 4th of November, was a national holiday.

Giles stood with Marianne on Tower Hill, watching as the great guns were fired from the Tower to celebrate the event, and he could not but remember that same day two years earlier. He had been with William aboard his flag ship, the Den Briel, on their way to England with a flotilla of nearly three hundred ships. The sails of every vessel had been slackened so that services could be held to celebrate the occasion, which also happened to be William and Mary's wedding anniversary, and Giles had been expecting to see the English navy sail into view at any moment. But no ships had appeared on the horizon. King James' fleet had been trapped in port by the 'Protestant' east winds.

They had arrived safely at Torbay and marched to London without opposition. William had become king and Giles, in gratitude for the part he had played in the venture, had been made an earl and appointed as William's aide. Giles, who had previously been wanted by the law in England on account of his involvement in the Duke of Monmouth's Rebellion, had achieved more than he could ever have dreamed possible.

So why, such a short time later, was he feeling so dissatisfied, he wondered. What had happened in Ireland had certainly played a part in it. He had not forgiven William for the ease with which the King had abandoned him, and he never would, yet he knew that, at one time, he would have borne that slight without complaint if it had been to his advantage to do so.

Now William was talking of going to Holland in February to hold a congress of the Allies at the Hague and Giles had been amongst those chosen to accompany him. He could no longer use his injuries as an excuse to be absent from his duties but he did not want to go, any more than he wanted to remain behind to assist the Queen during William's absence. He simply wanted no part of it. No part of William's wars or the power struggles at his Court. Giles was tired of politics and inspecting the royal building works, but he was especially tired of constantly being at William's beck and call.

"I fear I am turning into Philip," he said to Marianne.

"How so?" Marianne said, laughing

"Each time he achieves his aims he can never be content but must always be risking everything in some new scheme. I used to chide him for it but now I'm just as bad. We have everything we could ever want here, and yet…"

He did not finish the sentence, but there was no need. Marianne slipped her arm through his as they walked down the hill together. "You are nothing like him, my darling," she said. "I love Philip, as do we all, and I shall be eternally grateful to him for saving your life but, wonderful though he can be at times, Philip will always be a restless spirit. You, on the other hand, merely have sense enough to know when to change the direction of your life."

Giles smiled. "Is that what I have, my loyal little wife?"

"When we first left Morocco, you talked of staying in France and buying a chateau," she recalled, "but then you decided we should go to Holland instead. Now you are thinking of leaving William's service. You always know when it is time to move on."

"Perhaps, but what do we all live on if I no longer work for the King?" The fortune Giles had managed to get out of Morocco had long gone, invested not in a French chateau but in William's expedition, which had been short of funds. "We might be able to afford a country house but, unlike Philip, I will never own a profitable family estate, or a vineyard granted me by the King of France," he reminded her. "And it is highly unlikely that I can get by on my looks anymore!"

There had been a time, at King Charles' Court, when Giles' handsome face had made him the darling of the ladies, who had showered him with expensive gifts. But that was before a sword cut had given him the scar he bore on his cheek. In spite of that, he was still an attractive man if he could only see it but, for one who had once been so vain, it been hard to come to terms with what he considered to be his disfigurement. For a long while he had been bitter but he had come, if not to accept it, at least to realise that life could still hold much promise for him and much joy too. Especially since he had met Marianne.

And she was right – it was time to move on

Nanon was welcomed with open arms by Theresa and Maudie, as Philip knew she would be, and happily pitched in to help Bet with the festive preparations. The pair had taken to each other right away and when Philip saw Nanon outside cutting greenery for the decorations with Bet's little Gwen strapped, gurgling happily, to her side he knew he had made a decision which had pleased everyone.

She had looked in delight at what he had achieved in the house and gardens, which she thought looked even better than they had in his father's day.

When Giles, Marianne and Will, accompanied by Ahmed, arrived, in the middle of December, Philip truly felt that his family was complete.

"We need to talk," he told Giles, as they rode out of the tall gates, decorated with Philip's family coat of arms, to inspect High Heatherton's woods, Philip was riding his beloved black stallion, Ferrion, and Giles was on Scarlet, the horse Philip had bought for him when he had first become Giles' patron. Scarlet belonged to Thomas now but Giles still rode him when he stayed at the house. It was a fine, frosty morning and the horses were lively, their breath rising in the cold air. Philip felt pleased with life; satisfied with the progress they had made at Les Jacinthes and happy to be home and once more in Giles' company.

"We do?" Giles said.

"You did well here, when I was away," Philip said, indicating the amount of timber that had been felled whilst Giles had been in charge, "and you have evidently become quite the businessman. I heard you drove a hard bargain at the shipyard in exchange for guaranteeing the quantity they needed ahead of time. I told you that your trading experience in the Sahara would come in handy!"

Giles smiled. "I'm not sure about that, but your labourers were more than happy to work the extra hours for the bonus I was able to pay them on account of it, and it freed them up the sooner to help John with his harvest."

"He was grateful for that, for it was a good one this year, he tells me. I am grateful to you too, Giles," Philip said. "and not only for running the estate so profitably in my absence. It was also good to know that you were here, keeping an eye on everything. In fact, without you I would not have been able to stay away so long."

"It was my pleasure," Giles assured him. "Besides, I was in no hurry to return to William's service."

"And you are in no hurry now to accompany him to Holland, I imagine."

"I am not. He can't wait to go, of course. He's planning to put on a great show, I gather. He's even planning on taking an entire orchestra!"

"But you don't want to be part of his parade," Philip guessed.

Giles shook his head. "Not this time. He talks of going upon campaign against the French in the Spring as well. He reckons that morale went down amongst the Allies whilst he was in Ireland and that he should be seen to be leading them. I want to be done with it, Philip. All of it." They reined their horses in an area of the wood which, under his direction, had been cleared and planted with new saplings. "The problem now is what I should do next."

"Isn't it obvious? You should come into business with me."

Giles gave him a sideways glance. "Now you're beginning to sound like the Duke of Buckingham!"

Buckingham, who had once been Philip's patron at Court, had been constantly trying to involve Philip in what always turned out to be disastrous commercial ventures. Fond though he had been of the Duke, who had died several years before, Philip had never harboured any illusions about his abilities in that direction!

He smiled at the memory. "Dear Buckingham, I still miss him, but no, this is nothing like the propositions he used to offer me. If I can make a success of Les Jacinthes, which I am hopeful that I can, I see no reason why I should not ship our produce back to England. If the property you decide to buy is within reach of the Thames then you can easily get our wine to London by water. You could run the entire business from your estate."

"The estate I haven't bought yet?"

"But you will, I know you well enough to realise that when you have made up your mind to something you will see it through. Give it thought, Giles. With your head for business, and your contacts through the Court, you would be the perfect person to be in charge of the operation."

"Are you suggesting I go into trade?" Giles said archly.

For the son of a country squire, which Giles was, being a wine merchant was a perfectly acceptable occupation but he was an earl now and some members of the aristocracy would consider it below their station. Philip knew that his brother-in-law was not one of them, however, for even though he had achieved his lofty aims Giles was, above all, a pragmatist.

"Why not?" he said with a smile. "Some of the best people are doing it these days, Giles, including me!"

That year Philip did finally manage to spend Christmas at High Heatherton, and a wonderful one it was too.

A huge log had been selected from one of the loads bound for the shipyard and on Christmas Eve it was dragged into the house by some of John's labourers, accompanied by everyone on the estate in holiday mood, for there would be no more work done until after twelfth night. Philip lit it himself in the huge fireplace of the Great Hall. The room had been decorated with the holly that Nanon and Bet had gathered, whilst ivy festooned the magnificent portrait of him, which dominated the Hall. It had been painted when he was in his twenties, a proud young officer in the French army, resplendent in his uniform and mounted on Ferrion. Bet had not been able to find any mistletoe so, instead, she had made what she called a kissing bush, from branches of rosemary and bay, which had been hung from the rafters of the ceiling.

Another Christmas Eve tradition which Philip revived, much to the delight of all the country folk, was the wassailing of the apple trees, to persuade them to yield a good crop the following year. This was a new custom to a city-born girl like Bet but it was a familiar one for Theresa, who had been brought up in Dorset. A large bowl of cider, in which was floating pieces of toast, was taken out to the orchard and she and Maudie, with some of the other youngsters, laid pieces of the toast on the branches of the apple trees before pouring the cider on their roots. Philip watched his wife and daughter affectionately as they performed the little ceremony, accompanied by the singing of the onlookers. He loved those two more than he could ever have believed he could have loved anyone.

All who lived and worked at High Heatherton were invited to share the feast on Christmas Day. Trestle tables were brought in for the occasion and set out in a square around the sides of the hall, with Philip and his household seated at the top table, beneath his portrait. Every table was piled high with food. There was roast beef and wild boar, with the boar's head as the centre piece on a table in the middle of the room. There was goose too, and venison pasties as well as mince pies filled with mutton and prunes. There was also a plum porridge, made from Bet's own recipe of boiled beef and raisins, with sugar and wine. Spiced ale was plentiful and at the end of the meal, when all were replete, every man and woman raised their glasses and drank Philip's health amid loud cheers, showing that they had not forgotten how bleak their lives had been before he had managed to acquire the property.

They had not all warmed to him at first, even though many remembered him from his childhood. Philip had been a well-mannered boy, who had always made a point of being courteous to all the workers on the estate, but after the treatment they had received at Henry' hands they had come to distrust the family and fear that this Devalle would be no better than his mad brother. John Bone had stayed loyal to him and had helped to persuade the rest, and Philip had proved to them all that he was a worthy master.

Eventually the Hall emptied, but not before every person had given him their good wishes. He was pleased to see that Giles, too, had made himself popular whilst he was working amongst them and was receiving his own share of friendly greetings. The festivities were to carry on outside, with the Sussex game of stool-ball first, refereed by John in case it got too boisterous, followed by dancing and singing until it grew dark. Philip and his family, though, were happy to retire to the parlour, where Nanon and Marianne contributed a French touch to the day with some delicious pastries they had made, composed of layers of light, flaky pastry, filled with fruit and cream.

Theresa had always loved sweet things and Philip laughed as she attempted, unsuccessfully, to eat the delicate dessert without it dropping to pieces in her fingers. He glanced around at the rest of what he considered to be his true family, the people who meant more to him than any in the world, and he could rarely remember feeling so quite so contented.

"Well?" he said to Giles as they both sat with Morgan afterwards, sharing a bottle of wine whilst Marianne, Theresa, Bet and Nanon played at cards and Luc and Thomas were enjoying a noisy game of blind-man's bluff with Maudie. "What have you decided?"

Giles cast a questioning look at Morgan before he replied. They might not always have been the best of friends but Philip knew that Giles was grateful for the part Morgan had played in his rescue, just as he knew that Morgan had been impressed at the way Giles had run the estate during their absence.

The Welshman simply nodded, indicating his tacit agreement to the plan.

"You are asking me to hazard all I have worked my whole life to attain and throw in my lot with you," Giles said to Philip, "even though your schemes in the past have caused me to be injured, made an outlaw and nearly killed. I would need to be as mad as a Devalle to agree to it."

Philip said nothing. He knew Giles pretty well and felt certain he was about to agree.

Giles kept him waiting for a moment longer, then raised his glass. "But perhaps it is time to show that a Fairfield can be a little mad too. To our new venture!"

Philip smiled as the three of them touched their glasses together. "Now all you have to do is tell William!"

TWELVE

❧

Philip had not intended to return to France until March but a letter that his old friend Armand wrote to him from Versailles in February changed everything.

"Hell and damnation!"

"What is it?" Theresa asked him anxiously. "Les Jacinthes?"

"Not exactly". He handed her the letter. "Antoine has been taken."

"Oh no!" Theresa read Armand's letter. "Philip, I am so sorry. What will they do to him?"

"Since he is now in the hands of that bastard du Chayla I dread to think. If the wretched man had taken my advice, he would be safe in England now."

"But you would have taken a great risk to get him here," Theresa reminded him.

"And now I must take an even greater risk to save him."

Theresa's eyes met his. "Can you do it?"

Philip didn't honestly know. What he did know was that he had to try.

"He's my cousin, Tess. I have no choice."

Theresa put her arms around him and pulled him close. "I know."

Nanon listened tearfully as Philip told her what had happened. Armand had written that du Chayla's dragoons had captured Antoine when he was travelling the route to the mountains and that he was being held, along with some other rebels, at the Archpriest's chateau in Le Pont de Montvert.

"But how does your friend know that one of the prisoners was Antoine?"

"He knows because de Basville recognised him and told Madame de Maintenon, who, no doubt, took great pleasure in informing the King of the fact," Philip said bitterly. "Louis is furious with me, apparently, since de Basville also informed him that Antoine was observed leaving Les Jacinthes. Du Chayla's men were watching us, Nanon."

"And yet they never came to take him?"

"Not then, no. They were cleverer than that. They must have guessed he would attempt to run eventually so they waited until he was alone and vulnerable. I tried to tell him, Nanon, but he wouldn't listen to me."

"Oh, Antoine!" Nanon shook her head in despair. "Always so headstrong, but he had no guile. You, now, have much more sense."

"Maybe not," Philip said drily. "I'm going after him."

"No, you must not!" Nanon gripped his hand tightly. "It is far too dangerous. Think of your poor wife."

"Theresa expected nothing less from me. She is probably already packing my bags!" Philip said, with a flippancy he did not really feel.

Nanon was obviously not fooled. "You don't even like him," she said quietly.

Philip thought back to the last conversation he'd had with Antoine and he recalled the sight of him setting off bravely towards the forest with his few possessions, determined to fight for the cause which meant so much to him.

He turned away, before she could read anything in his expression.

"He's family, Nanon. I don't have to like him."

Morgan had already heard the news, for Theresa had told Bet. He was grim-faced when Philip saw him "When do we leave?"

Philip had never doubted that the Welshman would want to accompany him, especially since he seemed to have struck up a rapport with Antoine over the weeks they had worked together. Even so, this time he knew he had to offer him the choice to stay behind.

"This is likely to be a perilous enterprise, Morgan."

"Tell that to them," was all Morgan said, indicating Thomas and Luc, who were waiting to see him.

Philip knew that Thomas would insist on being part of the rescue mission but Luc was more of a surprise, since he and Antoine had barely ever said a civil word to one another.

"You too?" he said to the Frenchman.

Luc shrugged. "He's our cousin."

"That he is," Philip said heavily, "but I have no idea what we shall be facing. Think on that before the pair of you rush into this."

Thomas winked at Luc. "He's right. I say we stay here and let him and Morgan handle it on their own. After all, we're neither of us much good in a fight!"

"Just go and get yourselves ready," Philip ordered them, with mock severity. "We leave for France in the morning." The two young men were laughing as they went off to make their preparations for the journey. "They are good fellows," he said to Morgan, watching them fondly.

"That they are," Morgan agreed, "and they would both lay down their lives for you."

Philip shuddered. "I hope to God it never comes to that. For you either, my friend. I have led you into danger more times than I wish to remember."

Morgan gave a half-smile. "When you chose me to be your manservant, all those years ago, I hardly expected that I would lead a safe and ordered life!"

"As I recall it was *you* who chose me," Philip said, "and I have many times been thankful that you did! I only wish that Giles could join us on this enterprise. He is a useful man to have around when the odds are stacked against you."

Giles had written from London to say that William had insisted he accompany the royal party to Holland but had, reluctantly, agreed to release him from his duties once their official business was completed, which was expected to be by the end of February, after which William intended to spend some time in his palace of Het Loo. It was the best that could be expected under the circumstances, but it meant that Giles was out of the country now, and likely to be so for at least a month.

In any case, Philip feared it would have been risky for his brother-in-law to show his face in France at the present time. Despite Giles' friendship with Monsieur, who had given him sanctuary when Giles had been fleeing from the law in England, Louis had never much liked him and it was unlikely, now that he had served as William's aide, that Giles would be able to safely return to France for a long while.

Impatient though he was to get back to Languedoc, Philip knew he must go to Versailles first and try to make his peace with Louis. In spite of Maintenon's influence upon the King, Philip did not think Antoine's actions would have actually cost him Les Jacinthes, but Louis' patience was not limitless, even with those he favoured and Philip cursed Antoine for the awkward position in which he had been put on account of him. He cursed himself too, for allowing it to happen.

"Is this what you call not causing me any trouble?"

King Louis' first words damned any slight hope Philip might have had that the King would treat the matter lightly. He knew how to deal with Louis, however, and he also knew that any attempt to defend his position would only serve to infuriate him further.

"I greatly regret this incident and offer my most abject apologies if any actions of mine have caused your Majesty embarrassment."

"Actions such as concealing your cousin from Intendant de Basville and his Inspector of Missions?" Louis replied tartly. "You are a guest in my country, Philip, a guest, moreover, that many think I should not even be entertaining in France at a time when your own country is part of the Allied forces currently waging war upon us, let alone be rewarding with such a generous gift as I have given you."

Philip guessed that was the reason why, on this occasion, Louis had arranged to meet with him in the gardens of Versailles instead of inside the chateau, where his presence would have attracted more attention.

There was keen wind blowing, so few people were promenading in the gardens that day. Not that it would have been that much warmer inside the chateau for, thanks to Louis' insistence that none of the chimneys were visible from the gardens, the fireplaces gave out more smoke than heat! Quite apart from that, Louis, who loved fresh air and never minded the cold, always insisted upon windows being opened inside the chateau in all weathers, regardless of the discomfort of his courtiers. Philip didn't particularly mind the cold either. When he was in the French army, he had spent one bitter Winter fighting amongst Maréchal de Luxembourg's troops during the sack of Holland, struggling across frozen fields after William had opened the sluice gates at Muyden and flooded the countryside.

"I shall be eternally grateful, as well as forever loyal, to your Majesty for the return of my family's estate," Philip assured him.

"An estate which was legally taken from them when they refused to comply with my laws," Louis stressed. "The Pasquiers are outlaws who all fled to escape justice, or so I thought. Apparently, one did not. Were you aware of that before you took possession of Les Jacinthes?"

"No, your Majesty," Philip said truthfully. "I had no idea I even had a cousin. Your Majesty will recall that I had never had any dealings with the Pasquiers, for they refused to even acknowledge me as being a member of their family."

Louis did not seem convinced. "So he just appeared and introduced himself when you took over the property, did he?"

"Indeed not. He tried to kill me!"

Louis looked at him suspiciously. "And why would he do that?"

"He is a Pasquier," Philip said simply. "They are pig-headed and arrogant. He objected to my being given the vineyard."

"How did you persuade him to accept you as the new owner then?"

"By making him realise that, before your Majesty graciously gave Les Jacinthes to me, it was set to become the property of a member of de Basville's family, as the Intendant made sure to tell me," Philip said pointedly.

Louis looked at him sharply and Philip knew that the words had hit home.

They were in the South Parterre, its usually colourful flowerbeds looking bare, although gardeners were already busy preparing them for the Spring planting. Philip looked, with Louis, over the balustrade at the Orangery below them, although the orange trees, in their tubs, had all been moved inside the glasshouses that were built in beneath the many steps that led down to the Pond des Suisses beyond. There were usually courtiers to be seen upon those steps, talking, flirting or just out to be noticed, but not today. Today the whole place seemed deserted and strangely silent to Philip, without the sound of water cascading from the many fountains, for their ponds had been emptied in the icy weather.

"How had your cousin been able to evade capture for so long?" Louis said. "Someone must have been sheltering him. Who was it?"

"I have no idea."

It was obvious Louis didn't believe that for instant, but he did not press the point.

"But you gave him sanctuary yourself, even though you knew the penalties for harbouring a Huguenot?"

"We were about to leave for England, your Majesty, so I sent him upon his way. It is true that I did not turn him over to de Basville, and for that I must throw myself upon your Majesty's mercy."

They walked round a little further to look down upon the path that led to the Pond of Autumn, where Saturn and his cherubs reclined upon a bed of vines, which seemed appropriate to Philip, in view of the fact that they were talking about the vineyard! It was empty, like the others, but, from where they were standing, they could just pick out two artists at work, one painting the black fruit and the other gilding the leaves of Saturn's vines.

"Tell me, one thing," Louis said, "and try to make it the truth this time. According to de Basville, you have restored a vineyard which had been completely neglected for five years to such an extent that you are expecting to harvest a crop this year."

"That is so, your Majesty," Philip said, wondering where this was leading.

"So how did you do it?" Louis said. "I am certain that the only thing you know about wine is how to drink it!"

"My steward, Morgan, is a very knowledgeable man."

"He would need to be. I only wonder where he acquired this specialised knowledge. Are there many vineyards then in England where he could have learned such skills?"

"No, your Majesty," Philip was forced to admit.

"I also understand that you hired no local labour to assist you. Are you asking me to believe that the steward of an English estate, assisted only by your manservant, your bastard son and you, managed such a monumental task in just 3 months?"

Philip knew better than to insult Louis' intelligence by claiming any such thing. "Antoine did assist us," he admitted quietly," but everything else I have told you is the truth."

"Including the fact that you concealed him from de Basville," Louis stressed.

"De Basville is a tyrant," Philip said passionately, for he felt he had very little to lose now, "and du Chayla is a worse one. The Intendant runs the province like his own kingdom. I don't believe you can have any idea what atrocities are being committed in your name and it troubles me that you should be held responsible for the persecution of your subjects."

Louis' expression softened just a little. "And why should that trouble you?"

"Because you are the person I revere most in all the world and the only ruler I have ever been content to serve."

In that, if in nothing else, Philip was telling the truth, as Louis must have realised.

"What would you have me do, Philip? De Basville is an advocate from a family of eminent lawyers, a family in which I can place my trust. He was recommended for the post of Intendant at the time of the Revocation and he has served me loyally and dutifully since then."

And Philip could guess who recommended him, but he had more sense than to bring Madame de Maintenon into the conversation.

"I would have your Majesty investigate the actions of his Inspector of Missions, the Abbé du Chayla," he said instead. "He is an evil man who delights in torturing his prisoners before he kills them."

"He is the one holding your cousin?"

"Yes, your Majesty. I refused him permission for his soldiers to cross my land to patrol the route to the Cevennes. I believe this is his retribution."

"Come, Philip, the man's methods may be harsh but surely he is only doing the job for which de Basville appointed him."

"He threatened me," Philip said.

Louis looked shocked. "With violence?"

"No," Philip admitted. "with the loss of your Majesty's favour, and it appears he has succeeded in that."

"Nonsense! I have forgiven you much in the past and, no doubt, will do so again in the future but I am instructing you now not to interfere in the running of the province, is that clear?"

"Yes, your Majesty."

Louis lapsed into silence, appearing to be mulling over Philip's words as he regarded the Pond of Autumn and the Pond of Winter beyond it, where the outline of Neptune was just visible in the distance.

"I have decided I will ask the Comte de Rennes to meet you in Languedoc, since he is already there, conducting an investigation in Carcassonne," he said at length, turning to walk back to the chateau "It should not take him long to travel to Montpellier and he has my authority to investigate claims of unnecessary cruelty caused by any over-zealous officials acting on my behalf."

Philip was delighted, although he felt a little guilty at adding to poor Armand's problems when he knew his friend wanted nothing more than to be done with all of it and living happily on his Brittany estate.

"Thank you, your Majesty."

"You, however, do *not* have my authorisation and I do not wish to hear that you have played any part in this," Louis said sternly. "The last time we spoke you assured me that you are here merely to make wine, so do that and no more, if you wish to please me."

"I always aspire to do that, your Majesty."

Louis gave him a sideways glance. "I have always liked you, Philip, but don't push me too far." They paused beside a bronze statue of Apollo, the god who Louis had taken as his own symbol. "You had better go to Paris and please my brother now. He will be eagerly awaiting a visit from you, I'm sure."

Philip bowed and kissed the hand that Louis offered him. A

good sign, he felt, and a privilege he had not dared to expect on this occasion.

❧

"Louis didn't exactly forbid me to do anything," Philip said to Luc, as their carriage passed through the archway into the courtyard of the Palais Royale, Monsieur's Paris home. "He just said he didn't want to hear about it."

He had decided to take Luc with him on the visit this time, as he knew how much it would please Monsieur.

"You take chances, my Lord," Luc said, laughing.

"If I didn't, we would not be here now! Be pleasant to Monsieur, won't you. He was upset when Giles took you to England."

Luc pulled a face. "I'll try, for your sake. I just wish he wouldn't make such a fuss of me."

"Well he might not now. I told him who you claim to be. Naturally he told the King," Philip said, remembering Louis' reference to his bastard son.

Monsieur received them joyously. He gave Philip an affectionate hug and a kiss on both cheeks. "And you brought Luc this time. How wonderful! May I still kiss him?" he asked Philip.

Philip smiled, ignoring Luc's pleading look. "Of course!"

Monsieur chattered happily for an hour or so, mostly about the intrigues at Court, which took up the whole of his time when he was not organising a ball or some other social event, but it was obvious that he was bursting to tell them something else. A juicy bit of tittle tattle, Philip suspected, or maybe it was a secret that he was dying to reveal, although anyone with any sense never told Monsieur secrets, for he was notoriously bad at keeping them.

Philip thought that he had better humour him. "What is it, Monsieur?" he asked him. "Something is on your mind, I can tell."

"You were lucky to catch me still in Paris," Monsieur said, savouring the drama of the moment. "Another week and you might have missed me."

"Why, where are you going?"

"You'll never guess."

"Probably not!" Over the years Philip had been privy to a great many confidences that the Frenchman had shared with him.

Monsieur's next words surprised him however.

"I'm going to war."

"You are?"

"Yes, I shall soon be a soldier again. What do you think of that?"

Philip's first thought was that if Monsieur was truly going to fight then there was only one enemy he could be fighting. The Frenchman's next words confirmed it.

"I mustn't tell you more than that, even though I know you are no longer serving in the English army, but you won't breathe a word to anyone, will you?"

Philip promised, but he rather wished Monsieur had not told him, all the same. "Surely the campaign season hasn't started yet."

"That's the beauty of it, we shall take the Allies totally by surprise. I can't say anything else or my brother will be angry with me. He is going as well, and the Dauphin."

Philip gave Luc a significant look and received a long-suffering one in return. He had to know more. For one thing, Giles was still in Holland with William and he feared that if any actions did start unexpectedly his brother-in-law might be caught up in the middle of it with no choice but to play his part. He knew that Luc, being a Frenchman, and one with a talent for eliciting information, had a better chance of discovering what was afoot.

He stayed for a while but when Monsieur proposed a stroll around his gardens, he excused himself, saying that he needed to organise their transport down to Languedoc.

"Why don't I leave Luc here for a little bit longer," Philip suggested. "I'm certain he would love to see your gardens, wouldn't you Luc?"

Monsieur agreed happily and Luc, who evidently already realised what Philip expected of him, attempted to look enthusiastic at the prospect.

It was late before Luc got back to Philip's house, near the Place Royale, but he had managed to get the information that Philip wanted.

"They plan to attack Mons next month," Luc told him.

Mons was the most important fortress in the Spanish Netherlands and Philip knew that the previous year Louvois, Louis' Minister of War, had concentrated troops there. Not only did it appear that they were returning but it seemed they were returning early.

"Marshall Boufflers will be in command and Vauban is leaving ahead of them to plan the siege."

Vauban was Louis' military engineer. As well as being the army's expert on the art of siege warfare, the fortifications that he devised in order to protect France's acquisitions were triumphs of engineering. Philip had served with him on several occasions. "He always favoured attacking before the opposition was at full strength," he recalled. "He's a brilliant man, Luc. The town will fall for certain if William cannot get there in time to relieve it."

"Shall you warn him?" Luc asked.

Philip shook his head. "The Allies should have set scouts on the borders. I certainly would have done. From what Giles said, William will have finished his business at The Hague by now and have left for Het Loo, which means that Giles should be on his way home. With any luck he will be safely out of it and that, frankly, is all I care about at the moment."

"Then you are going to do nothing?" Luc said uncertainly.

"I'm going to go to Languedoc," Philip corrected him. "I shall be in enough trouble with Louis as it is if I succeed in rescuing Antoine. If I am found to have been in correspondence with France's enemies then not only would I be sure to lose Les Jacinthes but Louvois would be within his rights to have me executed as a spy."

∽

"I wish you to accompany me on to Het Loo," William told Giles.

Giles fought back a stab of annoyance. He had already made it clear that he wished to leave the King's service and William had grudgingly agreed. He had still expected him to be part of the delegation accompanying him to The Hague, which Giles had thought not unreasonable, since William had originally intended to leave in the first week of January, and there would not have been time to find a replacement for him. What was not reasonable, to his mind, was for William to expect Giles to follow him to his palace at Het Loo and help him entertain the Elector of Bavaria and his other royal guests on a hunting trip.

"I would prefer to return home, as we agreed, when you leave The Hague, your Majesty," he said firmly. "I have matters to attend to in England."

"Such as overseeing your brother-in-law's estate, which he should be there taking care of himself, and purchasing a house?" William said irritably. "There is surely no need to waste your time traversing the country to find a property you like when you could find a dozen that are suitable in London in a single day."

Giles had no intention of discussing his desire to move away from the capital, or Philip either. "I have fulfilled all my duties since we arrived here," he said instead, "and your Majesty knows that I have never been fond of hunting," he added, although he knew that hunting would be playing only a part of what, for William, would be a much longed-for holiday at his beloved Het Loo. Most would have considered it an honour to be invited there but it was an honour Giles could do without. Neither he nor Marianne had particularly liked Holland, or Het Loo, for that matter, during the period they had lived there whilst Giles had been helping with the preparations for William's invasion of England. Now all he wanted was to get home, but it seemed the King was not going to make it easy for him.

Not that any aspect of this trip had been easy, so far as Giles was concerned, but then, to his mind, crossing the North Sea in January was bound to be fraught with peril. Their first attempt had to be abandoned on account of the high seas and when they did eventually set sail, they had hardly left Gravesend before they found themselves in the teeth of a violent storm. William had refused to turn back, even though they had been blown off course, and it was nearly a fortnight before they had finally neared the coast of Holland. Even then their troubles had not been over, since dense fog and ice floes had prevented them from landing and Giles would not soon forget the freezing cold journey he had endured as one of those chosen to accompany the ebullient William and Hartevelt, the captain of William's yacht, when the King insisted upon leaving the vessel and launching his barge to reach land. The journey in the rowboat had taken them all of fourteen hours and might have taken still longer if Hartevelt, had not managed to jump overboard and clamber over the ice to fetch help.

William had been infuriatingly cheerful throughout the whole experience but it had been a journey from hell for Giles, who had felt the cold acutely since his years spent in the burning Sahara Desert.

Once they had finally reached The Hague, he had still to endure being a part of the formal entrance into the city, followed by fireworks and celebrations. Unlike his brother-in-law, Giles had never enjoyed being part of a parade.

Then had followed the Congress, which had meant days of talking and which had culminated in an agreement to raise an army of over 200,000 men to fight against France in the coming season. Giles' work was now done, and arduous work it had been at times, helping to sort out the divisions amongst the Allies, and it had all taken far longer than anyone had anticipated.

"Surely you can wait another week before you leave," William said petulantly.

Giles thought, and not for the first time, how differently the King addressed his English associates compared with the warm and friendly manner he used with his own countrymen.

It was already the first week of March and he had no desire to stay away from Marianne and Will, or delay his plans, any longer than he must, but neither did he want to part from William on bad terms. Whilst Giles knew that if he did not leave the King's service his life would never be his own, he was not foolish enough to risk losing his friendship.

He sighed resignedly. Exasperated though he was at the prospect, he felt he had little choice but to agree to go with William. After all, he told himself, it was only for a week.

And what difference could a few days possibly make?

THIRTEEN

❦

Armand had completed his business in the prosperous little town that had sprung up at the foot of the ancient citadel of Carcassonne. It had been a wasted journey in some respects for, despite rumours to the contrary, he had found no evidence of any defiance of the new laws. It was natural enough that the region would be regarded with suspicion, however, for it had certainly had its share of troubles in past years.

Once the seat of the Cathars, a religious sect regarded as heretics by the Pope and persecuted cruelly, it had also been the centre of religious dissent for over four centuries, but it had a thriving textile industry now and Armand had been pleased to find that the townspeople were more intent upon the running of their businesses than upon rebellion.

"Shall we pay a visit to the old city?" he asked his servant, Eugene, as they stood upon the bridge that crossed the Canal Royale and looked up at the towers of the fortress.

"I would like that, my Lord, but only if it will not cause you too much discomfort."

Armand's knee had been plaguing him lately, as it often did in damp weather.

"The King does not bother too much about my discomfort, Eugene," Armand said wryly.

"The King does not care about you as much as I do, my Lord."

Armand smiled. "I am sure that's true."

Eugene was a thin stick of a man, who had been with Armand for many years. He had been only fifteen when Armand had first engaged him as his servant, and he had wondered then whether the gangly youth would withstand the rigours of army life, but Eugene had proved to be tougher than he looked.

He had also proved himself to be a loyal ally and had been staunch by Armand's side, not only upon campaigns but throughout his recovery from his injury and now upon the gruelling journeys across France that he was forced to undertake in the King's service.

They had already made the long trek from Montauban, another city with a troubled history. During the religious troubles in the reign of King Louis' father, the royal troops had failed to take the place from the Huguenots, despite firing a bombardment of cannon balls at the city. It had capitulated eventually, when Cardinal Richelieu had ordered the destruction of the fortifications, but there were still some defiant Huguenots there.

As Armand and Eugene made their way up the hill, they could see that the walls of Carcassonne's citadel were crumbling, but the chateau, which those walls had once protected, was still a magnificent sight with its pointed turrets. To Armand's mind, nowhere in the south could ever compare with Brittany, of course, and no chateau could ever be so beautiful as his own beloved La Fresnaye but he had to admit that it was impressive.

He found the rest of the city to be a rather sad place, its streets, once bursting with life, now near deserted, for this place, which had been an impregnable fortress, was no longer an important border town since a treaty had made Roussillon a part of France thirty years before. Ivy was now growing up the walls, some parts of which were actually missing, where local people had made use of the stones.

They climbed up to the ramparts and sat down to rest on the stone seats positioned either side of an arrow slit in one of the towers. As a soldier, Armand could imagine how those long-dead archers had felt as they looked down, waiting for the enemy to scale the outer walls and be caught in the killing ground below. The wind was whistling through the opening and they walked on but, before they left the ramparts, Armand glanced out at the fields of vines that stretched out as far as he could see, for this was good wine growing country, and he was reminded of Philip.

Even though travelling on to Montpellier would delay his returning home, he was glad of an opportunity to help his friend, although he doubted very much whether de Basville would be happy to see him!

⁓

Armand was right. De Basville was not happy to see him when he called at the Intendant's house in the Rue du Cannau.

"Is it Philip Devalle who has raised some complaint against me?" he demanded. "If so, then I assure you that, no matter what he has told you, I have never shown him anything but the hand of friendship, even to inviting him here, to my own home, and I have sent men regularly to check upon his estate whilst he has been away, as he requested."

"I am pleased to hear it, but I assure you I am not here at the request of Lord Southwick," Armand told him, taking care to use Philip's correct title after de Basville had, impudently to his mind, referred to him by his name. "I am here at the express wish of his Majesty King Louis."

Armand let that one sink in, rather enjoying the worried look that crossed the Intendant's countenance.

"The King has no cause to doubt my obedience to his wishes or the loyalty of this region," de Basville protested. "Why, I have plans to commission a statue to him in Montpellier and erect a triumphal arch in the Place de Peyrou, honouring his achievements."

"Then I am sure his Majesty requires no further proof of either your obedience or your loyalty," Armand said, with a trace of sarcasm he could barely hide. "The reason I am here, however, is because he wishes me to investigate a recent incident."

"When Lord Southwick's cousin was arrested, I suppose," de Basville said. "I had nothing whatever to do with that, but if a man defies the King's law then, in my opinion, he should be treated as a criminal, no matter who he is. Or to whom he is related," he added peevishly.

Armand let the remark pass. He was not there to bandy words with this pompous official and he had no intention of letting the conversation deteriorate into an opportunity for de Basville to make snide remarks. "Some disturbing rumours have reached the ear of the King, rumours that will do your own reputation little credit, Intendant."

That got the de Basville's attention.

"What rumours," he asked, "and who is spreading them?"

"Never mind who," Armand said firmly. "The complaint was not made against you directly but rather against the person who you have appointed as your Inspector of Missions."

"Du Chayla?" De Basville looked relieved. "What's he done now?"

"Surely, since he is answerable to you, Intendant, you must already know." Armand looked him full in the face. He had reached the rank of Colonel whilst he was on active service and had intimidated far more formidable people than the jumped-up lawyer who sat before him now.

De Basville visibly crumbled. "The man is a law unto himself," he admitted.

"And who allowed him to become so?" Armand demanded. "Are you telling me that you did not grant this fanatical Archpriest permission to enlist and control his own army?"

"I did, but only in order that I might carry out the King's order to scour the region of any rebels," de Basville said defensively.

"And what were your instructions regarding those rebels that his soldiers manage to capture?"

"He was to ensure their conversion, which was the duty entrusted to me by Louvois. You know that man, he is interested only in numbers, not methods."

Armand knew Louvois well enough but the Secretary of State for War was only part of the problem, and Armand was looking now at the other part; Intendants like de Basville, puffed up with their own importance and ruling provinces as if they were their private kingdoms.

"And what of those he and his acolytes fail to convert?"

De Basville looked uneasy, which told Armand all he wanted to know.

Armand was a good Catholic but he was not particularly devout and he marvelled often at men's intolerance to one another. To fight an enemy of your country was quite a different matter, to his mind, than to cruelly persecute your fellow Frenchmen.

"Send word for him to attend upon me here, if you please."

"That might be difficult," de Basville protested.

"It was not a request, Intendant," Armand said pleasantly. "If, however, you propose to obstruct me in the duty entrusted to me by his Majesty…"

"No, no, not at all," de Basville hastened to reassure him, "but du Chayla is not always at Le Pont de Montvert. He travels around the region seeking out dissidents."

"Then find him."

Armand turned to go. De Basville disgusted him, as did all men who abused the power of their positions, and he had met many since he had begun the distasteful task Louis had set him.

"I tried to warn him not to go up against Lord Southwick, my Lord," de Basville said.

Armand smiled icily "Perhaps you should have tried harder."

∽

François-Michel Le Tellier, the Marquis de Louvois, had inherited the position of Secretary of State for War from his father, and he was now Louis' most influential minister.

Louvois had been determined to increase France's military presence in the Spanish Netherlands and had spent the Winter months moving men up to the region and seeing to the preparations for the siege. Supplies had been laid up in towns along the border and labourers employed to dig Vauban's earthworks.

But the true beauty of the plan lay in the fact that the attack was due to take place before the Allies had finished their own preparations for the coming campaign season. If all went well, King William would be taken completely unawares but Maréchal de Luxembourg's forces were already in position to intercept him if it looked like he would arrive with aid before Mons fell.

"Is everything in readiness?" Louis asked him.

"It is, your Majesty. I received confirmation today from Maréchal Boufflers."

"Excellent! You have exceeded all my expectations," Louis said delightedly, for he believed in giving praise when it was due and Louvois had certainly earned it on this occasion. "I shall be leaving very soon to join Boufflers," Louis said.

Louvois looked less than happy with that prospect, even though it was not the first time Louis had gone into battle at the head of his troops. "I beg your Majesty to reconsider. You will be in a vulnerable position there and I must confess I fear for your safety."

"Would you have it said that an upstart Dutch prince exposes himself to danger in battle whilst the king of France dares not?" Louis said.

"Of course not, your Majesty, but with you will be your brother and your son."

Louis knew the point Louvois was making. He was not just putting himself at risk, but two of his possible successors as well.

And not only them. Beside him also would be his illegitimate son, the Comte de Toulouse whilst elsewhere, on the front lines of the armies of both Boufflers and Luxembourg, would be no less than seven other members of the royal family.

Even so, Louis knew where his duty lay and he had never believed in asking others to hazard members of their families for the glory of France without being prepared to hazard members of his own.

"Philip Devalle presented himself to me last week," he said, changing the subject to indicate that the discussion was closed.

"So I was informed, your Majesty."

That came as no great surprise to Louis, who knew that his Minister of War was sometimes better informed about what was happening than he was himself.

"I understand there has been some trouble in Languedoc recently," Louis said.

"There is always some trouble in Languedoc," Louvois said dismissively. "I can usually rely on de Basville to sort it out."

"Well in this case he seems to have been the cause of it," Louis said. "You know that Philip's cousin has been arrested?"

"Yes, your Majesty."

"Of course you did! And you never imagined that the news would bring Philip hotfoot here from England complaining about the methods employed by your Intendant and his Inspector of Missions?"

"The man was a Huguenot," Louvois protested. "A criminal in the eyes of the law. It is hardly de Basville's fault if the arrest has caused Devalle any discomfiture."

"It is not Philip Devalle's discomfiture that is important here so much as mine, since it was on account of my decision to restore his family's property to him which caused him to be involved in the affairs of Languedoc in the first place," Louis pointed out.

If Louvois had any thoughts upon that subject then Louis knew he would not voice them. A man of bourgeoise upbringing, such as Louvois, would never have risen to such an important position if he had ever questioned any of Louis' decisions, which was the precise reason Louis chose such men for high office as opposed to those of the nobility, who were invariably more opinionated and harder to control.

"Is your Majesty saying that it would be better to have his cousin released?" was all Louvois said

"No. I am saying that it would have been better if he had not been arrested in the first place." Louis said tartly, "but since he was and the matter has, apparently, become public knowledge there is little I can do about it now." Louis was only too aware that Madame de Maintenon was one of those who was joyfully spreading the news. "I have, however, sent the Comte de Rennes to Montpellier to investigate the methods employed by this Inspector of Missions to whom de Basville gives such licence."

"Very good, your Majesty."

Louis knew that there was no love lost between Louvois and the Comte. When Armand had first left the army, he had been offered a position as Louvois' military adviser and had turned it down, preferring to retire to his estate. Later, it was Armand who had brought to Louis' attentions the atrocities being committed against the Huguenots by the infamous dragonnades, who were quartered forcibly in Protestant houses and allowed to act as cruelly as they pleased in order to obtain the necessary conversion figures.

Louvois had always strenuously denied that the orders for their behaviour came from him, but there could be no doubt that he was aware of what was happening and did nothing to prevent it.

Louis, urged on by Madame de Maintenon in his determination to turn France into a wholly Catholic nation, had been pleased with those conversion figures, until he had learned from Armand how they were being obtained. He had long ago abandoned his great vision of achieving a willing and peaceful conversion of his Protestant subjects but he was certainly not prepared to be held responsible for the actions of any fanatical archpriest.

"Philip visited Monsieur whilst he was in Paris, by the way," Louis told Louvois, although he guessed that he would already know that too. "He had Luc Santerre with him. Were you not the person who first introduced Santerre to my brother?"

"I was, your Majesty," Louvois said, a little cagily.

"Monsieur tells me that he is probably his son." He looked sharply at Louvois. "As I am sure you were aware at the time."

"There must be many young courtiers who like to claim kinship with Philip Devalle."

"Quite possibly, but they don't all get taken back to England with him.," Louis pointed out. "No doubt you employed him to spy upon what went on at my brother's Court. I believe he is still doing that, but for his father rather than for you."

Louvois looked horrified. "Do you imagine Monsieur told him of our plan for an early attack?"

"I am sure he did."

"What if Devalle sends word to King William?"

"He won't," Louis said confidently. "Philip is loyal to me and, besides, we had an agreement. I promised him the Pasquier vineyard if he pledged never to fight against France."

"How can you be sure he can be trusted to keep to his part of the arrangement? He was always devious," Louvois said

Louis smiled. He knew that Louvois liked Philip no more than he liked Armand.

"Devious he might be but I trust him because he is shrewd enough to see where his best advantage lies and because, no matter what you may think of him, Philip is an honourable man – in his own way."

꿎

"So, what did de Basville have to say for himself?" Philip asked when he and Armand met at the Inn of the Three Crowns in Montpellier.

"Other than that he had never shown you anything but friendship?" Armand said dryly. "He disavows all knowledge of du Chayla's methods and denies playing any part in your cousin's arrest. He also claims that he tried to dissuade du Chayla from antagonising you."

"That much may be true," Philip said, remembering the Intendant's worried reaction when du Chayla had made his threat.

"I shall shortly have the opportunity to hear what du Chayla has to say for himself, since I have ordered him to Montpellier to meet me."

"I am sorry to have inflicted the man upon you," Philip said.

"Hopefully I will not need to spend much time in his company. Just long enough to delay his return to Le Pont de Montvert," Armand said meaningfully.

Philip smiled, understanding. "You are a good friend, Armand."

"Am I? I wonder whether, as your friend, I should not be trying to dissuade you from this venture. Even if du Chayla is not there himself, his chateau will be heavily guarded. There are only four of you, after all."

"I am hoping we may have some help. There are a great number of Huguenot rebels hiding out in the Cevennes, according to du Chayla, and we already know that Antoine is not the only one held captive at his chateau. If some of the rebels are prepared to aid us, we might have a chance to free the rest of the prisoners."

Armand's look of horror made it plain what he thought of that prospect.

"This is like you, Philip, but have you truly thought it out? These are dangerous times. You would be hazarding everything, not only your estate and your favour with Louis but quite possibly your freedom, even your life. And for what? A member of the family who disowned you and a cause you don't truly believe in."

"I believe in justice, Armand, as do you, and I believe that tyrants should not be allowed to inflict cruelty upon the oppressed. I also believe in France. I love your country every bit as much as my own and the actions of bastards such as this Archpriest not only besmirch the King's name but call to question the honour of every noble Frenchman, be he Protestant or Catholic."

"You are a good man," Armand said quietly, "but how will you even locate these rebel bands. They will hardly be likely to announce their presence to strangers."

"Thomas may be able to find them." Philip glanced over at Thomas and Luc, who were chatting to the pretty serving maid. "It would probably be best if I don't tell you how!"

Armand nodded. "Agreed! He is a useful young man, your Thomas, but he needs to be careful. If he is caught with them there is little I would able to do to save him."

"I'll not be far away and Morgan and Luc would never let any harm come to him either."

"What of Luc? Is he useful too?" Armand had first known Luc as a companion of Monsieur.

"Very. For one thing he is my source of information about the Catholic community here. He has made a friend of one of the local priests."

"Does this priest realise who he is?"

"No. Luc told him he was Louvois' nephew!"

Armand laughed at that. "From the sound of him I would reckon that, no matter what you say, he very well could be your son."

"I'm beginning to think that too," Philip admitted, "but don't you dare tell him! Luc has discovered something else too," he said, becoming serious again. "and from Monsieur. I know about the siege they are planning at Mons."

"Then you probably know more about it than I, since I am no longer kept abreast of military plans," Armand said, with a trace of regret.

"They are all going; Louis, the Dauphin, even Monsieur, and they are going soon. Vauban has probably already started his earthworks."

Armand smiled at a memory of Vauban. "I recall the day he came to bid me farewell when I was leaving the army to return to Paris after my injury. He said he envied the retirement I was so dreading as all he longed for was to retire to his Burgundy farm with his wife and tend to his cows and apple trees!"

"Really?" The thought of the robust General desiring such a peaceful life caused Philip to smile too. "Yet he is still in the army."

"Because Louis won't let hm go."

"He is too valuable to him, I suppose."

"Not only that. He is somewhat outspoken, as you know, and he was foolish enough to criticise the decision to revoke the Edict. Now he, like me, is forced to remain in the King's service, but he told me he detested the bombardments he was ordered to carry out, and that it was his ambition to carry out a siege so successfully that the enemy would yield without a shot being fired, as he would rather preserve a hundred French soldiers than kill three thousand of the enemy."

"Amen to that," Philip said with feeling. "I have seen too much of death in war, Armand. At the Boyne I saw Schomberg fall and I lost a young lieutenant whose life held so much promise. When I wrote to inform his family of his demise it was hard to find any words that would come close to justifying their loss. They both perished leading a charge across a blasted river, Armand, whilst King James, who was responsible for all of it, was fleeing for his damned life."

Armand nodded sadly. Philip knew that he, too. must have had to write similar letters to the families of officers he had lost in battle.

"My brother-in-law was nearly killed too, Armand." Philip shuddered to think how close his own family had come to suffering such a devastating loss. "William would have left him to die, you know."

"Monsieur told me what you did. Thank God you managed to save him." Armand looked at him uncertainly. "Have you informed King William about the siege?"

"Have I hell! I want no part of this war with France. My only concern is that Giles gets safely home from Holland before it all begins."

"If William finds out that you knew and did not warn him things might become difficult for you in England," Armand reminded him.

Philip shrugged. "Then he had better not find out, had he?"

He spoke carelessly but he was well aware of the difficult situation Monsieur's confidences to Luc had placed him in. By not sending word to William he was being a traitor to England but if he did, and it was ever discovered, then he would not be welcome in France again. Louis never forgot and seldom forgave.

Armand and Vauban were proof of that.

"The French have opened a siege at Mons." William told Bentinck, his chief adviser, angrily. He passed him the letter he had received from the Marquis de Gastañago, the Governor, who had written begging for his help. "Boufflers has brought three French armies into Flanders under our very noses."

"So early in the season?"

"They thought to catch us unawares and they have succeeded," William said bitterly. "It seems my precious time at Het Loo has ended all too quickly. I must send word to the Allies today and order them to assemble their troops. Tell Giles he will need to be ready to accompany me back to the Hague immediately."

"The Earl of Wimborne left for England an hour ago, your Majesty."

"He's gone already?"

"He set off at crack of dawn." Bentinck said, with a trace of disgust. He had little regard for Giles or any of the English courtiers, for that matter, as he did not feel they were loyal enough to William. He had been William's friend since childhood and he was fiercely protective of him. "He said he was hoping to catch the morning tide."

"Did he indeed!" William said crossly. "Well he'll have to miss it. I need him, so have him fetched back!"

Giles arrived at the port of Rotterdam to find it a bustle of activity. "What's happening?" he asked one of the port officials as he prepared to board the boat waiting to set sail for England, for there was clearly panic in the air.

"Have you not heard the news?" the man said. "There is talk that the French army is attacking Mons."

Giles' heart sank. This was exactly what he had not wanted to hear before he had left Holland.

"Are you certain? I have just come from Het Loo," he told him, "and there was no word of it."

"Word will have reached there now. Do you still wish to board? I cannot hold the boat or it will lose the tide."

Giles hesitated, but only for an instant. "I'll board."

He'd had two narrow escapes upon the battlefield, one at Sedgemoor, fighting beside the Duke of Monmouth, and one in Ireland, where he knew he would have died had Philip and Morgan not found him in time. Giles was no coward, but neither did he imagine he was indestructible. He had a wife and child to consider and he had no wish to tempt fate for the third time.

Even as the boat prepared to pull away, he saw the people on the quay making way for a horseman arriving in great haste.

Giles did not need to see the colour of the man's uniform to guess that he bore an order recalling him to William's side.

Five minutes later and the messenger would have missed him. Giles would have been looking down at the widening stretch of water between him and the shores of Holland.

"Damn and blast!"

FOURTEEN

❧

"What do you want here, English!" Emile Tartours looked at Thomas with the expert eye of one well used to assessing men.

Thomas was unperturbed. The man who sat before him was probably the most dangerous in Montpellier, the ruthless head of the city's criminal fraternity, but Thomas had been brought up in the roughest part of London and had lived his early life amongst criminals. Had a happy chance of fate, under the unlikeliest of circumstances, not brought him and Theresa together when he was a twelve-year-old orphan of the streets, and had Philip not agreed to take him in, he knew he would have probably ended his days swinging from a rope by now.

As a member of the Devalle household he had been fed, clothed and taught to behave but, more importantly, given the chance of a better life. Very few who knew him now as the manservant of a duke would have guessed at his lowly beginnings, but Thomas had not forgotten those beginnings, and they were a part of him that he could call upon when he needed to, in the service of his master.

He cocked is head to one side and gave Tartours a cheeky grin. "I'm looking for work and I'm told that, in this city, you are the man to whom I must pay respect."

"That's so. What's your trade?"

"Thieving. Street work mainly but I've done some housebreaking, and I'm nimble."

"I can see that." Tartours looked him up and down. "Where have you worked?"

"Paris and London."

"Who did you answer to in Paris?" Tartours asked straightaway.

"François Delaporte." That was a lie, but Thomas knew enough about the seamy side of Paris to know it was a name which would impress Tartours.

"So why did you leave?"

"Things got tricky for me there."

"Why?"

"I'm English," Thomas reminded him. "We're at war."

"Oh, that," Tartours said dismissively.

Thomas had guessed correctly that, whilst the war with England was on everyone's lips in the capital, down here in the provinces the people knew little of its progress and cared still less so long as it did not interfere with their lives or their livelihoods.

"What about London? Did things get tricky for you there too?"

"Very. I had to get out in a hurry. The new king is scouring out Alsatia so there's nowhere left to hide. His men are worse than La Reynie's."

La Reynie was the Chief of police in Paris and Tartours nodded sympathetically. "I hear it's bad in Paris now. Citizens forced to show a light outside their houses and regular patrols. It must be hard to make a living there but this city has enough cut-purses."

"I can do other things."

"Like what?"

"I was led to believe you run guns up to the rebels in the mountains."

Tartours gave him a sharp look. "Where did you learn that?"

"Here and there."

"Then you know we can only move the merchandise when de Basville's Inspector is out of the Cevennes."

"He'll be in Montpellier this week."

"Where did you find that out?" Tartours asked, then answered the question for himself. "I know. Here and there! You're a crafty little bastard, aren't you, English?"

"So I've been told!"

Thomas was aware that Emile Tartours was sizing him up. He was slightly built but he was agile and wiry and the Frenchman was obviously satisfied with what he saw.

"You might be right for the job. There'll be two of you and you'll need to watch each other's backs. It's risky having dealings with the Huguenots," he warned. "The penalties are harsh but what can we do? Business is business. If you're right about du Chayla we can shift some weapons tomorrow. Do you know the Place d'Oeuf? "

"I can find it," Thomas said.

"Be outside the first house by six in the morning, and, English…" Tartours's expression was genial but there was no mistaking the steel in his tone, "Don't let me down."

In reply Thomas raised his left hand to Tartours and made the international hand gesture that only those who lived outside the law knew, signifying unity and respect, a bond of honour between criminals of every country and class.

"What happened to the finger?" Tartours asked, for Thomas was missing the little finger of that hand.

"A lady slammed her carriage door on it as I was trying to take her purse. I was just a small child," he added, seeing Tartours smile,

"This," the Frenchman said, nodding philosophically, "is how we learn."

"It's on for tomorrow," Thomas said to the others when he got back to the inn.

"Good work!" Philip said. "I don't suppose he told you where you were going."

"Sorry, no, and I could hardly ask without arousing his suspicions."

"Quite. I'm surprised he trusted you in any case."

"I don't think he does really. I expect he's warned the other man to keep an eye on me but I think he recognised me as one of his own kind!"

"Be careful," Philip instructed him. Whilst he had every faith in Thomas' ability to carry this off, he was well aware than no-one got to become the head of a crime organisation by being good-natured!

"But am I not about to do exactly what he has paid me to do, my Lord, which is to help deliver weapons to the rebels in the mountains?" Thomas fished out the bag Tartours had given him and rolled some coins over the table.

"He's paid you already?" Luc said, surprised.

"He said it was usual for this job, in case we get spotted and have to make a run for it. The last thing he wants, I imagine, is us returning to Montpellier for our money and leading the law back to him if we are being watched."

"Even so, what if you were to cheat him?"

Thomas shook his head. "I've met the man, Luc. I don't think anyone does that!"

"Fifteen livres," Philip said, counting the money. "I'm impressed. At rates like that for a few day's work I might have to watch you don't slip back into your old dishonest ways! In the meantime, maybe you can spare 3 sous of your new-found wealth to buy the wine, for once."

It was barely light when the four of them neared the Place d'Oeuf, on the outskirts of the city. It was oval-shaped, which, Philip realised, accounted for the odd name, and lined with houses that had passageways leading to courtyards behind. There was a covered cart backed up to one of these.

"Guess that's the house," Thomas said, dismounting and handing the reins of his horse to Morgan. The Welshman had been like a father to him since Thomas had joined the household and they exchanged a long look. No words were spoken, nor did they need to be.

They watched him cross the street to disappear into the courtyard.

"He will be alright, won't he, my Lord?" Luc said quietly.

"Of course," Philip said with more confidence than he felt, for he knew Armand had been right when he had said that if Thomas was caught aiding the rebels there would be little that even he could do to help him. But Philip wasn't going to let that happen. He cursed Antoine once again. It was only because of him that he was having to send his beloved servant into danger.

He felt better about it when Thomas emerged a little while later, talking casually with another man, who got into the driver's seat. Thomas fastened the door to the passageway, then climbed up to join him. Philip and the others watched the vehicle as it headed out of the city in the direction of the river.

They let it get a little way before following but, fortunately, the area that side of the city was heavily wooded and they were able to keep out of sight.

It was all up to Armand now, Philip knew. If du Chayla could not be kept occupied for the next few days then everything could still go horribly wrong. but his friend had never let him down yet and he was certain that he never would.

"Have you done this run before?" Thomas asked his companion, whose name he had learned was Marcel.

"Twice, but not for several months. It rains here a lot in the Winter and the route gets muddy."

It was raining at that moment and Thomas couldn't help but wonder how Philip and the others were faring. Morgan and his master had spent years in the army and were well-used to such discomforts but he could not resist a little smile to himself as he pictured Luc, who had come to consider himself a gentleman during his time at Court, and who was quite particular about his appearance!

They were making their way through a thick wood called the Bois de Valène and Thomas wondered whether Antoine had walked these same tracks to the mountains. It seemed likely, for they were well-hidden by the trees on both sides. He only hoped that Philip, Morgan and Luc were managing to keep them in sight.

"You handle the cart well," Thomas said, for some of the tracks were narrow and had been made uneven by the tree roots that grew beneath them.

"Driving was my work once. What about you?"

"I never had a trade before I took to stealing," Thomas said truthfully.

They had been travelling for quite a while, although Thomas had no idea where they were, and Marcel had avoided the few settlements they had come upon.

"You can't trust anyone," Marcel warned him as they skirted around the village of Murles. "Du Chayla has paid informants who will fetch the soldiers down here in a trice."

"You've managed before," Thomas pointed out.

"By being careful. I don't even trust the Huguenots. Their leader is a strange one. I reckon he'd slit your throat as soon as look at you."

"But they need us, surely," Thomas said.

"They need us now," Marcel stressed, "but if they ever get sufficient strength, I wouldn't want to come up against them in a fight. They're fanatics, fired up by religion, like du Chayla's lot. There'll be blood spilt here, you mark me. Not yet, perhaps, but it's coming."

"And we're taking them the weapons for it," Thomas pointed out.

Marcel shrugged. "If it wasn't us making money out of them then it would be someone else."

Thomas wanted to ask Marcel the question that was mystifying both him and his master, and that was who was paying Tartours for his services. It was not a subject he could broach, however, not without incurring suspicion. Marcel was a little older than him, in his thirties, Thomas guessed, and he seemed friendly enough, but Thomas guessed that he must be in a trusted position in Tartours' organisation to be chosen to lead the job they were on, which meant that he was probably as ruthless a bastard as they come!

They had still not reached the mountains when they stopped for the night and unhitched the horse. It was too damp to attempt to light a fire, but they made a meal from the bread and cheese that Marcel had brought along for them both and shared a bottle of wine, which warmed them a little, before they settled down beneath the cart, for protection from the weather. Marcel soon fell asleep and directly Thomas heard his breathing becoming more regular he slipped out from under the vehicle and started back in the darkness along the way they had come. He had not gone far before he saw a light shining through the trees. It was coming from a lantern, hung from a branch, and it was the signal which told him what he wanted to know – that the others were close at hand. He would have dearly liked to have gone to speak with them but, if he was not to incur the suspicions of his travelling companion, he dared not be absent for any longer than it would reasonably take to relieve himself in the woods so he returned as quietly as he could and slid back under the cart.

"I demand to know by what right you have summoned me here." Du Chayla's hard eyes glittered as he fixed on Armand a glare that, Armand guessed, would have struck terror into the hearts of his victims.

Armand, however, was totally unperturbed.

"By the power invested in me by his glorious Majesty King Louis, whom we all serve," he reminded the Archpriest and de Basville.

That took the wind out of du Chayla's sails for a moment but he soon recovered his arrogance. "It is scarcely in the interests of King Louis for you to drag me to Montpellier when I would be better employed in serving those interests in Le Pont de Montvert."

"It is your activities in Le Pont de Montvert that I wish to discuss, Inspector." Armand deliberately chose to use du Chayla's title of Inspector of Missions rather than that of Abbé. He might be a Catholic himself but he felt no common bond with this fanatic and had no desire to dignify him with his religious title.

Du Chayla reacted with a tightening of his lips and Armand knew that the slight had hit home.

"I fail to see what there is to discuss. I am performing the duty for which the Intendant appointed me, which is to help ensure the conversion of every Protestant in Languedoc, a duty which is being carried out by priests in all regions of France, as no doubt, you are aware," he said sneeringly, "since your own wife, I believe, is herself a Huguenot convert."

Armand would have dearly loved to knock du Chayla off his feet for having the impudence to bring Marguerite into their conversation, but he had more control.

"My Comtesse," he said evenly, "was attacked before she became a convert and would have been raped by Louvois' brutish dragonnades had I not arrived in time to save her. It is atrocities towards the Protestants, and the indifference to them shown by some of the intendants," here Armand shot a glance at de Basville, who had the grace to keep silent even though he looked put out at being included in the conversation, "which the King wishes me to investigate. His Majesty abhors the use of such methods."

191

"Yet he is pleased enough with the results," Du Chayla said tartly. "How else do you imagine that I am to get them, especially in a region as troublesome as this?"

"I am not here to tell you how, but only to remind you that you are accountable," Armand said, "to me in the first instance and, ultimately, to the King. I understand that you have been aggressively seeking out the Huguenots and that those you capture are kept incarcerated in your chateau."

"I keep some there in order to save their souls by instructing them in the true faith," du Chayla said piously. "I am doing God's work."

"I've heard you keep them prisoner and subject them to all manner of tortures," Armand snapped back. "and that you, Intendant," Armand gave de Basville a withering look, "allow it to continue. The King is concerned and I need to be able to reassure him that matters have been resolved satisfactorily, so I want a list of all the prisoners currently undergoing 'instruction' at your chateau."

"A list?" Du Chayla sounded outraged. "That is unthinkable. I am a busy man with important duties to perform." He turned to de Basville for support.

"Don't look to him for help," Armand warned. "The Intendant's only concern is to remain on the right side of the King."

De Basville did not argue the point, although he looked unhappy at the situation he had been placed in.

"He has more to lose than you," Armand reminded du Chayla, "and even having friends in high places at Court may not be sufficient to protect his position, should his Majesty decide to replace him," he added pointedly, for he knew that although Madame de Maintenon had Louis' ear he would not always heed her. "I want a list of names and of the progress," he stressed the word, "that you are making with their conversion. I can supply you with one name already, if it helps, that of Antoine Pasquier, but I am sure there must be others."

Du Chayla looked up sharply but Armand kept his face expressionless.

"I would need to return to Le Pont de Montvert to obtain such information," du Chayla said sullenly.

"I would not put you to such inconvenience," Armand assured him. "I would have been prepared to travel there myself but it is a difficult journey by coach and I fear that my leg would prevent me from travelling so far on horseback these days. However," he added, anticipating the pleasure from seeing du Chayla's expression change from smug satisfaction to annoyance, "my servant is a fit young man who can be trusted to make the journey in my stead and has my authorisation to collect the information I require. He will, of course, be accompanied by the small force I have at my command, for fear that these dangerous rebels I hear spoken of may attack him on his journey. You, meanwhile, I am certain will find plenty of godly work to occupy you in Montpellier whilst he is gone, you being such an important and busy man," he said, in a voice dripping with sarcasm, "and I would be most interested to accompany you to the churches where the priests you have trained in your seminary at Saint-Germain-de-Calberte preach their uplifting words to the newly converted."

Eugene, was waiting for him in the Rue du Cannau, with the six men who provided their armed escort as they travelled the country. Good, stout fellows all and hand-picked by Armand from amongst those who had served well under his command during his years at war.

"I am ashamed to say that I rather enjoyed that," Armand confided to him. "I don't know which of that pair is the worst, one driven by what he feels is his divine mission and the other by a desire to retain his position of power. I believe I managed to disconcert both of them a little!"

"I guess the meeting went well then, my Lord," Eugene said with a smile.

"It did, but now, I must endure the man whilst you play your part." The truth was that Armand could very well have managed the three-day journey into the mountains, despite his leg, but Eugene was both able and willing to go in his stead, and Armand felt he needed to remain in Montpellier, where he could keep a watchful eye upon du Chayla. "I think I have given Philip a few days grace to attempt a rescue but, even though he may be able to save his cousin and the others held there, I fear there is little I can really do to maintain control over du Chayla, not while he has the blessing of de Basville. I may have been able to curb his shameful activities for a short while but I am certain there will be many more in the future who will suffer at his hands."

FIFTEEN

✍

"What is it" Thomas asked, as he hitched up the horse ready for an early start on the third, and final, day of the journey.

Their travels had been uneventful so far. Even the rain had mercifully ceased after the first day and they had made good time, encountering few other travellers, and none of those had taken much notice of them or given them more than a cursory greeting as they passed by. This morning, however, Marcel seemed edgy.

"We are nearing St. Germain-de-Calberte. We are in du Chayla's territory now," he explained, laying his pistol on the seat beside him. "He trains his Jesuit disciples up there and his soldiers patrol the area." He smiled grimly. "This is where you may have to earn your money, English."

They gave the village a wide berth, even though the detour would cost them some time but, even so, when they had got a little further down the road, they heard horses behind them and Thomas turned to see soldiers rapidly approaching.

He tensed ready, as they drew nearer, but he feared they might fare badly in an exchange of fire, for he counted three of them.

The weapons that he and Marcel were carrying for the Huguenots were hidden beneath a false bottom in the cart and covered over with heavy sacks of grain but he knew that would not deter the soldiers from searching it if they had a mind.

"Let me do the talking," Marcel told Thomas. "Let's hope they are not bored and looking for someone to stop."

But it seemed they were. As the soldiers drew level, they signalled Marcel to halt.

He swore under his breath.

"Now what?" Thomas whispered.

"Now we pray, English!" He doffed his hat to the leader of the troop. "Good day to you, Sergeant."

The sergeant did not return the greeting. "What might you be about so early in the day, fellow?"

"We are delivering grain to the good people of Cassagnas," Marcel said, adopting the slow way of speaking that was common to the country folk of the region.

The sergeant spat on the ground, plainly indicating his opinion of the residents of Cassagnas. "You'd be better letting them starve."

Thomas looked about him nonchalantly, appearing to be disinterested in what was going on and merely taking in the view but, in reality, he was scanning the woods and hills around them. They had moved off earlier than usual that day and he hoped that the others had been sharp-eyed enough to notice them leaving.

"Get down, both of you," the sergeant ordered. "Take that cover off the cart. I want to see for myself what's under there."

They pulled back the tarpaulin and showed him the sacks of grain.

"You see, it is just grain, as I told you," Marcel said.

"Is it? Let's find, shall we?" The sergeant pulled out a knife and used it to slit one of the bags. He laughed as he watched the contents spill out onto the muddy track. "That's one bag the 'good people of Cassagnas' won't be getting." When the bag was empty and he had made was sure it had contained nothing but grain he turned back to them. "Unload the rest."

They both knew that if they did that the game would be up for certain.

"But I have to deliver this before noon, or I will lose my job," Marcel protested, still in the character of a farm labourer.

"Listen, you country dimwit," the sergeant snarled at him, "it will be your life you lose if you don't do what I say. That goes for you too." he said to Thomas, who was keeping quiet, as Marcel had asked him to do, although his brain was racing as he tried to think of a way out of their predicament. With the sergeant's two soldiers now pointing their pistols at them it seemed they had little choice, no matter what the consequences.

But Marcel was still stalling for time, and Thomas' could have cried out for joy as he saw why.

"What do you hope to find?" Marcel asked the sergeant.

"Never mind that," the sergeant snapped. "Just get to it before we shoot the pair of you and see for ourselves what you are carrying. In fact," he levelled his own pistol at Marcel's head and laughed, "I might just do it anyway."

"I don't think that would be very wise."

The laughter died on the sergeant's face as he spun round to see that a tall, blonde man had emerged from the woods behind them, his own weapon trained upon the sergeant himself. His men spun around, only to find that the stranger's two companions had their pistols trained on them.

The odds now more than evened up, the soldiers lowered their weapons reluctantly.

"That's better," Philip said, without lowering his. "Now, what is happening here and why are you threatening my men?"

"Your men?" the sergeant said suspiciously. "This is your grain?"

"That's right."

Philip's command of French was good enough to convince any that he was a Frenchman, particularly in Languedoc, for he had learned the language first from Nanon and he still had a trace of her southern accent. Dressed in a plain, brown woollen coat, as he was, he could easily be taken for a gentleman farmer by any who did not know him.

"We're on the watch for Huguenot scum and any who are helping them," the sergeant said, eyeing Philip warily.

"And that is your excuse for harassing loyal Catholics about their lawful business?"

"They might have had weapons hidden in those sacks for all we knew," the sergeant said, his voice rising defensively.

"But they didn't, did they?" Philip pointed to the grain spilled out in the dirt. "So you thought you would have a little sport and threaten some innocent locals."

"We were doing our duty," the sergeant protested.

"No, you weren't, but I would be doing mine if I treated you as you were about to treat them. The Inspector of Missions is even now in Montpellier, being held to account for his conduct toward the people of this region, and I would have a care if I were you. In order to excuse himself, he will likely deny giving his soldiers free reign to threaten honest citizens for no better reason than for entertainment."

"How do you know where he is?" the sergeant said sullenly.

"Word travels fast in these parts. Now I would suggest you took yourselves off and allowed my men to pass in peace."

The sergeant seemed about to argue, but Philip glared at him and he evidently thought better of it.

"We're moving on," he told the soldiers. "These wretched peasants are not worthy of our time."

Philip guessed that the sergeant's parting remark was made to save his face in front of his men, and he allowed him that.

"I doubt they'll return," Philip said to Marcel, as Luc and Morgan went back into the trees to fetch the horses, "but we'll stay behind you on the road for a while, as we are going your way."

"I'm grateful to you, sir, whoever you are, but you must think me a fool if you reckon I'll believe you just happened to appear when we needed you and made up that tale for the soldiers out of the goodness of your heart." Marcel looked at Thomas. "You're in on this aren't you, English?" His hand moved towards the pistol on the seat.

"We mean no harm to you or to the rebels," Thomas quickly reassured him. "These are my friends, and they have reasons of their own for wanting to find them. I'm here to do what I was paid to do, which is to help you deliver the weapons, and they have been following us here."

Marcel glanced from him to Philip and back again, but he made no further move toward his weapon.

"Père Tartours said he thought you were a crafty little bastard. He didn't know the half, did he?"

"He hasn't lied to you completely," Philip said. "He might work for me now but he was once everything he claimed to be."

"I know that, I can spot one of our own," Marcel said dismissively. "I care not what he is, or what the four of you are about. I only want to know what happens now."

"You make your delivery, as planned. We'll stay out of your way until you have completed your business and are on your way back to Montpellier although, if you take my advice, you will choose a different route. I cannot guarantee the sergeant won't return with reinforcements, in fact, it might be wise to move on now," he said, as Luc and Morgan returned with the horses.

Thomas waved to the pair before climbing up beside Marcel.

"You're not going with them, then?" Marcel said, sounding surprised.

Thomas shook his head. "We still have a job to do, and I'd hate for Père Tartours to think I did not earn my money." He gave a questioning glance at his companion.

"He'll hear no different from me." Marcel assured him, taking up the reins. "I reckon, one way or another, you have earned your money well enough, English!"

࿔

Following the River Mimente through the valley, Thomas and Marcel arrived before long at Cassagnas, whose dark-roofed houses were set into the side of the mountain. This village Marcel did not trouble to go around, but followed the track that led through the houses towards rocky crags which rose high above them.

"No-one here will betray us," he explained to Thomas. "This is Protestant territory, although the people here are Catholic converts now, or pretend to be."

"They still don't look too friendly," Thomas decided, as a woman who had been on her way out of her house with a shopping basket saw them coming and dodged back inside, slamming her front door shut. There was not a soul to be seen as they drove through and he noticed some shutters being hastily fastened.

"They're not. They turn a blind eye to what we do, but if du Chayla ever discovered that they know where rebels are hiding out then the people of Cassagnas would be treated no better than them, so they keep out of our way. Our business is not with them but with the ones up there." He pointed to the steep, red mountains towering over them.

"That's where the rebels are, in the mountains?" Thomas said in surprise, for he saw no dwellings perched on the rocks.

"They live in the caves," Marcel said. Thomas could just pick out what could have been caves, well hidden amongst the trees that grew upon the slopes.

"How do we get the cart up there?" he wondered.

"We don't. They come down for the goods. They know me so I'll go up and tell them we are here. You wait with the horse and make sure your friends stay well out of sight, or this lot may give us more trouble than the soldiers."

Thomas took the horse's reins and watched as Marcel made his way up what looked like an old goat track which went around the mountain before going out of sight amongst the trees that grew upon the lower slopes. He returned in the company of a dozen or so others. Thomas helped them unload the grain and removed the false floor of the cart, then the boxes were lifted out and taken up the track. The whole operation was managed swiftly and efficiently and within half an hour there was nothing to be seen of the weapons or the grain, which Marcel said they could take as well.

He turned to Thomas, when the last of them had gone.

"Well, English, I guess this is where we part company."

"Will you be alright?" Thomas asked. During the three days they had spent in close company he had come to rather like Marcel, and to respect him too. Thomas knew that, tough as he was, Marcel would be helpless alone if the soldiers should return.

"Don't you worry about me, English. I'm going to take your friend's advice. I'm heading north and I'm thinking it might even be wise to get out of the region altogether for a while. This is my third run and a man's luck can only hold out for so long in our game. You'd be welcome to come with me if you didn't have other plans."

They shook hands and Marcel climbed back into the driver's seat. "I hope you know those friends of yours well. They don't look the sort you should mess with," he said as he drove off.

Thomas smiled. "They're not!"

⁂

"It's done," Philip said, relieved. "Let's go."

From where they were hidden amongst a clump of the chestnut trees that grew along the valley, Philip, Morgan and Luc had been keeping watch on the proceedings. Philip had no better opinion of these desperate rebels than he had of the soldiers that patrolled the area, and he did not intend to have Thomas put in any more danger.

Thomas and Luc greeted each other enthusiastically. Philip was pleased that they had become such good friends. Their relationship had been a little uneasy in the beginning but they had quickly got the measure of one other.

"You did well," Philip told Thomas, "and now I have job for you, Luc."

"What's that," Luc said eagerly, "and please don't tell me I have to go to church. Catholic I may be, but I have never attended so many services in my life as I have had to do lately!"

Philip laughed. "It is good to know that I am helping to save your soul, but no. I fear the priest of the church in Le Pont de Montvert will be some fanatical Jesuit specially selected by du Chayla and you will stand no chance of making a friend of him. I need to discover more about the chateau, the best place to approach it, how many soldiers are there and where the prisoners are kept. You will need to observe the place, from a safe distance, and perhaps talk to some of the locals."

"I can do all that," Luc assured him.

"I know you can." Philip showed him the rough map Armand had drawn for them of the area. "Meet us in St. Julien d'Arpaon, tomorrow. If all goes well, we should have some of the rebels with us." Philip had not allowed himself to think on what he would do if he could not persuade any to join them. "Be careful and for God's sake stay out of trouble. We don't want to end up having to rescue you as well!"

Luc tipped his hat to them and set off along the road at a canter.

"He's been worried about you," Philip told Thomas.

"And now we all need to worry about him, my Lord."

"He'll be fine," Philip said, partly to reassure Thomas and partly to reassure himself. "He's French and he's a Catholic."

"And he has absolutely no regard for danger."

"That too," Philip allowed, "but the fact remains that he is the only one of the four of us who has any chance of finding out what we need to know without incurring suspicion. Besides, I have a feeling that he will not be made too welcome by the Huguenot rebels."

"We don't know that they will welcome us either," Morgan

said as they dismounted and led their horses up the narrow track.

As they climbed higher, they could see that many caves had formed in the mountain. None of those they passed were inhabited but they peered into a few of their dark depths.

"Antoine told me the local people say that thousands of years ago the centre of the earth boiled out of the tops of these mountains and that when it cooled it formed these caves," Morgan volunteered as they walked along.

Philip and Thomas both looked at him sceptically.

"And you believed that?" Philip said.

"Not really, no," Morgan admitted, "although I do come from a land of strange legends myself."

"Is it true that you once had dragons in Wales?" Thomas wanted to know.

"That's true," Morgan assured him, ignoring Philip's exasperated look.

Philip was about to reply but then he caught sight of a small clearing not far ahead and motioned the other two to silence.

He could see figures moving about in front of a massive cave, larger than any they had so far come across.

"I had better go first," Thomas said. "They know me."

"They know you as a criminal trading in stolen weapons," Philip pointed out. "They may not be so pleased to see that you have led us here. Do they leave none outside to watch for strangers approaching?" he asked, looking around him, for he could see no sign of anyone.

"It seems not," Thomas said. "They appear to be very trusting."

"Or very stupid," Philip reckoned as they entered the area and saw an encampment with what looked like a cooking fire lit, with a pile of charcoal by the side of it. The contents of the large kettle on the fire did not smell like food, but it was a smell he recognised.

"Saltpetre," he said. "They are making gunpowder!"

A few people, including some women, could be seen around the fire, but no-one challenged them.

They still proceeded cautiously, for they had reason to know that the rebels were armed. One man obviously recognised Thomas and called out to him but at the sound of a harsh voice, which rose above the rest, everyone else fell silent.

"What are you doing back here?"

"That's Raoul, their leader. He helped unload the cart," Thomas said quietly to Philip. "I have brought some friends to meet you," he told Raoul.

"I see that." Raoul studied them. "You have the look of one of Emile Tartours' felons," he said to Morgan, then turned to Philip, "but not you, so who the hell are you and what is your business here?"

Philip had already decided that it would be safer not to disclose his identity.

"If I had the time I would make it my business to teach you some better manners," he said, with an amused glance at Morgan, who did, indeed, look every inch a villain to anyone who did not know him, "but I don't, so I will simply say that I am here to attempt to free one of the prisoners in du Chayla's chateau and I am hoping to join forces with anyone amongst you who has friends or relatives also captive there."

There was an immediate murmur of interest amongst the others but, once again, Raoul's voice silenced theirs.

"It cannot be done."

Those four words gave Philip the measure of a man who would take on the rôle of a leader and yet would not do his utmost to protect those he led.

"Have you tried?" he asked, although he already suspected what the answer would be.

"Any who attempted to enter the chateau would be in danger of suffering a similar fate," Raoul said, without answering the question.

"So you haven't," Philip said disgustedly. "And what of the poor wretches incarcerated in that hell-hole, enduring God knows what before they are executed?"

"It is in God's cause that they suffer," Raoul said. "Each person here knows that they may be called upon to make the ultimate sacrifice for that cause."

Philip looked at those who had gathered around them. There were old men, young children and many women among them and their faces reflected only too well the horrors they had seen and the losses they had suffered. Some looked weary, some despairing and some fearful, but there was only one fanatic that Philip saw among them, and that was Raoul himself.

Anger rose inside him, an anger he saw reflected in the expressions of both Morgan and Thomas. "Why exactly are you here, man?"

"I am leading my people in the fight for freedom."

"Is not one of the first duties of a leader to keep his people safe?" Philip said.

"That is the very reason I will not attack the chateau."

"Are those imprisoned there no longer counted as your people then? Surely you have a duty to them too."

Raoul scowled. "It is not for you, an outsider, to tell me my duty. When the time is right, we shall rise up and avenge all those who have given their lives for our cause."

"If you do that then many more of your people will probably die for your cause," Philip warned him.

"Of course, they will," Raoul said, "but it will be a glorious death."

"There is no such thing," Philip said flatly, remembering those he had lost, and very nearly lost, on the battlefield "I have seen enough of death to know that. If you truly want to free your people you would surely be better leading them over the mountains to Italy or Spain. You have weapons. You might stand a chance if you all went together."

"De Basville's tyranny will not be allowed to go unpunished," Raoul insisted stubbornly. "He and du Chayla must be made to pay for their crimes against us."

"I agree, but this is not the way."

"Then what is?" Raoul demanded. "They are answerable to no-one."

"They are answerable to the Comte de Rennes," Philip corrected him, "and he is even now investigating their activities."

"What use is that to us?" Raoul sneered. "De Rennes was a soldier, the same as the dragoons who rounded up our men and took them away to spend the rest of their lives chained to a galley's oar. Now he is just another Catholic agent of King Louis." He almost spat the words.

"He may be Catholic, but he is a good and honest man," Philip said. "It is true that he was appointed by the King, but to watch over the intendants to ensure that Protestants were treated fairly. You should not assume all Catholics are cruel bastards like du Chayla."

"You might too if you had endured what we have at the hands of those of their accursed faith," Raoul said hotly. "Even before the edict that protected us was revoked, the King's lawyers searched it and declared that anything not granted in it was illegal."

Philip had heard that from Armand, although he kept silent.

"Do you have any idea of what that meant?" Raoul asked him. "The Edict of Nantes did not authorise that Protestant burials could be carried out during the hours of daylight and so it was decreed that we must bury our dead by night; it did not state which subjects could be taught in our schools, which meant our schoolmasters could teach our children little more than how to read and write. Then the Jesuits seized our schoolrooms and threatened to take our children from us if we would not let them be converted to their faith. We could not carry out any trade or profession not mentioned in the Edict and so skilled men were forced from their livelihoods. Even after that they must take the bread from the mouths of the rest of us by forbidding any Huguenots to take on apprentices until, eventually, we were forced to give up our businesses and lose our homes if we were not prepared to submit to their oppression. Can you wonder at my hatred of Catholics? They will not even let our sick into hospitals yet they take them forcibly from their families when they are dying in order that a Papist priest can perform the final rites over them. Do you not think a man should be allowed to die in the faith of his choosing?"

"I believe it is more important that a man should be allowed to *live* in the faith of his choosing," Philip said, "but I have no say in the law and neither have you. I agree that you have been severely wronged but you will right nothing by venting your spite upon every Catholic in France. I feel sorry for you, Raoul, not because you are a Huguenot but because you cannot see who are your real friends. The Comte de Rennes is a man of honour, of principle and of reason. You should not despise him but rather treasure him, for it is only with the help and influence of people like him that you and your people will survive. You cannot beat those in authority by might; they outnumber you and all the power is in their hands, but you should not suppose every one of them to be without compassion."

Philip could tell that his words were wasted on Raoul, as he had guessed they would be, and he turned, instead, to appeal to those who had drawn closer to better hear him. "I wish to enlist the help of any who care to join me in freeing the unfortunate wretches held captive by Archpriest du Chayla. Who is with me?"

About twenty men stepped forward immediately. A few of them looked warily at Raoul but he nodded his assent, although he did not offer to accompany them, for which Philip was extremely grateful!

"Well, they are coming with us," he said to Morgan as those

who had elected to accompany them made haste to gather weapons, although he doubted whether they had been properly instructed on how to use them.

"I thought they would, my Lord. They are brave men."

"Brave they may be but how much good will they be, I wonder?" Philip looked dubiously at the assorted group that were falling in line behind them. They were obviously drawn from every walk of life, but not one of them looked, to him, as though they had ever been in a fight before. "I would exchange the lot of them for five trained soldiers!"

"They may surprise you," Morgan reckoned.

Philip hoped they would, for he had no choice but to work with what he had. He also hoped he was not leading lambs to the slaughter.

They set off through the trees at dusk, led by one of the men who knew the forest tracks well. A young lad caught up with Philip, who was leading his horse just behind their guide, and fell in step beside him. Philip put his age at no more than fourteen or fifteen, a farmer's boy by the look of him, although most of the rebels were dressed in simple rustic clothes.

"I have brought a weapon, look," he said proudly, showing Philip a leather sling and a woven bag filled with stones.

"I see that." Philip shuddered at the thought of this fresh-faced youngster hurling his stones at soldiers. armed with pistols and swords. "How far can you throw?" he asked him.

"A long way." The boy pointed to an outcrop of rocks ahead of them. "As far as those."

"Then that is the distance away that you will stay," Philip told him. "It is where you will be of most use," he explained, seeing the boy's face fall. "You will be able to pick off soldiers who are attacking our men."

The boy brightened again. "I'll do that, sir." He lapsed into silence and then, suddenly, looked Philip full in the face. "Will the prisoners in there be still alive, do you think?"

Philip saw pain in his eyes and knew that the mission was a personal one for him. "What's your name?" he asked him.

"Jean-Paul, sir."

"The truth is, Jean-Paul, that I do not know. Who is it you hope to find?"

"My father. He was caught leading a party of refugees to the border a month ago, when he was trying to earn some money to support my mother and my little brothers."

Philip regarded him pityingly. "If your father is in that accursed house then I swear to you that I will do all that I can to free him, and any others we find in there."

"I know you will, sir," Jean-Paul said, his eyes shining in obvious admiration. "You are a good man, who God has sent to aid us in our fight against oppression."

There was only so much hero-worship Philip could take, especially since, in this case, he felt it was undeserved. He was here for one reason and one reason only – to free Antoine. In order to do that he had talked the others into helping him and used the possibility of freeing their friends as an enticement but, in truth, that had been incidental to his plan. Until now.

"I'm not that good a man," he admitted, "but I will do my best."

Thomas had been near enough to hear the exchange. "You do realise," he said, when Jean-Paul had re-joined the others, "if you succeed in this then the rebels will probably celebrate you as a saviour."

"And if I fail, and some of these men are taken prisoner too, they will very likely try to string me up," Philip reminded him.

"You won't fail, my Lord."

"Don't you start," Philip warned him. "It's bad enough that Jean-Paul reckons me as a liberator sent by God. I am as flawed as the next man, and don't you forget it."

"Oh, I would never claim you were not flawed, my Lord," Thomas said brightly, "just that you never fail."

"You have evidently forgotten the times that I have nearly got you killed," Philip said.

Thomas shrugged. "I'm still here, aren't I?"

Philip smiled at him fondly. "Yes, you are, and I am very glad of it!"

SIXTEEN

Luc entered the village of Le Pont de Montvert and rode his horse along the narrow street that ran beside the River Tarn. On one side of the street there was a row of grey stone cottages and on the other side he saw a washhouse on the river bank. There were two women inside the little tile-roofed building, scrubbing their laundry. One was a young girl of around his own age, and other, from her age and the likeness between them, could have been her mother, but what caught Luc's eye was the soldier lounging against the wall. It was obvious from the women's expressions that his presence was unwelcome. The younger one looked near to tears and the other was plainly angry.

Philip's last instruction to him had been to stay out of trouble, but he brushed that aside. His mother, though only a lowly actress, had taught him to always respect and defend women.

He tied his horse to a rail by some steps that led up to the door of one of the cottages, then walked over to the washhouse.

The soldier turned and looked at him warily. "What do you want?"

"Merely to ensure that you are not bothering these ladies," Luc said, doffing his hat to the women, who looked relieved to see him.

"It's no business of yours what I'm doing," the soldier snarled.

"I could make it my business," Luc said.

"I wouldn't, if I were you." The soldier's hand moved to his sword, but Luc's was out of its scabbard first.

"But I am not you, and I suggest you get back to doing whatever you soldiers do in this town, other than annoying its womenfolk."

"Why should I take any notice of you, you arrogant young popinjay?"

"Perhaps because I am an arrogant young popinjay who has a sword pointing at you?" Luc suggested, waving it menacingly at him.

For a moment the soldier still faced him defiantly but then he obviously thought better of it. "The girl's not worth the trouble anyway," he sneered, "much less the old hag."

When he had gone the older woman put her arm around her daughter, and smiled at Luc gratefully.

"That was kind of you, young sir, to put yourself at risk for us."

"Not so much risk," Luc said, sheathing his sword. "He didn't seem to want to take me on. Do you get much of that?"

"I fear so. They swagger about the place, full of their own importance. They are bored most of the time and they are growing more and more insolent. They work for the Abbé but he does nothing to stop them."

"What are you doing here, sir," the young girl asked him shyly.

"Just passing through. So, what's the gossip, ladies?"

Luc knew that the wash house was the place where all the local news was broadcast.

A lot of what they told him he already knew, for it was about the goings-on at the Abbé's chateau, although he was gratified to learn that du Chayla was still out of town. The women shook their heads sorrowfully when they spoke about the prisoners that they had heard were kept in the cellar there and the treatment they received.

"The Abbé is a cruel man," the mother said. She crossed herself quickly, as though fearing that to speak ill of a man in holy office might bring down heaven's wrath upon her.

"Where is his house?" Luc asked her.

"If you take the bridge over the River Tarn you will come to the bridge across the River Rieumalet, which runs just beside it. You can plainly see the back of the chateau from there, but have a care, I beg you, for they watch who travels over that bridge."

"I'll be careful," he assured her, treating them both to a courtly bow. "Now I must be on my way."

When he stood upon the second bridge, Luc could, indeed, plainly see the back of the house, as plainly, he guessed, as any watching from one of its many windows would be able to see a group of armed men crossing that bridge.

It was a three-storey building and it had a wall surrounding a courtyard at the rear. That would be the most convenient way of gaining entry, he knew, but there was also a row of windows set into the roof, from which soldiers could fire upon intruders.

As he stood there leaning on the rail of the bridge, as though taking in the view of the river, he saw three soldiers appear briefly in the courtyard, but no other sign of movement. He looked behind him at the other side of the bridge. There was a tower and some houses close by on that side but there were no windows facing him, so far as he could see.

It might be possible to cross the bridge unobserved, in the half-light of dusk. It wouldn't be easy though.

Philip listened as Luc described du Chayla's house and its position. They had made camp in the ruins of an ancient chateau near the village of St. Julien d'Arpaon and they were less than twelve miles now from Le Pont de Montvert, which he hoped to enter on the evening of the following day. The rebels were in good spirits and he had given them what rudimentary training he could in the brief time they had been there.

"Is there no other way to reach the house? he asked Luc.

"Not without a much longer journey to come into the town, and not without passing the front of the house, which, I was told, is guarded, night and day."

"Very well. I trust your judgement," Philip said. "We will just have to create some kind of diversion to cover our approach. How many soldiers are we likely to come up against?"

"The Abbé keeps only a small company there, just a dozen or so men, and sends the others out to patrol the area, according to folk I met at the inn where I stayed in the town last night. Whilst he is away, though, those at the house apparently tend to be less vigilant, so they said."

"That's good news," Philip said. "We should be able to take them. Are we likely to face any resistance from the locals, do you think?"

"I doubt it. They are terrified of him but, from what I could gather, none would raise a hand to help him."

It seemed he was right. They reached the outskirts of the town just before dusk and not a soul ventured out into the street to challenge them.

"Do you think we should sing psalms when we get near the house?" Jean-Paul asked Philip.

Philip looked at him in astonishment. "Don't be ridiculous!"

"But Raoul says we should always let the Catholics know that we are fighting for God."

"Does he indeed!" Philip looked into his earnest face and edited what he really wanted to say. "In this instance it would be better if they did not know that we were fighting them at all," he said instead. "Our best chance of success, indeed possibly our only chance, is to take them by surprise. It is stealth we need on this occasion, not psalms."

When they reached the bridge across the River Tarn, they tied up the horses and Morgan went on ahead, moving quietly as a shadow. He was carrying a large ball that he had fashioned roughly out of twigs, woven around a rock and stuffed with pieces of cloth he had cut from his sleeping blanket. Philip sat upon a low wall by the side of the bridge and drew the others around him.

"You have come this far with me, and I respect your courage and your resolution," he told them, speaking softly. "Now you will need both in full measure. This is the hardest part and I know that none of you have ever come up against trained soldiers, but you have three advantages over those soldiers. The first is that you outnumber them." He hoped this was true. "The second is that you will be catching them unawares and the third, and most important, is that you are fired with the strength that comes from passion, not for any cause, however just, but for the deliverance of those poor souls held prisoner inside that accursed house. What you do this night will be long remembered and be spoken of by your children and your grandchildren."

He had given many stirring speeches to soldiers before a fight, and they had usually been followed by loud cheers, but he was relieved that those listening to him this time had the sense to keep quiet! All the same, he could see their faces glow with pride at his few encouraging words.

They stayed where they were until he saw the signal for which he had waited. On the darkening hillside just above the house there was a sudden flash of bright light and a fireball started down toward the building, gathering momentum as it rolled.

"We move now!"

They crossed both bridges at a run. Philip heard shouts coming from the front of the house and knew that Morgan's ingenious invention had worked. He realised it would not occupy the soldiers for long, but it was long enough for the rebel band to reach the walls of the empty courtyard.

"We must try draw them all outside," Philip told them. "What we don't want is to give any the time to get up the stairs and fire at us from those top windows, or they will pick us off one by one. You stay here, behind this wall, where you will be of most use," he ordered Jean-Paul. "You can aim over it and take out any who come within range. The rest of you, follow me."

They scaled the wall and almost immediately met with a soldier who burst into the courtyard and shouted out to his comrades. He ran at Philip, but a knife hissed through the air, catching him squarely in the chest.

"That was a good diversion," Philip said, holding off with his sword a second man, who went for Morgan as he retrieved his knife.

"I thought so," Morgan said, laying about him with a cudgel he had made while on the march.

More soldiers now poured into the courtyard. One of them obviously recognised Luc.

"You!"

The man went straight for him, sword in hand, but Philip saw Luc step aside easily before taking up a stand, ready to fight.

"He knows you?" he said, engaging with one of the soldier's companions.

"I crossed paths with him when I first came here."

"How do you do it?" Philip muttered, as they fought side by side. "How do you manage to provoke people wherever you go?"

Luc only grinned, turning his back and ducking down as the blade passed over the space where his head would have been, then springing up to take the swordsman unawares upon the opposite side.

"Not bad," Philip admitted, as the man collapsed to the ground, clutching at a bloody wound in his shoulder at the same time as Philip himself succeeded in dispatching his own opponent. "Giles taught you that move."

"How did you know?" Luc said, panting slightly as he looked about him, ready to face his next assailant.

"Because I taught it to him. Thomas, on the other hand, has a style all his own!" Thomas had climbed up onto the wall and was running surefootedly along the top of it before delivering a killing blow down onto a soldier who was heading in their direction. Philip watched him leap down nimbly and attack another from behind. "Can't seem to stay on the ground to fight though!"

He turned his attention back to the action around them.

The rebels were fighting well, better than Philip had dared to expect. They had formed small groups, as he had told them to do, and were attacking the soldiers bravely, with a strength drawn from anger and hatred, and he saw at least one downed by a stone from Jean-Paul's sling.

They had engaged with the enemy and it looked as though they were winning the fight, but that was not the reason they were there and he had not lost sight of their mission.

He searched around for Morgan, who, true to form, was still sturdily dispatching with his knife and cudgel any who came close to him.

"Go down to the cellars with Luc," he shouted to him. "We can hold them off here now. Get the prisoners out."

The rest of the fight was short-lived. Seven soldiers soon lay dead and, under Philip's direction, the rest were driven back into a corner of the courtyard. The strength and fury of the Huguenots' attack had taken them by surprise as much as it had Philip himself. Only two of the rebels had injuries and neither were badly wounded, so the mood was jubilant.

Until Morgan emerged supporting two of the prisoners.

A gasp went up as more came stumbling out.

The Welshman's face was grim.

"Antoine?" Philip said.

"He's coming. He's alive."

Luc came out then, half carrying a limp figure that Philip barely recognised as his robust cousin. He rushed forward to help and together they managed to place him gently on the ground. He was filthy dirty, like the rest, and emaciated but, worse, his bare back was a mass of lacerations where he had been repeatedly flogged.

Antoine looked bemusedly from one to the other, as though finding it difficult to take in what was happening.

"Philip? Luc?" he said. "You came for me?"

"Well of course we bloody well did," Philip said, trying, unsuccessfully, to keep the emotion out of his voice. "No-one hurts a member of my family, no matter how cussed and troublesome he is."

Antoine managed a weak smile. "Help the others. There's worse than me in there." He reached up and tugged feebly at Luc's coat as he turned to go. "And thank you."

"What was that for?" Philip asked as he accompanied Luc back into the house.

"I killed the guard who tried to stop me taking him. You'll want to kill them all when you see in there," Luc warned him.

He was right. Philp had witnessed harrowing sights upon the battlefield but the scene that confronted him now was one he would not forget in a hurry.

There were heavy wooden stocks in the cellar where prisoners had been chained upright and instruments of torture next to a brazier in the centre of the room. One man still hung in the stocks, for he had died there, his body covered in burns. Philip hoped he was not Jean-Paul's father. Two guards lay dead upon the floor, one had died from a sword thrust, which he knew would have been Luc's handiwork, and he could see that Morgan's knife had slit the throat of the other. Philip felt no compassion for either of them, only disgust that soldiers of the King could stand by and see men treated so abominably.

One prisoner they had released sank to his knees in front of him in gratitude, holding up hands that were raw and disfigured.

"What happened to you?" Philip asked him, helping him to his feet.

"They made me hold the hot coal, sir, but I did not break,"

the man assured him, sobbing with relief at his rescue. "I did not break," he said again.

Philip's thoughts were dark as he watched him being led away to freedom. To his mind it was not only the Archpriest who had caused their suffering or the soldiers who had obeyed his orders but also Raoul, who had left them there and done nothing to aid them.

They searched the rest of the building and found no more prisoners or guards and Philip knew that it was time to leave. There was a wagon in the stables and he had Thomas hitch it to one of the horses they found there. Those who were not strong enough to walk were lifted onto it, together with the two wounded rebels.

Philip was hailed by Jean-Paul, an exuberant Jean-Paul who was helping an older man, who Philip guessed was his father, onto the cart.

He ordered the soldiers they had captured to be taken down into the cellar. You will not be shot," he told them, for, seeing their dead companions, some already looked resigned to their fate, "even though, in my opinion, it would be no more than you deserve."

Instead he had them chained to the stocks where their erstwhile prisoners had suffered, which he felt was a just punishment, for it could be hours, or even days, before any discovered them.

It was night by the time they crossed the bridges over the two rivers and made their way out of Le Pont de Montvert with Morgan, Thomas and Luc forming a mounted guard with him around the wagon and around the weary men who trudged beside it. If any saw the triumphant procession pass their houses, with torches blazing to light their way, then none acknowledged it and no move was made against them.

They had succeeded, but he did not feel joyful, only sickened at the cruelty men could inflict upon each other in the name of their religion.

And sadness that, despite their victory, the fight was far from over and many more, he knew, would suffer and die before it was.

cₒₒ

Philip insisted that Antoine was one of those travelling in the wagon for, although his cousin was not in as bad a state as some of the other eighteen prisoners they had rescued, Philip was genuinely concerned for his health. The untreated lash marks on his back were beginning to fester and he was weak from hunger, but what worried Philip far more was that Antoine's pugnacious spirit, the very thing which Philip had found constantly annoying, seemed to have deserted him. He stared ahead dully, as though barely taking in what was going on around him.

As dawn lit the sky, they stopped to rest in the forest by the side of a little stream that ran swift and clear through the mountains and was called the Sapet by the locals in the party. Philip filled his water bottle and took it over to his cousin.

"What happened to you, Antoine?" Philip asked him gently

"The Abbé treated us as though we were the scum of the earth," Antoine said. "We are good and loyal Frenchman, as good as he, but he called us heretics, devils, who were destroying France and we must be cleansed of our sins. I was going to be sent to the galleys when they had collected enough men together."

Philip could understand his terror at the prospect of spending the rest of his life chained to a galley's oar, at the mercy of the whip of a cruel overseer.

"Well that's not going to happen now, Antoine. You are free," Philip reminded him. "The cuts on your back will heal, as have those on mine, which were inflicted by my brute of a brother." Philip removed his coat and shirt and showed Antoine the scars which remained from the beatings he had received as a child at the hands of his brother, Henry.

Antoine looked shocked. "I had no idea."

"You now know why your family feared the 'Devalle sickness' tainting their line," Philip said wryly as he dressed again. "I have showed you this because although, like me, you will never lose your hatred of the man responsible for your suffering, you must let that hatred give you strength, not weaken you. You have survived and your life is once more your own."

"Because of you, cousin. I still can't believe you came all the way from England to rescue me."

"Nanon insisted upon it," Philip lied.

Antoine managed a half-smile. "No, she didn't. Nanon would have told you that you were far too important a person to put yourself at risk on my account. I've been a fool Philip. I should have listened to you."

"You should," Philip agreed. "Perhaps you will in the future, but I doubt it!"

"I'm not sure quite what the future holds for me now," Antoine admitted. "I never even got as far as joining with the rebels but, from what I learned from those unfortunates I met in that house of hell, I fear the war against Catholic oppression is not as glorious as I thought."

"Wars rarely are, Antoine. Most of those Huguenots who were able to, have already left France, including your own family. There is no shame in it."

"I did not want to run away," Antoine said quietly. "I wanted to be a soldier, like you, and fight for what I believed in."

"You think that is why I fought? I joined Louis' army for adventure and I stayed because fighting the Dutch was the only way I knew to make a living."

"But you were acclaimed a Hero of France."

Philip shrugged. "I was good at it. I serve a Dutchman now, and you cannot fail to see the irony in that! If you need a cause to fight for then fight with the other Huguenots alongside William. He's a good soldier, and a good man at heart."

"Then why are you not still fighting beside him?" Antoine said.

"Because he fights against France now. I fought James for him and I would follow him against any foe but King Louis."

"In case Louis takes Les Jacinthes away from you?"

"That's part of it." Philip knew he could never hope to make him understand the respect and admiration he felt for the man Antoine had come to hate with such fervour. "I still have some influence with William, however, and my brother-in-law stands even higher in his esteem. For the sake of he and I, and for what you have suffered at the hands of this fanatical archpriest, I am certain he will welcome you to his ranks, if you are willing to join him."

Antoine, for once, made no attempt to argue. "Very well. I'll do it your way this time."

"Good. All I have to do now is to get you out of France."

"And how do you propose to do it, Philip?"

"I haven't worked that out yet," Philip admitted.

"You haven't?" Antoine said in mock surprise. "I thought you were the one who always knew exactly what he was doing!"

"Not this time. To be honest, I didn't even know if you were still alive, let alone whether I could free you," Philip said.

"So you came over here with no plan other than to get du Chayla out of town and then try to enlist the help of rebels living in the mountains?"

That about summed it up. "Well it worked, didn't it?"

Antoine's eyes met his and Philip knew that from that moment their differences would be forgotten.

"I have spent my life hating my magnificent cousin," Antoine said quietly, "and now, it seems, I actually owe him that life. I swear from this day forward you shall have no truer friend."

Philip took the hand that Antoine offered him.

"Thank you, but I haven't got you out yet!"

Jean-Paul's father sought Philip out before they arrived back at the rebel camp.

"My son tells me it is to you we owe our freedom, sir," he said.

"Jean-Paul is a fine, brave boy. You should be very proud of him. Where were you taking the people in your party when you were arrested?" Philip asked him.

"To Italy, for there are Waldensians in the Piedmont region who welcome our people into their midst. They have even raised funds for us to buy weapons."

That answered a question that had been puzzling Philip from the start.

"It is a difficult route, over the Ardèche mountains to the Alps," Jean-Paul's father explained, "and the border is guarded by the King's troops, but it is still possible to get across, if you know the right places."

That sounded like a long and arduous journey to Philip, and certainly not one he would want Antoine to attempt in his present state of health.

"Try to get your own family to safety when you are strong enough," he advised him. "This is no life for them, or for you."

"I fear it will be too dangerous to attempt it for a while, even by the hidden mountain tracks, sir. The Archpriest's soldiers are patrolling everywhere now."

"Do you consider it more dangerous than remaining in Cassagnas?" Philip said.

"I fear so. They were lying in wait for us. Almost as though they knew we would be coming."

Philip was well aware of how perilous it could prove to be for himself if there was indeed a spy in the camp, even though none knew his identity. When they reached the rebels, he mentioned the possibility to Raoul, who bristled immediately.

"No-one here would betray their brothers and sisters. We are united as friends in the true faith."

"Are you? It seems to me that anyone who can sing psalms is considered to be a friend," Philip said. "We walked into your camp unchallenged when we first came here. You had not even set sentries."

"We have no need of sentries." Raoul insisted. "The angels of the God we serve will watch out for our enemies."

Philip shook his head in disbelief. He was finding it hard to even be civil to the Huguenot leader, who had made little of the fact that they had freed prisoners who would most certainly have been condemned to death or a life of slavery upon the galleys.

Mainly, Philip suspected, because he had maintained that the deed could not be done.

"If this is, as you say, a war that you are fighting then you must fight it in a proper military fashion or you are doomed, as are the men who blindly follow you," he said.

"Not if God is on our side."

"I dare say the Archpriest of the Cevennes believes that God sides with him. Both Protestants and Catholics will go into battle convinced that God is with them," Philip said, remembering the men under his command saying their prayers on the night before the Boyne. "Good men will fall upon both sides, men with families who will mourn them, and God will be nowhere near that place of death."

"That is blasphemy."

"It is the truth and you well know it, or should. War is not about causes, just or otherwise. It is about strategy and discipline, leadership and courage, and it is about pain and death."

"What do you suggest?" Raoul asked sneeringly, "that we all capitulate and convert to their faith?"

"It would ensure the safety of your families and enable you to return to your homes," Philip said.

"Even those who have converted are not granted the privileges the Catholics have themselves," Raoul said. "They will never be considered as their equals. We would rather fight for our beliefs."

Philip, looked at the men and women in the cavern who had gathered round him and he feared for them. He knew they had courage, for he had seen how bravely they had fought to free the prisoners, but he also knew they would be pitifully outmatched if Raoul decided to throw them at a troop of trained soldiers.

"We were fortunate this time," he said. "There were only a few of du Chayla's men there and we caught them by surprise, but if you truly intend to face an army one day then you must be properly prepared."

"We shall be prepared. We already have weapons, as you know, and we shall acquire more."

"There is more to making war than having arms and ammunition," Philip said. "You need to gather and train a proper army, for the soldiers you will be fighting will be the best trained in the world and they will destroy you if you come up against them unprepared. What are you?" Philip looked at the faces around him. "Farmers, shepherds, merchants, maybe we have a lawyer here, or a doctor? Those soldiers are fit and strong, they are skilled at what they do and, above all, they are disciplined. You may be able to learn to load a cannon or to fire a musket, but you have not been trained to fight, and I doubt that any of you have been trained to kill. Your beliefs, will count for nothing if you are not organised into a proper fighting force."

"*You* could train us," Jean-Paul ventured.

"I could," Philip said, "but I won't."

"But your faith is our faith," another man protested. "Don't you want us to win?"

Philip sighed. How could he ever make these earnest people, who had been treated so unjustly, understand that, although he was a Protestant like them, he was no psalm-singing, religious fanatic. And how could he tell them that, in his opinion, they had not got a hope in hell of winning?

"I will have no part in your fight," he said instead, "but I wish you well with it and I will give you the benefit of one piece of advice. You need to attack from different places so that they cannot concentrate their forces against you. You should raise other bands across the region and elect a separate leader for each one."

Philip sincerely hoped that the other leaders would be less driven by heavenly fervour and more rational in their approach to battle than Raoul, but he rather doubted it. What he did know, however, was that he needed to step away from the rebels and their cause now, before he became any more involved. He had got what he came for.

He nodded to Thomas and Luc, who helped Antoine to his feet.

Raoul made a move towards them but Morgan blocked his way.

"You should leave him here, with his own kind," Raoul maintained.

"No," Philip said emphatically. "He is coming with me." He looked over at Antoine, who, for once, made no attempt to disagree with him, indeed he barely looked in a fit state to do so, even though one of the women had bathed the cuts on his back and bandaged them for him.

"We can care for him," Raoul said "If he stays with us, he will one day go gloriously into battle for our cause."

"If he stays with you, he will be dead before the year is out," Philip predicted, "and if I had wanted this man dead, I could have killed him myself the first day I ever met him!"

SEVENTEEN

❦

"My servant has returned from Le Pont de Montvert," Armand told Du Chayla, savouring the moment.

"About time," du Chayla muttered crossly, for Eugene had followed Armand's instructions and taken as long as he reasonably could to make the return trip.

"Unfortunately, he had a fruitless journey." Armand watched du Chayla's expression change to one of obvious relief.

"He found nothing amiss then?" du Chayla said smugly.

"He found nothing at all." Armand waited for a second before he delivered the blow. "There were no prisoners held at your house. It appears that a successful attempt was made to set them free. The only people there when one of your patrols returned were your own soldiers, those that survived the attack, and they had been restrained in some of your," Armand paused, "instruments of correction."

Du Chayla's face was red with fury as he rounded upon Armand. "You knew," he hissed. "That is the reason you detained me here. I will see that you pay for this."

Armand was unmoved by his threat. "You cannot touch me, du Chayla, as you must well know. Any complaint you raise with Louvois will cause an official investigation. What that will discover would most certainly bring the King's wrath down upon de Basville, who appointed you his Inspector of Missions. If he is removed from office you will no longer wield such power here, that is if he does not incriminate you to save his own position, of course."

"This is an outrage, my Lord," du Chayla protested. "The law allows me to send to the galleys any rebel heretic who refuses to convert and take the sacrament."

"But it does not allow you to inflict torture upon them in order to obtain their conversion, and nor does it allow you to send young girls into a convent and then demand money from their families for their release," Armand countered swiftly, for he had been conducting his own investigation into du Chayla's activities and discovered some disturbing things.

Du Chayla glowered at him but he was beaten, for the moment, and he obviously knew it.

"Since you have finished your investigations into my affairs I will return to Le Pont de Montvert, my Lord," he said stiffly.

Armand nodded. "As soon as you like, Inspector. I may pay you a visit there the next time I am in the region."

In fact, he had no desire to ever see du Chayla again, or de Basville for that matter. He was going home himself and he intended to remain in Montpellier only until he had received word from Philip. He did not have long to wait. Luc arrived at the inn the following day.

"He has him safe then," he said, when Luc had related to him all that had happened.

"For the moment. I am going to meet them at Alès. We were told that many of the population there are sympathetic to the Huguenots. After that we are going to try to get him on a boat to England."

"Alès is not as safe as it once was," Armand warned him. Although it had once been a place of toleration for the Protestant community, much had changed there, as it had in many places, since the Revocation. "Philip needs to get him to the coast without delay and I may be able to help."

"He sent me to you to give you his thanks, not to ask for help," Luc assured him.

"I realise that but he takes great risks for this man, as do you all. I know du Chayla better than he does and believe me when I say he is not a man to be trifled with and nor is he a fool. Philip let the soldiers you took prisoner at the chateau live, which was the honourable thing to do, but they are sure to remember him, even if they did not learn his name. Frankly, I fear for his life, and the lives of all of you, should you be captured whilst Antoine is still with you," Armand said. "A man like du Chayla is more than capable of taking the law into his own hands, as he has already proven."

Antoine leapt up in alarm, the pistol Philip had given him ready in his hand, as they saw Luc approaching the small inn at Alès, ahead of a coach flanked by six soldiers. "What treachery is this?"

Philip stayed his arm, for he had already recognised who was in the coach.

"Luc would never betray you," he promised him, "and neither would the Comte de Rennes."

"That's de Rennes?" Antoine said disbelievingly. "I know of him, but why has he come here, with his soldiers, if not to arrest me?"

Philip was as mystified as him, despite being delighted to see his friend.

"I am on my way home to Brittany," Armand told him, when he had described his meeting with du Chayla. "I thought your cousin could accompany me. I know a boat master in St. Malo who I can bribe to take him over to England and land him somewhere on the Sussex coast, if that is what he wants."

Philip was staggered at the generosity of the offer, but well aware of the perilous position in which he might be putting Armand and his wife.

"I can't let you do this, Armand. Think of Marguerite."

"You can," Armand said firmly, "and as for Marguerite, she may have become a Catholic in order to remain with me but her sympathies have always been with those of her old faith."

"But supposing you are stopped?" Philip said.

"Who would dare to detain the Comte de Rennes when he is travelling with his two servants on the King's business?" Armand asked archly, indicating Antoine, standing in the yard with Eugene.

Philip, who had himself posed as Armand's servant on a previous adventure, looked at him in gratitude.

"What about your escort though?" he asked him.

"My soldiers are all Brêton and are loyal only to me," Armand assured him. "They will ask no questions and they will obey my orders."

Loath as he was to involve Armand any further in the matter when he had already played such a vital part, Philip felt as though a great weight had been lifted from his shoulders. "What can I say, my friend?"

"You will say yes," Armand said, in a tone that brooked no argument. "I think I have persuaded du Chayla not to take the matter any further but there is nothing to stop de Basville reporting it to Madame de Maintenon, who would delight in telling the King. With luck, Louis should be on his way to Mons by now but, even so, I suggest the four of you make all haste down to Les Jacinthes. If Intendant de Basville should decide to pay you a neighbourly visit it might be judicious for you to be seen innocently at work in your vineyard!"

Antoine looked a little apprehensive when Philip told him of the plan.

"Armand is my oldest friend, and one of the finest soldiers you could ever know," Philip said. "I would trust him with my life, and yours. When you reach England, you have only to send word to Theresa at High Heatherton."

"Will she be pleased to see me?" Antoine asked hesitantly.

Philip recalled all the people Theresa had welcomed into their family over the years; Thomas, Marianne, Ahmed, Luc and, most recently, Nanon.

"She will be delighted," he said, "and so will my brother-in-law's wife, Marianne, another Huguenot from the south. You will see Nanon again too."

"Nanon is going to scold me, I expect," Antoine said, pulling a wry face.

"And with good reason, causing me all this trouble!"

Antoine laughed, but then, abruptly, he looked sad.

"What is it?" Philip said.

"I shall never see France or Les Jacinthes again, shall I?" he said, sighing at the sudden realisation.

"Probably not, but neither will you see the inside of a galley," Philip pointed out. "You can be a soldier now, or whatever else you choose to be. What you will see is life."

"Thanks to you."

"Not only to me," Philip reminded him.

"He's seems quieter than I expected from your description of him," Armand said, as Antoine made his goodbyes to Thomas and Luc and had a few moments of earnest discussion with Morgan, who clapped him reassuringly on the shoulder.

"He is still a mite subdued by all that happened to him, but I doubt it will last long, and he obviously still doesn't trust us with the damned vineyard!"

The soldiers remounted and Armand and Eugene climbed back into the coach.

Philip and Antoine looked at one another and then, for the first time, embraced as cousins.

"How can I ever repay you, Philip?" Antoine said huskily, as he turned to go.

"I'll try to think of a way," Philip promised him with a smile. "Do whatever Armand tells you to do – and for God's sake, behave yourself!"

❧

Louis looked with satisfaction at the bombardment taking place in front of him. In the ten days since he had arrived at the front, the French army had blasted the town of Mons with cannon balls and mortar shells. Thanks to his Maréchal de Camp, Boufflers, who had made full use of Vauban's trenches, the town was surrounded and its garrison, of less than five thousand men, was powerless to defend it. Unless the Allied forces managed to reach them in time, and Louis was certain they would not, for Luxembourg's army was positioned to intercept them, he reckoned that the citizens of Mons would be beating the drum for a parley within a week.

He had determined this year upon early attacks on both northern and southern fronts and he hoped that the forces he had sent down to Nice would have similarly taken the Italian city by surprise, but it would give him particular satisfaction to outwit King William, who had been a thorn in his side for twenty years. Louis wanted to establish that it was one thing to claim a victory against his inept cousin, James, who had failed to defeat William despite the French troops Louis had given him, but quite another to come up against Louis himself. James had wanted to accompany them on this campaign, but Louis had made it plain that such a request would be denied. He needed people around him now who he could count on, like his handsome brother, who was mounted on his horse beside him.

Monsieur went into battle dressed as immaculately as he went everywhere else, but Louis knew that beneath the layers of lace, the perfumed curls and the diamond earrings was a man who was brave and ever loyal to him.

There were times when Louis felt a little guilty that he had deprived his brother of what might have been a dazzling army career, and this was one of those times, for Monsieur loved the military life and had shown a real aptitude for it when he had led his troops to victory at the battle of Cassel. Louis did not regret his decision, however.

People had always made a great fuss of Monsieur. Even as a

child he had been talkative and amusing, with a way about him that had charmed everyone. Their mother had been aware of that too and had feared his popularity might one day allow him to compete for power with his more serious-minded brother, as had their uncle Gaston with their father, so she had seen to it that he never had the chance. She made him constantly defer to Louis' will and, to ensure that he would be the weaker one, Monsieur was treated as she would have treated a daughter. She even dressed him sometimes in girl's clothes and encouraged him to play girl's games but Monsieur, for all his outward affectations and his petty ways, had a strength of character and a sensitivity that few perceived.

Louis knew that Philip Devalle was one of those few, for he had always been a real friend to Monsieur and never tried to take advantage of him as so many did. That was one of the reasons Louis had rewarded him so much and forgiven him so often. The other reason was that, having witnessed first-hand Philip's effectiveness as a fearless leader during the time he had fought for France, Louis did not want him for an enemy.

"We can be thankful that Philip will not be at William's side when the Allies finally appear," he said out loud.

Monsieur was certainly thankful for that, but not for quite the same reasons. He just could not bear the prospect of seeing Philip wounded or perhaps even killed, although Giles might well be there, he realised worriedly, and Giles was also Monsieur's friend. He wondered where he was.

Giles was on his way to Halle, where William had arranged for the Allied troops to assemble.

"Your brother-in-law should be here, playing his part," William grumbled to him.

"You gave him permission to leave the army, your Majesty," Giles reminded him, only too aware that he might not be there himself, if only the news of the attack on Mons had reached the King an hour later! It had been a trying couple of weeks arranging the movement of troops and the situation was not made better by William's constant complaining.

"I should have recalled Philip after Christmas," William said testily. "His duty is here, not taking his ease on his damned country estate."

Giles very much doubted whether Philip was either taking his ease or at High Heatherton, for he knew that his brother-in-law had been planning to return to Languedoc in March, although he realised William would have been furious to learn that he was in France, the very country they were going to fight. Giles also knew that Philip would have wanted to be nowhere near this conflict.

The prospect of losing the most important outpost in the Spanish Netherlands, coupled with the knowledge that King Louis was there in person at the head of the French forces, was making William impatient to get to the battle, and even more irritable than usual when faced with any delay.

When they finally reached Halle, William found he had nearly forty thousand soldiers under his command and, for the first since he had left the Hague, was in a good mood. It did not last long.

The Spaniards had promised to provide him with a thousand transport vehicles. The vehicles were not there.

William was furious.

Giles knew this would cost them time they did not have, for it was over a week since their scouts had reported that the siege had begun and it seemed unlikely now that they would get to Mons before it was forced to capitulate.

More transport was organised in haste but it was another three days before the Allies were in sight of the action.

To find that it was all over.

The citizens had capitulated only hours earlier. They were too late.

EIGHTEEN

❧

Giles was back at High Heatherton in April. William had returned to the Hague, after he had distributed his troops to various garrisons, but Giles had made straight for Rotterdam before anything else could delay his return home!

He had feared that Marianne might have been summoned back to the Queen's side during his long absence. He had left Ahmed behind to take care of her and Will in the eventuality of their returning to London without him but, to his delight, they were still there.

The months of clean Sussex air had done her good There was colour in her cheeks and she looked more beautiful than ever to him. There was something else too – she looked happy, far happier than he had ever seen her look whilst they had lived in London, and it reinforced his determination to find a house for them in the country just as soon as he could.

She was not the only one to have a healthy glow. Theresa was positively radiant and he understood why when she told him that she was expecting another child. Giles knew how joyful Philip would be when he learned that splendid news.

Theresa had written to Giles whilst he was at Het Loo, telling him about Antoine's arrest, but she had received no word from Philip since he had left for France and she had no idea where he was or how successful he had been.

"He will have everything under control by now," Giles said, although more to comfort her and Nanon, who was sick with worry about them both, than because he was really convinced of it. He could recall several times in the past when Philip had taken chances that had nearly ended in disaster and he could think of too many ways in which becoming involved in religious strife in what was now an enemy country could go wrong.

Their uncertainty did not last long. A week after Giles' return a message, written in French, was delivered to Theresa. She shook her head in disbelief as she read it. "Antoine is in England, Giles. He says he is in Selsey."

"How did he get here?" Giles was as surprised as her.

"Armand arranged his passage on a fishing boat. God bless that dear man, he's a true friend."

"What of Philip?" Giles said.

"The note says he's gone to Les Jacinthes. He did it, Giles. He rescued him."

"I told you he would," Giles said, more relieved than he wanted to show her. "I suppose I'd better go and find this bothersome cousin of his then!"

He had heard a great deal about Antoine and during the lengthy journey in Philip's coach to Selsey, a fishing village at the tip of Bracklesham Bay, Giles had plenty of time to wonder what the Frenchman would be like.

There was only one inn and it was crowded, but Giles had no problem in picking out Philip's cousin. Tall and blonde, his handsome Pasquier looks were unmistakeable.

He stood up warily as Giles approached him.

"I'm Philip's brother-in-law," Giles told him, speaking in French.

"Lord Wimborne?" Antoine said, his eyes drawn involuntarily to the scar on Giles' face.

It was a reaction that, over the years, Giles had become accustomed to when he met people for the first time and it no longer troubled him the way it once had.

"Giles to you, Antoine." Giles held out his hand, which Antoine eagerly clasped.

"Philip never told you about this, did he?" Giles guessed, indicating the mark on his cheek.

"No, he didn't," Antoine said, looking a little embarrassed. "I'm sorry, but it took me by surprise."

"You'll get used it," Giles told him matter-of-factly. "I am pleased to see you safe in England."

"And I am happy to be here, Giles."

Antoine did not look too happy, but Giles could well understand that.

"I am sure you would rather be living safely in your own country," he said quietly. "I know how you are feeling, for I was once an exile myself."

"Why was that?" Antoine asked him as he followed Giles to the coach.

"For much the same reason as you have been forced to leave France, fighting for a hopeless cause," Giles said with a wry smile. "One day I will tell you about the Duke of Monmouth."

Antoine's eyes opened wide when he saw the magnificent coach, with its Negro coachmen and the matching pair of black trace horses.

"He is rich, my cousin?"

Giles had noticed that Antoine had no bags and guessed the man had lost everything he had ever owned.

"He is now, but it was not always so," he said as they climbed into the coach. "It must be galling for you that Philip also has the vineyard that would one day have been yours."

"I hated him for it when we first met," Antoine admitted.

"Do you still?"

Antoine shook his head. "Never again. He risked his life to rescue me, Giles."

"Of course he did. He has accepted you as part of his family, which means that he will protect and take care of you."

Giles had not known quite what to expect, from the description Philip had given them of his belligerent cousin.

The Antoine sitting opposite him as they set off towards High Heatherton was nothing like what he had imagined he would be. Indeed, the Frenchman seemed subdued, although, Giles figured, that was not to be wondered at considering what he had endured.

"Philip will probably get you into quite a bit of trouble too though," Giles warned him, smiling.

"As he has you?" Antoine guessed.

"I fear so. Philip and my lives have been linked ever since I first met him, when I was just sixteen years of age, although there have been times when I might have wished they were not. But for him and his scheming I might still be handsome, although that no longer troubles me as it once did. There have certainly been times when I have had good reason to curse my brother-in-law over the years and yet I know that without his friendship my life would have run a very different course. I would never have had the opportunity to rise so high, in fact I might have ended up a country squire living in a small village in Dorset!"

"That does not seem too likely, to see you now," Antoine reckoned, for Giles, despite the loss of his good looks, still cut an elegant figure.

"Once Philip touches your life it will never be the same," Giles said, serious again. "Only see what he has done for Morgan and Thomas, a murderer he protected in France and a thief he plucked from the streets of London. Both are good men that most would have condemned and both would gladly give their lives for him now."

"And what of you," Antoine asked. "Would you give your life for him?"

"But for him, like you, I would not have a life to give, for I would have died in Ireland last year," Giles said, "so yes, Antoine, I would, but you don't have to tell him that!"

When they arrived back at High Heatherton Theresa ran out to meet them and threw her arms around Antoine. "Welcome, cousin. This is your home now for as long as ever you want, and I am happy to have you here."

She meant it too, Giles knew that, for his sister had a great capacity for love. He had never really understood it. Giles himself took to very few people and had always been of a suspicious nature.

Over the next few days, as Antoine settled in to his new life, Giles was pleased to see a little of his spirit returning. Nanon fussed over him constantly and Bet, who was proud that her Morgan had played a part in his release, inspected his back daily and treated the deeper lacerations, which had not yet quite healed, with some of her primrose salve.

Maudie took it upon herself to teach him some basic English, for his knowledge of it was scanty. Although only 8 years old, her French was perfect for, like her father, she had been brought up to speak both English and French and she was determined to help him to learn the language that he would need to be able to speak as well as his own, if he was to prosper in his new country.

It was with Marianne, though, that Antoine soon formed a special bond, as Giles had hoped he would, being herself once a southern Huguenot.

Marianne had been forced to convert at the beginning of the troubles, along with the rest of those who had lived in her small town, near Marseilles. Louvois' dragoons had marched everyone into the Catholic church and threatened them at gunpoint. Those few who had refused were taken away, never to be seen again.

"We were not as brave as you," she told Antoine. "You wanted to fight them."

"I still want to fight them, Marianne," he assured her, when he had heard her story, "more than ever after what happened to me."

Just over a week after Antoine's arrival Giles received word that William was back in London and requesting his presence.

Cautious though he always was in his dealings with others, Giles had already assessed Antoine's character and made his decision.

༄

Philip walked with Morgan along the rows of vines. He felt more contented than he had for a long while. From where they were, he had a splendid view of the house and the woods behind it, woods that were now colourfully carpeted with bluebells, the 'Jacinthes des Bois', which had given the chateau its name.

"Fleurs de Languedoc," he said suddenly. "That's it, Morgan! That is what we will call our wine."

"Flowers of Languedoc." Morgan nodded approvingly. "That's good, my Lord."

They inspected the fruit and also the rose bushes that the Welshman had planted at the front of each row before they had left to go home for Christmas. "Antoine told me that if the rose is diseased then it is a sign that the row is diseased and must be destroyed in order to save the rest of the crop," Morgan told him, scrutinising the healthy new shoots that were appearing on the roses.

"They look fine to me," Philip said.

"They look fine to me too," Morgan said. "This variety of vine makes a lot of leaf though, which can shade the fruit from the sun, so we shall need to watch for signs of mildew later."

Now that they were no longer hiding Antoine, Philip had been able to hire some labourers to help Morgan in the fields as well as a local woman who came each day to take care of the house whilst Nanon was in England.

There was plenty of work for Morgan to do. As well as the Spring planting of the new vines, he and his little workforce of five men were engaged in training and pinching out the shoots of the plants he and Antoine had pruned the previous Autumn.

There was little Philip could contribute to that so he left

them to it and took a trip to Marseillan, where he was planning to load their harvest onto a barge to be transported on the canal. It was only a day's ride away, although Philip realised that it would probably take two days for the crop to reach Marseillan by cart. Even so, the journey to the port was less than half of the distance to Fontfroide Abbey and using the canal would be far quicker and less risky than taking the precious, perishable cargo the whole way over land in the hot sun, and on poor roads.

The Abbot had advised him to pick the fruit directly into barrels ready for transportation and Philip designated the task of organising the barrels to Luc whilst he was gone.

He took Thomas with him, partly for company and partly because Thomas was attempting to keep out of the way of Emile Tartours. Whilst he and Marcel had fulfilled their task, he had not been completely straight with Tartours and thought it would probably be wiser not to show his face in Montpellier for a while.

They rode for the last part of the way beside the Etang de Thau, a lake so big it looked like a sea, for there were waves upon it and barely a sign of land on the horizon. They reached the town of Marseillan by nightfall and found an inn in the Place Carnot, where they enjoyed a good meal of fresh-caught fish, with a bottle of the local Muscat wine. It had seemed sweet to Philip's palate when he had first come to the region but he had grown accustomed to it and had discussed the possibility with Morgan of reinstating Muscat at Les Jacinthes.

"I wonder how Antoine is," Thomas said, as they started upon their second bottle.

"I am quite sure he is safe at Heatherton by now and that Giles will have taken him in hand."

"That was a wonderful thing you did, my Lord," Thomas said.

"*We* did," Philip stressed. Once again, his little band had unhesitatingly followed him into a perilous situation. In the twelve years since Philip had rescued Thomas from a life of crime, the young man had never let him down, and Philip had always vowed he would never let Thomas, or the others close to him, down.

That did not necessarily mean he would never again place them in danger!

They were awakened early by the sounds of the traders setting up their stalls in the covered market in the Place. After buying some bread and some country cheese to eat upon their journey home, they rode to the port. A barge was just leaving, its horse plodding beside the Etang towards Les Onglous, the mouth of Riquet's famed Canal Royale en Languedoc.

They stopped there for a while and watched another vessel being loaded ready for its voyage.

. "The port of Sète, is on the far side of this lake," Philip told Thomas. "It is on the coast and the big, ocean-going vessels sail from there. We could use it to ship our wine all over Europe one day, Thomas. The Dutch are usually good customers, I understand, although probably not at the moment! Apparently, they like the sweet wines and in Languedoc we can produce them cheaper than in Bordeaux."

"You're getting quite knowledgeable, my Lord. I'm impressed," Thomas said, giving him a cheeky grin.

"It's good to know that I can still impress you!" Philip said, smiling. Thomas was allowed considerable licence when they were on their own. "Actually, it was the Abbot of Fontfroide who told me that. He also told me the Romans were making wine in this area over a thousand years ago."

"Really? I've heard people say it was the Romans who built the walls around London," Thomas said. "How did they build things so long ago that are still there?"

"I know no more about them than you do."

Philip's education had been sadly neglected. None of the tutors which his father had engaged for him as a child had stayed long enough to teach him much and Philip could not really blame them, for it had been Henry's threats and rages which had driven them all away. By the time he had been enrolled at St. Paul's school in London he had been so far behind the other boys of his age that lessons had been a torture to him and the short time he had spent there before going to Court had not inspired him with a thirst for knowledge.

"The teachers at school tried to make me learn their language," he recalled to Thomas.

"What's the point of learning the language of dead people?" Thomas said incredulously.

"Precisely, although my Latin book came in handy once."

Thomas gave him a suspicious look. "It did?"

"I hurled it at a boy who was annoying me," Philip told him. "I caught him on the head with it and knocked him out!"

Thomas laughed. "Is that why you were expelled?"

"One of the reasons!"

What Philip did not tell him was that the incident occurred on the day that Nanon had come to London to inform him she was going back to France, and the reason why. Philip had been just thirteen years old at the time, but his fury at what had happened to her at Henry's hands and the fact that he would probably never see her again had caused him to demonstrate how he felt about his fellow pupils and the head master of the school he hated. He did not regret it. Philip's father, realising he would never be able to exert any control over his rebellious son and wracked with guilt over what he had suffered at the hands of his violent brother, had finally relented and agreed to let him go to Court.

The port was busy. Although it had been in use throughout the previous reign, it had acquired new significance since King Louis had instigated the opening of the canal ten years before. Philip went to see the harbour master in his office to explain the reason for their visit and found him most eager to assist. Leaving with his promise that, when the time came, transport could be obtained for his crop, Philip and Thomas started back to Les Jacinthes.

They reached home late that night and only just in time, it seemed, for the clouds had turned black over the mountains and there were rumblings of thunder.

Whilst they had been away Luc had located a local cooper and arranged to employ him at harvest time, but he had other news to report too, for the young priest at Luc's church had been replaced by one of du Chayla's acolytes.

"The new one is a Jesuit and he is inspired with more than heavenly zeal," Luc told them with a shudder.

"No chance of your posing as Louvois' nephew to him, I am guessing," Philip said, hoping that the change had not been brought about by their actions. "Do you know what happened to your friend?" he asked, for he knew that Luc had felt sympathy for him.

"Only that he has been turned out of his living. This Jesuit upstart told me there was no place now for any priest who does not do his heavenly duty and force the heretics to partake of the Holy Sacrament. He is reporting any converts who do not attend every service to du Chayla. If it's all the same to you, my Lord, I have decided I will cease going to mass from now on."

Philip agreed. The least contact they had with any of du Chayla's servants the better.

He was weary, for it had been a long ride back from Marseillan, and he was ready for his bed but, as they were all about to retire, he looked out of the window and saw a flash of lightening in the distance. Another clap of thunder followed almost immediately. Then he noticed it.

Tired though he was, he was instantly alert.

"Fire!"

Morgan, Thomas and Luc ran outside with him. Even from where they stood, it was obvious that the trees on the side of the mountain were ablaze and that the flames were sweeping down towards the vineyard that adjoined their own.

The stream that divided Les Jacinthes from the forest would

form a natural fire break, Philip knew, but his neighbour had no such protection.

"He'll lose his crop," Morgan said grimly.

Philip knew he was right.

Their neighbour, whose name Philip had learned from Antoine was Devereaux, had made no attempt at friendship, and Philip had been relieved by that during the time he had been keeping his cousin hidden from prying eyes. Indeed, he suspected that Devereaux was the neighbour who de Basville had told him was anxious to acquire Les Jacinthes for himself, but this was a calamity that overshadowed any petty issues of property or religion.

The gusting wind was sending the fire speeding towards the rows of vines. He knew what he had to do.

"We must help them," he said.

No-one argued with him.

Their workforce had gone home and they were the only ones in the house but the four of them grabbed up as many leather buckets as they could find and they ran though their own fields towards their neighbour's vineyard.

As they drew closer, they could see men laboriously drawing water from a well and attempting to douse the grass that separated the precious fruit from the inferno.

"Use the stream," Philip shouted to them as they drew closer.

They looked up looked up at him uncertainly.

"The stream," he told them again, as he and Morgan pushed down a section of the boundary fence then started drawing water from the stream whilst Thomas and Luc formed a chain to pass it along.

Those closest to them realised straightaway what they were doing and hastened to join the chain, whilst others rushed over to the take the water to where it was needed.

As he worked, Philip had memories of a different time and a different place, when he and the Duke of Monmouth had laboured through the night, alongside hundreds of others, in the streets of London to help fight the fire that was engulfing the city. Despite the seriousness of the threat to the capital, it had seemed a fine adventure to the two young men, but this was different. This felt almost personal, for Philip had reason to know how much time and effort had gone into producing the crop and how devastating it would be to lose it.

The storm finally broke and the heavens opened, aiding their efforts as they toiled beneath a sky illuminated by flashes of lightening. At last, it seemed, their labours were rewarded. A great cheer went up and they knew the fire had been halted. Philip guessed that by morning the mountainside would be a smouldering mass of blackened trees, but the vines had been saved, and their job was done.

He looked at the others and laughed at their disreputable appearance for, like him, they were soaked to the skin and filthy dirty.

"Let's go home!"

William's cold eyes regarded Antoine as Giles presented him. Giles had arranged for them to have a private audience with the King and had given the Frenchman very precise instructions as to how to behave.

Fortunately, William disliked any excessive form of salutation, reckoning it false and unnecessary, which was just as well, for Antoine had never been to Court or received any instruction in the formal behaviour that was usually required there. Philip had been schooled in these matters by his patron, the flamboyant Duke of Buckingham, and Giles by Philip himself, and he was extremely thankful that he was not presenting him to a king like Louis, who insisted upon having every point of etiquette not only observed but perfectly performed!

"I am honoured to meet your Majesty," Antoine said, using the exact words and pronunciation he had practised so many times with Maudie before he and Giles came to London. "It is my sincere hope that you will accept me into your service in order that I can aid you in your fight against Catholic oppression."

William nodded, plainly sizing him up.

"Lord Wimborne has told me that you wish to join the army," he said to him, speaking in French.

Giles was surprised at this concession but relieved too for, despite Maudie's best efforts, Antoine's English was still halting at best.

"Yes, your Majesty."

"If you are anything like your cousin you will, at least, make a fine soldier," William said dryly.

Giles recognised the barb in that remark even though Antoine did not.

"It is my only wish, your Majesty, although I may never become like him."

William gave a half-smile at that. "I rather hope you don't."

Antoine looked puzzled. "But is he not a hero, your Majesty?"

"Yes, Philip is a hero," William agreed. "I would even go so far as to say that without him on my side I would have had a far more difficult time of it when I first came over to England. Philip helped pave the way for me and he has fought for me, but we both know to which King he owes his true allegiance. You, on the contrary, I imagine have neither love nor respect for King Louis, Antoine Pasquier."

"I hate the man from the depths of my being," Antoine said passionately. "Because of him my family was forced to flee France and I was arrested, although, luckily, I was able to escape."

He glanced up at Giles, who nodded imperceptibly. They had already decided that the least said about Philip's part in his rescue the better, since it had occurred at a time when Philip would not have wanted William to know that he was in France.

William looked from one to the other and Giles feared he would press the point, but he did not.

"I am surprised that your cousin did not present you to me himself," he said instead to Antoine, although it was upon Giles his gaze was resting.

"He has recently left for Languedoc to attend to matters at the vineyard, your Majesty," Giles said.

"Has he indeed? Then I assume that, like yourself, he will not be accompanying me when I leave for Flanders this month," William said stiffly. "You, however," he turned to Antoine, "can enlist in one of my French Huguenot regiments, if that is your wish."

"It is, your Majesty," Antoine said delightedly.

"Very well. Giles can arrange everything for you."

Giles thought that William looked harassed again. Certainly he was a far different man from the one who had arrived in Holland at the beginning of the year. He supposed it was probably not to be wondered at, for the Jacobites, emboldened by the news of the French victory at Mons, were causing trouble again. There were rumours of a plot and the Queen had been openly insulted in her carriage. In addition to that, William had been forced to endure a constant round of meetings with politicians since he had been back in England, which always put him in a bad mood, and, to top it all off, there had been a fire at Whitehall whilst they had been away and a large part of the old palace had been destroyed.

At one time Giles would have felt that he could not desert William whilst he was beset with so many problems, but not now. Besides, it had lately become quite a fashionable thing for members of the nobility to accompany the King on his campaigns, and there was no shortage of willing volunteers eager for adventure and to prove themselves in battle. Giles felt he had no further need to prove himself and that he'd had more than his share of adventures in his twenty-eight years.

William had become accustomed to having him at his beck and call but, throughout his life, Giles had always had his own best interests at heart and he knew that the time had come to look out for himself and his family.

He remained in London with Antoine until William left in the middle of May. Giles taught him all he could in the short time he had and introduced him to some of the others who would be going to war, placing him in the care of Richard Lumley, the Earl of Scarborough, who had once been a supporter of King James but who was now one of William's trusted friends.

When the moment finally came for Antoine to leave, the Frenchman embraced him like a brother. "I will never forget the kindness you and your family have shown me, Giles, or that of the Comte de Rennes and his wife, who took such risks for me in France. I owe you all so much, and Philip most of all, of course. Tell my cousin I will make him proud that he is a Pasquier!"

Giles smiled. "I'll tell him that when I see him."

"And tell him, too, to take good care of my vineyard!"

NINETEEN

༄

"We have a visitor, my Lord."

"De Basville?" Philip asked Thomas.

The Intendant had not been near them since they had returned from Le Pont de Montvert, for which he was extremely grateful.

"No, my Lord. Someone else."

Whoever it was, Philip figured it could not be good news. He watched the man entering the courtyard. He had white hair and he was riding a fine horse, but he was not armed, so far as Philip could tell. Nor was he dressed as a gentleman, although his clothes appeared to be of good quality.

"I dare say I can manage him. He looks to be twice my age!" he said as their visitor dismounted.

Despite that, the stranger looked agile, and had the complexion of one who has spent his life out of doors.

"Good day to you, sir," Philip said, approaching him.

"My Lord, it is an honour to meet such a famous hero."

That was certainly not what Philip had expected. "And who have I the honour of meeting, pray?"

"I am Jacques Devereaux, your neighbour."

That was another surprise. "You are most welcome here, Monsieur Devereaux."

Thomas took their visitor's horse to the stables whilst Philip led Devereaux into the house.

"I fear that I can offer you little by way of refreshment, Monsieur Devereaux," Philip said apologetically, taking him into the room which Antoine had rather grandly called the salon, although, in his opinion, it did not compare with the salon at High Heatherton, or even the one at his house in Paris. "My present housekeeper prepares only the most basic necessities for us, but I have some excellent brandy, if you would care to partake of it with me."

Devereaux's eyes twinkled. "Most certainly I would, my Lord. Nanon did not return with you, then?" he asked, as Philip filled two glasses from the bottle which stood on a side table in the room.

"You know Nanon?" Philip said, surprised.

"Naturally. The Pasquiers and their household were my neighbours. I probably know her better than you."

"I doubt that," Philip said with a smile. "I have known her all my life."

"Forgive me, I was forgetting that she went to England with your mother."

Philip stared at him as a sudden realisation hit him. "You knew my mother?"

"Certainly."

"What was she like? Philip asked him. "She died when I was very young," he explained, seeing Devereaux's surprised expression, "I don't remember her."

"She was a lovely young girl, so spirited and full of life. Everyone around here loved her. She was a true beauty too, especially when she came back from Court in all her finery. I had high hopes of her for my son, to tell the truth, but she fell for your father and the next thing we knew she had gone to England and no-one was allowed to speak of her." He made a point of looking at his now empty glass, which Philip quickly refilled for him, and his own. "I never understood how a man could treat his daughter in such a way, my Lord. Your family and mine have grown our vines side by side for many generations and we have always co-existed peaceably but, I'll be honest, your grandfather was a difficult man to like."

"I can imagine!"

"Say what you will about the old man, though, he knew his business and so did his son."

"What about his grandson?" Philip said.

"Antoine?" Devereaux made a deprecating gesture. "He learned it dutifully enough, I think, but his heart was not in it. He never had the passion. All the same, he obviously made a good teacher, looking at the way your man has restored the vineyard."

Philip looked at him sharply. "You knew?" he guessed.

Devereaux laughed. "Of course I knew. You cannot hide a man like Antoine Pasquier from folk who have known him since he was a child, not even by making him wear a wig and a hat!"

"Thank you for not giving him away to de Basville," Philip said sincerely.

"Our families have been friends for too long to become enemies now. As for de Basville, I would not give a dog I liked to him," Devereaux said. "I have as little as possible to do with the man."

"He told me that you wished to buy Les Jacinthes," Philip said, wanting to clear the air about that.

"Only because the alternative was to have some member of his wretched family purchase it for next to nothing," Devereaux snorted. "My life would never have been my own with one of his cronies spying on me." He held his glass out again and Philip obligingly refilled it. "This is damn fine brandy," Devereaux reckoned. "You've got good taste – for an Englishman. Did he get away?"

It took Philip a second to realise that Devereaux was talking about Antoine again. Much as he was beginning to like the old man, he did not yet know him well enough to trust him. "I believe he made it to England," was all he said.

"Good! Hot-headed young idiot, that one, always was, but I never wanted to see harm come to him. You took a chance, having him here, my Lord."

Philip shrugged. "He's family. I owe you a debt of gratitude for your discretion, Monsieur Devereaux."

"Nonsense! It is rather I who am in your debt. But for your aid on the night of the fire much of my crop would have been destroyed. I should have thanked you sooner but I am here now to offer you my friendship and to repay your kindness in any way I can."

Philip clasped the hand that Devereaux held out to him. "Your friendship I accept, and gladly, monsieur, but I did not act in expectation of any repayment," he assured him.

"I know. You did it because you are an honourable man, whose reputation precedes you."

"A man who some would not wish to call friend whilst our two countries are at war," Philip reminded him with a wry smile.

"You are no enemy of France, my Lord." Devereaux said emphatically.

"True, although that does not endear me too much with my own king, I fear! There are two favours I would ask of you, Monsieur Devereaux, since you seem to feel indebted to me."

Devereaux spread his hands. "Ask them, my Lord, I beg you."

"The first is this. I have not seen my wife and daughter for over three months and would dearly love to go home for a while. Morgan, my steward, will remain here to continue the work but, frankly, I distrust de Basville now and I would feel much easier in my mind to know that a friendly neighbour was keeping an eye upon the place."

"I would be pleased to do that, my Lord. It looks like a fine crop you have and it would be a shame if any harm came to it. Mourvèdre has never been the easiest of vines to grow, for it likes its face in the sun and its feet in water, but it is a good-flavoured fruit and your family have always done well with it, thanks to the stream that crosses your land."

"Thank you, I would appreciate it greatly," Philip said. "Luc will be remaining here as well."

"I have seen Luc at Ste. Anne's church, a handsome boy. He is your son, is he not?"

"So he says."

"I see!" Devereaux gave him a broad wink. "Still, it doesn't hurt to have a good French Catholic in the family at present. Not that his religion would have made any difference if he'd been caught helping to hide Antoine," he added more seriously. "The authorities might even have dealt with him more harshly than they did the rest of you, being foreigners."

"He knew that."

"A brave man, then, like his father. What is the other favour you would ask of me, my Lord?"

Philip refilled their glasses for the fourth and final time. Although a hardened drinker himself, he was quite surprised at the old man's capacity for the spirit. "Simply that, when I return, you will tell me more about my mother."

"Gladly, although you may need to provide some more 'refreshment'," Devereaux said, eying the almost empty bottle. "They don't let me drink the stuff at home," he explained. "The only thing I am allowed is watered wine ever since my wretched physician told them brandy was causing an inflammation of my liver."

Philip raised his eyes heavenwards.

"Now you tell me?"

✑

Theresa's slightly swollen belly was barely discernible yet, but the knowledge that there was new life in there again was the best news Philip could have had waiting for him when he arrived home.

"Maudie and I will be coming with you when you go back to Languedoc," she said, "and don't argue," she warned him, before Philip could protest.

"Believe me, Tess. nothing would please me more," he said truthfully, for he had missed them both whilst he had been away, "but will it not be a risk?"

"You cannot keep me in a glass case, my darling," she laughed. "Besides, this time it is different. I am fit and well."

He thought she certainly looked a picture of health. "It's a long journey," he reminded her, "and there are few comforts at Les Jacinthes compared with Heatherton. What if you should have the baby whilst we are there?"

"Nanon will be going back with us and Bet is coming too, and bringing little Gwen. She says it's about time Morgan saw his wife and child again before he forgets what they look like! With them fussing round me I shall be quite as safe there as I will be here."

Philip already realised the futility of arguing the point. When Theresa had made up her mind, he knew from experience that she could be very determined.

Giles shook his head incredulously when Philip told him. "You will be travelling to France with three women and two children?"

"It would appear so! Fortunately, Thomas will be with us as well, to help keep an eye on them."

"I'd come too, if I could," Giles said.

"I know you would, but your part in this venture will need to be played here for the time being," Philip said.

Giles had been typically secretive about the house that he and Marianne had found. All Philip had managed to learn from him was that it was a riverside property in Gravesend, at the mouth of the Thames Estuary, and he was eager to see it when he and Giles set off in his coach for Kent.

"I trust Luc has made himself useful," Giles said as they went along.

Philip was about to make some light remark but Giles was watching him closely and he thought better of it.

"He has been invaluable," he admitted honestly. "It was actually he who killed the guard to rescue my cousin."

"Antoine told me that," Giles said. "You still have not acknowledged him as your son?"

"I have accepted him as part of my family," Philip said, "so what does it matter?"

"I think it matters to him," Giles said quietly.

"I wonder how life as a soldier is suiting Antoine," Philip said, to change the subject.

"Very well, I would imagine. He told me it was what he had always wanted."

"Thank you for what you did for him," Philip said sincerely.

"I saw promise in him and, frankly, I liked the man, better than I had thought I would."

"Also, presenting William with a willing volunteer might make him look a little more favourably upon your own departure from his army," Philip guessed, for he knew his brother-in-law very well.

"That too," Giles said admitted, with a slight smile.

Philip had been horrified to learn that Giles had been at Mons after all and he was more pleased than ever that William had learned of the siege too late to arrive in time for what could have been a bloody battle.

"Even so, I am surprised that William let you go so easily," he said.

"He didn't let me go entirely," Giles said with a sigh. "There is unrest in Scotland."

"There has always been unrest in Scotland," Philip pointed out. James still had many supporters amongst the Highland clans and William had always had as little as possible to do with this unruly part of his kingdom. "What does he expect you to do about it."

"Whilst he is away, he has instructed John Dalrymple, the Scottish Secretary, to issue an order for the clan chiefs to swear allegiance to the crown and he has appointed me to aid him."

"You certainly get the best jobs," Philip said dryly. "What if they will not sign?"

"Then," Giles said, in a grim voice, "they are to be punished."

Philip knew well enough what that meant.

"William wants the matter handled amicably if possible," Giles assured him, "but he fears Dalrymple will ignite the situation rather than pacify it."

"It is a pity that our King cannot concern himself with matters closer to home and deal with this himself, instead of appointing others to keep order in his absence," Philip reckoned.

"He wants no part of it. He told me once he wished that Scotland was a thousand miles away! The truth is, though, that with so many problems on the continent he cannot risk more here at home, for any Jacobite uprising in Scotland is certain to add to his troubles with the Irish."

"But why you?"

"He says there are so few that he can trust now, for the Commons do nothing but argue and the Whigs and Tories are constantly at each other's throats. I have been promised that, directly he returns home, I shall be free of all official duties, excepting at times of national emergency."

William had freed Philip under the same terms, and he knew exactly what that meant in his own case – his leash might have been lengthened but it was still held by a monarch he no longer truly respected, one who had once been his bitter enemy.

Now Giles was being held at the whim of that same monarch.

Foxfield Hall exceeded all Philip's hopes. Not only was it by the river but it already had a substantial wharf, which had ample space on it to construct a warehouse.

"The place used to belong to a timber merchant," Giles explained. "He used to ship wood upriver to London apparently."

From where they were standing, Philip could see a little single-masted hoy working as a ferry between Gravesend and Tilbury, on the opposite side of the estuary.

"A boat like that would be able to transport our wine from here to the capital in a matter of a few hours," he reckoned. "It's perfect, Giles. You have done well."

The house itself was a neat, brick building which had been built in the previous century. It was smaller than High Heatherton, but it was attractive and, although usually not much given to enthusing about anything, Giles looked happier than Philip had seen him for a long while as he showed him round and told him how excited Marianne had been when she saw it.

"Congratulations, Giles," he said, when the tour was complete. "You are now a country gentleman!"

Giles shook his head, laughing. "No, Philp, *you* are a country gentleman. *I* am a gentleman wine merchant!"

"I understand that you have recently become a father, Comte," King Louis said to Armand.

"Yes, your Majesty. I am delighted to say that my wife presented me with a healthy baby boy two weeks ago," Armand said, hoping that he had not been summoned from Brittany to be sent on yet another mission when he wanted nothing more at the moment than to be able to spend time with Marguerite and his little son.

"That is excellent news, and I have more news for you. I beg you to be seated." Louis indicated a chair in front of the desk where he sat. "I would not have you suffer any discomfort on account of the injury you received in your illustrious service for France. Does it trouble you much these days?"

"Mostly on long journeys, your Majesty," Armand said. He was honoured at the concession to sit in the King's presence, although he found it somewhat amusing that Louis should show concern about him standing in his cabinet for a few minutes and yet had been quite prepared to send him chasing over the length and breadth of the country for the last six years! He was hopeful, though, as to what Louis' news might be.

"In that case I am sure you will be relieved to know that, after due consideration, and discussion with Louvois, I have decided to release you from your duties."

That was, indeed, the best news Armand could have had, especially now. Far from wanting to sit down, he had an absurd desire to stand up and cheer! "Your Majesty is most gracious," he said, instead.

"What shall you do now?"

"Retire to my estate in Brittany, your Majesty," Armand told him.

"I trust we will not lose your company altogether," Louis said. "Be assured that you will always be a welcome visitor here."

Armand had never considered himself to be, or desired to be, a courtier, but he dutifully promised that he would not become a stranger, even though he doubted that Louis' words were sincere. His years of faithful service to France counted as nothing, he feared, against his transgression, in Louis' eyes, of marrying a Huguenot, not even after Marguerite had renounced her faith. He knew enough of the ways of the world, however, to realise that, from Louis' point of view, his occasional appearances at Versailles would demonstrate to the rest of the Court that the King never truly relinquished control of his servants.

But that was a problem for the future and he was in a happy frame of mind as he left Louis' cabinet. The door to it was behind one of the many mirrors in the Galerie des Glaces, whose magnificent ceiling depicted the battles which had been won during Louis' reign, in some of which he himself had played a part before his injury.

Those had been the glorious years, before he had been forced to perform such distasteful duties in Louvois' name, but at last he felt as though his life was truly his own again.

Almost on cue, he spotted a man looking out of one of the open windows at the Fountain of Latona, in the gardens below. One he recognised only too well, even before the man turned toward him.

Armand realised it could be no coincidence that Louvois was in the Galerie at the very moment he had left his meeting with the King.

The only question in his mind was whether or not Louis was aware that Louvois would be there waiting for him.

Apparently, the games had not yet ended.

Louvois greeted him with his customary outward show of deference to his title. Despite the importance of the office he held, the Secretary of State for War came from a bourgeoise family and needed to observe the proper respect due to one of Armand's rank, much as it obviously pained him at times to do so.

Armand returned his salutations with the merest nod of his head, impatient to learn the reason Louvois had waylaid him.

"I expected you would be travelling to Brittany as soon as you were able and I wanted to find the opportunity to talk with you before you left."

"You seem to have found it," Armand said heavily.

The Minister's face looked a little flushed but it was a warm day, even for the middle of July, and Armand thought that was probably the cause.

"I needed to speak with you concerning Languedoc."

"Indeed?"

Armand kept his expression bland but he had wondered how long it would be before the recent events there were brought to light.

"Madame de Maintenon has received some troubling information from Intendant de Basville."

Armand knew that Maintenon was no friend of Louvois. Philip had managed to learn that he had been the sole witness to her secret marriage to Louis and, to her annoyance, Louis had taken Louvois' advice not to publicly acknowledge her as his wife.

"What is he saying?"

"That there was an insurrection whilst you were in the region, and yet I found no mention of it in your reports."

"Hardly an insurrection," Armand said dismissively. "A handful of rebels attacked Inspector du Chayla's chateau at Le Pont de Montvert and freed their friends, who were being held prisoner there."

"One of those freed, apparently, was Antoine Pasquier. Do you not find that a coincidence, since it was his arrest which prompted the King to request you to go there?"

Armand shrugged. "I can only assume that he had friends amongst the rebels."

"He had friends somewhere, that is for certain," Louvois said tartly. "His cousin, Philip Devalle, was in Languedoc at the time, so de Basville said. Another coincidence?"

"I scarcely think that Philip, being an Englishman, could have made any connections with rebels living in the remote mountains of the Cevennes," Armand said. "Even du Chayla has been unable to flush them out, notwithstanding that he seems to have a private army at his disposal."

Louvois ignored that. "Maybe not, but it is a curious thing indeed that, at the time Pasquier and the others were freed, du Chayla was in Montpellier, summoned there, it seems, by you."

"I was merely carrying out an instruction which came directly from his Majesty," Armand pointed out. "He asked me to investigate the activities of de Basville's Inspector of Missions, particularly with regard to his treatment of those prisoners held at his house. In the event, I was unable to do so, since there were none by the time my servant arrived there."

Louvois eyed him for a long moment. Armand had no idea if he believed any of it, but he did not much care.

"Where do you think Pasquier would have gone after his escape?" Louvois asked Armand. "Into the Cevennes with the other rebels?"

"I doubt that," Armand said evenly. "More likely he used the escape route over the Ardèche."

"The border is patrolled now," Louvois reminded him.

"Nevertheless, those who are determined to get out of France still find a way through, it seems."

"So you think he is out of the country?"

"I am almost sure of it."

Armand had no idea why Louvois was getting so agitated about this, but he plainly was. He was breathing heavily and trembling a little as he spoke.

"Why is Pasquier of such interest to you?" he asked the Minister.

"He is of interest to Madame de Maintenon because he is the cousin of your friend, Devalle."

"I see," Armand said, for he did see now. Maintenon hated Philip almost as much as she did Louvois, all because Philip, many years ago, had publicly ordered her out of his Paris house after she had insulted a dear friend of his. She had tried to have him killed two years before and Armand knew she would stop at nothing to disgrace him. To have a close relative brought to justice would sour his reputation and undermine his position with Louis.

"She is demanding now that I make an example of the man," Louvois said, sounding angry.

And, in doing so, she was making yet more trouble for Louvois with the King, Armand guessed.

Armand could almost feel sorry for him, having such a powerful enemy. Almost but not quite.

The following day Armand made preparations to leave Versailles. He and Eugene packed up the few items they usually left in the small apartment that had been allotted to him for his frequent visits to the palace for, despite Louis' words, Armand had no intention of returning there for some time.

Eugene took the boxes to the coach and rushed back with some news. "Monsieur de Louvois has been taken ill."

"When was this?"

"Just now, my Lord. He collapsed as he left the King."

Armand thought back to his last conversation with the Minister. Louvois had certainly not seemed himself and he wondered now whether his high colour and the obvious agitation he had shown could have been, after all, an indication that the man was ill.

"People are already saying he's been poisoned." Eugene said.

"Well they would." Armand knew that any sudden, unexplained illness was put down to poison and he did not know enough about the early symptoms of it to determine whether the signs he had seen could be an indication of that. What he did know was that Louvois had made many enemies in his rise to power. And Armand also knew that the most influential one of them was vengeful, despite her outward air of piety.

It would be irony indeed, he thought, if Louvois, who had headed the Chambre Ardente in its investigation into the poisons scandal twelve years before, had succumbed to it himself.

Louvois died that day despite, or maybe because of, the attentions of his physician, Seron. The official cause of his death was apoplexy, but Armand, along with the rest of the Court, would never be sure.

Philp received a letter from Armand at the end of July, telling him the news about the birth of his son. Philip was pleased for him, especially since he knew that Armand had lost his only other child when his first wife had died whilst she was carrying it. The letter also mentioned Louvois.

Philip had clashed with him on more than one occasion. The rules and regulations Louvois had introduced, and some of the decisions he had made, tended to be unpopular with soldiers who fought France's wars with weapons on the battlefield, not with a pen behind a desk, but Philip knew what a great loss his death would be to Louis.

There were other aspects to consider too. Armand had once told him that Louvois had been opposed to aiding James in any attempt to take back his crown, but it was possible that Louvois' son, the Marquis de Barbesieux, who now held his father's post, might take a different view.

Even so, he guessed the news would cause great rejoicing for William and his troops and he guessed, too, that it would mark the end of the Summer campaign.

He was right upon both counts. Word reached him in August that William was on his way back to the Hague and Philip suspected that it would not be too long before the King was home in England and demanding his presence at Court. Much as he would have liked to wait and meet up with Antoine again, Philip knew that it was time for him to return to France.

And this time his family was going with him.

TWENTY

❧

Languedoc was wonderful in September. The days were warm and the fruit hung heavy as it ripened in the sunshine.

Theresa fell in love with the house as soon as she saw it.

Philip put his arm around her thickening waist as they stood by the open window in what Antoine had informed him was once his mother's room. "There are about twenty-five acres all told," he said as they looked across the vineyard, stretching out as far as the mountains beyond. "Morgan has managed to restore a good ten of them and he thinks the rest can be saved in time. He's done so well."

"And so have you, my love." Theresa leaned her head against him. "It is your spirit that has brought Les Jacinthes to life again, just as it did Heatherton."

He smiled. "If you say so. Will you be able to regard it as our second home, do you think?"

"I already do," she assured him, and so does someone else, by the looks of it!"

From where they stood, they could see their daughter leading Gwen by the hand through the rows of vines. She stopped to taste one of the black fruits and popped another into her little companion's mouth before they both broke into a joyous run, going as fast as Gwen's small legs could manage.

"This is Maudie's inheritance," Philip said, watching her lovingly. "I want her to marry a Frenchman one day, you know that don't you? Then no-one can ever take this away from her and our grandchildren."

Theresa laughed. "She's only eight! It's a little early to be talking about your grandchildren, don't you think?"

Philip knew how reluctant she would be to have Maudie living so far away from them, but he also knew how uncertain the future could be.

The life he had led had been precarious at times. What fate had in store for him he could not predict but he vowed that, whatever might happen, he would ensure that his little girl would be safe, and under the protection of the only monarch he felt he could trust. And that was King Louis.

Devereaux came to visit them as soon as they sent word of their return.

"Any problems whilst we were gone?" Philip asked him.

"De Basville has stayed away but you had a visit from du Chayla's soldiers. They were eyeing the barrels. Some of my men spotted them and went over. Your Luc had already threatened to cut off the hand of any who touched them," he said with a chuckle.

"I can imagine!" Luc had organised the making of fifty of the oak barrels and he was proud of the impressive stack.

"More than a bit of Pasquier in that one, I'd reckon! I thought they might be going to fire them," Devereaux said, growing serious.

That thought had never occurred to Philip. "Would the bastards do that?"

"It's been known."

"Then the sooner we get this crop picked and away the better," Philip reckoned. "Morgan estimates it will be ready in another two weeks."

"He's right. Mourvèdre can stay on the vine longer than others, for its thick skin can withstand the rain that comes in Autumn, but, once it is ready, you must not delay or the flavour will be impaired."

"When I speak with someone like yourself, with so much knowledge and experience, I realise how arrogant I was to believe that a soldier like myself could come to Languedoc and run a vineyard," Philip said, in all honesty.

"And yet you have," Devereaux said, "and I am certain that the King would not have given Les Jacinthes to you if he did not think you could make a success of it."

Philip doubted very much if Louis gave a damn whether he made a success of Les Jacinthes or not, since his main reason for giving it to him was to ensure that he did not use his soldier's talents against him, but he would not say that in front of Devereaux.

"Morgan runs it truly, not me," he admitted, "and all credit must be his. By the way, his wife has brought you a preparation she made up for you before we left England. I expect it will taste foul," he warned him, "but it will likely do you more good than anything your physician prescribes."

Devereaux looked dubiously at the mixture in the bottle when Bet handed it to him.

"It is wild thyme and rhubarb powder boiled in vinegar," she told him crisply, "It will cleanse your liver. Take a spoonful every morning on an empty stomach."

"Best do as she says," Philip advised him. "We generally do!"

The next two weeks went by quickly.

Philip hired a temporary labour force of locals to swell the numbers of Morgan's own men for the harvest and he also organised four wagons with drivers to take the barrels the thirty miles to Marseillan.

Meanwhile, he dispatched Thomas to the port to make arrangements with the harbour master for a barge, and Luc to Fontfroide to sort out the transport they would need to take the crop from the canal to the Abbey. He knew he could safely trust both young men to fulfil those tasks for him and he felt his own continuing presence at Les Jacinthes was necessary, just in case any more of du Chayla's soldiers were considering paying them a visit.

By the evening before the harvest everything was in readiness. Whilst Theresa, Bet and Nanon were preparing food to sustain the workers the following day, Philip went out alone and looked across the fields of perfectly ripe fruit. It occurred to him that his mother would have seen that same sight many times and, even though there was little left of her in the house, the thought suddenly made him feel close to her. Morgan came out to join him after a while, then Thomas and Luc and they all stood in easy silence, taking in the peaceful scene until the sun finally disappeared behind the mountains.

A year ago, Philip had not even been sure whether any of this would be possible, but he had done it, thanks to Antoine and the three loyal men who stood by his side now, and he was grateful to them all.

The whole household was up and waiting in the fields before dawn the following morning, for Morgan wanted to get as much picked as possible by the time the sun was high overhead and the heat of the day began in earnest.

To the Welshman's annoyance, none of the workforce had arrived by 5 o'clock, not even his regular labourers.

Philip began to get an uneasy feeling.

"Something's wrong."

Even as he said it, he spotted a two-wheeled open carriage, pulled by a couple of horses, approaching them along the road that bordered the field.

"Who the devil is this?

An armed soldier rode upon either side of the vehicle and driving it was a man who Philip had sincerely hoped he would never have to meet again. Archpriest Du Chayla.

Philip knew that du Chayla could be in no doubt as to who had freed the prisoners at Le Pont de Montvert, both from the description of him the surviving guards would have given and the all too convenient fact that his cousin had been amongst those liberated. Philip also knew that the priest had been warned by Armand not to take any action against him through official channels and he had wondered several times what form of revenge de Basville's Inspector of Missions would attempt to take.

He was about to find out.

Du Chayla brought the horses to a halt beside him.

"I understand that it was your intent to employ some of the locals to do your picking today, my Lord," Du Chayla said, getting directly to the point, "but they are all good Catholics round here. Whilst exceptions may have been made for you in the past, it is my sad duty to remind you that it is against the law for any Protestant to employ a Catholic."

Philip stared at him as the full import of du Chayla's words hit him. "Are you telling me I will not be able to harvest my crop?"

"Yes, my Lord, that is exactly what I am telling you, for there is no-one around here, I am certain, who would be prepared to take the risk of working for you, not when there is ample work available upon the other estates."

"You can't do this," Philip said angrily.

"Indeed I can, my Lord, for I have been given full authority by Intendant de Basville, who represents the law in Languedoc and, at my suggestion, he has sought advice from a friend in a position of influence."

Philip did not need to ask him who.

"Maintenon," he guessed. "She is behind this."

"It seems that, as well as allies, you have some enemies in high places, my Lord. You could of course appeal to the King, who would no doubt overturn the Intendant's ruling, but, alas, it is a long journey to Versailles and I fear that by the time you were able to put your case before him and return here with his answer your fruit would be spoiled." Du Chayla allowed himself a smirk of triumph as he flicked the reins and drove on. "Such a pity, for it looks a fine crop."

Philip did not often feel defeated, but he felt it now as he looked out upon the acres of full-ripened fruit and the stack of newly-made barrels ready to transport them to Fontfroide. He had planned for everything but this.

He turned to Morgan, who had heard it all and was casting murderous glances in the direction of du Chayla's disappearing carriage.

"Has it all been for nothing, Morgan? All my hopes and your hard work?"

"It has if you let him win."

The others came over to join them and stood around him in dejected silence. All he had to do was get the fruit on a boat at Marseillan. The problem was he didn't know how. He knew what was expected of him, what was always expected of him, some plan to make things turn out right. But he didn't have one. Not this time.

Morgan spoke first. "We'll just have to pick it ourselves."

"The two of us?" Philip smiled sadly at him. "We'll never do it before it rots on the vine."

"Three of us," Thomas said, stepping forward.

"And me," put in Luc. "That's four."

"Five," Theresa said, slipping her arm through his. "I'm a country girl, I can manage it."

"So can a Londoner," Bet assured him. "Six."

"I'll help too," Maudie declared. "So, it's seven."

"Eight," Nanon added. "You know I would never let you down."

"I know it sweetheart." Philip looked affectionately at her and the others, and then at the fields of ripe fruit stretching as far as he could see. Even with eight of them he knew there was no chance of saving it.

That was when he saw men approaching them along the road.

There were about two dozen of them and some were carrying long poles with hooks at the top

"More trouble?" Philip asked Morgan, who had moved to stand beside him.

"Maybe not. I have seen a couple of them before. They work for Devereaux."

"That doesn't explain why they are here, and bringing weapons – if that is what those are."

He felt a little easier in his mind when he spotted Devereaux himself riding alongside the men.

"You have done well," the old man said, looking around him.

"Any praise due belongs to Morgan," Philip looked over to the Welshman, who was handling one of the long, hooked poles interestedly "but it seems his efforts are in vain, since the bastards are not going to let me harvest it."

"I heard. What shall you do?"

"What can I do? I have only my family to help me now. What are those, by the way?" he asked Devereaux, pointing to the poles.

"Antoine may have taught you how to care for your crop but what he evidently didn't teach you was how best to pick it," Devereaux said. "Those are what we call grappes."

"And did you come to lend them to me," Philip asked uncertainly.

"And the men to wield them, my Lord."

"But de Basville has forbidden me to hire any labour," he reminded him regretfully.

"As to that, you will not be hiring them," Devereaux said. "These men work for me at harvest time and, since my crop is now almost all safely in, I can spare some men. They are yours for as long as you have need of them."

Philip looked at him in amazement. "Why would you do this for me?"

"Because we are neighbours, my Lord, and neighbours around here help each other, especially during la vendange."

"La vendange?"

Deveraux laughed. "Don't tell me I have finally found a word in French that you do not understand! Your mother would have known it well enough. It is the harvest, my Lord, the most important event in our year. You must not refuse my help for, without yours on the night of the fire, I would have lost a good deal of my own crop."

Philip said nothing for moment, a little overwhelmed by the offer, coming as it had at a time when, for once, he had feared he was beaten. Some of the experiences in his rich and varied life had caused him to cease believing in the innate goodness of his fellow men and he could scarcely credit that Devereaux, who he really hardly knew, would do so much for him. He was not accustomed to accepting charity, however, even when it was well-meant, and it angered him that, after all their efforts, he would need the help of a neighbour because of du Chayla's spite.

Theresa, looked at him and he knew she understood. She gave Devereaux an impulsive little hug, her eyes moist with tears. "You are kind and generous, Monsieur Devereaux. My husband is a proud man so, before he turns down your offer, I want to thank you most sincerely and accept on his behalf."

Despite his dark thoughts, Philip could not help but laugh. "I wasn't going to turn it down," he protested. "I may be a proud man but I am not a stupid one!"

Harvesting the crop was a slow and back-breaking job, even with the aid of the grappes. Philip and all his family laboured alongside Devereaux's men for the whole of that day in hot sun and Philip's heart swelled with pride as he watched them. Morgan, who had been brought up to farming, toiled methodically, like a true son of the soil, but Thomas and Luc, their sleeves rolled up, plunged into this new task with the enthusiasm they had shown for every aspect of the enterprise; Bet worked with her usual dogged determination and little Maudie picked as steadily as the rest, whilst Nanon, standing up occasionally to stretch her back, kept pace with the younger ones.

Philip cast several anxious glances in Theresa's direction during the course of the day. She was, as she said, a country girl and had always been strong, in both body and spirit but, with his baby due in only two months, he could not help but be concerned. Even so, he knew how useless it would be to suggest that she rested whilst the others worked and he took some comfort in the fact that both Bet and Nanon were close at hand.

Although, like all of them, she was plainly exhausted when they finished for the day, he thought she looked wonderful. Her unruly red curls were loose about her shoulders, her dress, which she had hooked up above her knees, was stained with juice and her face was streaked with dirt.

"My little duchess," he said, kissing the top of her head. "what would King Louis say if he saw you now?"

"Probably that I was too good for you," she joked, for Louis, who had always had a fondness for her, often told Philip that.

"And he would be right!"

They all collapsed wearily into their beds that night and were back out into the fields at daybreak the next morning but by midday the vines were stripped clean and forty-eight of Luc's fifty barrels were full and loaded onto the four wagons.

La vendange was complete.

Philip prepared to set off for Marseillan immediately with Morgan. The Welshman would not let the crop out of his sight after the many months of hard work he had put into it and Philip could think of no-one he would rather have with him in the event that they encountered any trouble along the way, for he was watchful now for any further sign of Du Chayla's soldiers. Thomas and Luc were remaining behind to look after the women and children, and he knew they could be in no better hands.

Despite Philip's fears, the journey to Marseillan was uneventful. As soon as they arrived, on the afternoon of the following day, the wagons were swiftly unloaded and the barrels put into the hold of a barge by the owner and his son. Philip felt a rising excitement as the bargee's wife made the strong old barge horse ready and untied the ropes that held the vessel to the quay. He glanced over at Morgan as they mounted their horses, ready to follow the barge, and saw that even he was smiling.

"We did it, Morgan!"

"Yes, my Lord. We did indeed."

Philip already had some experience of travelling with a barge. After the attempt upon his life two years before, he had been pulled from the River Seine by a bargee, whose daughter had nursed him back to health. Whilst he was recovering his strength, he had walked many miles leading their horse along the side of the canal and had helped her with the locks.

These locks looked a little different, for instead of having straight sides they were oval in shape, but the workings were the same and, as he and Morgan rode along the towpath beside the barge, he was happy to help the bargee's son with closing the lock gates and lifting the paddle to raise the level of the water. They joined the River Herault for a short while on the approach to their third lock, at the old town of Agde. This was a round lock, with three gates, two for entering or leaving the river and one to re-join the canal, and Philip found himself beginning to truly appreciate the engineering skill which had gone into the creation of Riquet's Canal Royale de Languedoc.

They managed three more locks before it grew dark and moored at the town of Bezier. It was a warm night so Philip and Morgan laid their blankets out on the deck of the barge.

"Not the first time we have slept out under the stars, my old friend," Philip said, remembering the many adventures they had shared over the years and the many occasions when he had been glad to have Morgan by his side.

"That's so," Morgan agreed, "but at least no-one is trying to kill us this time!"

The next morning, just after they left, they encountered more of Riquet's marvels, first a canal bridge that took them right over the River Orb and then, at a place called Fonserannes, there was series of seven locks, each chamber leading to the next, and forming a stairway to raise the water level. Not far from that, the barge passed through a tunnel hewn straight through the rock and Philip and Morgan looked up at the cavernous space in awe as they carefully led their horses through behind the patient, plodding barge horse.

There were no more locks before they arrived at Capestang and Philip left the boat there to ride the few miles along the towpath to Le Somail, where Luc, on the advice of the Abbot, had arranged for their transport to Fontfroide.

Although only a hamlet, Philip had learned from the bargee's wife that the Canal Royale had brought trade to Le Somail, for passengers on the mail barge, that often ran from Agde to the city of Toulouse, stopped there to rest. He located the owner of the wagons and, whilst they were made ready and brought down to the quay, he went to watch for the barge from the pointed-topped bridge that spanned the canal. It was a little while coming, but he was not impatient. He had rather enjoyed the gentle pace of the journey on the canal, after all the activity of the few days that had preceded it, and he reckoned they would easily arrive at Fontfroide by nightfall.

They would have completed the journey in three days, as opposed to taking the better part of a week to transport the crop upon the country roads and allowing time for frequent stops to rest the horses. He was feeling exultant as the boat came slowly into view around the bend and he waved to Morgan, riding by its side.

The barrels were taken from the hold and loaded upon the wagons then, with Philip and Morgan riding escort, they set off to travel the short distance to the Abbey of Fontfroide.

It was not the route he and Luc had taken when they had ridden to the Abbey from Narbonne, but was one that the lead driver evidently knew well and Philip was content to follow him. He was still vigilant for he was a soldier and his instinct for danger had never left him but, so near their journey's end, he began to relax a little.

That was until they entered a steep, narrow valley.

Philip looked up at the tree-covered hills on either side of them and his nerves began to tingle. Anyone might be concealed amongst those trees. He glanced over at Morgan and saw that he, too, was looking warily from side to side. They both moved nearer to the wagons, their pistols ready in their hands, but there was no way of hastening the vehicles through, loaded as they were, and no place to defend them in the event of an attack.

The perfect place for an ambush.

It was Morgan who first spotted a movement in the trees.

"Get under the wagons," Philip shouted to the drivers.

The light of the setting sun was reflecting on what could have been a weapon and, as the four drivers scrambled for cover, he took aim and fired. A man screamed. Morgan's pistol sounded and another man tumbled down the hill but, at the same moment, a shot rang out upon the opposite side. They were surrounded.

Philip's anger rose. "Damn du Chayla! Does he never give up?"

They had overcome so many problems since he had taken possession of Les Jacinthes and it had taken them a year of arduous work to make a success of the enterprise. He was determined that no-one was going to rob him of that now. No-one on God's earth.

He dismounted and, ducking down beside one of the wagons, he reloaded and fired again as he saw another figure emerge from the wooded slope. The man dropped where he stood, but Philip knew that he was himself an easy target, for the wagons offered little real protection. This was a fight he needed to take to the enemy.

Drawing his sword, Philip, leapt up and ran to the slope. Morgan was already off his horse and running into the trees on the other side of the valley, his knife in his hand.

With no idea of how many they were facing, Philip knew they would be taking a risk but there was little choice. He took comfort in the fact that these men did not appear to be soldiers, probably local mercenaries, he guessed, hired for the job. He realised that would not necessarily make them less dangerous but he hoped it would make them less disciplined.

A sword was not an ideal weapon to wield in the close confines of the woods but Philip had another weapon at his disposal, and it was just as deadly. When John Bone had been his childhood friend, during his early years at High Heatherton, John's father, Sam, had taught Philip to fight with nothing but the strength and agility of his own body. Those lessons had stood him in good stead many times during his eventful life and any foolhardy enough to make the mistake of underestimating him on account of his appearance soon paid the price of their error. Philip might look and behave as a gentleman but he could brawl with the best.

The trees hampered his opponents' ability to shoot him but he saw three men coming down toward him as he reached the woods. They had the benefit of the higher ground but Philp was unperturbed. Giving the first man no chance to fire the pistol in his hand, Philip ran at him and thrust his sword directly into the man's gut. He collapsed, screaming, onto the ground, clutching at the blade as his life-blood gushed out from the wound.

The other two, hesitated, having witnessed their companion's fate, and Philip was thankful he was not dealing with trained soldiers. Even a few seconds delay gave him the advantage in this situation, and he took it.

The branch of a tree was just above his head and he jumped to grasp it, bringing his feet up to kick out at his nearest assailant.

Philip's boots caught him full in the face and he staggered back, clutching at his nose, which was plainly broken.

Before the remaining assailant could react, Philip had thrown himself down, landing upon him with his full weight and driving the breath from the man's body. They rolled over twice as his opponent threshed about, desperately trying to throw him off, but Philip's strength prevailed and he managed to pin him down and sit astride his back.

Philip's pistol was useless, for he had not had the chance to reload it a second time but, he pulled it out and smacked it with his full force on the back of the man's head. Philip heard his skull crack.

There was no time to savour his victory, for the other man was coming at him again, blood streaming from his ruined nose. He was holding a pistol but he was plainly dizzy and his hand was shaking as he aimed it. Philip never gave him the chance to fire. Leaping up, he charged him and head-butted him hard in the stomach. His pistol fell from his hand as he gasped for breath and Philip seized it up.

"Mercy," The man cried, scrambling backwards in a futile attempt to distance himself.

Philip shook his head. He knew exactly how much mercy this assassin would have shown him. "I don't think so."

He fired and, before the man had even dropped to the ground, he bent to retrieve his sword from the body of the dead man who lay a few feet away.

His first thought now was for Morgan and he hastened back down to the road. The carts were still there, to his relief, and he was even more relieved to see the Welshman coming down from the other side of the valley.

"Only two?" he said lightly, as he viewed Morgan's gruesome handiwork. One man lay with a knife wound to his heart and the other had his throat cut. "What was it you said last night about nobody trying to kill us?"

Morgan gave a grim smile. "They weren't du Chayla's men."

"No?" Philip removed a couple of leaves and a small twig that had got caught in his long hair during his tussle on the ground. "Who then?"

"De Basville sent them," Morgan said. "This one tried to buy his life with that information, just before I slit his throat."

"Really?" Philip decided to ponder upon that later. It was already dusk and they still had forty-eight barrels of wine to get to Fontfroide Abbey before nightfall. The drivers had all crawled out from beneath the wagons and were only too eager to be out of the valley and upon their way before it grew dark.

It was late by the time they arrived at Fontfroide and most of the monks had retired but the lay brothers were summoned to help them. The wagons were directed round to the doorway that led into the storeroom, where the barrels were unloaded.

Afterwards, the horses were led away to be stabled and the four drivers, who seemed to have recovered from their experience to the degree that they were keen to tell the brothers all about it, were taken to the lay brothers' refectory, where they would be fed before being given beds for the night. Philip and Morgan had been invited to dine with Abbot La Rochefoucauld and were escorted to his quarters, an elegant building just off the main courtyard.

The Abbot made them welcome and poured them each a glass of the Abbey's own wine, which Philip thought was amongst the best he had ever tasted.

"I hear you met with some problems on your way here, my Lord," La Rochefoucauld said conversationally, as they waited for the food to be served.

Clearly news travelled fast within the Abbey, mainly, Philip suspected, because so little of any excitement ever happened within those sheltered walls.

"Nothing we could not handle," Philip said guardedly, appearing to study the wine in his glass with extraordinary care.

He trusted no-one at the moment, although he couldn't see any reason for the Abbot to be involved in their attack since the Abbey, or rather the Abbot himself, Philip guessed, stood to make a financial gain from their business together.

"Obviously, but there are those, it would seem, who do not wish you well."

"Such as Intendent de Basville and his Inspector of Missions?" Philip suggested bluntly.

"Quite. You should know that I have been approached by Archpriest du Chayla, who demanded that I render you no assistance with your crop."

That was exactly what Philip had feared, but he regarded him coolly. "You have already entered into an arrangement with me," he pointed out.

"An arrangement which I shall honour," the Abbot assured him.

"For the agreed amount, I hope," Philip said sharply, relieved, but suspecting that this might be a ploy by this astute man of the cloth to drive up the price. He knew that he was really in no position to haggle over terms either, not with a perishable crop on his hands and no other options.

He need not have worried.

"Du Chayla cannot tell *me* what to do," La Rochefoucauld said, with more than a touch of disdain in his voice, "and nor can the man who employs him. De Basville may be puffed up with his own importance but he is only a lawyer." He managed to make the word sound like an insult. "So yes, my Lord, at the original price and may we have a jointly profitable association over many years to come."

The Abbot raised his glass to that and Philip raised his in return.

He looked over at Morgan who slowly lifted his own, although during the conversation he had been looking ready to thrust his knife into the Abbot's ample belly if it had seemed like the man was contemplating double-crossing them. Philip was well aware that, whilst Morgan had felt an immediate affinity for the Huguenot rebels, La Rochefoucauld was not the type of man the Welshman would ever esteem or understand. Philip did, for he had met his like throughout his varied career; men who used their position to advance their own interests, regardless of law or loyalty.

He decided that, as far as he was concerned, he might have finally met a priest that he could actually respect!

Philip drank to the toast then raised his glass again. "And to 'Les Fleurs de Languedoc'."

TWENTY-ONE

⁓

Philip smiled as he thought back to when he had last been at the palace of Fontainebleau. This time he was there hoping to see the King, but the previous occasion had been very different, for it was shortly after someone had tried to kill him in Paris. Then he had entered the palace grounds with caution, partly because he was dressed only in a dirty shirt and ragged trousers and he had feared being shot as an intruder, but more because, at that time, he was unsure of who wanted him dead – and whether they would try again.

Now the coach he had hired for the journey from Languedoc drove him and Thomas boldly through the main gates and he entered the palace unchallenged through the doorway beneath the imposing twin staircases that curved down from the first-floor balcony above.

Philip knew he had taken quite a chance coming here on this occasion too. He had been given no invitation to join the royal party on their traditional Autumn visit to the palace, but he had been one of the guests invited to join them in past years and he was gambling on the favour in which he was still held by Louis. After the problems he had recently encountered in Languedoc, Philip felt it was imperative to see him before he returned to England and he considered that Fontainebleau, where the King did less official business and tended to be slightly more informal, to be preferable to Versailles where, he felt, his presence was unwelcome whilst England and France were still at war.

He was not really sure how welcome he would be here either,

but there was one person who he felt sure would be pleased to see him and that was Monsieur, so that was who Philip requested to see when he was shown into the anteroom.

Monsieur was not in the palace, he was informed, but was watching a display on the canal.

"Shall you wait, my Lord?" the servant enquired.

Philip was certain that word of his arrival would swiftly reach the King but he needed to speak with Monsieur first, to see how the land lay. "I'll go and find him."

It was a long while since he had been dressed in elegant Court attire and, once he was outside the building, he could not resist a quick glance at his reflection in one of the windows, for Philip's looks had always been one of his greatest assets. Lately he had not had time or opportunity to pay much attention to his appearance, but he was still satisfied with what he saw.

Thomas watched him knowingly. "You wear it as well as ever, my Lord."

"Of course I do!"

They walked through the large formal gardens, laid out by Le Nôtre in the style he had designed for Versailles with little box hedges enclosing beds that were bursting with late flowers. The gardens led out to a rectangular pool which had fountains playing at varying heights around the edge and, beyond that, stretched the canal. Two galliots were sailing on the canal, surrounded by half a dozen smaller craft, their coloured sails fluttering gaily in the slight breeze.

There was a large crowd of courtiers gathered there, some standing in groups and others watching from their carriages. It was easy to spot Monsieur's carriage amongst them and Philip could see that he was surrounded by his usual circle of admirers, some of who turned hostile gazes upon him as he walked toward them.

"Looks like a few of them are not too happy to see you, my Lord," Thomas said.

Philip was totally unconcerned by that. He had spent too

many years at Court to be affected by the opinions of his fellow courtiers, most of whose lives, particularly at Louis' Court, revolved chiefly around petty intrigues and tittle tattle.

"The only thing which matters, Thomas, is whether Monsieur will be happy to see me."

That question was quickly answered.

Monsieur saw him approaching and cried out in delight. He did not even wait for Philip to reach the carriage before climbing out to greet him and then threw his arms round him in a tight embrace, kissing him upon both cheeks.

"What a wonderful surprise!"

"I'm glad you think so!" Philip was grateful once again for the friendship that had been his protection and opened so many doors for him over the years. "I haven't been invited here," he admitted.

"Well you have now." Monsieur said unhesitatingly, leading him into the gardens. Thomas followed at a discreet distance, like a dutiful servant, and Philip knew he would be alert for any sign of danger. Despite the welcome Monsieur had given him, Philip realised he was still in a precarious position in the Court of a country at war with his own.

"We may be annoying your friends," Philip warned him, but Monsieur gave a dismissive shrug. "Doesn't hurt to make them jealous! Have you presented yourself to my brother?"

"Not yet. I wished to see you first."

Monsieur laughed. "You're not in trouble with him again are you, you naughty man?"

"I hope not," Philip said sincerely, "but I've certainly *had* some trouble."

Monsieur listened intently as Philip related what had recently happened to him.

"Maintenon," he said decidedly when Philip had finished. "She put de Basville up to this, without a doubt."

"That is exactly what I thought."

"She did her best to prevent my brother from granting you

the vineyard in the first place, you know. Fortunately for you, I still have greater influence on him than she does." Monsieur linked his arm through his. "What are you going to do about it?"

"I'm not sure," Philip admitted. "I am reluctant to bother him further, especially since it would seem that the person most responsible for my problems is his consort." Philip refrained from referring to Madame de Maintenon as Louis' wife since she was not publicly acknowledged as such. "I fear he will soon regret his generosity to me but, even so, I cannot be thwarted at every turn by de Basville's Inspector of Missions. Who knows what the man will try next? I have no wish to impose further upon the goodwill of my neighbours but I must return to England soon and, frankly, I am loath to leave Les Jacinthes without adequate protection now."

"Yes, I can see why you would be." Monsieur lapsed into thought for a few moments, then he brightened. "I have an idea. A truly brilliant one."

Philip looked at him indulgently. Monsieur could be giddy-headed at times and he wondered what outrageous suggestion was about to be voiced. "Go on."

"Dear Giles is your partner in this venture, is he not?"

"He is, but 'dear Giles' cannot set foot in France at the moment without running the risk of being arrested," Philip reminded him.

"So you both need to acquire another partner, a Frenchman and a Catholic, one whose authority none will challenge."

Philip shook his head. "I can't ask Armand. He has helped me enough and he deserves to enjoy his retirement in peace."

"I didn't mean Armand."

"Alas, there's no-one else in France I could truly trust at the moment."

Monsieur's peal of merriment could be heard even over the sound of the cascading water of the fountains, causing several heads to turn. "What about me?"

Philip stared at him. "You?"

"Yes, me. Would it be so terrible to go into business with the First Gentleman of France?"

Philip was still not sure whether he was a victim of Monsieur's sometimes wayward sense of humour.

"Are you being serious, Monsieur?"

"Completely," Monsieur assured him. "Armand St. Jean is not the only friend you have here you know. If I was to invest a small sum of money into the place then no-one would dare to interfere with it."

Philip was astounded. Once again, it seemed, Monsieur was prepared to come to his rescue, as he had been when Philip was in danger of losing his Paris house. Les Jacinthes was even more important to him and Monsieur's involvement would not only ensure its safety but resolve the tricky issue of his being able to employ labour on the estate.

"It is the perfect solution, Monsieur, but why are you so good to me?" he asked him.

Monsieur laughed. "I've always been a little in love with you, you know. Besides, it will annoy Maintenon!"

"It will," Philip agreed, smiling, "but, apart from that, what do you expect to get out of it?"

Monsieur gave an airy wave of his delicately perfumed hand. "Oh, name a wine after me someday. I would like that."

Their walk through the flowerbeds had taken them back to the canal and, as Monsieur re-joined his friends, Thomas caught up with Philip again.

"Success?" he guessed.

He let out a low whistle of appreciation when he had heard Monsieur's proposal. "Is there anything that man wouldn't do for you?"

"I hope not! What I need now is for Louis to be in a good mood and sanction it."

Louis certainly looked more relaxed, and a good deal more amiable, than when Philip had last met him, in February.

"I trust your Majesty will forgive my presumption in attending upon you at Fontainebleau uninvited," he said, making the low, elaborate bow that was required whenever a courtier greeted the King of France. "Before I leave again for England, I wanted to offer you my grateful thanks We had a fruitful harvest, which we have successfully delivered to be processed at the Abbey of Fontfroide."

In view of Monsieur's offer, Philip had decided to make no mention of the problems he had recently encountered, for there was no longer any need to risk Louis' displeasure by complaining once again about the behaviour of one of his officials.

If Louis had any inkling of what had occurred, he gave no sign of it. "I am pleased for you. It would seem your enterprise is a success."

"So much so that Monsieur has expressed a wish to come into the business with me." Philip spoke lightly. He thought it was important to present the matter to Louis as one of Monsieur's frivolous whims, rather than as an arrangement to protect Les Jacinthes from Maintenon's spite.

He was right.

"An excellent idea, and one which has my approval. As my brother's guest, accommodation will naturally be found for you in the palace for the duration of your visit."

Philip was gratified to learn that, for he had expected they would have to find a room somewhere in the town, which would already be full of visitors attending upon the King, or hoping to catch a glimpse of him.

"Your Majesty is gracious, although I regret I shall not be able to stay for too long. Theresa is expecting our second child next month and I would like to get her home to England before it is born."

Louis looked concerned. "She ought not be travelling so near her time. You should not even have brought her to France with you," he chided him.

Philip knew that Louis had always had a soft spot for Theresa. "I know, but she insisted upon accompanying me. It was all I could do to dissuade her from coming here today, for she so longed to see your Majesty again." There was an element of truth in that and he knew how much it would flatter Louis.

"Bring her when you come again," Louis instructed him, "and it is about time your daughter was presented at my Court. How old is she now?"

"Nearly nine, your Majesty."

"Then you are to bring her too. Has she been presented at Whitehall yet?" Louis asked sharply.

"No, your Majesty."

The fact was that, although Philip had lived at Court from the age of thirteen, Theresa had wanted Maudie's childhood to be free of the restrictions and formality of Court life. A direct command from the King of France was a different matter entirely, however. It would have to be obeyed, and Philip was secretly rather glad of it.

"Why not?" Louis demanded.

"In truth, I rarely go there myself," Philip told him honestly. "I don't believe King William holds me in particularly high regard."

"Then the man is a fool, after all you have done for him," Louis declared.

"By the way," he said, as Philip prepared to take his leave of him, "when the Comte de Rennes went to Languedoc to investigate the matter we discussed at our last meeting, he discovered that, strangely, there were no prisoners being held by Intendant de Basville's Inspector of Missions. Not even Antoine Pasquier."

"So Armand told me," Philip said carefully, wondering quite what was coming next.

"I don't suppose you have any idea what might have happened to Pasquier?" Louis persisted.

"I can only assume he managed to escape, your Majesty."

Louis' searching blue eyes met his and held them there for several seconds before he spoke again. "He is a lucky man," he said at length.

"To have escaped? Yes, your Majesty, he certainly is."

"And," Louis said heavily, "to have you for a cousin."

✑

Philip had feared his journey to Fontainebleau might prove to be a futile one. He was not even sure whether Louis would be prepared to grant him an interview, but matters had turned out better than he had dared to expect and everyone gathered around to welcome him back and congratulate him.

It was a fine October evening, still mild for the time of year, even though the sun was getting low, and Theresa was seated on a stone bench in the little courtyard garden in front of the chateau. She was certainly looking heavy with child now, he thought, and, recalling Louis' words, he knew he had to start their journey home as soon as possible.

She looked in amazement at the drawn-up document, formally stating Monsieur to be part-owner of Les Jacinthes with a token investment of just 100 livres. Philip had signed it, just below the extravagant flourish that plainly bore the name 'Philippe d'Orleans'.

Maudie was sitting beside her mother. "I've some news for you too," he told her. "You, young lady, are to be presented to King Louis when we next come back to France. He insisted upon it."

Maudie clapped her hands. "I shall make him a proper Court curtsey," she declared. "Nanon has taught me how."

She leapt to her feet and, going over to him, made a deep curtsey, as gracefully and as naturally as if she had done it all her life.

"I used to watch your mother practise that," Nanon said to Philip, looking fondly at Maudie. "She is so like her, but I never truly thought she would get to meet his Majesty."

"Well I never doubted it for a moment, although I little thought he would take an interest in her so soon," he admitted. "Still, if we are to find a handsome Frenchman to be her husband one day, I suppose the sooner the better!"

Maudie giggled. "I want him to be as handsome as you, Father."

"Now that might be difficult, but I will do my best! You will have to learn the correct way to behave at Court," he warned her, "especially if you hope to find as good a catch as your mother found in me."

"Maybe you could find one who is not quite so vain,"Theresa retorted." I thought your father was insufferable when I first met him," she said, much to the amusement of the rest.

"But you still married him."

Philip and Theresa exchanged glances.The truth was that they had not had any choice in the matter. He had been dependent on the Earl of Shaftesbury at the time and Theresa had been the Earl's mistress. When her involvement in Shaftesbury's scheming had caused Theresa to be in disgrace with King Charles, the Earl had insisted Philip marry her, as his title would enable her to remain at Court. They had been fortunate for, despite the circumstances, they had fallen in love, but neither of them would ever force Maudie into an arranged marriage that might make her unhappy.

Theresa smiled at him. "Yes, I did, and I am very glad I did, but I think it is far too soon to know whether you want to be a courtier, Maudie."

"But I already know. Luc has been telling me all about it, haven't you, Luc?"

"Has he now?" Theresa said, with mock severity. "I'll thank you, young man, and you," she said to Philip, "not to fill my daughter's head with this nonsense. Two courtiers in one house are quite enough, in my opinion!"

In answer Luc made her a perfectly executed Court bow and raised her fingertips to his lips as the others laughed. "Whatever you say, my Lady!"

Their happy mood was spoiled when they heard the sound of horses approaching at a fast pace. A carriage was nearing them, followed by a troop of mounted soldiers.

"De Basville!" Philip recognised him.

"Does he know about Monsieur?" Morgan asked Philip.

"He will have received word of it by now," Philip reckoned, "so what the devil do you suppose brings him out here?"

"Nothing good," the Welshman guessed.

"Have you come to congratulate me upon my good fortune in acquiring a partner?" Philip asked him, when de Basville had climbed out of his coach and made the necessary civilities.

"You are blessed indeed in your friends, my Lord," de Basville replied tersely. "However, you are less fortunate in your enemies. It is my sad duty to inform you that a complaint has been made by Archpriest du Chayla against a member of your household. I am here to arrest Luc Santerre."

That was totally unexpected.

Philip heard Theresa gasp in shock and saw Thomas move instinctively to Luc's side. Morgan joined them as two of de Basville's men stepped forward to seize Luc, who had already drawn his sword.

"On what charge?" Philip demanded.

"From the description that was given by one of du Chayla's surviving guards, he has reason to believe that Santerre led those who attacked his chateau in Le Pont de Montvert and freed some Protestants who were being held there for interrogation."

"What?" Philip knew that du Chayla must have guessed his own part in the incident and that the priest had been subtly cautioned by Armand to take no further action against him, so this new move was pure spite. "My household is under the protection of the King," he reminded de Basville hotly.

"Only your family and your *English* servants are under his Majesty's protection, my Lord," de Basville corrected him. "That does not include Santerre. He is a French citizen, one who has betrayed his Catholic faith and Archpriest du Chayla intends that he be taught the error of his ways."

Philip gave an involuntary shudder as he remembered how closely du Chayla had watched Luc during that first meeting.

"You bastard! This is a low trick, even for you."

"I am only obeying the letter of the law, my Lord," de Basville maintained.

"I know exactly what, or rather, shall we say, who you are obeying, de Basville. This is her last desperate attempt to wreak revenge upon me, isn't it?"

"I don't know what you mean," de Basville said stiffly. "If you value Santerre's life you will tell him to put down his weapon and I advise all of you to stand aside and let my soldiers do their duty."

There were ten men with him and all now had their muskets raised. Philip feared he could not prevent Luc's arrest without bloodshed.

There was only one thing he could do.

"Order your men to put down their weapons, de Basville. You cannot take him." He swung round on the Intendant. "Luc Santerre is not my servant."

"Really, my Lord," de Basville scoffed, "you cannot think to so easily thwart the course of justice by such a feeble denial. Why is he here if you do not employ him?"

Philip sighed before making the admission he had always vowed he would never make.

"He is my son."

Luc's eyes opened wide in surprise and Philip saw his expression mirrored on the faces of the rest of his household.

Theresa struggled to her feet and came over to him, slipping her arm through his. "Well done, my darling."

De Basville looked at both Philip and Luc suspiciously, then motioned for the soldiers to lower their weapons. "He could be but, if he is, why have you not acknowledged him before?" he demanded.

Philip shrugged. "Do you acknowledge all your illegitimate offspring?"

"I have none." The Intendant said indignantly.

"What a boring life you must have led! Get your men off my property, de Basville, and tell your Inspector of Missions that the next move he attempts to make against me will be his last."

"You would be wise not to threaten him," de Basville warned.

"Just tell him."

As the carriage and its escort headed back out to the road Philip felt Theresa's hold upon his arm tighten.

He looked at her and saw that her face was contorted with pain.

"What is it, sweetheart?" he asked, concerned.

"I think it's the baby. Philip, the baby's coming."

Bet had already spotted what was happening and rushed to her side, closely followed by Nanon and, between them, they supported her as she doubled over clutching her swollen belly.

"We need to get her indoors now," Bet said, taking charge of the situation.

Without a word, Philip gathered Theresa up in his arms and carried her into the house. She was slight of build and, even full with child, was easy for him lift but he dared not attempt to take her upstairs and, instead, laid her gently down upon the long couch in the parlour.

"Don't worry," Nanon said, as the two women got to work. "Even though it is a month before her time, she is fit and healthy."

"He'll worry," Bet retorted, as she came in with an armful of sheets. "He was such a nuisance last time I had to make Morgan take him out of the room."

Theresa managed weak smile and held out her hand to him. "I'm so sorry, Philip. I know how much you wanted this one to be born at Heatherton."

"I don't mind where it's born," he assured her, kissing her hand. "My only concern is for you."

"I could not be in better care." She gripped his hand hard as she was overtaken by a second contraction.

"Fifteen minutes," Nanon said to Bet, looking at the clock.

"The pains are coming fast. This one is in a hurry to come into the world!"

"Can't you give her something to ease the pain?" Philip asked Bet.

He had never believed in the old wives' tale about placing the husband's hat upon the wife's belly to ease the pain. Neither did Bet, but she shook her head.

"All women must suffer pain in childbirth," she told him. "Anything that dulls the pain would sap her strength and she is going to need all she has to bring your infant out."

"Then what's that?" Philip asked, seeing Bet place one of her familiar, stoppered bottles on the table by the couch.

"A syrup I made from Pennyroyal which will help clear her out afterwards," Bet explained "I brought it to France with me, because I had a feeling we would need it. Now, are you going to get in my way and pester me with questions again, like you did before?"

"Go be with Maudie, my darling. She needs you," Theresa said when her breathing had returned to normal.

"And we don't," Bet said. "Take him out, Nanon."

Nanon put her arms around him, the arms that had comforted him so many times when he was a child. "We'll take good care of her."

"As you did me," Philip said quietly, allowing her to lead him from the room. "I'm thankful you're here with us."

"I never dreamed I would be fortunate enough to be present when a child of yours was born," she said. "It is I who should thank you, Lord Philip. Go sit with Maudie. I don't believe it will take long."

Philip found Maudie seated between Thomas and Luc. She raised scared eyes to him.

"She will be fine," he said, as reassuringly as he could manage when his own fears were filling his head. "The baby is just a little early, that's all."

"It was the shock, wasn't it?" Luc said wretchedly. "This is all my fault."

"Yours?" Philip shook his head. "No. Those who came to arrest you, perhaps, but it is chiefly mine. I should have got her home and not taken the time to go to Fontainebleau, then none of this would have happened."

Fontainebleau was a long journey away and, even though he had stayed there the minimum time good manners allowed, the trip had delayed their return to England by a nearly a month. He was wracked with guilt to think that his concern for Les Jacinthes might have put Theresa and his unborn child in jeopardy.

"You did what needed to be done," Morgan said simply. "You secured the future of your mother's vineyard and your daughter's inheritance."

Maudie had come to perch upon Philip's knee and he stroked her golden curls. He knew the Welshman was right, but he still could not help but feel responsible for the situation.

"This has certainly been an eventful homecoming," he declared.

"Indeed it has, my Lord. You saved my life today," Luc said. "I shall never forget that."

Philip gave him a wry smile. "But you should also never forget is that it was I who put you in danger in the first place. You could be safely in England with Giles now, but for me."

"I'm thinking of remaining with Giles myself next time," Thomas said cheekily, with a wink at Maudie, which made her laugh.

Philip looked at him warmly. Thomas could always be relied upon to lighten the mood in any situation. "You," he told him, "have no choice. I have no intention of ever training another manservant, I assure you. Not after the struggle I have had with you and Morgan, and, God knows, I never did succeed in training him!"

"I am glad I came with you," Luc said, laughing with the others.

"Then you truly must be a mad Devalle!"

"What you told the Intendant, though," Luc ventured, "was that just to thwart du Chayla's plans?"

Philip was tempted to say that it was, for he had already regretted making the admission, but a glance at Luc's earnest face made him realise how unfair that would be to the young man. Regardless, he had no intention of getting into any serious discussion on the subject.

"Luc, you know that I disliked you intently at the start and that I was opposed to my brother-in-law's decision to take you to England," he said, amused to see Luc's long-suffering expression as he realised he was about to be the butt of Philip's humour. "I decided you were arrogant, resentful and hot-headed and I resolved to have as little to do with you as possible."

"I didn't like him either, my Lord," Thomas chipped in, picking up on the tone of the conversation. "And nor did Morgan."

Morgan grunted his assent.

"However," Philip continued, more gently, "since then you have shown loyalty and courage. You have proved yourself to be a person who can be relied upon and you have earned the friendship of Thomas and Morgan, two men whose judgement I trust implicitly. Those, and your good looks, are the qualities I would hope to find in any son of mine and *that* is the reason I said what I did to de Basville."

Luc's face lit like the sun.

"Don't let it go to your head," Philip warned him, "Nothing changes."

"Yes, my lord," Luc said happily.

"And you are still hot-headed!"

"Does that mean he is now really my brother?" Maudie, who missed very little of any conversation, looked at Luc in mock horror. "He teases me all the time," she complained to Philip. "Can't I have Thomas for my brother instead?"

"Good Lord no! I am not prepared to take any responsibility for that one!"

They all laughed again, but their laughter stopped abruptly when another sound could be heard from the next room.

It was a baby's cry. A strong and lusty baby's cry.

Philip did not wait to be summoned but went straight through, relieved to see Theresa looking exhausted but happy.

He raised her from her pillow and clasped her thankfully in his arms.

"We have a son, my darling," she said softly.

A son. An heir to his title and High Heatherton, a boy to carry on the Devalle name. Philip looked delightedly at the bawling infant and at the two women who had helped this miracle to take place.

Nanon was crying tears of joy and Bet, who was matter-of-factly wrapping the baby in a blanket, glanced at her companion in exasperation. "She's French," she said to Philip, as though that explained it. "He is a fine and healthy boy, my Lord, despite being a few weeks before his time."

"Thank you, Bet," Philip said sincerely. He recalled his daughter's birth as Maudie hugged her mother now and placed a gentle kiss on the tiny baby's forehead. He was grateful once more for Bet's medical knowledge, which had benefitted them all in the past, as well as her down-to-earth common sense. "I realise it would have been much easier for you if we had managed to get her home to High Heatherton."

Bet shrugged. "Perhaps," she admitted, "but better here, my Lord, than in a coach on the way to Calais!"

TWENTY-TWO

꒰ఞ꒱

"The King says he will see you now," Giles told Philip.

"Good of him, since I am here at his 'request'!"

Philip put emphasis on the word. He had delayed his return to England until the New Year, being unwilling to cause Theresa and his little son, who they had called Simon, to endure the journey too soon. It had meant them spending Christmas at Les Jacinthes, but he had not minded that too much. Although it was a much simpler affair than it had been at High Heatherton the year before, he'd had the pleasure of knowing that it was the place where his mother had spent her earliest Christmases.

Directly he had arrived in England he had received word that William wished to see him and that he was expected to present himself at Kensington Palace at his earliest opportunity.

So here he was.

His words didn't raise a smile with Giles, not even one of sympathy and Philip looked at him closely.

"What's wrong?" He knew his brother-in-law very well.

"One of the Scottish clans did not sign the Oath of Allegiance in time," Giles said. "The MacDonalds of Glencoe arrived too late."

The Scottish Chieftains had received King James' permission to sign the Oath now that the Jacobites had been defeated in Ireland, first at Aughrim, which was said to be the bloodiest battle of the whole campaign, and then at Limerick, which had finally fallen in October.

"But did they intend to sign?" Philip asked him.

"It appears so. They were told they could still sign in Edinburgh and they walked forty miles, in freezing weather, and gave their oath there."

"Then surely the timing is immaterial in the greater scheme of things."

"You would think so, but William has bowed to pressure from the Earl of Breadalbane, who is a Campbell, and they are bitter enemies of the MacDonalds," Giles said. "He will use this as an opportunity to settle old grievances, I fear. I have come to know a great deal more than I wanted to about the clans, Philip. Some of them hate each other even more than they hate us, whilst Secretary Dalrymple hates all the Highlanders."

Philip had always known that Scotland was a troubled nation but, thankfully, he had never needed to become involved in Scottish affairs.

"What will happen now?"

"William has washed his hands of it. He has signed an order giving full authority to Dalrymple."

"Bastard," Philip said with feeling. Once again William had delegated his responsibilities in Scotland, and this time, it would seem, he was careless of the consequences so long as he had succeeded in his determination to bring the clans to heel. "You are not responsible for this," he reminded Giles. "You had no choice but to follow his orders and your part in the business is done."

"I know, but it sickens me just the same. When William first came to power, he was all for tolerance and uniting the people. He has united Ireland certainly, but at the cost of so many lives, and he fights abroad not for land or justice but because he is obsessed with besting Louis. He cares not how much blood is spilt to achieve his aims, and now this. I can't believe it of him."

Philip was more cynical. Many years ago, he had seen the other side of King Charles, the affable and charismatic ruler who he had admired until he discovered that he had made a secret treaty with France behind his ministers' backs. It was a treaty that, if he had been allowed to have his way, would have forced Catholicism on the nation. Philip had seen King James in his true colours long before he had come to the throne and he had also seen the callous way in which William would have abandoned Giles after the Boyne. He had no illusions about any of them.

William did not even glance up from the documents he was reading when Philip was shown into his presence. "Good of you to bother to return home."

Philip bit back the reply he wanted to make to a king who had not bothered to return to his kingdom for two months after the end of his last military action in Europe. "My wife was only delivered of a son in October," he said instead, "and I was loath to move them too soon."

If Philip had thought to receive any kind of congratulations, he was to be disappointed.

"It might have been preferable for your son to have been born in England," was all William said, before raising his head and giving Philip a stony stare.

Philip could not help comparing the reception he was receiving from his own King to the warmth of the ones he received from the King of France, even on the occasions when Louis had reason to be displeased with him. The real difference, he knew, was that Louis actually liked him, whilst William obviously did not, as his next words plainly showed.

"Can you think of any reason why I should not have you arrested as a traitor?"

William had never been one for unnecessary pleasantries but, even so, Philip was a little taken aback by this bluntness.

"Perhaps because I have not committed any treasonable acts, your Majesty," he said.

"Yet you spent the greater part of last year in a country with which we are at war and, I have reason to believe, actually visited the Court of the monarch who is your country's greatest enemy."

So William still had spies at Versailles. Philip was not too surprised. "My business in France is personal, not political, your Majesty."

"Yes, your wretched vineyard. A gift from the very king whose troops are fighting mine. Any man truly loyal to his own country would have thrown that gift back in his face," William said.

"That 'gift' is my inheritance," Philip reminded him mildly, "and I believe I have already given ample proof of my loyalty both to my country and to you, your Majesty."

William regarded him coldly. "I have no illusions about you, Philip Devalle, you may be assured of that. I know that the only reason you ever gave me your support was because your life under my father-in-law's reign was intolerable for you."

That much was true and Philip saw no point in denying it.

"Whatever my reasons at the start, I have served your Majesty well since then," he reminded him, "both here and in Ireland."

"I can't deny that yet, I'll be frank, I can put no trust in you whilst you still retain the friendship of King Louis."

"What is it you require of me, then?" Philip said. "My oath of allegiance?"

If William recognised any barb in those words, he gave no sign of it. "I know that King Charles didn't trust you," he continued. "That is why he kept you at Court, where he could keep an eye on you."

It was a fact that, even after Philip had been released from the Tower and cleared of the charge of conspiring against him, King Charles had insisted that Philip remain with him at Court for the remaining two years of his reign.

"I wonder sometimes if any of the English are to be relied upon," William said pettishly. "I intend to speak to Marlborough next. Did you know that he moved an address in the House of Lords last month demanding that I remove all foreigners from my service?"

Philip did not know, but he could guess how infuriating that must have been for William, who always gave the most important posts to his own countrymen.

"Besides that," William continued, "I have now good reason to believe that he has been in secret correspondence with King James in an effort to get back into his favour."

That was news to Philip too, but he was not entirely surprised. Marlborough, had once been one of James' staunchest supporters but he had changed sides and switched his allegiance to William when it became obvious that James had no chance of retaining his crown. Philip suspected William had never trusted Marlborough either, and with far more cause, it appeared.

"Your Majesty cannot possibly believe that I would conspire with King James," he said. "Not when I raised an army to help you gain his throne."

"No," William admitted. "for it would scarcely be in your interests to do so and I have not forgotten what I owe you, but it would please me greatly now if you were to break off all ties with France."

Philip had been expecting that.

"It would be difficult since I own property there," he said firmly.

William made a deprecating gesture. "I am certain that your vineyard could manage to run itself without your presence."

"In due time, perhaps, your Majesty, but it is early days and there is still much work to be done to restore it. We have yet to reap the rewards of our first harvest," Philip told him.

"And is that of more worth to you than fighting for your country?" William asked him tartly. "I am ordering you to take up arms for me again. I have had word that the French may try to take Namur this season and I am offering you a command with the Allied Forces in Flanders. It is a post that will not endear you to King Louis but it is one that may bring you glory and renown, things which were once of some importance to you, I believe."

Philip saw that offer for exactly what it was – a chance for William to demonstrate that he, not Louis, owned him. On the other hand, if he refused it, then he realised that not only would his military career effectively be over but William, in his present frame of mind, would be likely to take reprisals.

"Think carefully before you say any more," William warned him, "and return here before I leave in March. This year I vow the French will not succeed in getting a head start upon us."

In the anteroom to William's chamber Philip came face to face with the Earl of Marlborough, John Churchill, waiting to be called in to speak with the King.

They had known each other for years and Churchill had always been jealous of his success, and especially of the title and the rank William had given him. William had employed Marlborough only once in Ireland, and that for a less important battle, and he had always passed him over when it came to naming those in high command on the Continent.

"It seems, Devalle, that your affairs in France have displeased the King," Churchill said, sounding smug. "Were you summoned here to be reprimanded?"

"Not at all."

"Then why did he send for you?" the Earl demanded.

"Not that it is any of your business, Churchill, but he has offered me a command of the Allied campaign in Flanders."

From the look on Churchill's face, Philip guessed that it was a command he had hoped to get for himself this time. That fact almost made Philip want to accept it. Almost but not quite.

"Enjoy your success whilst you can, Devalle." Churchill said. "My day will come."

Philip had no doubt of that. Mary had still not managed to give William an heir and it was beginning to look more and more likely that the throne would one day pass to Mary's sister, Anne. Churchill's wife, Sarah, was cultivating her in readiness and it was not difficult to see how the pair of them would rise to prominence in her reign. When that happened, it wouldn't matter a damn that Philip had campaigned for William on the borders of France and lost Louis' favour and probably even Les Jacinthes, by doing so.

"In the meantime, you would do well to watch your own back," he said to Churchill.

"I don't know what you mean," Churchill said stiffly

"I think you do. Remember, if William's spies can report on my activities they can also report on yours."

Churchill's usually bland expression flickered, betraying a moment of concern. "Why would you warn me?" he asked looking at him suspiciously.

Although they had both been young courtiers together, they had never been friends.

Philip laughed. "Because, Churchill, I no longer give a damn!"

"Have you decided what you are going to do?" Antoine asked Philip.

"Well I'm not going to lose the vineyard," Philip said decidedly.

"If you refuse to go will you not incur King William's wrath?"

"Probably, but if I do go, I will most certainly incur the wrath of King Louis. Then what will become of Les Jacinthes and all our hard work?"

"And what if King William follows through upon his threat to have you arrested?"

"He won't," Philip said, with more conviction than he felt. He was seeing a different side to William lately and was learning that the once-reasonable and fair man could be vengeful if he did not get his way.

Antoine was visiting him at High Heatherton. He had been inspecting the new warehouse Giles had built and had travelled down with them from Kent.

Antoine was a captain in the Huguenot regiment now and looked dashing in his uniform, a far cry from the pathetic wretch Philip and the others had rescued from Le Pont de Montvert.

"It looks as though life is treating you well," Philip told him.

"It is, and I have managed to get in touch with my family," Antoine said happily. "I contacted them through some friends of theirs who settled in Carolina at the start of the troubles. My father has written to me that he bought some land there and that most of the vine stock he took with him survived the long voyage. He says it has taken well to both the soil and the climate, so they hope to be able to begin again."

"That is excellent news," Philip said. He was genuinely pleased, particularly for Antoine's sake. "Did you tell him I now own Les Jacinthes?" he asked wryly, for he little thought that piece of news would please his uncle.

"I did, and I also told him everything you have done for me and the great debt that I owe you."

Philip had long since put their adventure in the Cevennes out of his mind and he certainly did not intend Antoine to feel forever indebted to him "I didn't do very much," he insisted

"No, not much at all," Antoine agreed. "You merely hid me from the Intendant, rescued me from certain death or slavery and enabled me to come to England and be a soldier."

Philip smiled at his earnestness. "Well, yes, I did do that, I suppose! Has it put me in your father's good graces?"

Philip didn't honestly care whether it had or not. He had lived for too long without the acknowledgement of his mother's family to crave their approval now. Even so, he was unprepared for Antoine's next words.

"He wishes me to convey to you his grateful thanks and his regret that he was estranged for so long from the son of the sister who was the dear companion of his youth and who he never ceased to love," Antoine said. "He wishes you every success."

"Does he now?" Philip said, surprised.

"As do I," Antoine said. "I still can't quite believe that our wine is to be shipped to England."

"Soon it will be drunk in some of the finest houses in London," Philip predicted, smiling. "Morgan seems to think it was a reasonable harvest, all considering. He proposes to continue with the new planting this year."

"That's good. By the third leaf you will truly discover what Les Jacinthes is capable of giving you."

A wistfulness had entered Antoine's voice as he spoke of his old home and the third leaf which, Philip knew, referred to the three years they would have to wait before the new vines which Antoine had helped Morgan to plant bore their first crop. A crop his cousin would never get to see.

"Do you miss it?" Philip said quietly.

"Sometimes, but I am fulfilling my life's ambition now, thanks to you and Giles."

"You are not planning to join your family then?"

"Indeed not! I am happy here. Besides, I have fallen in love with a young lady at Court," he admitted, somewhat shyly. "She is in love with me, too."

"Yes, the uniform will do that for you," Philip teased him. "You must bring her with you next time you come. Of course, you may have to bring her to meet me in the Tower, if William gets sufficiently annoyed with me!"

Antoine laughed but soon grew serious again. "You can't defy him, you know, Philip."

"Don't tell me you are worried about me, Antoine!"

"A little," Antoine admitted, "and so is Giles."

"That's nothing new. If I had ever listened to Giles' advice, I wouldn't even have paid the visit to France on the occasion when Louis offered me the vineyard."

"Was that the visit when everyone thought you had been murdered?" Antoine asked him in an innocent tone

Philip shot him a look. "He told you about that, did he? Where would any of us be if I did not sometimes take risks?"

He was no nearer to figuring out a solution when Antoine left to re-join his regiment.

"I trust no-one has told him about Monsieur," Philip said to Giles when they went back into the house after he had gone.

"Of course not." Giles said. "I hardly think he would be pleased to learn that the brother of the man who caused his family to be dispossessed is now a part-owner of their vineyard! You should listen to what he says about the King though. William will be furious if you don't report for duty."

Thomas agreed with him. "He may well decide to have you arrested just to make an example of you, my Lord."

Philip knew they were right.

"I'll think of something," he assured them. "Don't I always?"

This time, however, the answer to his problem seemed to elude him and by the end of February, with William's deadline fast approaching, he was no closer to knowing what he should do.

Then he received Antoine's letter.

It was a short note, written in haste, for Antoine's regiment was preparing to leave for Flanders but, after Philip had read it, he began to laugh.

Thomas, who had handed him the letter looked bemused "What is it, my Lord?"

"I think, Thomas, that my cousin might have just repaid his debt to me!"

This time William's greeting was far more genial and the look that momentarily crossed his pale countenance actually seemed like one of relief.

"So you decided to obey my order."

"Did your Majesty doubt that I would?" Philip said. He'd had the presence of mind to wear his uniform to meet the King and it was evident that the decision had pleased William.

"Frankly, I have come to doubt a great many people lately, but perhaps I should not have doubted you, Philip."

From William that was tantamount to an apology, even if it was spoken with his customary stiffness of manner.

He did not say any more for few seconds as his thin body was wracked by a violent fit of coughing. Philip had become used to this during the time he had spent with him and stood quietly by until the coughs subsided. Although William was only the same age as him, Philip had always doubted that he would make old bones. He saw a spot of blood on the handkerchief the King had held in front of him, although he knew better than to make mention of it.

"Have you heard the news?" William said, when he could speak again. "The French are gathering in great numbers at La Hogue and King James is on his way there to join General Sarsfield, at the head of an Irish army."

Philip had heard, thanks to Antoine's letter. "Yes, your Majesty."

"There can only be one reason for that – my father-in-law intends to invade us."

"Then we must gather troops and raise the militia to protect the south coast without delay."

"We must," William agreed. "I might have entrusted the defence of England to Marlborough but I have had to dismiss him, for Portland has proof now that he is trying to ingratiate himself with King James. He is a vile man," he said, "and I despise him for the traitor that he was in deserting my father-in-law when he did, even though I profited from it."

It came as no surprise to Philip that the haughty Churchill had not had the sense to heed his warning. In fact, he had been counting on it to be the one sure thing to goad him into being even more rash. "I will undertake the task whilst you are in Flanders, if your Majesty wishes," he offered.

Philip had taken part in a similar enterprise some twenty years before alongside the Duke of Monmouth but, on that occasion, they had been attempting to defend the country from an attack by the Dutch!

"I do wish it," William said. "Marlborough has many friends here and, frankly, I am loath to leave the Queen at the mercy of those who may decide to give their allegiance to James, should he succeed in landing upon our shores."

"Your Majesty can rely upon me to protect both her and our country," Philip said.

"I know I can and, believe me, the irony of the situation has not escaped me. I might not be able to trust you to fight against King Louis but I would trust you more than any other to fight King James, should it come that," William said, looking him full in the face. "We may not like each other very much, Philip Devalle, but I believe we understand each other. We met first as enemies and then as friends. It would not benefit either of us to become enemies again."

Philip fully accepted the wisdom of that. "I'll not let you down," he promised him.

"Of course you won't. Forming men into an effective fighting force and leading them into battle is precisely what you are best at." William allowed himself a slight smile as he could not resist adding. "Not running a damned vineyard!"

TWENTY-THREE

There had been a late fall of snow and the distant Downs were white with it, but High Heatherton's parlour was warm and cosy with the fire built up high.

"This has all worked out rather well for you hasn't it?" Giles said. "You can now keep your promise to Louis by not going to fight him in Flanders and still retain your position with William."

Philip was just thinking the same thing, and marvelling at the way that the perfect solution to his problem had appeared just when he had almost despaired of finding one.

Not that he was ever going to admit that!

"Didn't I tell you I would think of something?"

Theresa, sitting with little Simon on her knee, laughed. "Even you could never have devised this, my love."

"Maybe not, but fortunately King James has been my salvation, for once!"

"Does this mean you are going away again?" Maudie, keeping a sisterly eye upon the baby from a footstool at her mother's feet, looked up at him.

"Not very far," he promised her. "And I shall be quite safe because your Uncle Giles is coming as well."

Philip had persuaded his brother-in-law to join him, partly because it would keep Giles in better favour with William but more because Philip knew he was going to need officers he could trust not to defect to the Jacobites, should James succeed in landing his forces.

"And me," Thomas reminded him. He had positively refused to be left behind this time.

"Yes, you too," Philip said, with a long-suffering sigh, "since it was the only way I could get any peace!" He winked at Thomas, who grinned.

"What about Luc?" Maudie said.

"That's rather up to your uncle."

Luc was still officially a part of Giles' household and he glanced plaintively over to him now. Giles nodded.

Luc's reaction was a whoop of glee before he snatched up Maudie from her little stool and whirled her around the room, much to her delight.

Philip watched him tolerantly. No further mention had been made of his admission to de Basville, and he suspected it never would be. Luc had heard him say it, and he guessed that was all Luc had ever really wanted.

The only person Philip had already decided should not accompany him this time was Morgan, who had Spring tasks to do at Les Jacinthes. The Welshman still looked far from happy about it but he had already grudgingly agreed.

"You will serve me better there, my friend," Philip reminded him gently.

"So I suppose it will be up to us women to run this place again while they're all away," Bet complained to Marianne and Nanon, drawing the curtains across and shutting out the view of the windswept gardens.

Philip knew she was not really grumbling. "I'm sure you'll manage, Mistress Bet!"

"Probably better," Bet retorted, and they all laughed.

Philip looked around the room at the people who had become so dear to him. During his childhood at High Heatherton, ill-treated by his brother, with no mother but only a father too indecisive to protect him, Philip had felt he had no family. Now he had two, his mother's family and those he had gathered about him over the years.

It had been an eventful eighteen months, but they had overcome every obstacle set before them. He had needed to rely on them, as they had him, and he knew they were his strength, just as he was theirs. He also knew that they would be able to face whatever may lay ahead. Together.

These uncertain years would pass and the future looked bright. Les Jacinthes was flourishing, their first harvest was safely in and he was eager to return to Languedoc. But first he had to defend the coast of England.

For Philip was a soldier, and he was going back to war.

ALSO BY THE AUTHOR